Provided as a generous gift of the
Orange County Library Foundation
2007 Campaign

MARK TWAIN.

TOM SAWYER

STERLING AND
THE DISTINCTIVE
STERLING LOGO ARE REGIS
TERED TRADEMARKS OF STERLING
PUBLISHING Co., INC.

LIBRARY OF CONGRESS
CATALOGING-IN-PUBLICATION
DATA AVAILABLE

2 4 6 8 10 9 7 5 3 1

PUBLISHED BY STERLING PUBLISHING Co., INC.
387 PARK AVENUE SOUTH, NEW YORK, NY 10016
© 2008 BY BEN CALDWELL
DISTRIBUTED IN CANADA BY STERLING PUBLISHING
C/O CANADIAN MANDA GROUP, 165 DUFFERIN STREET
TORONTO, ONTARIO, CANADA M6K 3H6
DISTRIBUTED IN THE UNITED KINGDOM BY
GMC DISTRIBUTION SERVICES
CASTLE PLACE, 166 HIGH STREET, LEWES,
EAST SUSSEX, ENGLAND BN7 1XU
DISTRIBUTED IN AUSTRALIA BY
CAPRICORN LINK (AUSTRALIA) PTY. LTD.
P.O. BOX 704, WINDSOR, NSW 2756, AUSTRALIA

PRINTED IN CHINA
ALL RIGHTS RESERVED

STERLING ISBN-13: 978-1-4027-3399-4
ISBN-10: 1-4027-3399-2

FOR INFORMATION ABOUT CUSTOM EDITIONS,
SPECIAL SALES, PREMIUM AND CORPORATE
PURCHASES, PLEASE CONTACT STERLING
SPECIAL SALES DEPARTMENT AT
800-805-5489 OR
SPECIALSALES@STERLINGPUB.COM

MARK TWAIN. TOM SAWYER

ADAPTED BY

TIM MUCCI
WRITER

RAD SECHRIST
ARTIST

STERLING

New York / London
www.sterlingpublishing.com/kids

To
ANDREA,
WHO SHOWS ME
EVERY DAY THAT
WE CAN BE WHO
WE WANT TO BE.

— T. M.

FOR MY ALWAYS
WONDERFUL
WIFE MANDY.

— R. S.

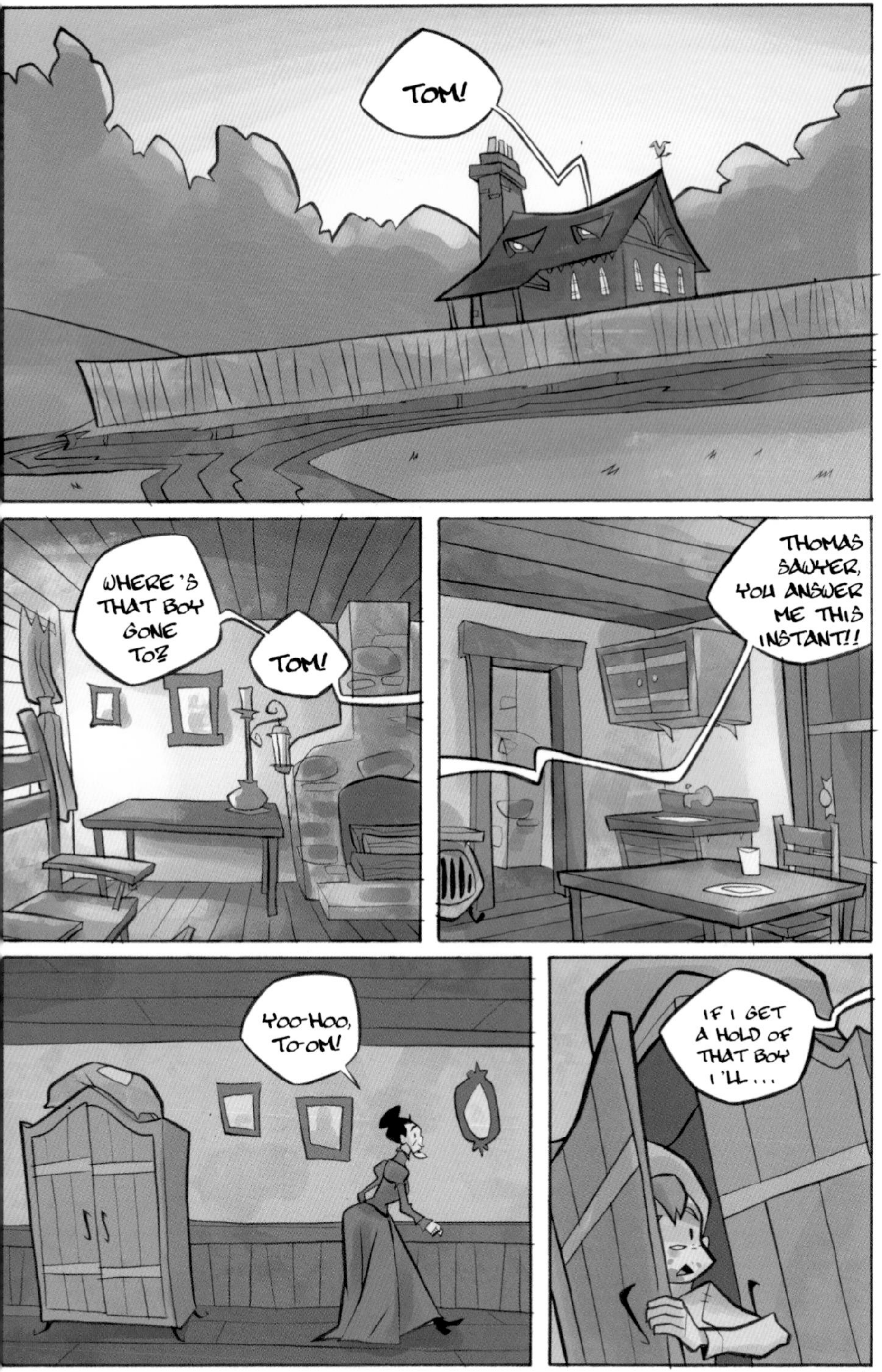
TOM!
WHERE'S THAT BOY GONE TO?
TOM!
THOMAS SAWYER, YOU ANSWER ME THIS INSTANT!!
YOO-HOO, TO-OM!
IF I GET A HOLD OF THAT BOY I'LL...

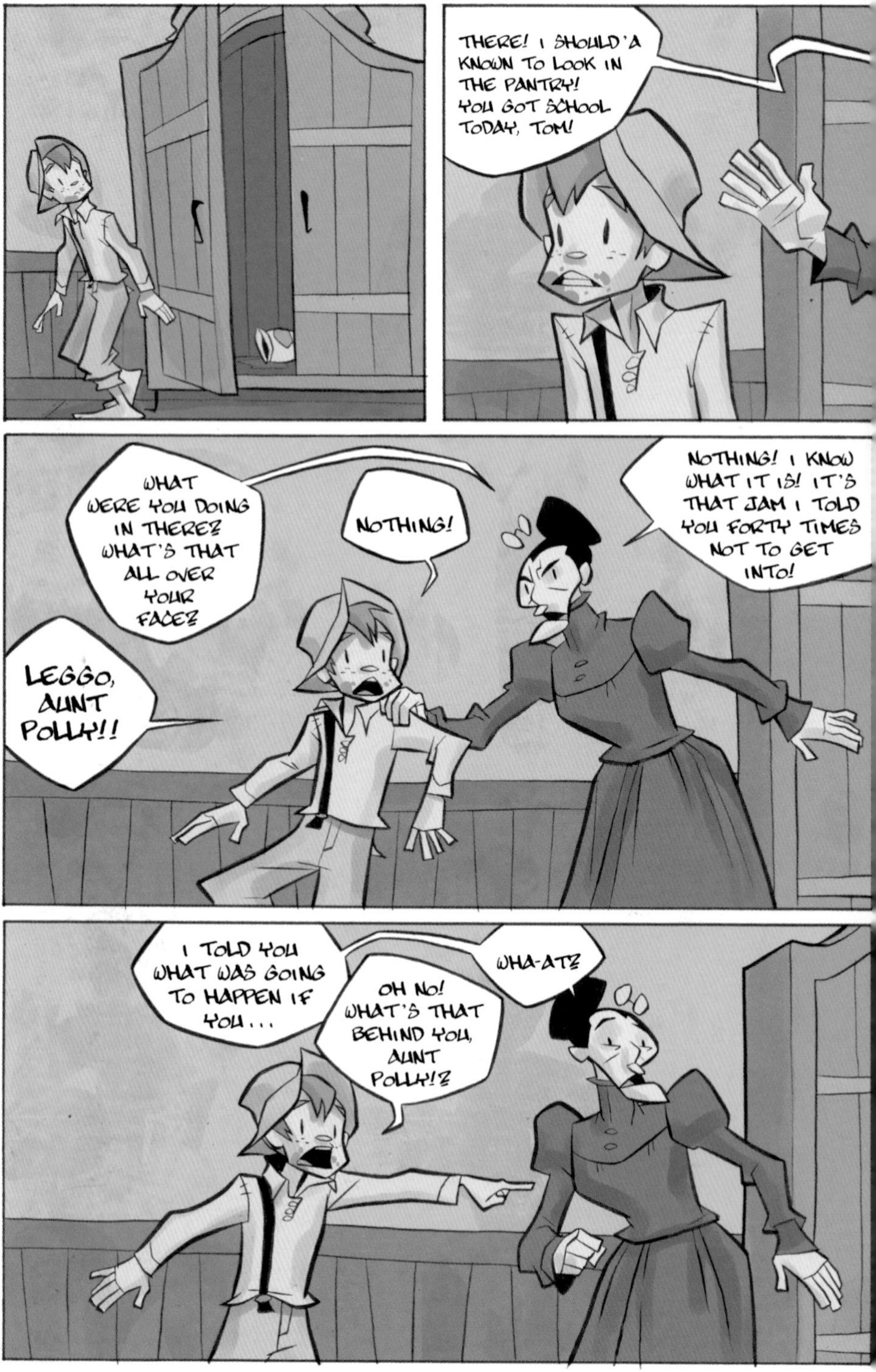
THERE! I SHOULD'A KNOWN TO LOOK IN THE PANTRY! YOU GOT SCHOOL TODAY, TOM!
WHAT WERE YOU DOING IN THERE? WHAT'S THAT ALL OVER YOUR FACE?
NOTHING!
NOTHING! I KNOW WHAT IT IS! IT'S THAT JAM I TOLD YOU FORTY TIMES NOT TO GET INTO!
LEGGO, AUNT POLLY!!
I TOLD YOU WHAT WAS GOING TO HAPPEN IF YOU...
OH NO! WHAT'S THAT BEHIND YOU, AUNT POLLY!?
WHA-AT?

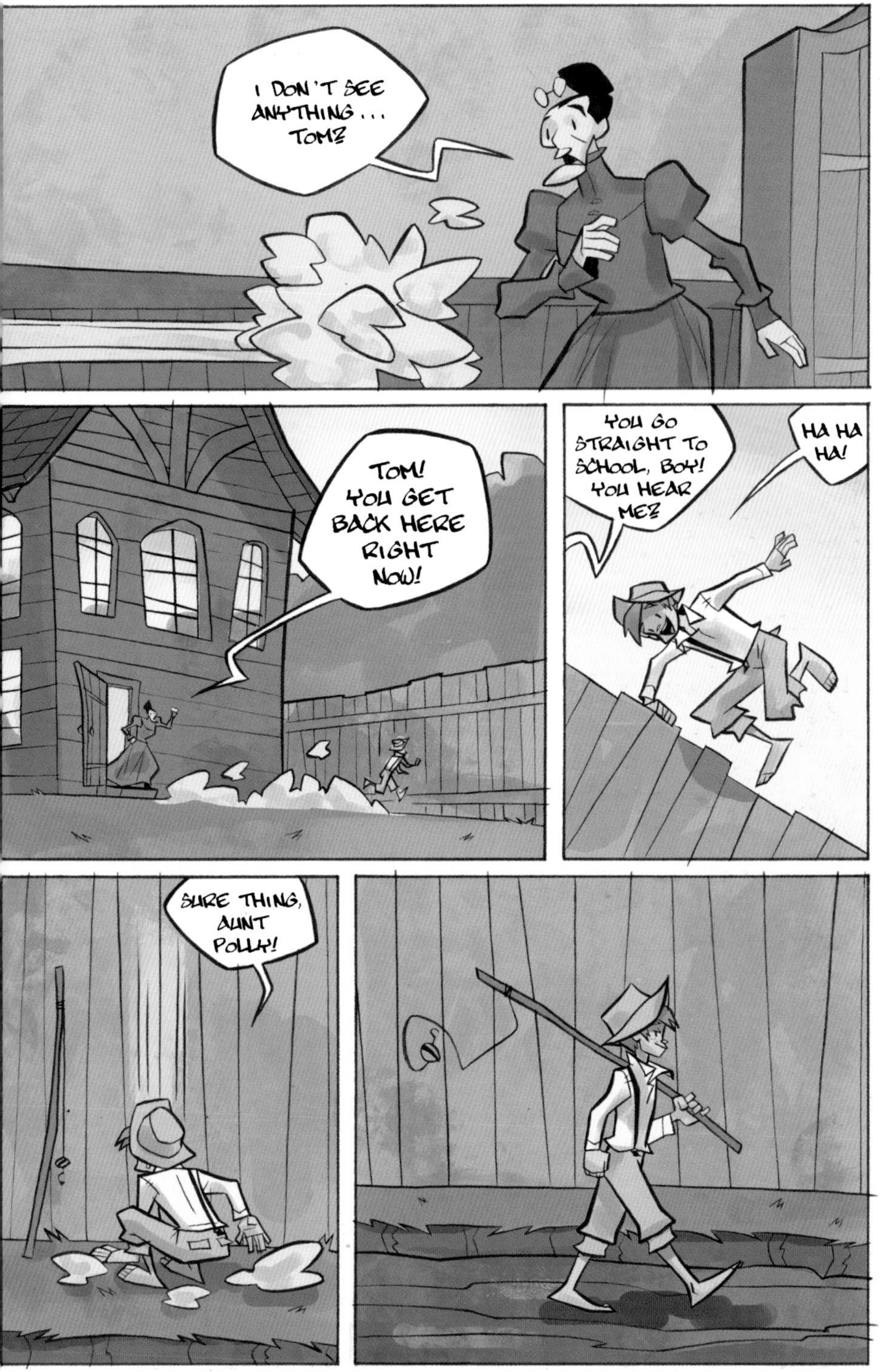
I DON'T SEE ANYTHING . . . TOM?
TOM! YOU GET BACK HERE RIGHT NOW!
YOU GO STRAIGHT TO SCHOOL, BOY! YOU HEAR ME?
HA HA HA!
SURE THING, AUNT POLLY!

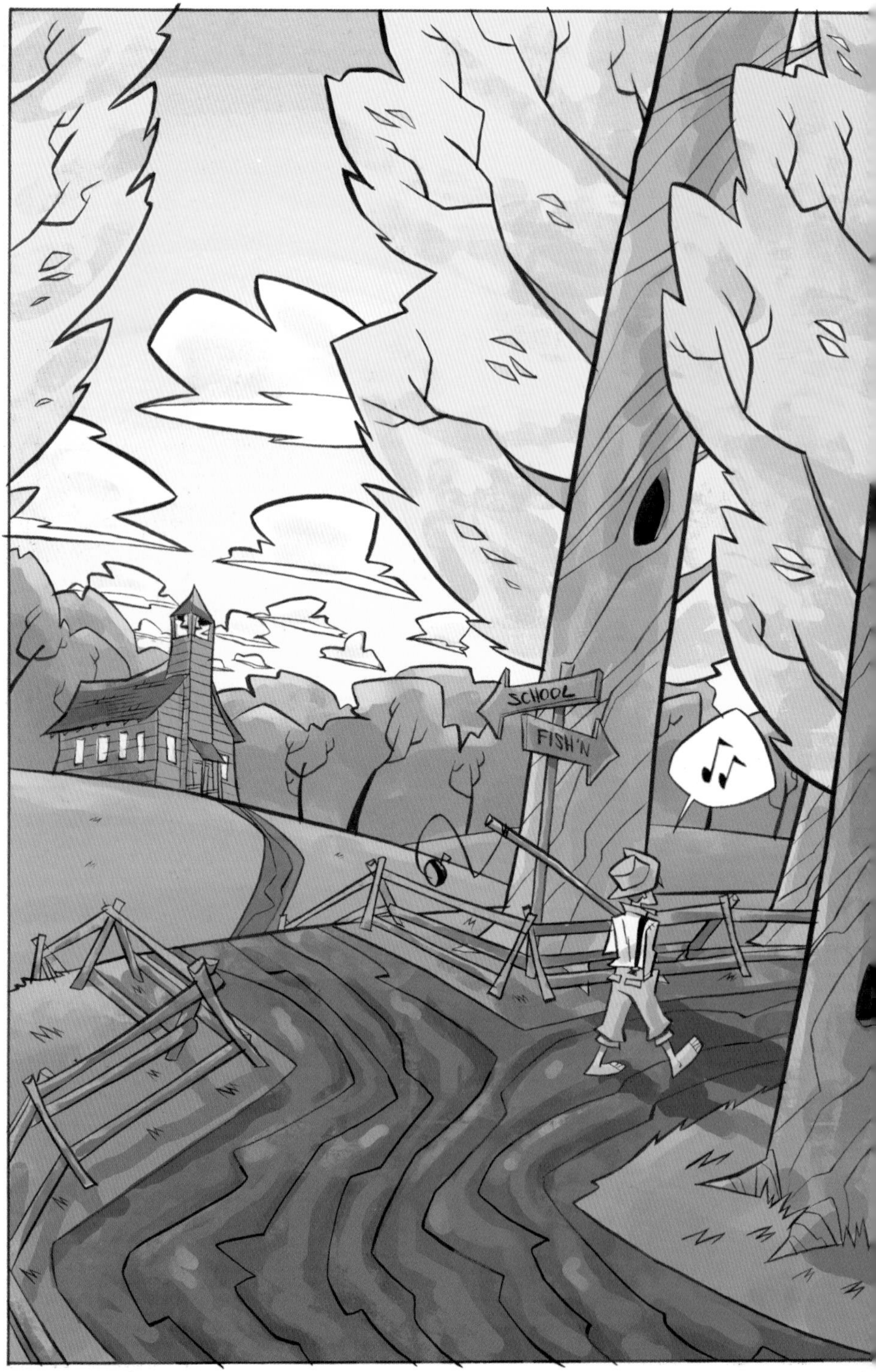
SCHOOL
FISH'N

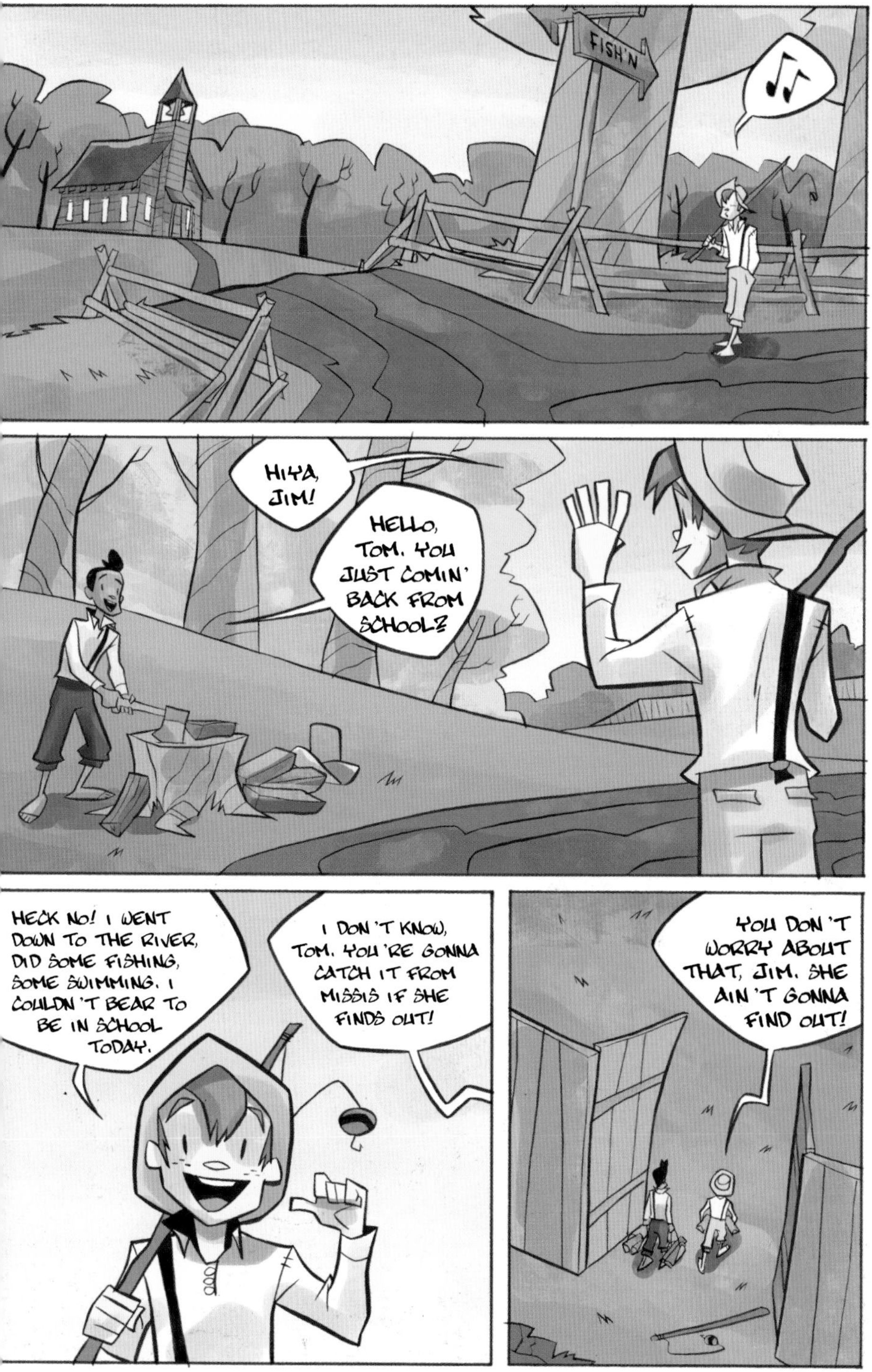
FISH'N
♫
HIYA, JIM!
HELLO, TOM. YOU JUST COMIN' BACK FROM SCHOOL?
HECK NO! I WENT DOWN TO THE RIVER, DID SOME FISHING, SOME SWIMMING. I COULDN'T BEAR TO BE IN SCHOOL TODAY.
I DON'T KNOW, TOM. YOU'RE GONNA CATCH IT FROM MISSIS IF SHE FINDS OUT!
YOU DON'T WORRY ABOUT THAT, JIM. SHE AIN'T GONNA FIND OUT!

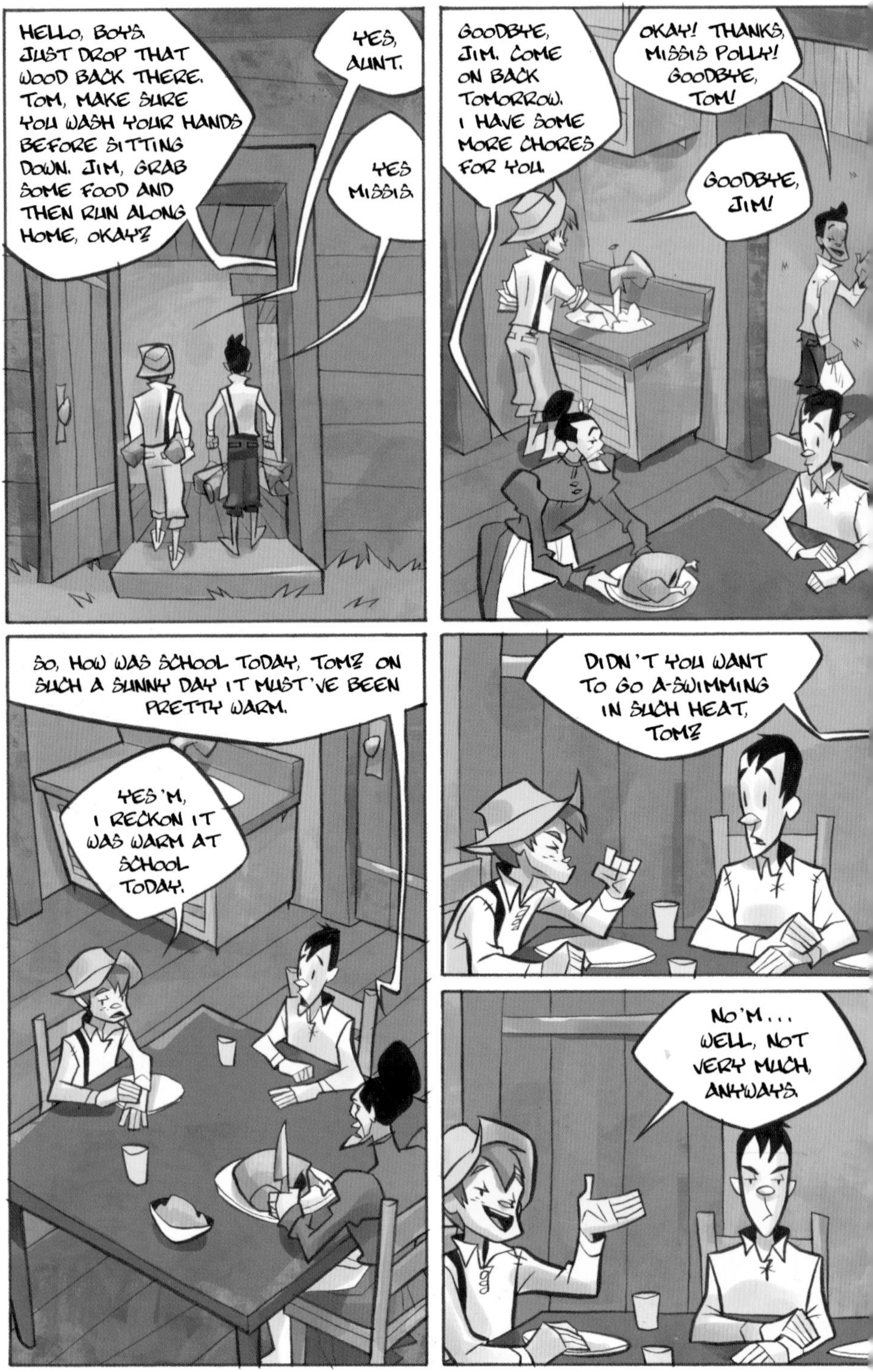
HELLO, BOYS. JUST DROP THAT WOOD BACK THERE. TOM, MAKE SURE YOU WASH YOUR HANDS BEFORE SITTING DOWN. JIM, GRAB SOME FOOD AND THEN RUN ALONG HOME, OKAY?
YES, AUNT.
YES MISSIS.
GOODBYE, JIM. COME ON BACK TOMORROW. I HAVE SOME MORE CHORES FOR YOU.
OKAY! THANKS, MISSIS POLLY! GOODBYE, TOM!
GOODBYE, JIM!
SO, HOW WAS SCHOOL TODAY, TOM? ON SUCH A SUNNY DAY IT MUST'VE BEEN PRETTY WARM.
YES'M, I RECKON IT WAS WARM AT SCHOOL TODAY.
DIDN'T YOU WANT TO GO A-SWIMMING IN SUCH HEAT, TOM?
NO'M... WELL, NOT VERY MUCH, ANYWAYS.

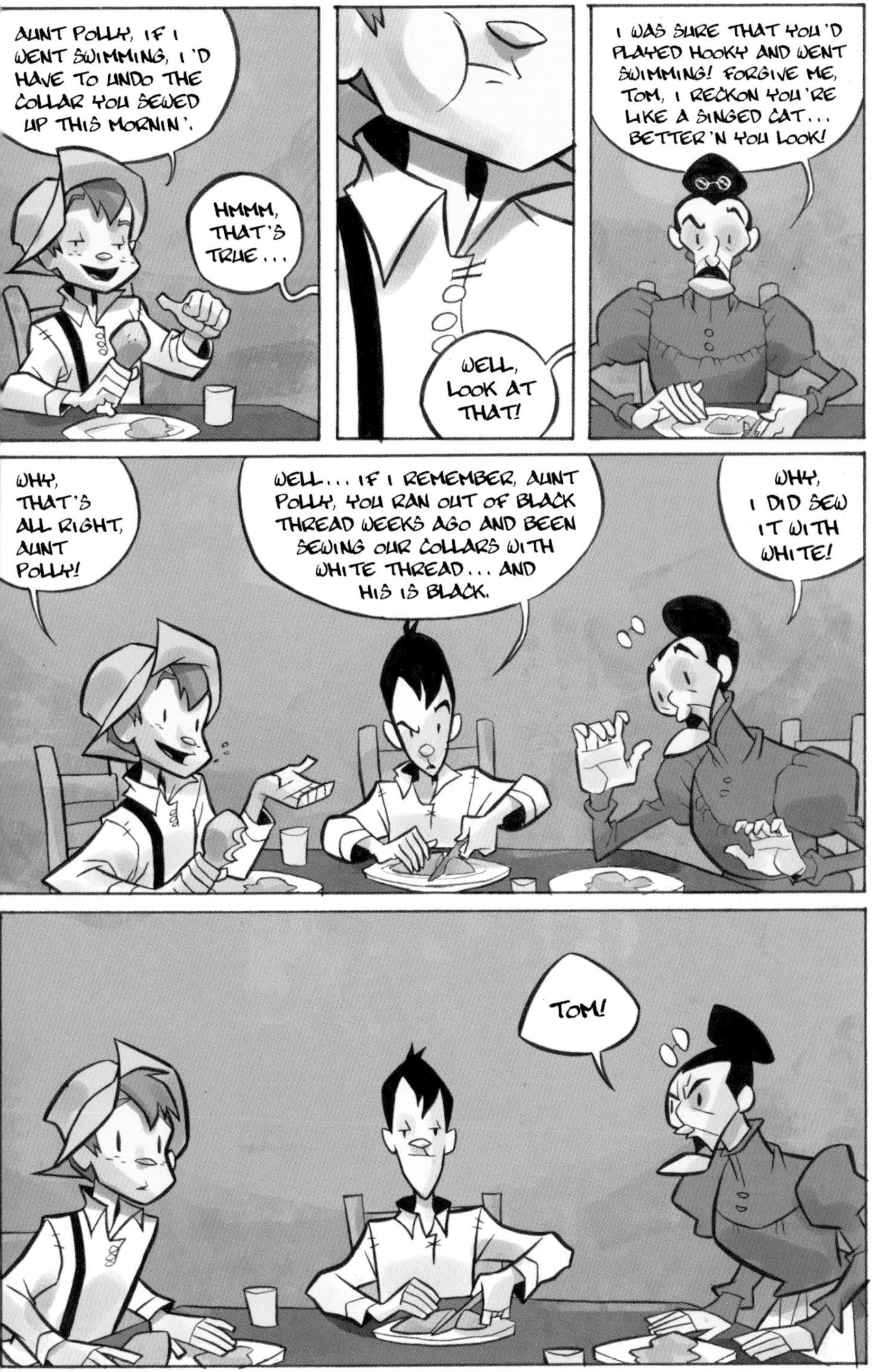
AUNT POLLY, IF I WENT SWIMMING, I'D HAVE TO UNDO THE COLLAR YOU SEWED UP THIS MORNIN'.
HMMM, THAT'S TRUE...
WELL, LOOK AT THAT!
I WAS SURE THAT YOU'D PLAYED HOOKY AND WENT SWIMMING! FORGIVE ME, TOM, I RECKON YOU'RE LIKE A SINGED CAT... BETTER'N YOU LOOK!
WHY, THAT'S ALL RIGHT, AUNT POLLY!
WELL... IF I REMEMBER, AUNT POLLY, YOU RAN OUT OF BLACK THREAD WEEKS AGO AND BEEN SEWING OUR COLLARS WITH WHITE THREAD... AND HIS IS BLACK.
WHY, I DID SEW IT WITH WHITE!
TOM!

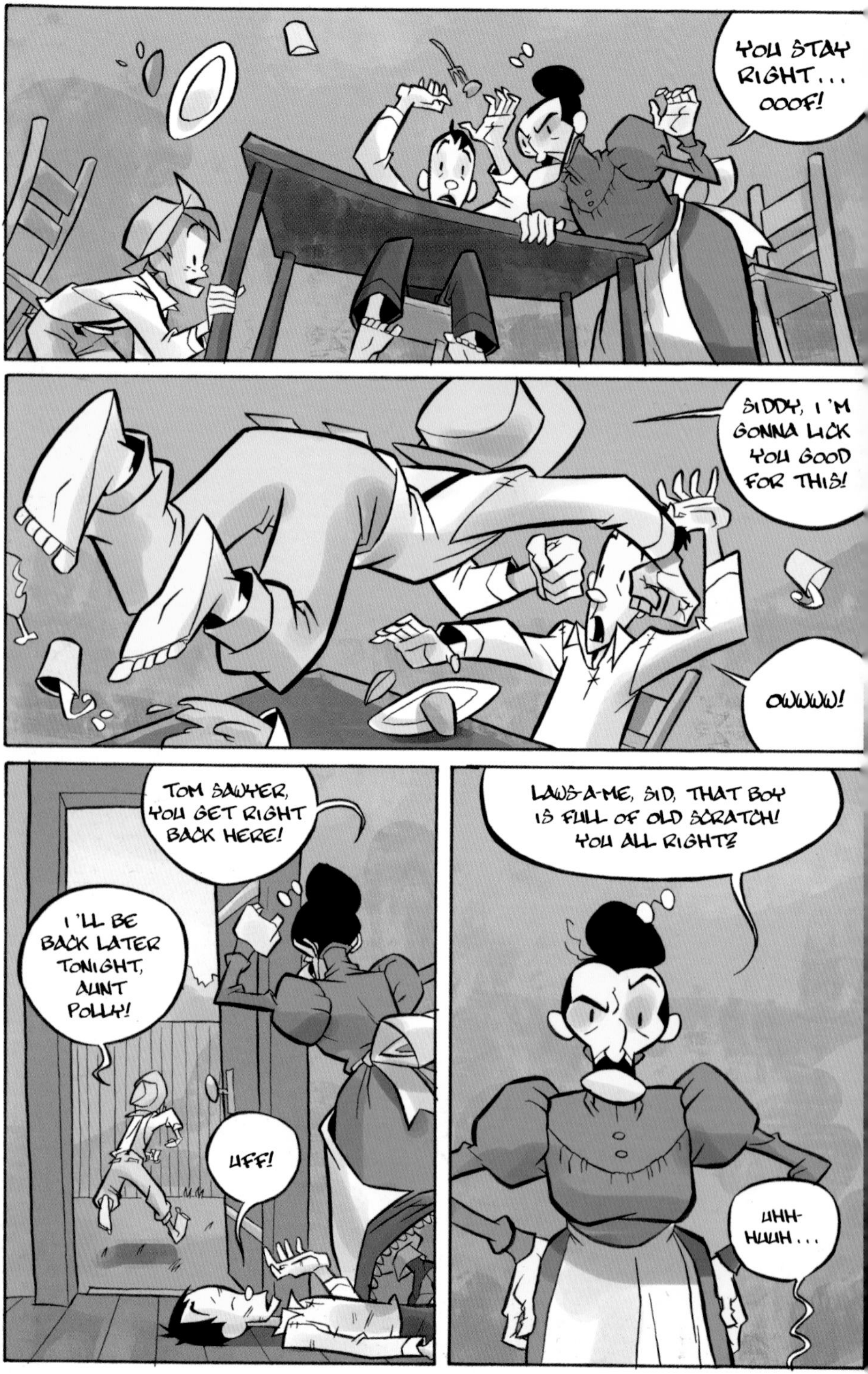
YOU STAY RIGHT... OOOF!
SIDDY, I'M GONNA LICK YOU GOOD FOR THIS!
OWWWW!
TOM SAWYER, YOU GET RIGHT BACK HERE!
I'LL BE BACK LATER TONIGHT, AUNT POLLY!
UFF!
LAWS-A-ME, SID, THAT BOY IS FULL OF OLD SCRATCH! YOU ALL RIGHT?
UHH-HUUH...

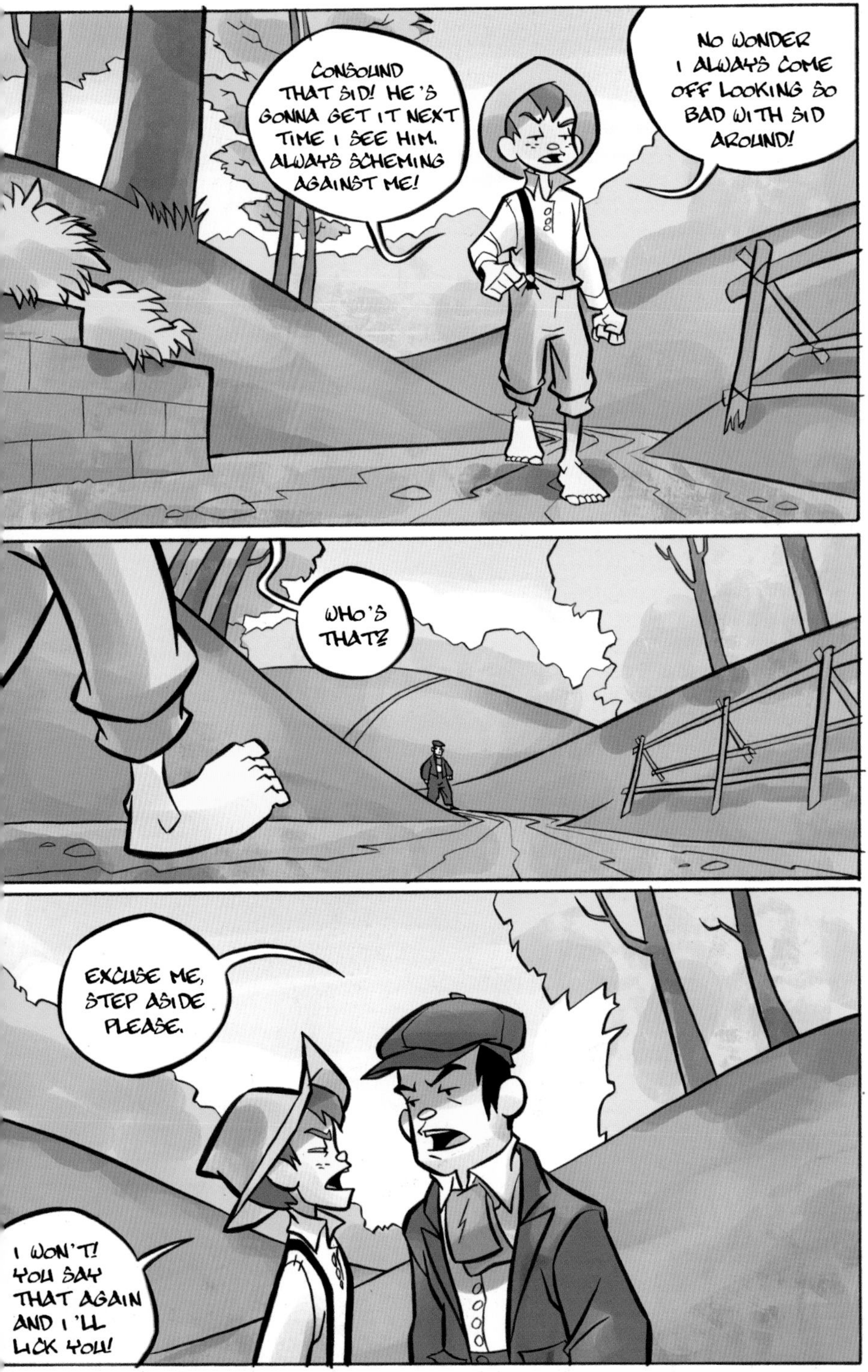
CONSOUND THAT SID! HE'S GONNA GET IT NEXT TIME I SEE HIM. ALWAYS SCHEMING AGAINST ME!
NO WONDER I ALWAYS COME OFF LOOKING SO BAD WITH SID AROUND!
WHO'S THAT?
EXCUSE ME, STEP ASIDE PLEASE.
I WON'T! YOU SAY THAT AGAIN AND I'LL LICK YOU!

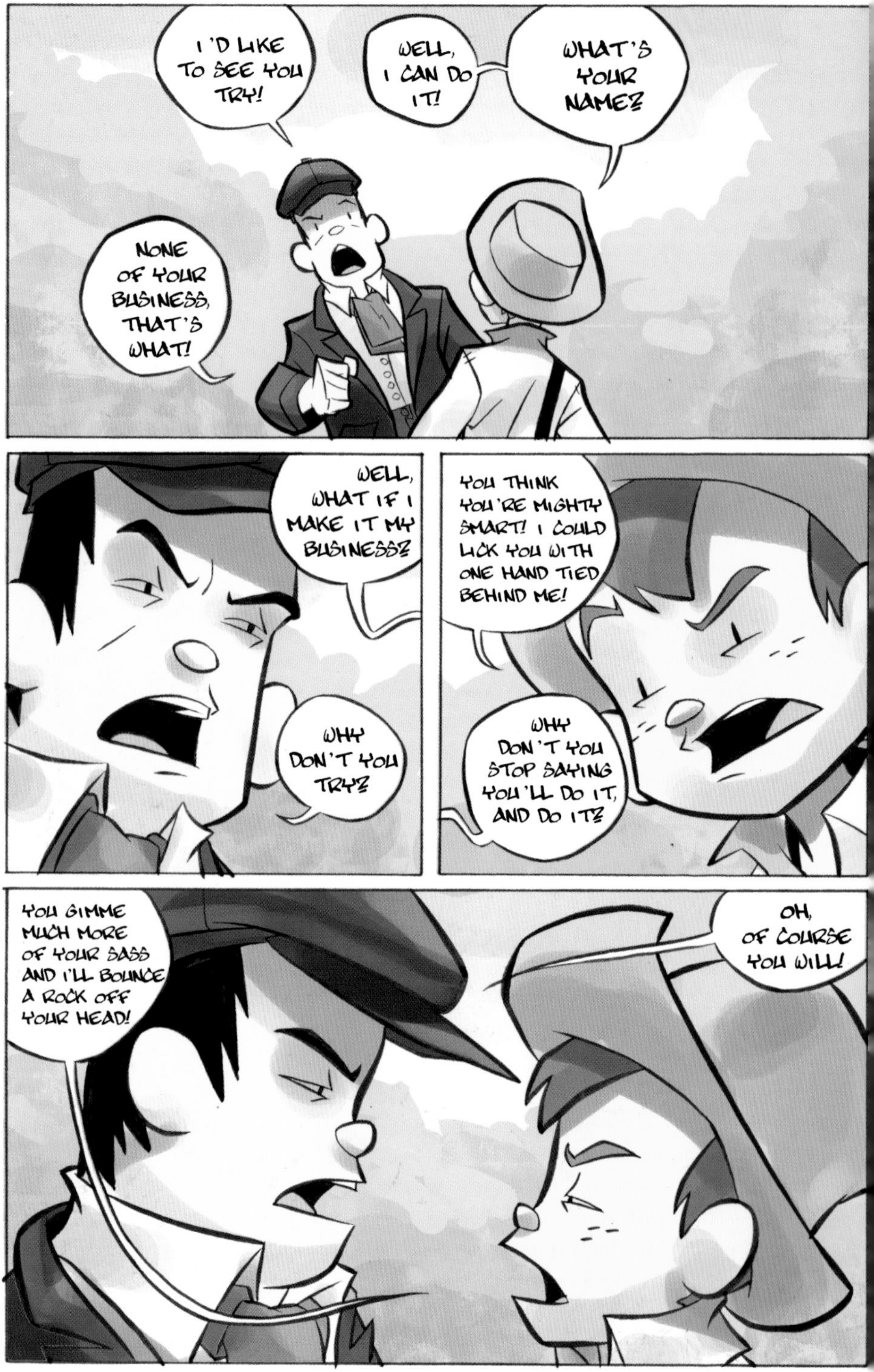
I'D LIKE TO SEE YOU TRY!
WELL, I CAN DO IT!
WHAT'S YOUR NAME?
NONE OF YOUR BUSINESS, THAT'S WHAT!
WELL, WHAT IF I MAKE IT MY BUSINESS?
WHY DON'T YOU TRY?
YOU THINK YOU'RE MIGHTY SMART! I COULD LICK YOU WITH ONE HAND TIED BEHIND ME!
WHY DON'T YOU STOP SAYING YOU'LL DO IT, AND DO IT?
YOU GIMME MUCH MORE OF YOUR SASS AND I'LL BOUNCE A ROCK OFF YOUR HEAD!
OH, OF COURSE YOU WILL!

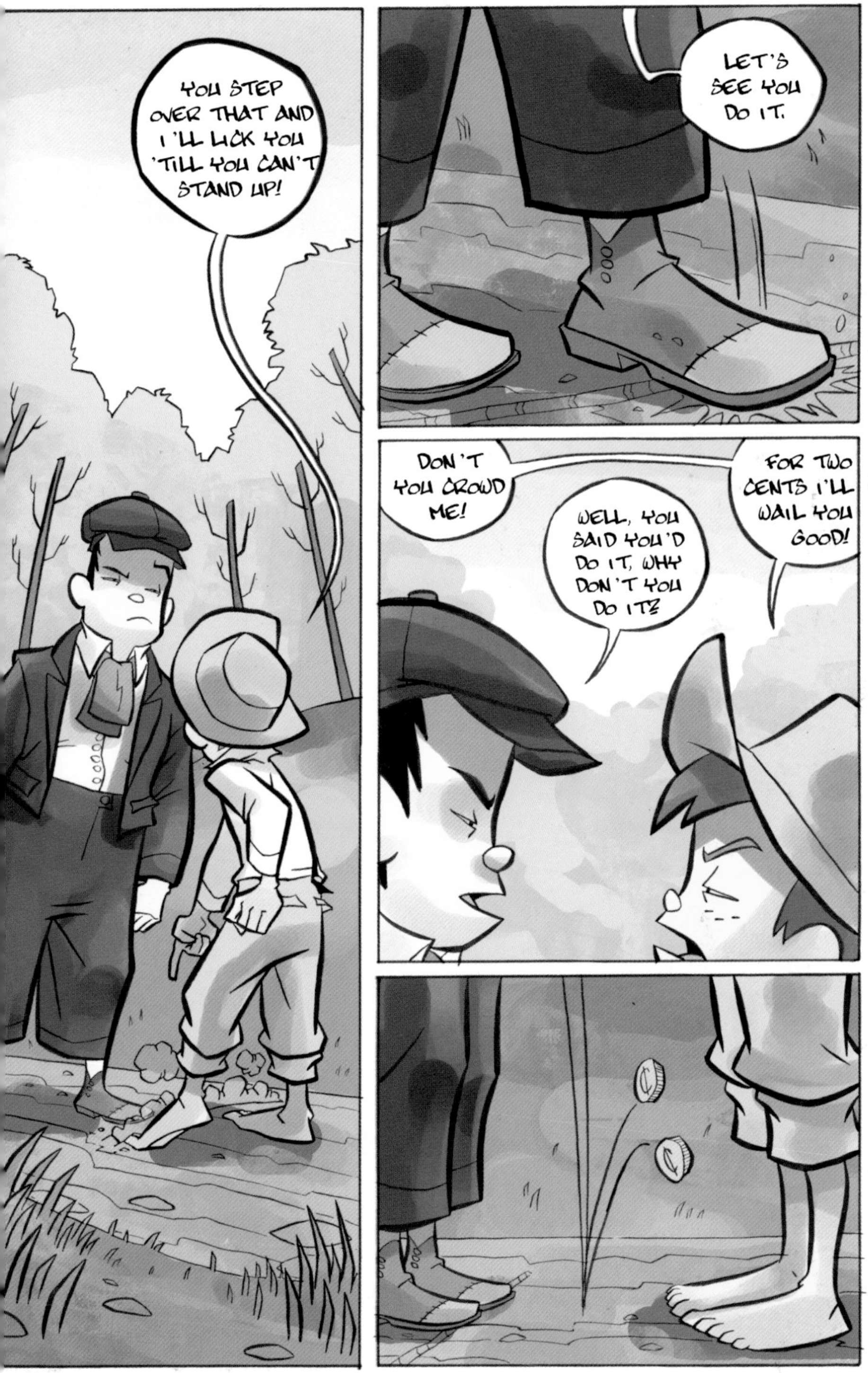
YOU STEP OVER THAT AND I'LL LICK YOU 'TILL YOU CAN'T STAND UP!
LET'S SEE YOU DO IT.
DON'T YOU CROWD ME!
FOR TWO CENTS I'LL WAIL YOU GOOD!
WELL, YOU SAID YOU'D DO IT, WHY DON'T YOU DO IT?

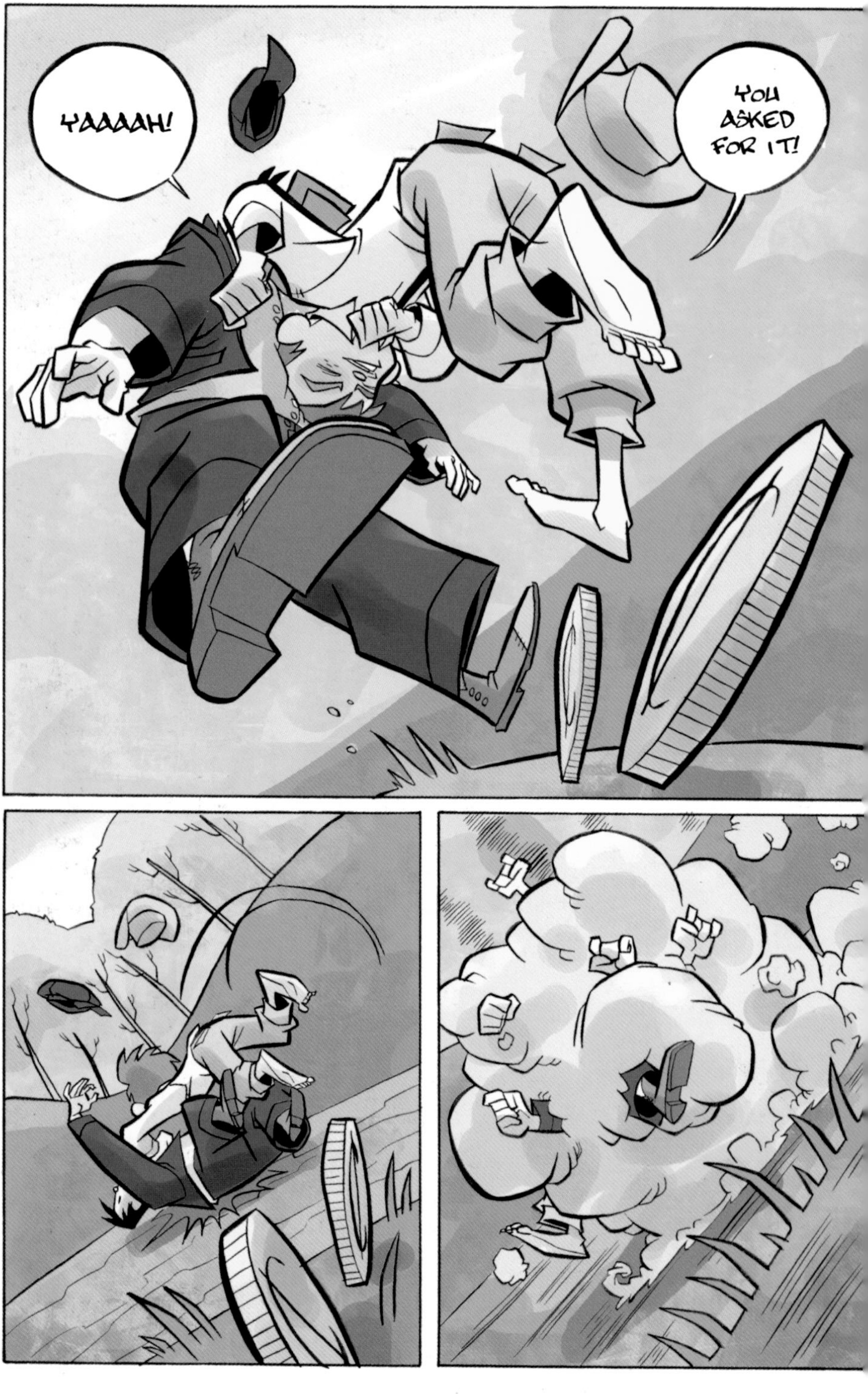
YAAAAH!
YOU ASKED FOR IT!

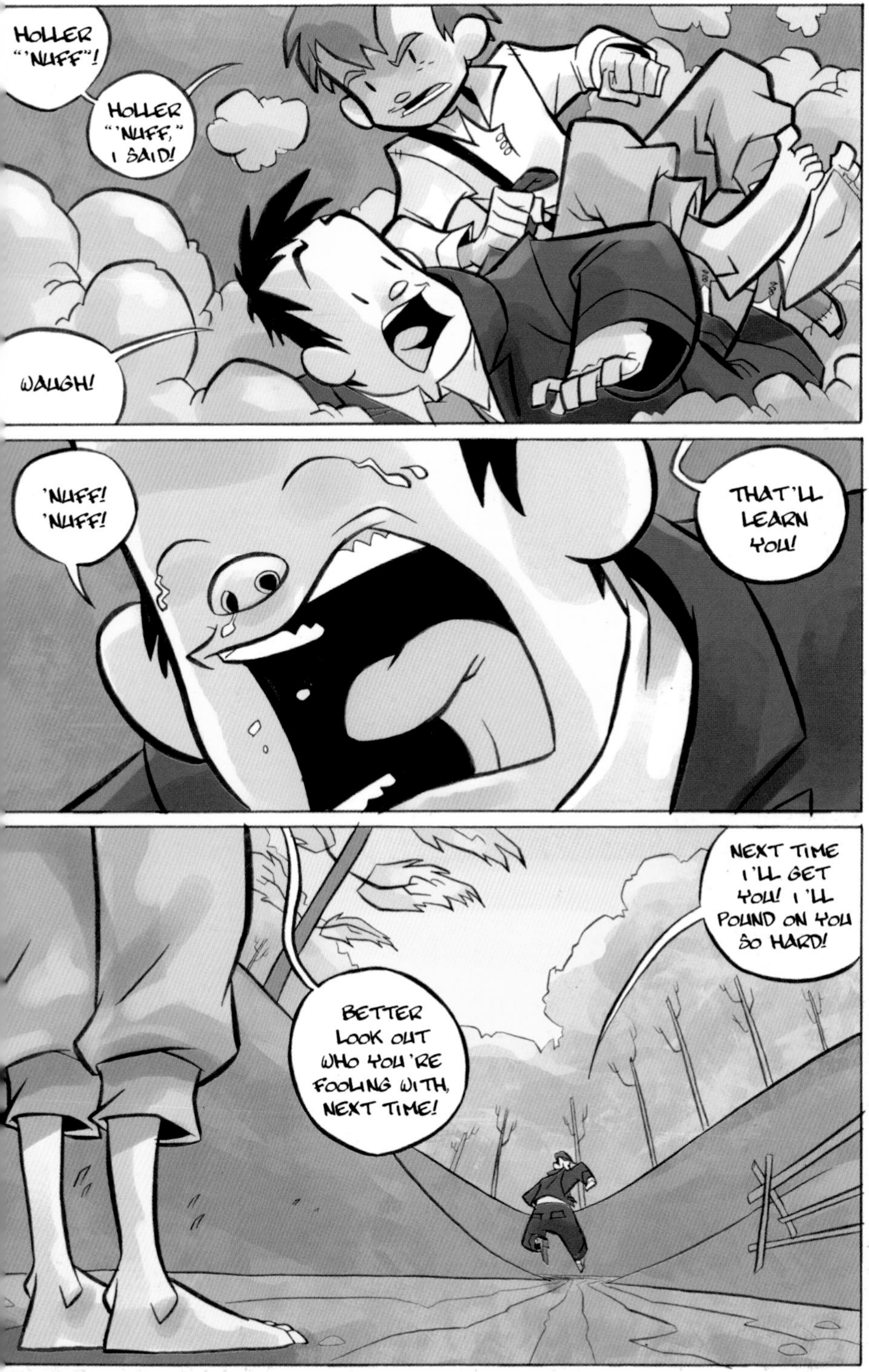
HOLLER "'NUFF"!
HOLLER "'NUFF," I SAID!
WAUGH!
'NUFF! 'NUFF!
THAT'LL LEARN YOU!
NEXT TIME I'LL GET YOU! I'LL POUND ON YOU SO HARD!
BETTER LOOK OUT WHO YOU'RE FOOLING WITH, NEXT TIME!

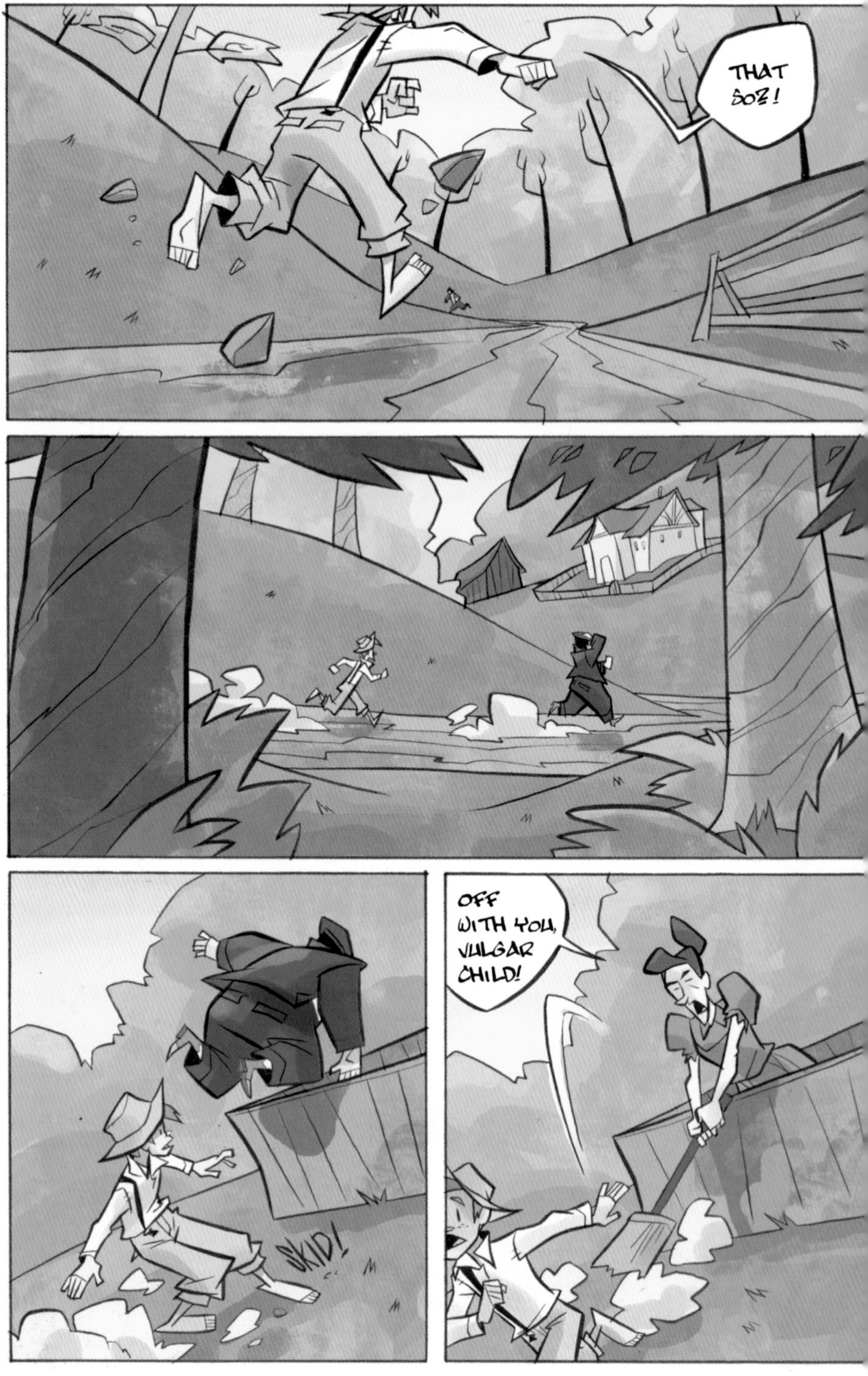
THAT SO?!
SKID!
OFF WITH YOU, VULGAR CHILD!

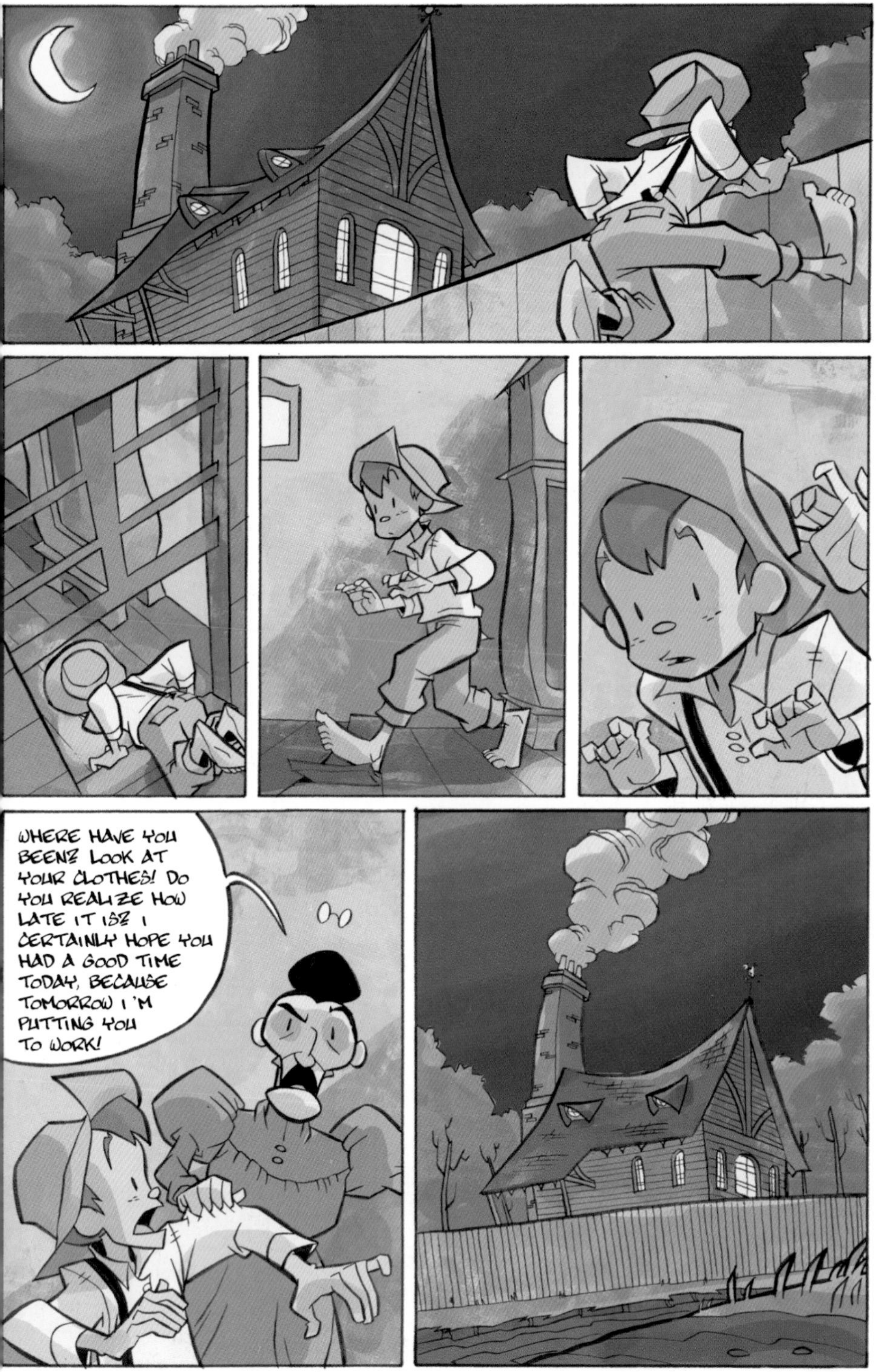
WHERE HAVE YOU BEEN? LOOK AT YOUR CLOTHES! DO YOU REALIZE HOW LATE IT IS? I CERTAINLY HOPE YOU HAD A GOOD TIME TODAY, BECAUSE TOMORROW I'M PUTTING YOU TO WORK!

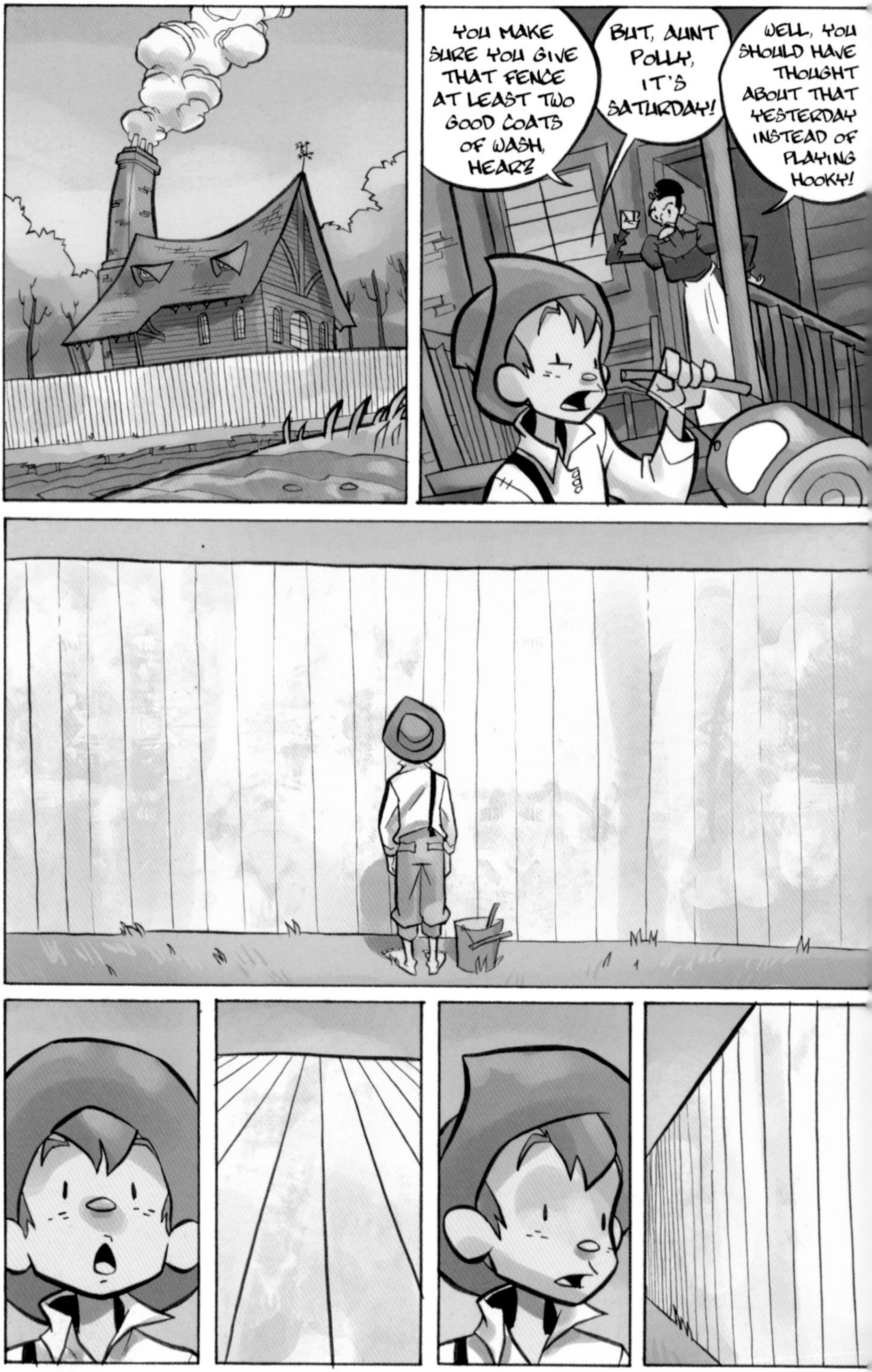
YOU MAKE SURE YOU GIVE THAT FENCE AT LEAST TWO GOOD COATS OF WASH, HEAR?
BUT, AUNT POLLY, IT'S SATURDAY!
WELL, YOU SHOULD HAVE THOUGHT ABOUT THAT YESTERDAY INSTEAD OF PLAYING HOOKY!

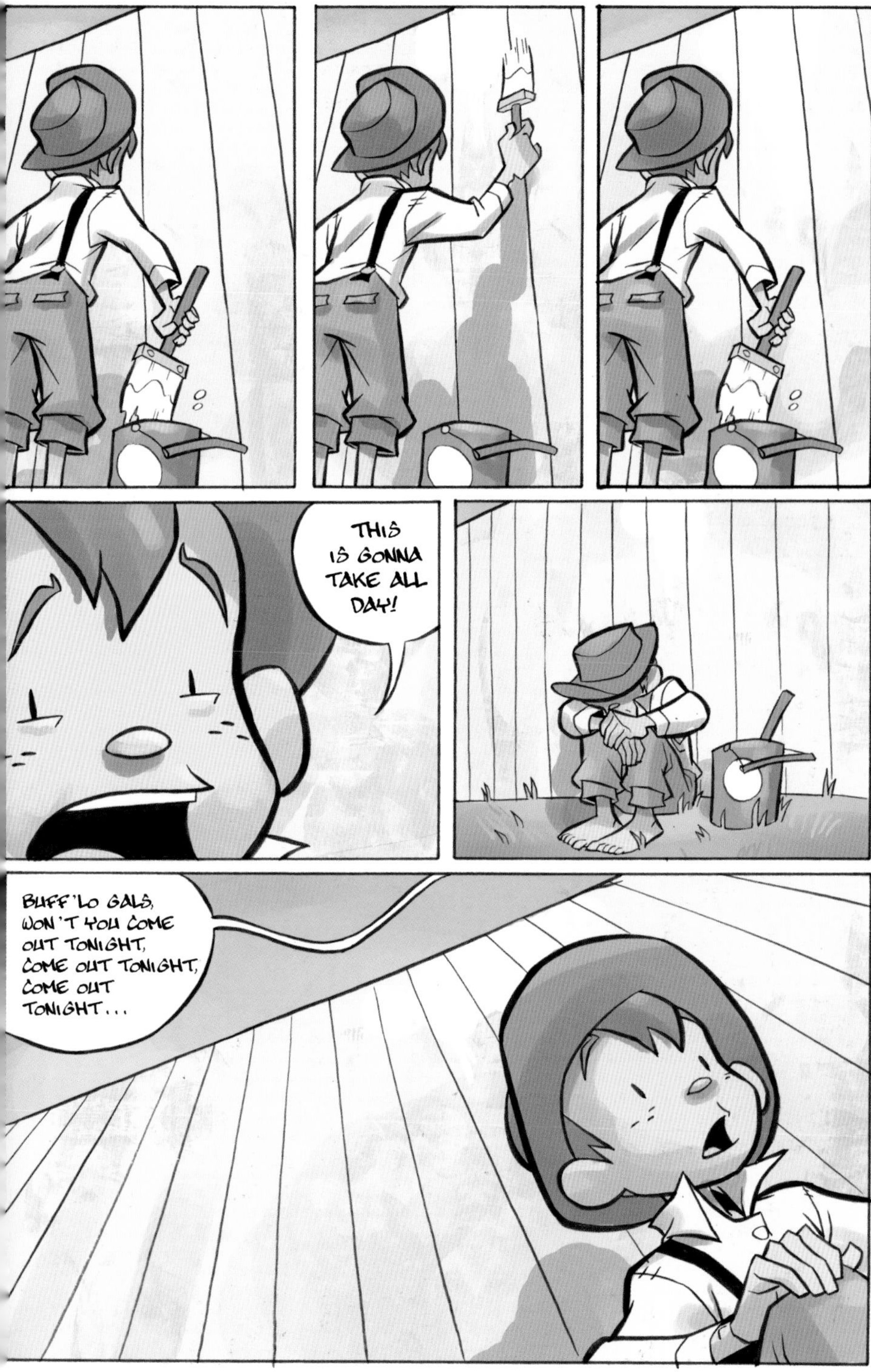
THIS IS GONNA TAKE ALL DAY!
BUFF'LO GALS, WON'T YOU COME OUT TONIGHT, COME OUT TONIGHT, COME OUT TONIGHT...

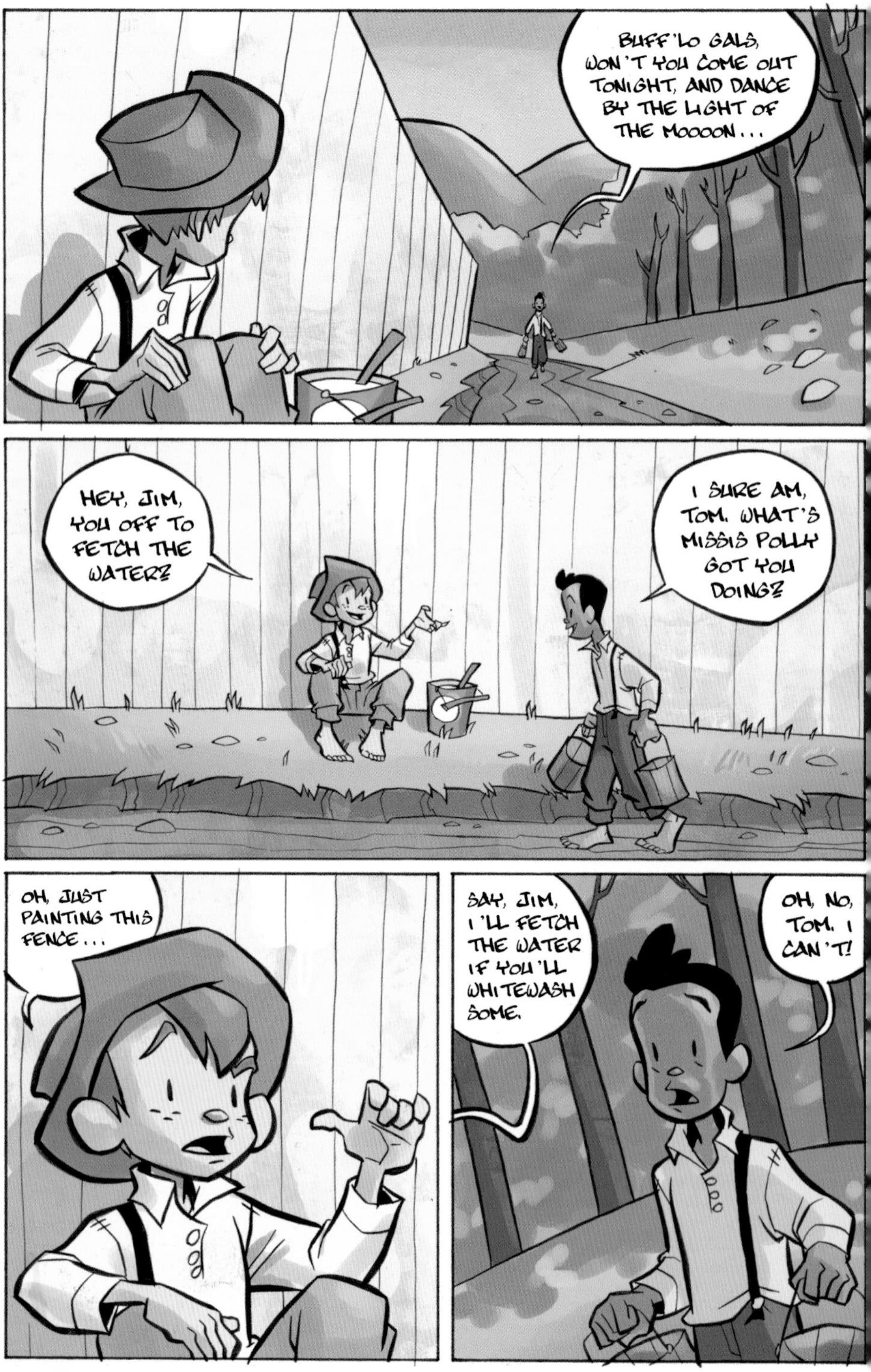
BUFF'LO GALS, WON'T YOU COME OUT TONIGHT, AND DANCE BY THE LIGHT OF THE MOOOON...
HEY, JIM, YOU OFF TO FETCH THE WATER?
I SURE AM, TOM. WHAT'S MISSIS POLLY GOT YOU DOING?
OH, JUST PAINTING THIS FENCE...
SAY, JIM, I'LL FETCH THE WATER IF YOU'LL WHITEWASH SOME.
OH, NO, TOM. I CAN'T!

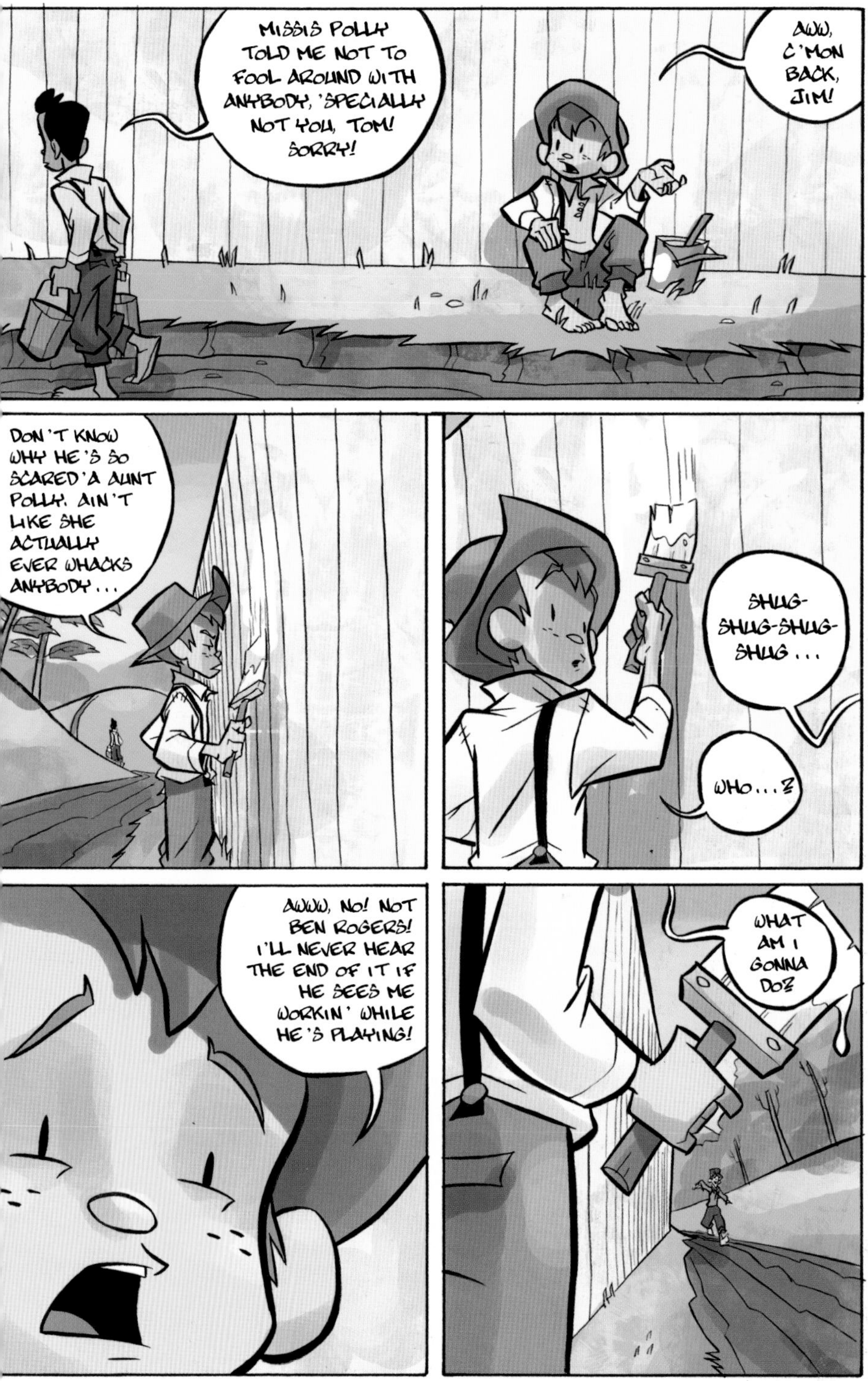
MISSIS POLLY TOLD ME NOT TO FOOL AROUND WITH ANYBODY, 'SPECIALLY NOT YOU, TOM! SORRY!
AWW, C'MON BACK, JIM!
DON'T KNOW WHY HE'S SO SCARED'A AUNT POLLY. AIN'T LIKE SHE ACTUALLY EVER WHACKS ANYBODY...
SHUG-SHUG-SHUG-SHUG...
WHO...?
AWWW, NO! NOT BEN ROGERS! I'LL NEVER HEAR THE END OF IT IF HE SEES ME WORKIN' WHILE HE'S PLAYING!
WHAT AM I GONNA DO?

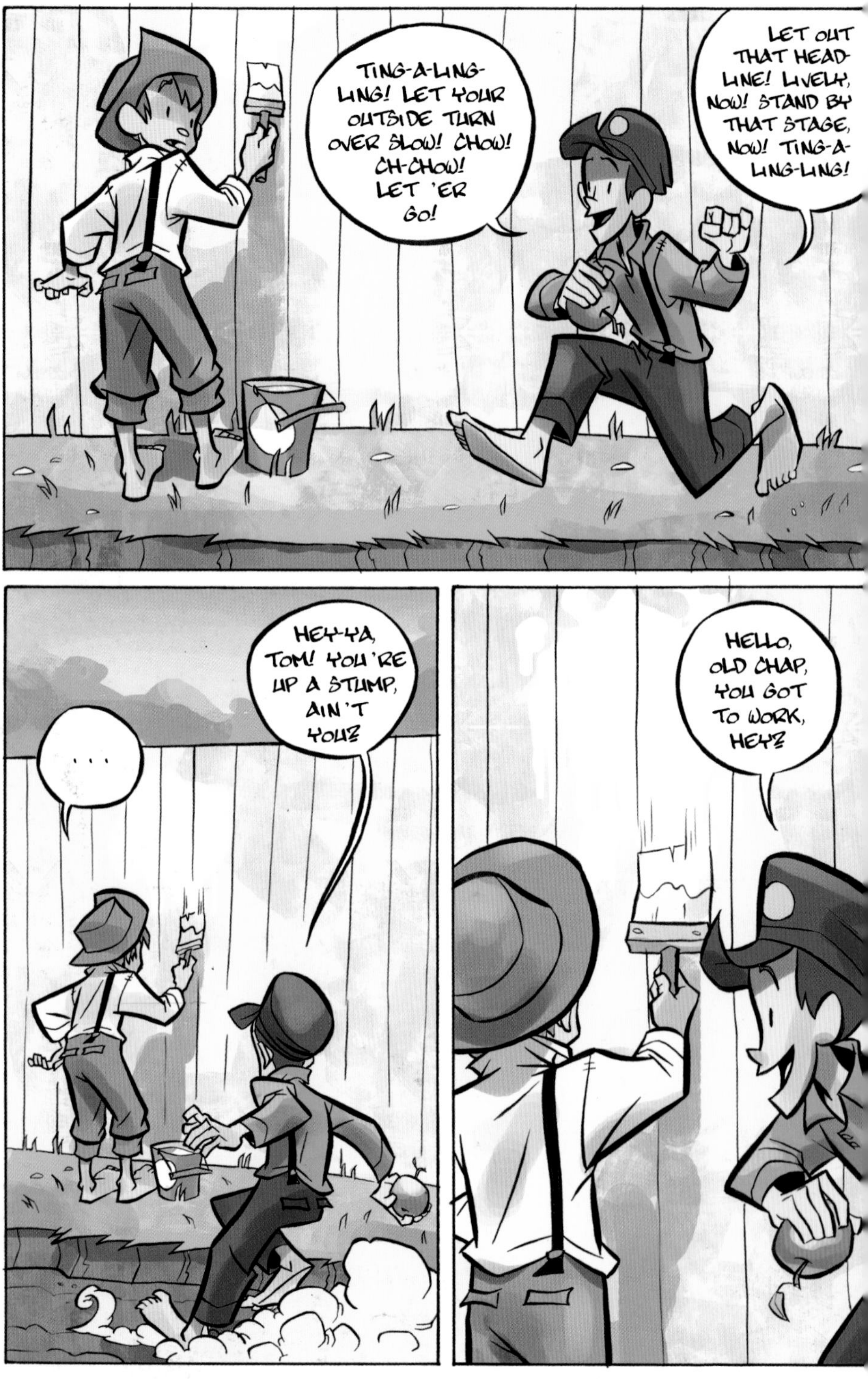
TING-A-LING-LING! LET YOUR OUTSIDE TURN OVER SLOW! CHOW! CH-CHOW! LET 'ER GO!
LET OUT THAT HEAD-LINE! LIVELY, NOW! STAND BY THAT STAGE, NOW! TING-A-LING-LING!
. . .
HEY-YA, TOM! YOU'RE UP A STUMP, AIN'T YOU?
HELLO, OLD CHAP, YOU GOT TO WORK, HEY?

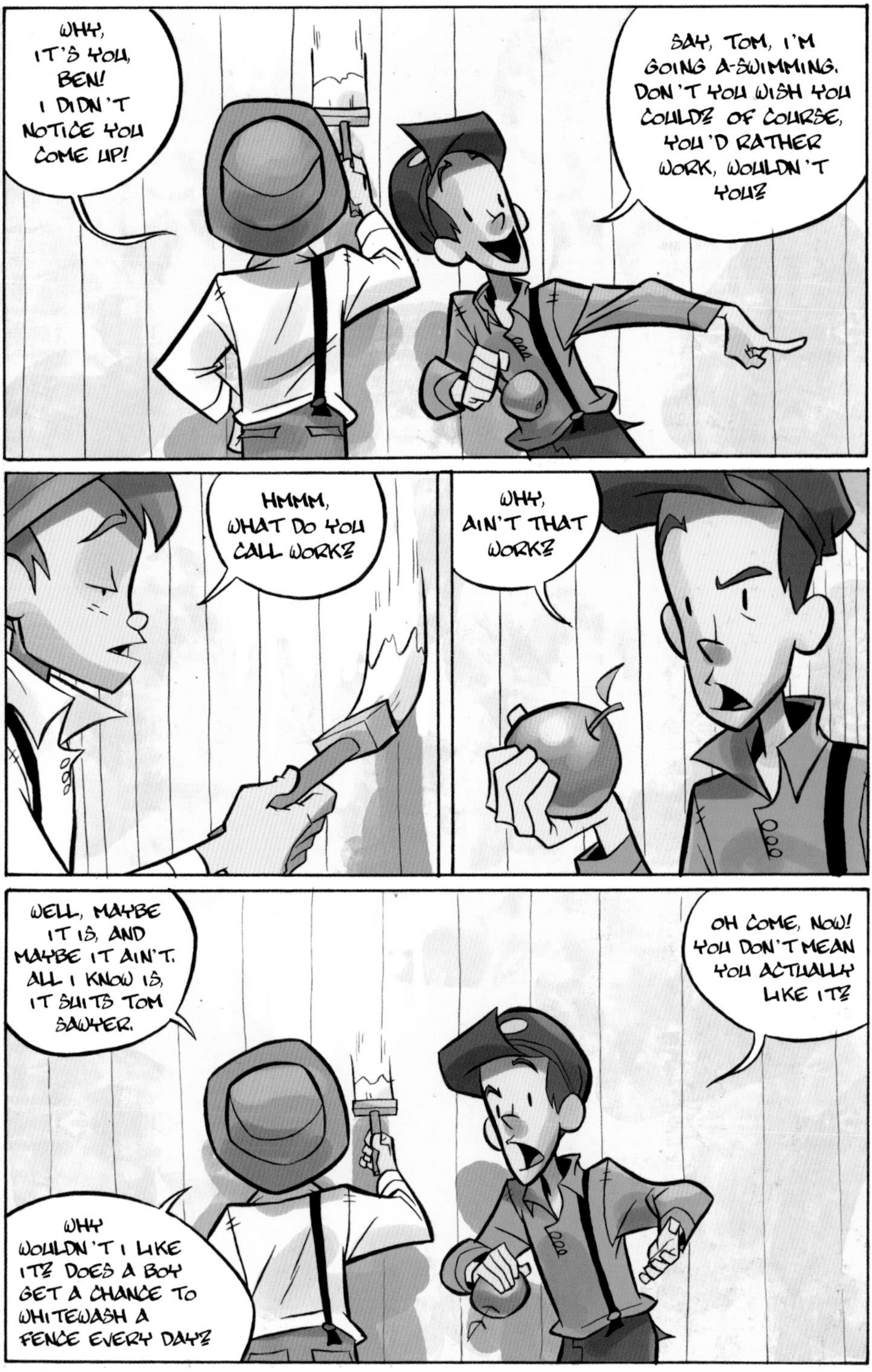
WHY, IT'S YOU, BEN! I DIDN'T NOTICE YOU COME UP!
SAY, TOM, I'M GOING A-SWIMMING. DON'T YOU WISH YOU COULD? OF COURSE, YOU'D RATHER WORK, WOULDN'T YOU?
HMMM, WHAT DO YOU CALL WORK?
WHY, AIN'T THAT WORK?
WELL, MAYBE IT IS, AND MAYBE IT AIN'T. ALL I KNOW IS, IT SUITS TOM SAWYER.
OH COME, NOW! YOU DON'T MEAN YOU ACTUALLY LIKE IT?
WHY WOULDN'T I LIKE IT? DOES A BOY GET A CHANCE TO WHITEWASH A FENCE EVERY DAY?

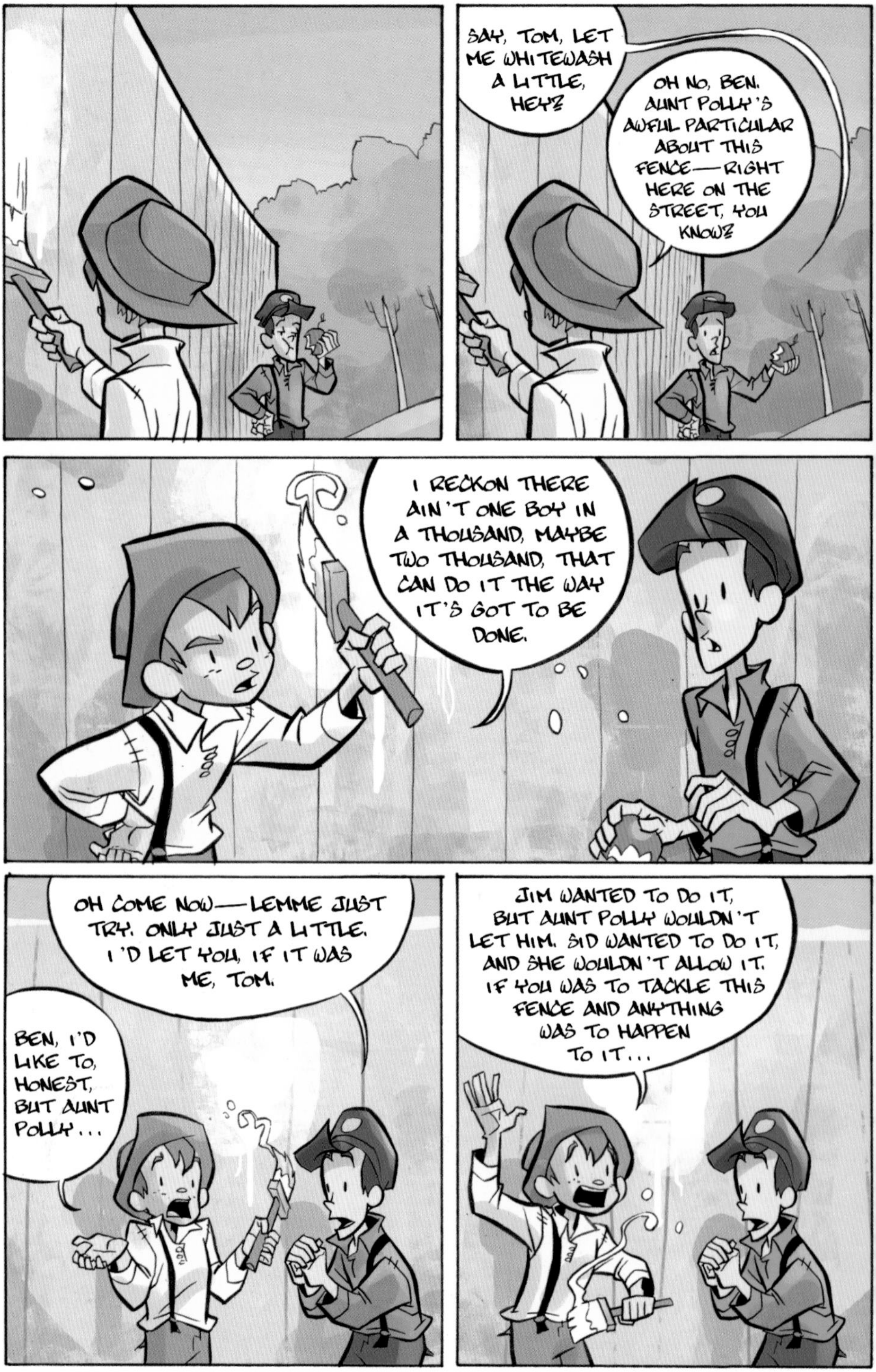
SAY, TOM, LET ME WHITEWASH A LITTLE, HEY?
OH NO, BEN. AUNT POLLY'S AWFUL PARTICULAR ABOUT THIS FENCE—RIGHT HERE ON THE STREET, YOU KNOW?
I RECKON THERE AIN'T ONE BOY IN A THOUSAND, MAYBE TWO THOUSAND, THAT CAN DO IT THE WAY IT'S GOT TO BE DONE.
OH COME NOW—LEMME JUST TRY. ONLY JUST A LITTLE. I'D LET YOU, IF IT WAS ME, TOM.
BEN, I'D LIKE TO, HONEST, BUT AUNT POLLY...
JIM WANTED TO DO IT, BUT AUNT POLLY WOULDN'T LET HIM. SID WANTED TO DO IT, AND SHE WOULDN'T ALLOW IT. IF YOU WAS TO TACKLE THIS FENCE AND ANYTHING WAS TO HAPPEN TO IT...

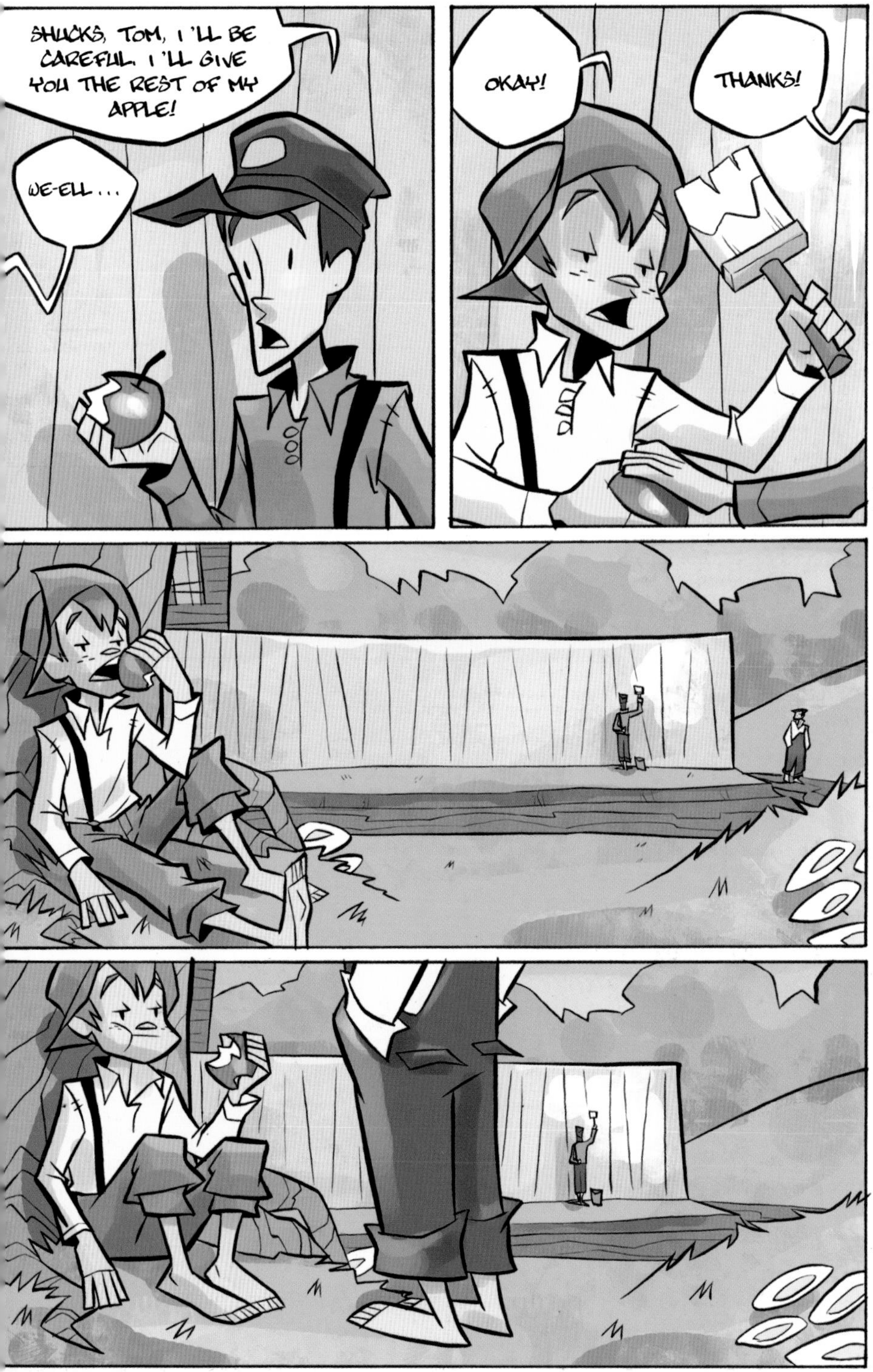
SHUCKS, TOM, I'LL BE CAREFUL. I'LL GIVE YOU THE REST OF MY APPLE!
WE-ELL . . .
OKAY!
THANKS!

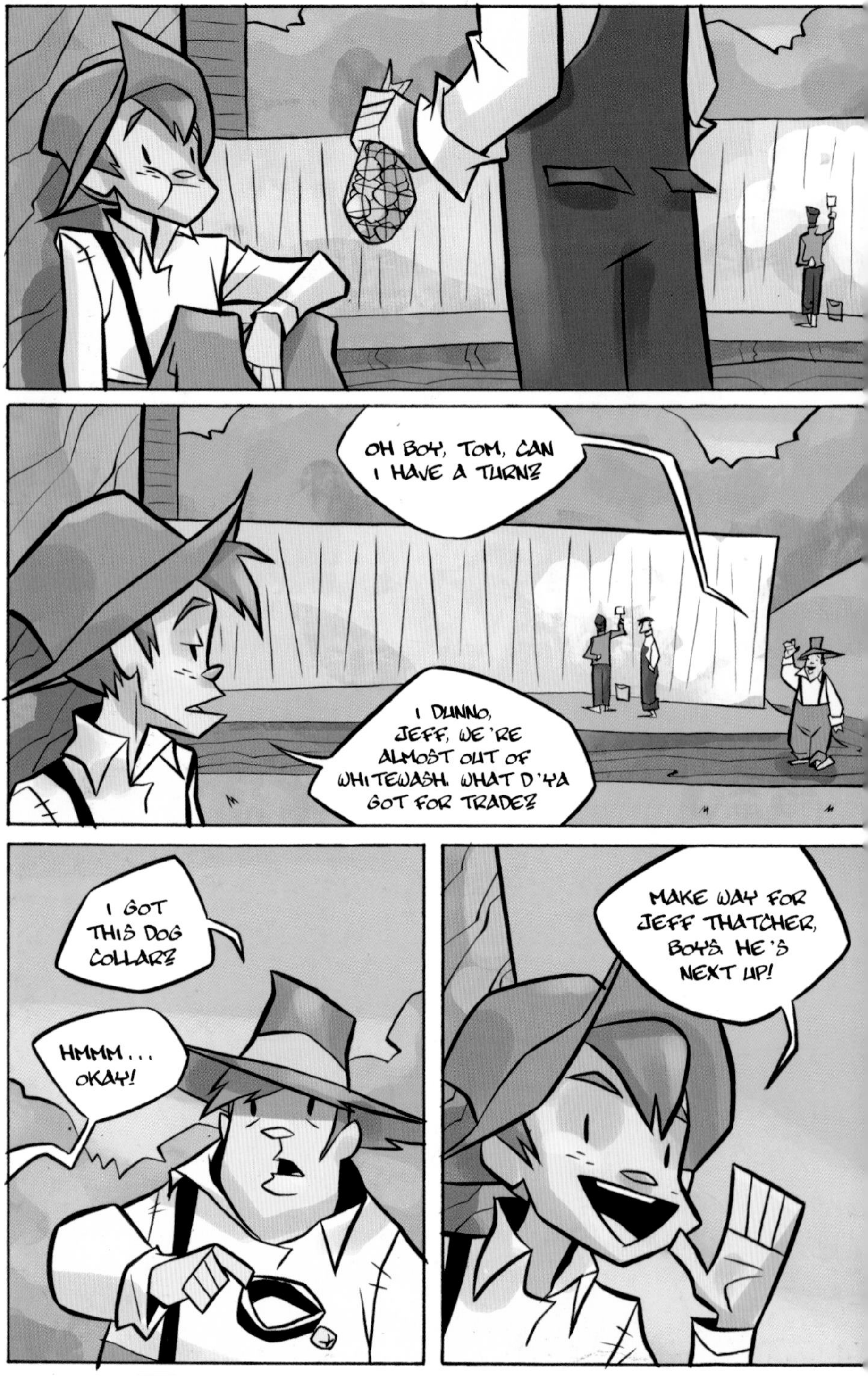
OH BOY, TOM, CAN I HAVE A TURN?
I DUNNO, JEFF, WE'RE ALMOST OUT OF WHITEWASH. WHAT D'YA GOT FOR TRADE?
I GOT THIS DOG COLLAR?
HMMM... OKAY!
MAKE WAY FOR JEFF THATCHER, BOYS. HE'S NEXT UP!

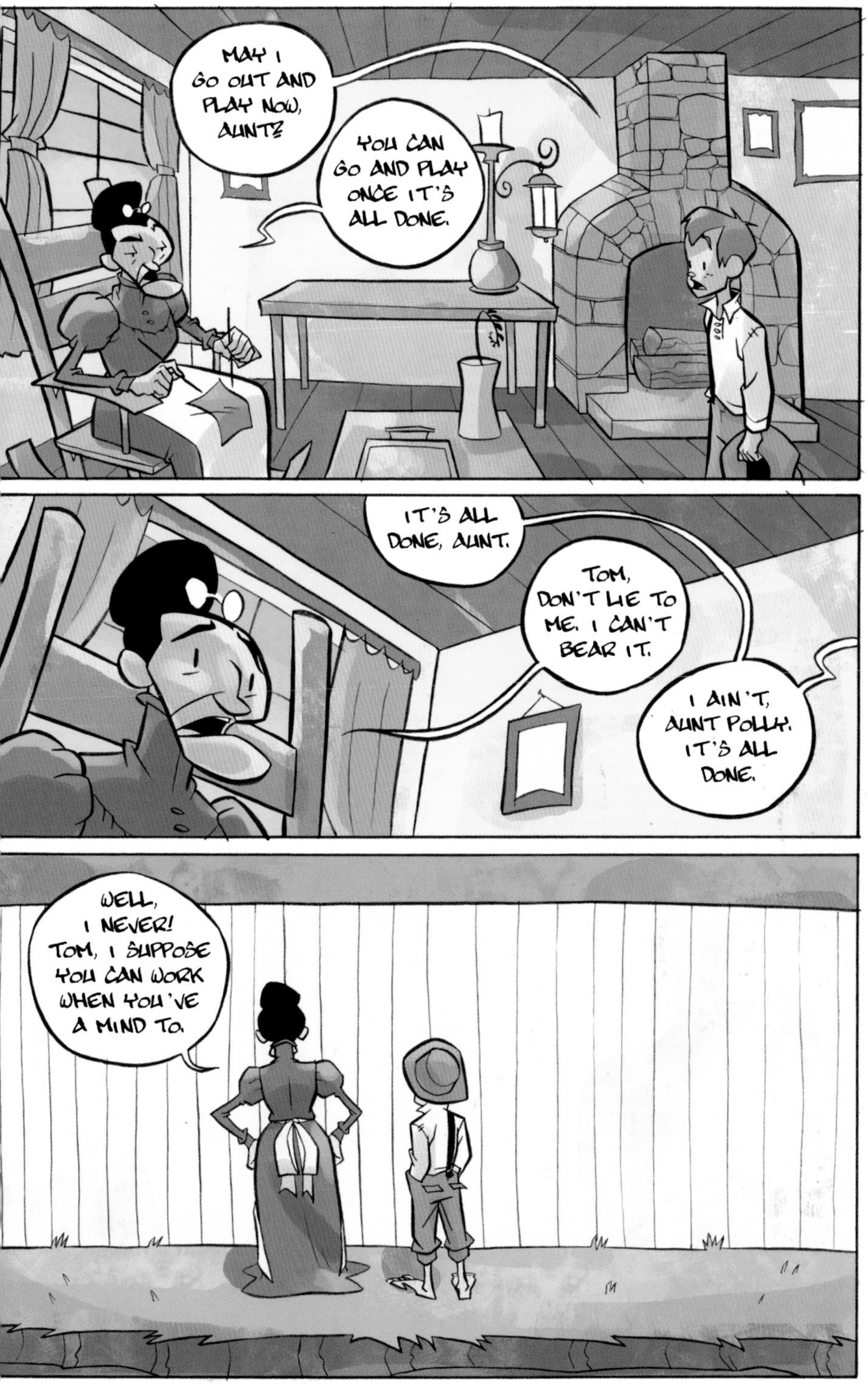
MAY I GO OUT AND PLAY NOW, AUNT?
YOU CAN GO AND PLAY ONCE IT'S ALL DONE.
IT'S ALL DONE, AUNT.
TOM, DON'T LIE TO ME. I CAN'T BEAR IT.
I AIN'T, AUNT POLLY. IT'S ALL DONE.
WELL, I NEVER! TOM, I SUPPOSE YOU CAN WORK WHEN YOU'VE A MIND TO.

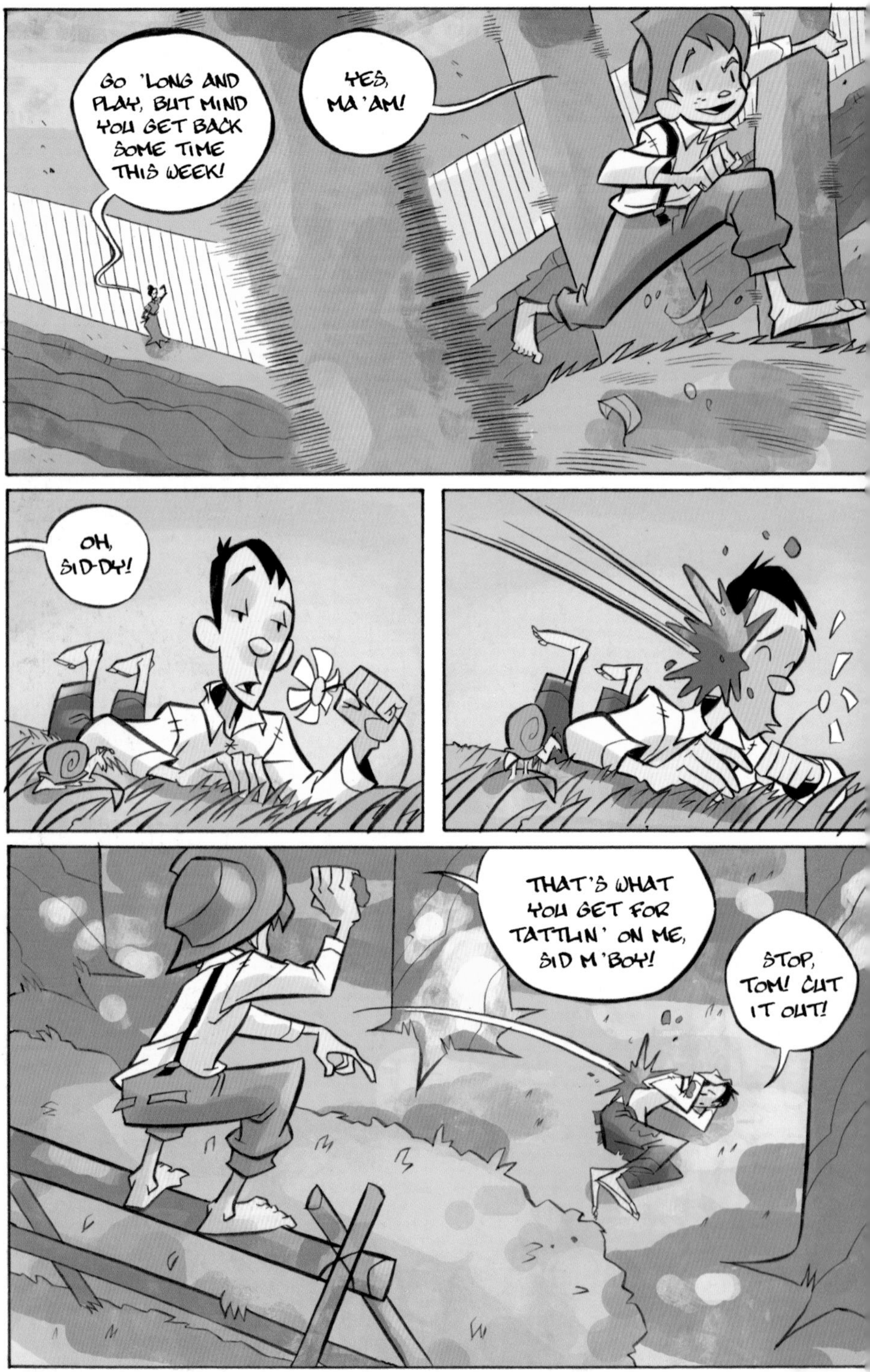
GO 'LONG AND PLAY, BUT MIND YOU GET BACK SOME TIME THIS WEEK!
YES, MA'AM!
OH, SID-DY!
THAT'S WHAT YOU GET FOR TATTLIN' ON ME, SID M'BOY!
STOP, TOM! CUT IT OUT!

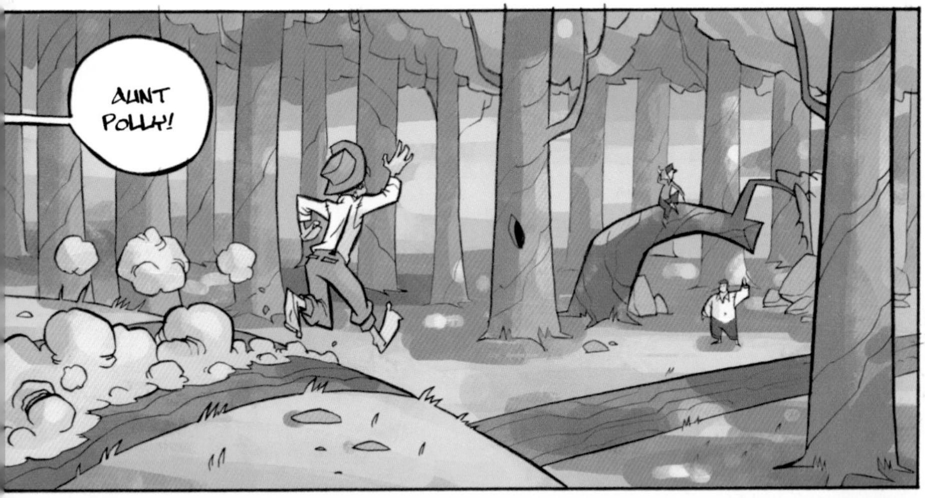
AUNT POLLY!

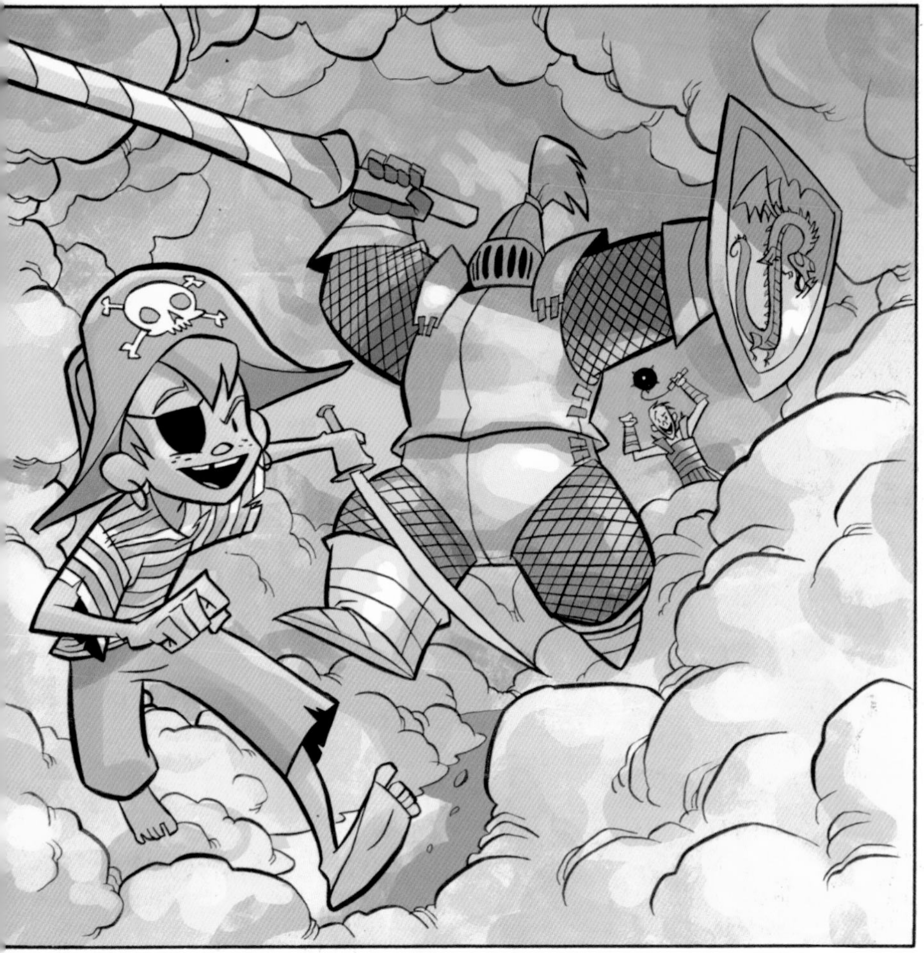

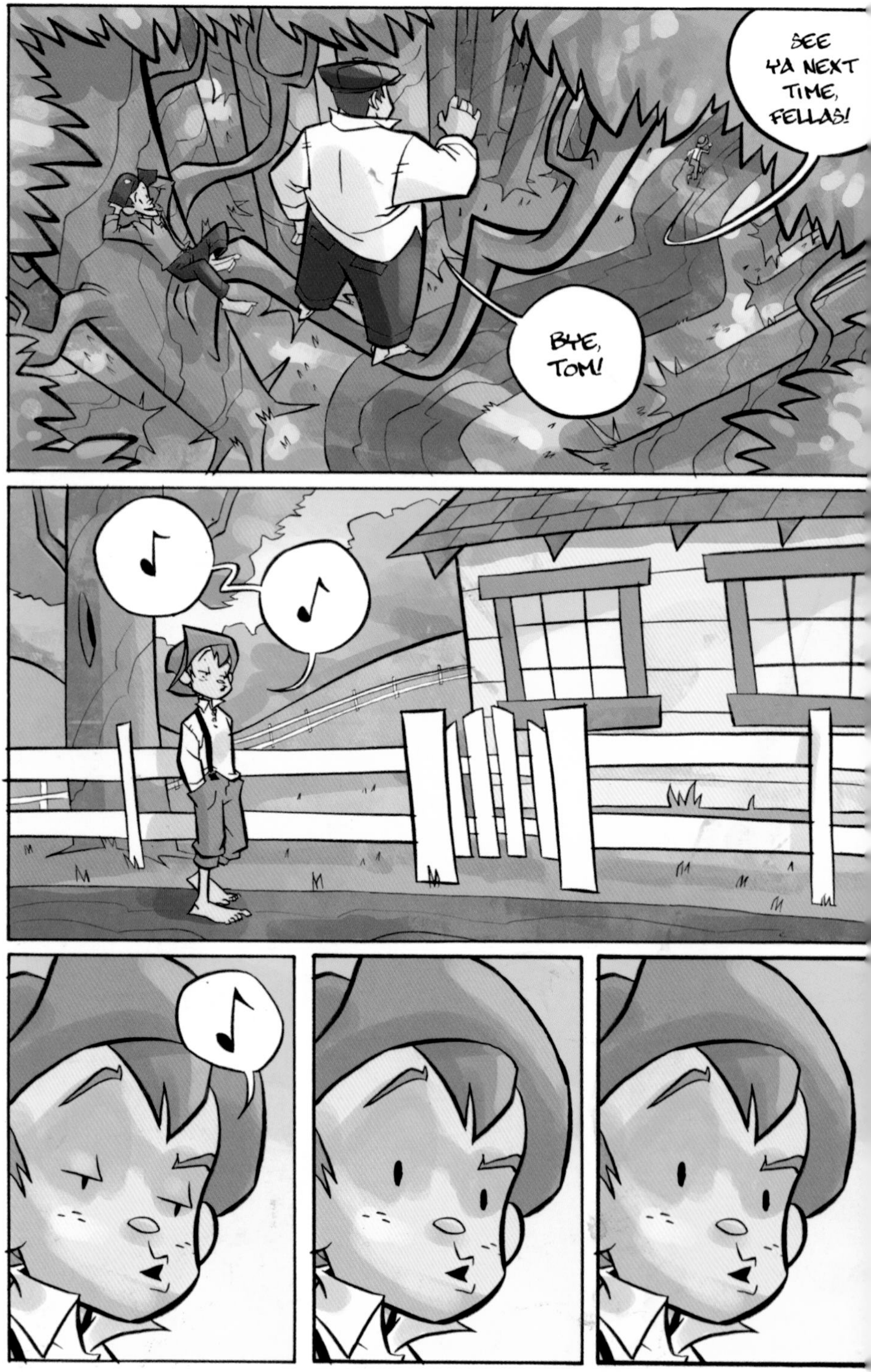
SEE YA NEXT TIME, FELLAS!
BYE, TOM!
♪
♪
♪

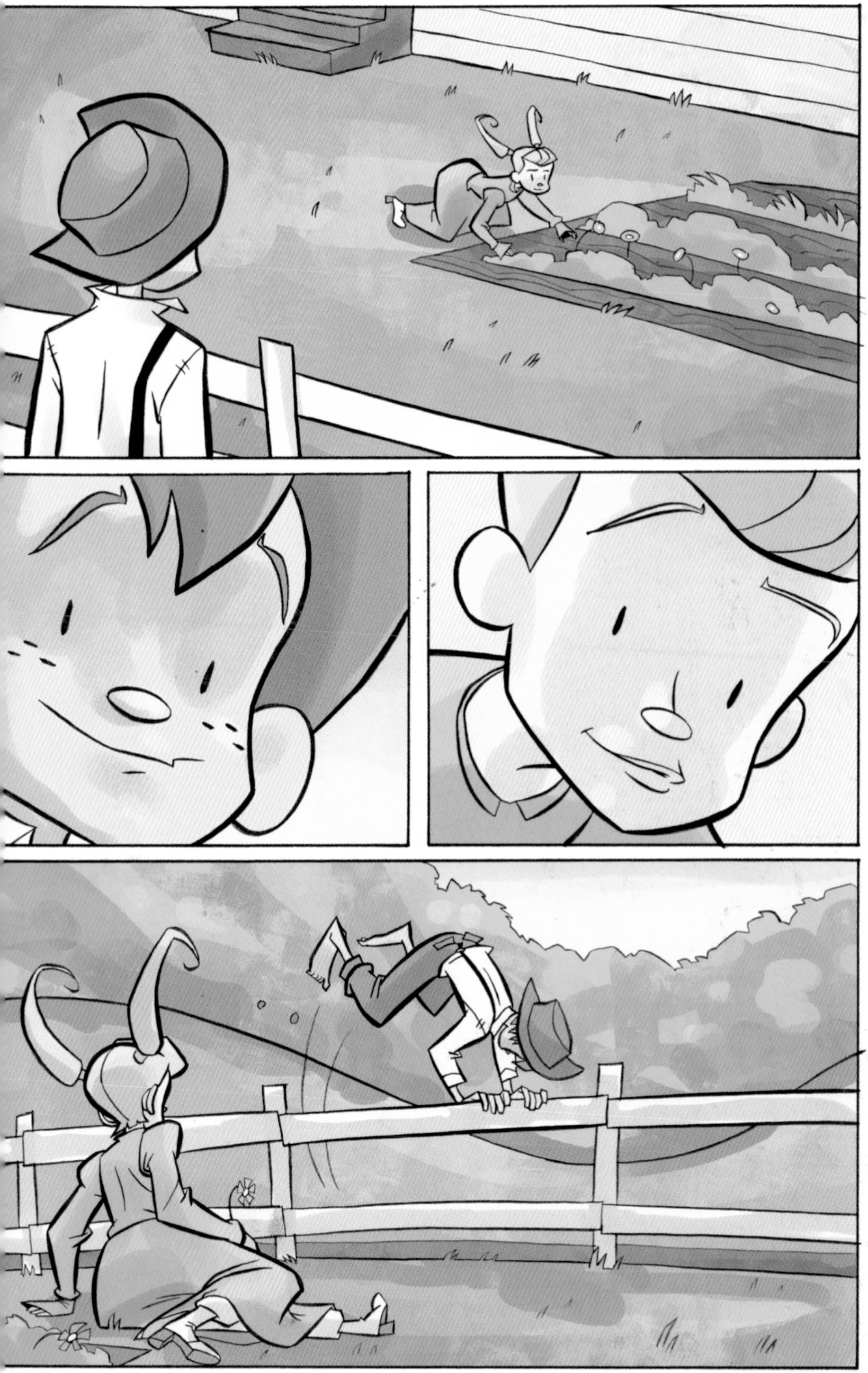

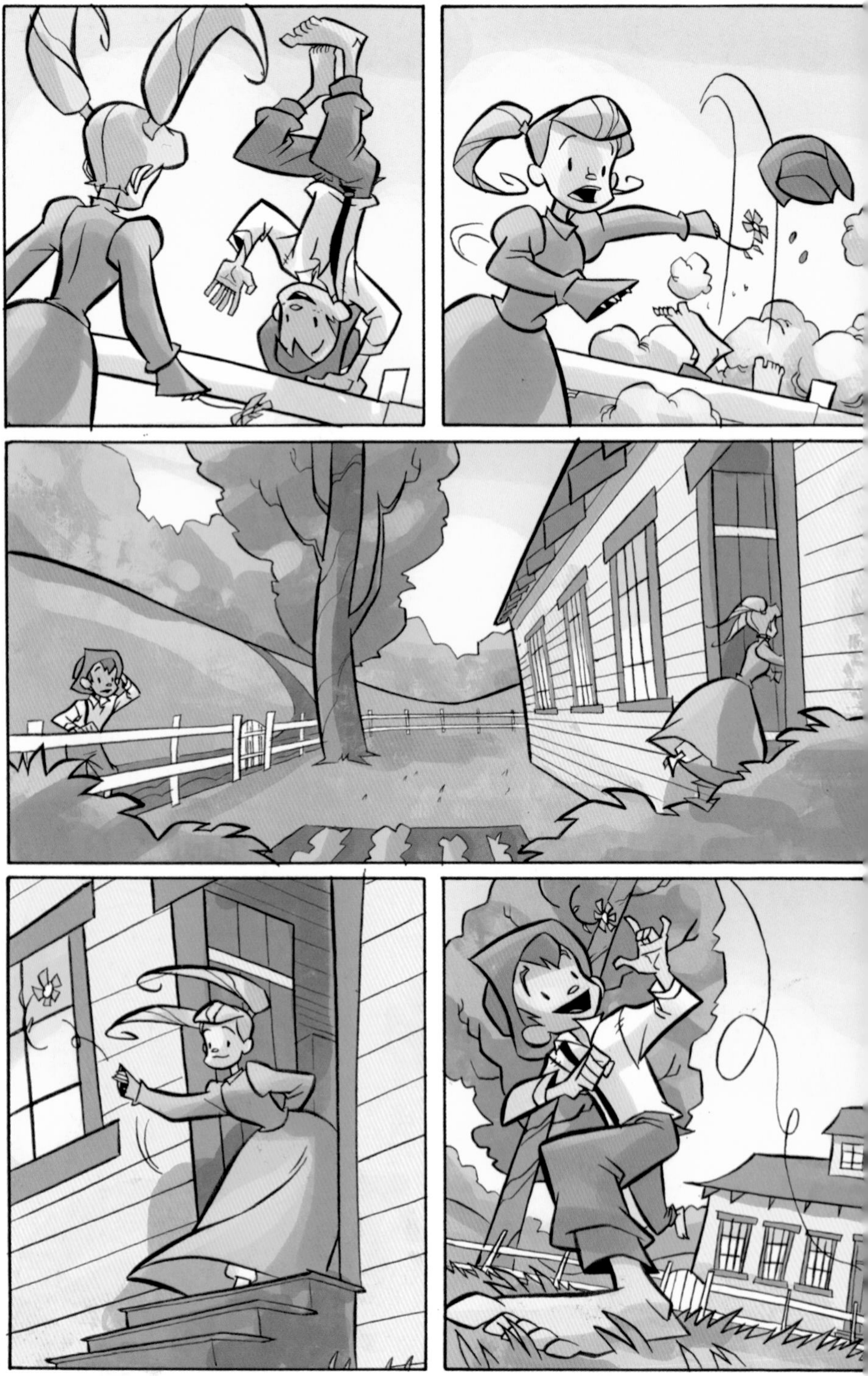

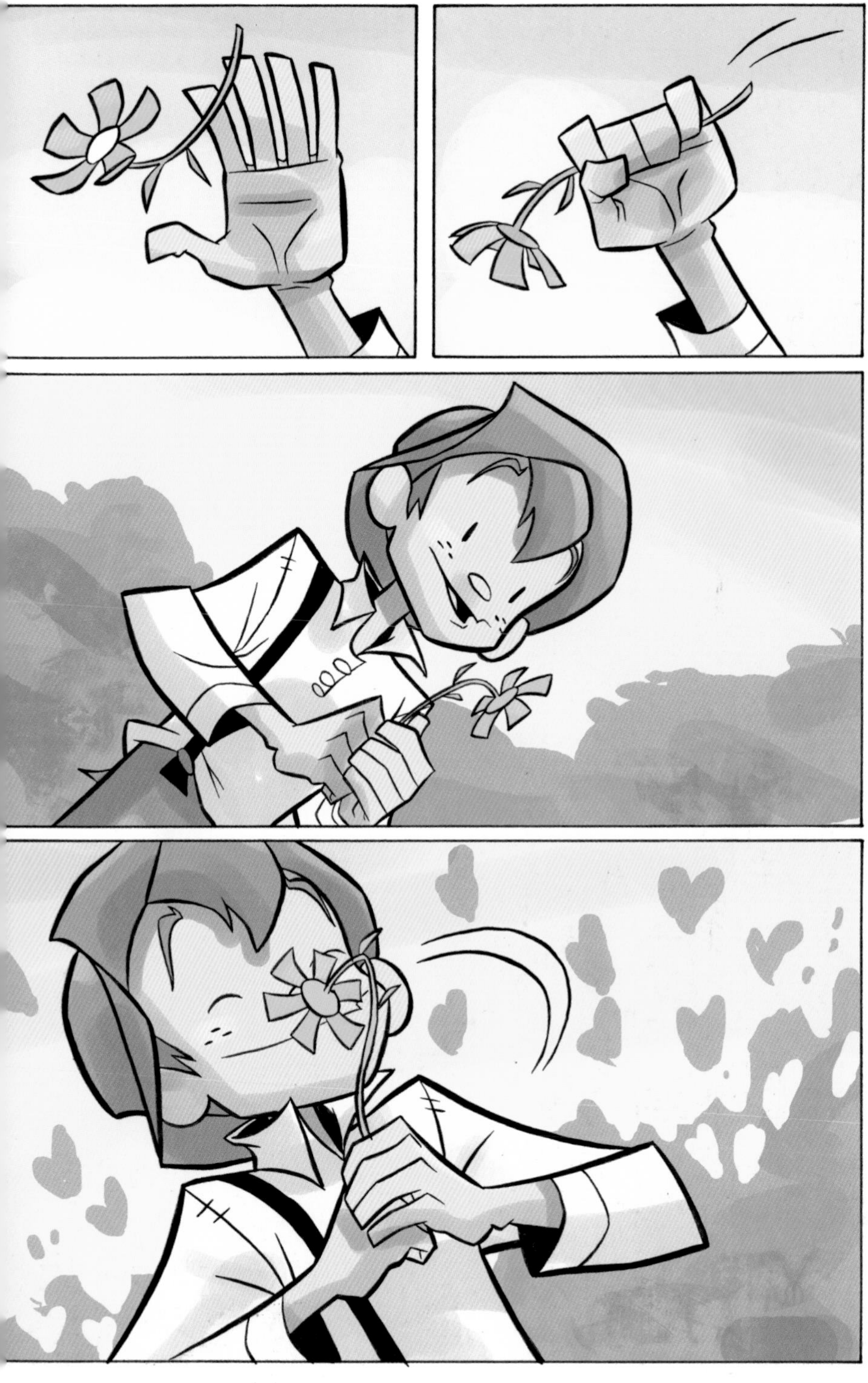

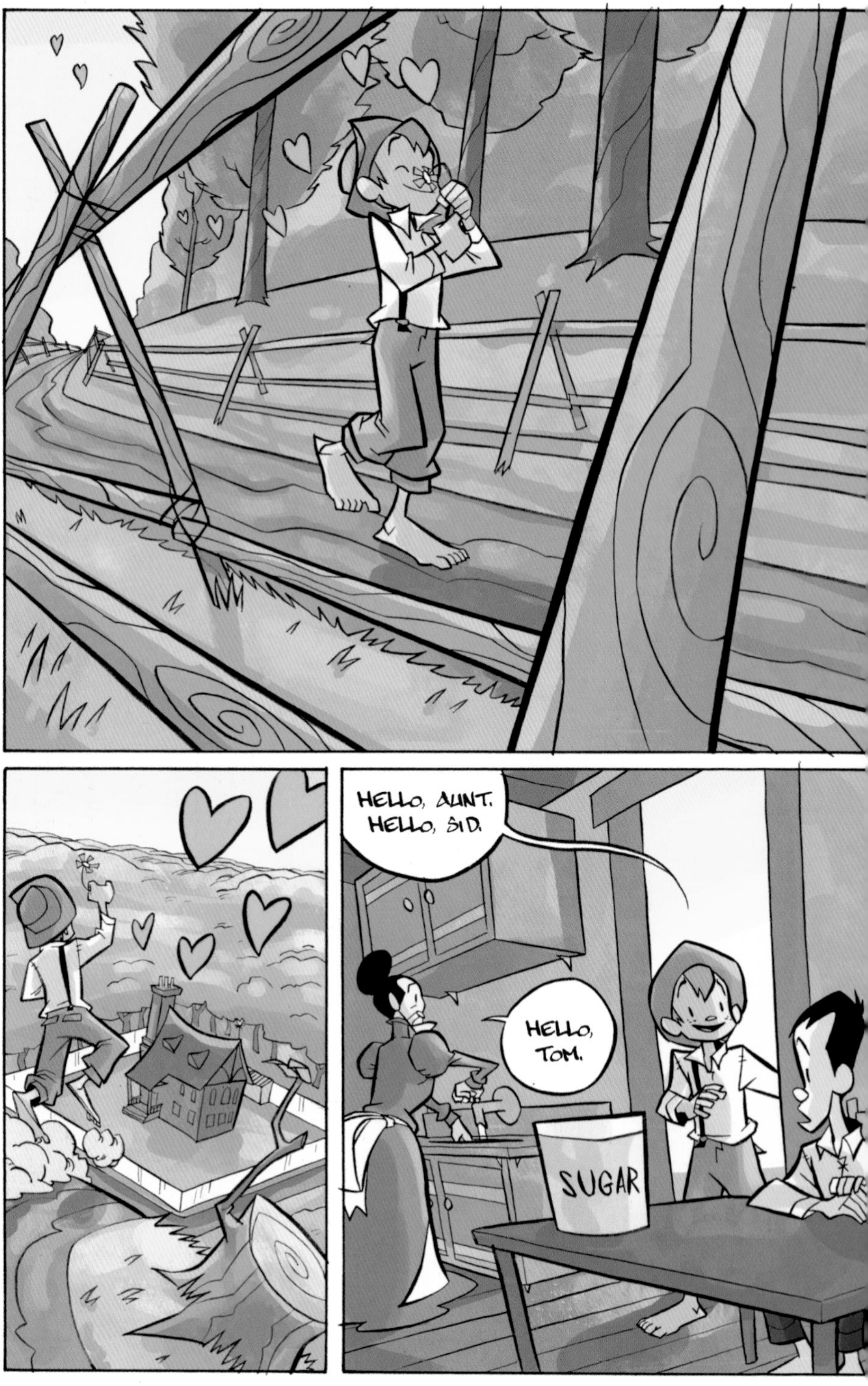
HELLO, AUNT.
HELLO, SID.
HELLO, TOM.
SUGAR

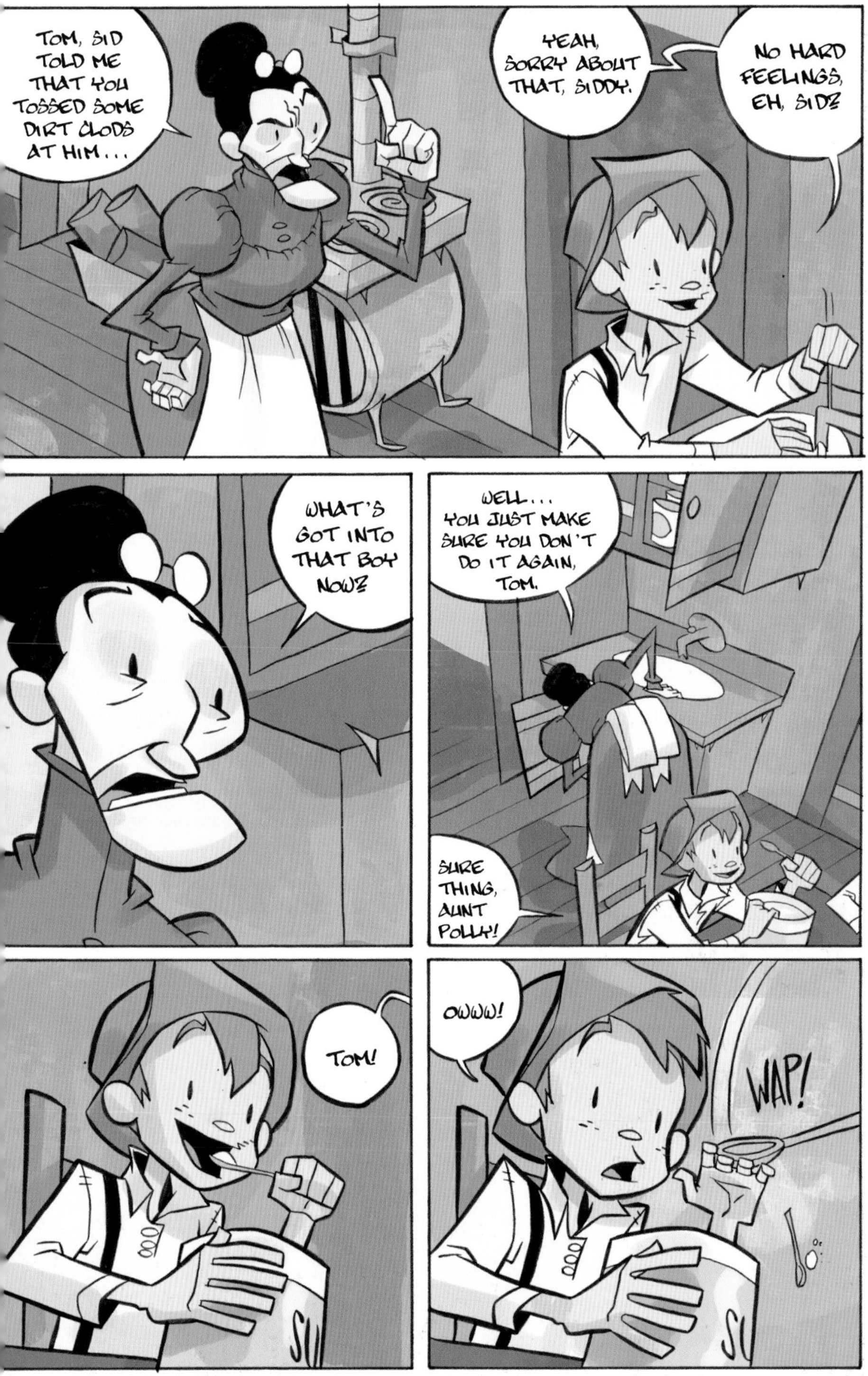
TOM, SID TOLD ME THAT YOU TOSSED SOME DIRT CLODS AT HIM...
YEAH, SORRY ABOUT THAT, SIDDY.
NO HARD FEELINGS, EH, SID?
WHAT'S GOT INTO THAT BOY NOW?
WELL... YOU JUST MAKE SURE YOU DON'T DO IT AGAIN, TOM.
SURE THING, AUNT POLLY!
TOM!
OWWW!
WAP!

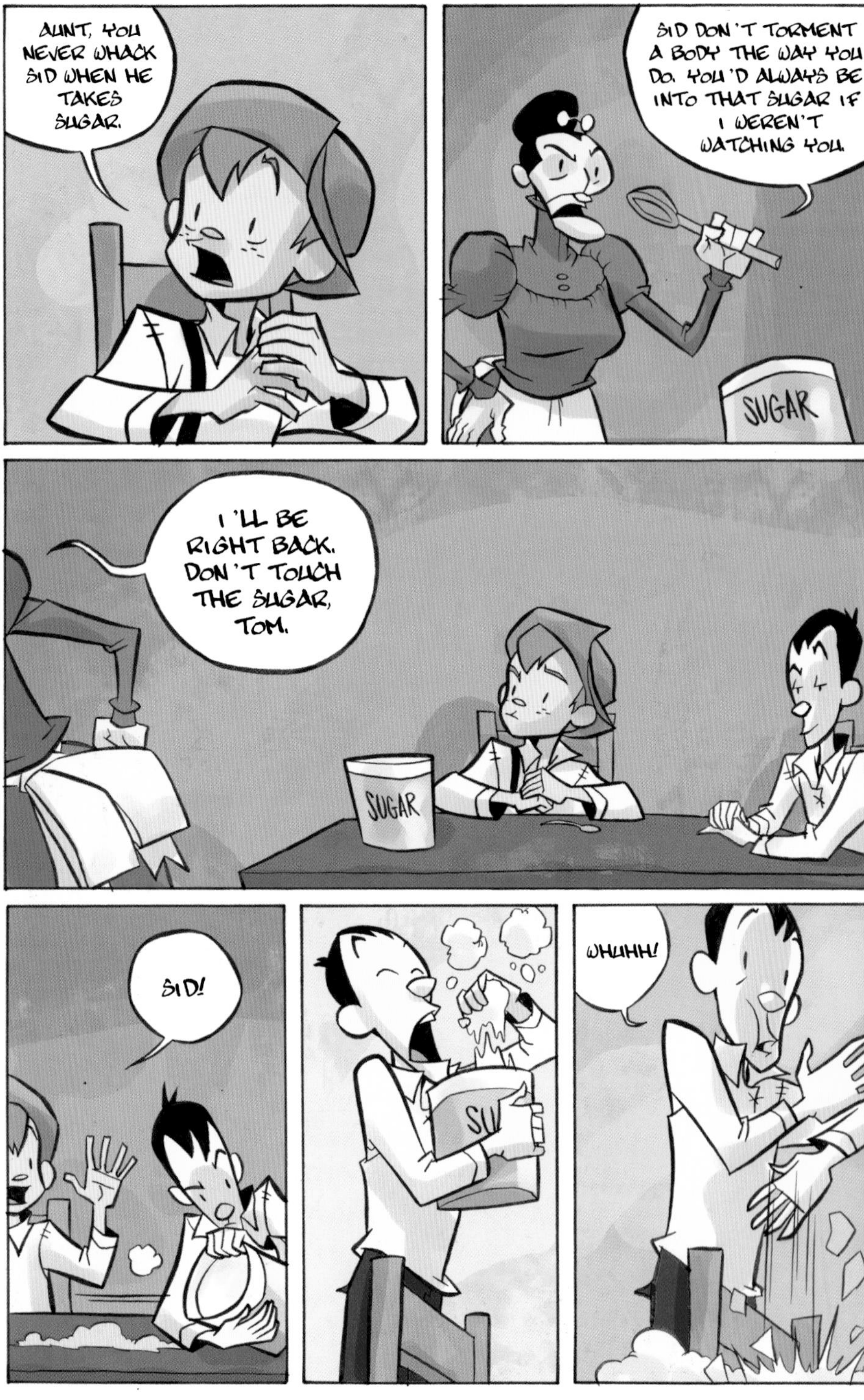
AUNT, YOU NEVER WHACK SID WHEN HE TAKES SUGAR.
SID DON'T TORMENT A BODY THE WAY YOU DO. YOU'D ALWAYS BE INTO THAT SUGAR IF I WEREN'T WATCHING YOU.
SUGAR
I'LL BE RIGHT BACK. DON'T TOUCH THE SUGAR, TOM.
SUGAR
SID!
WHUHH!

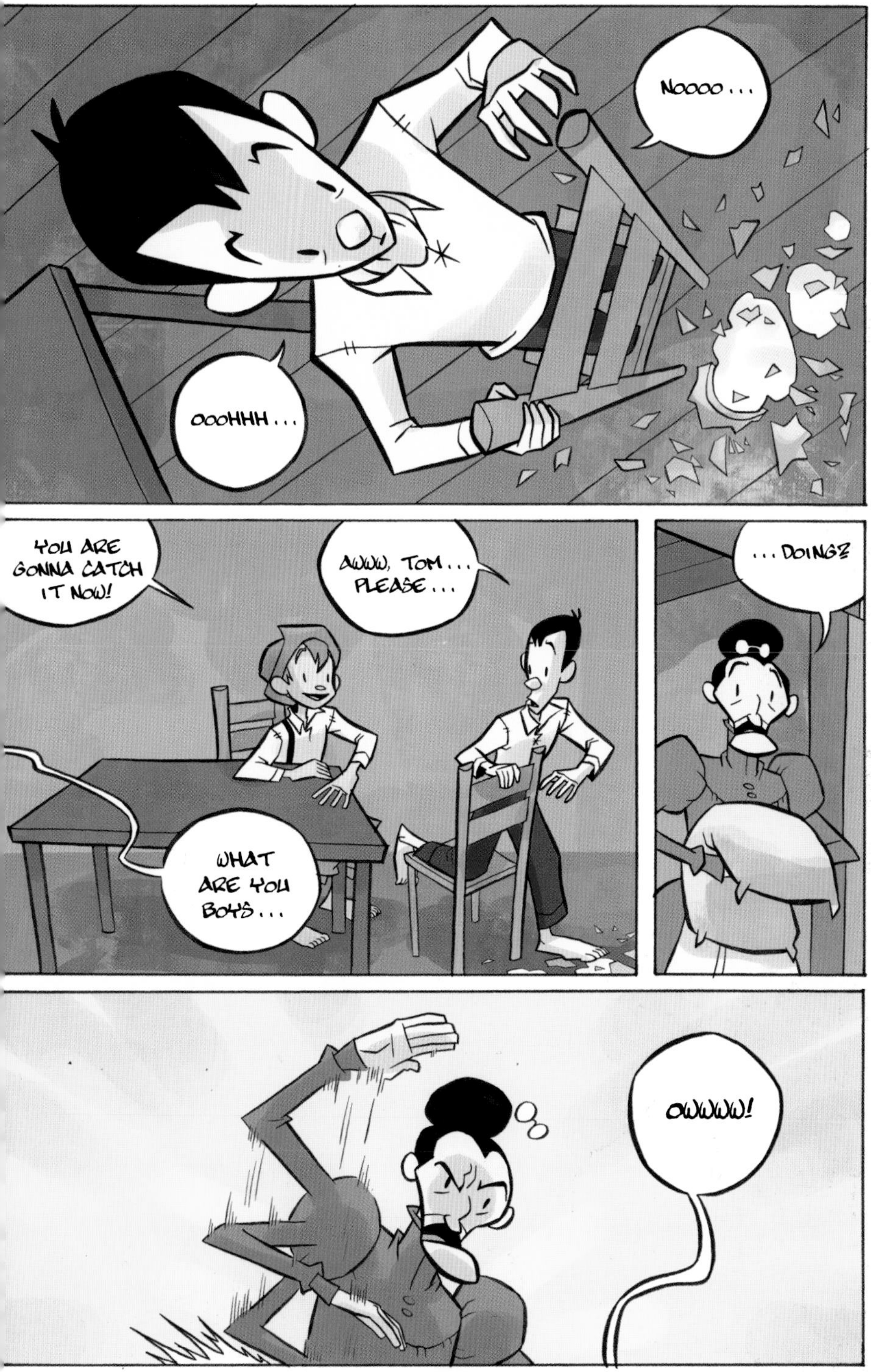
NOOOO...
OOOHHH...
YOU ARE GONNA CATCH IT NOW!
AWWW, TOM... PLEASE...
WHAT ARE YOU BOYS...
...DOING?
OWWWW!

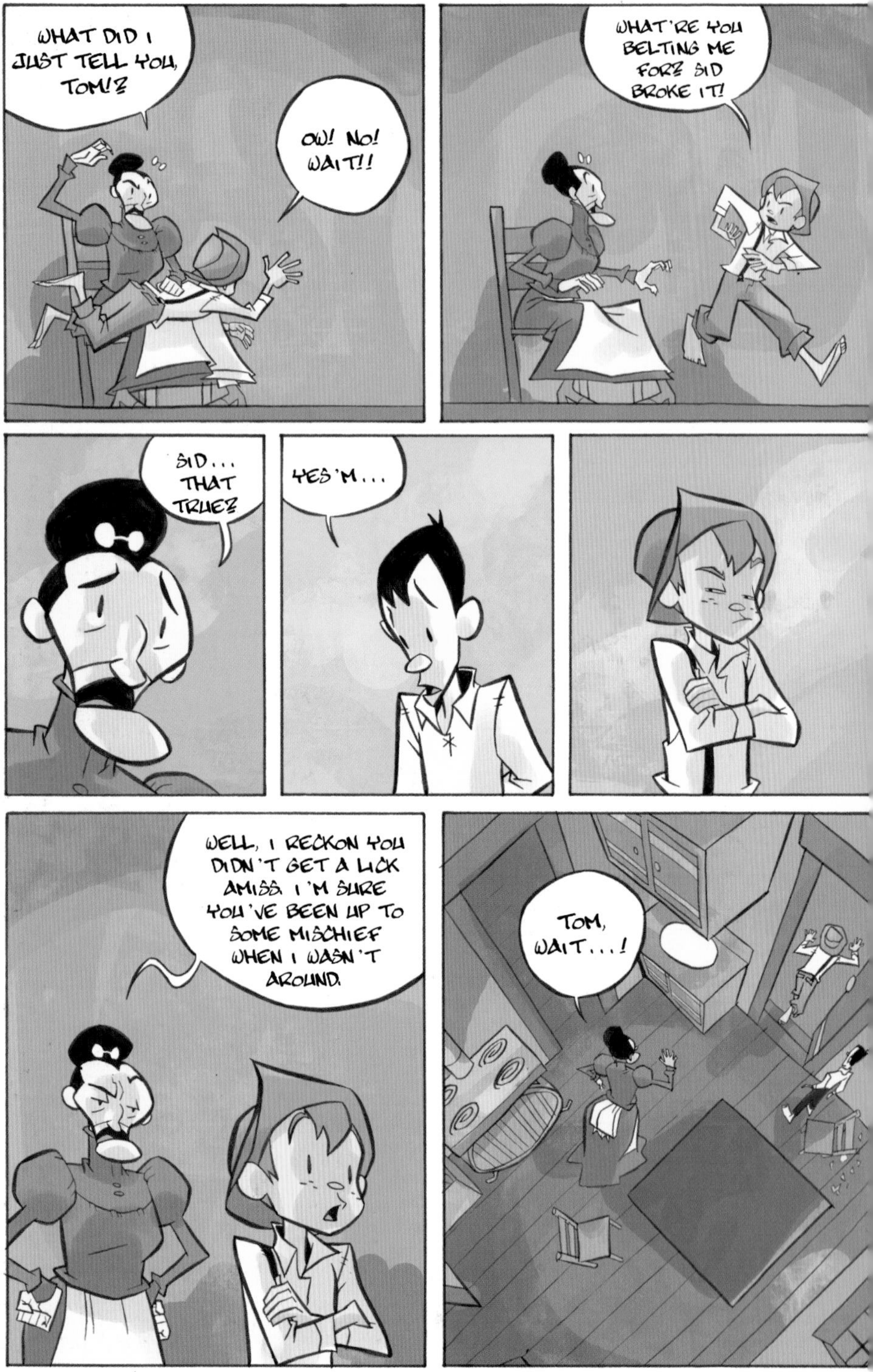
WHAT DID I JUST TELL YOU, TOM!?
OW! NO! WAIT!!
WHAT'RE YOU BELTING ME FOR? SID BROKE IT!
SID... THAT TRUE?
YES'M...
WELL, I RECKON YOU DIDN'T GET A LICK AMISS. I'M SURE YOU'VE BEEN UP TO SOME MISCHIEF WHEN I WASN'T AROUND.
TOM, WAIT...!

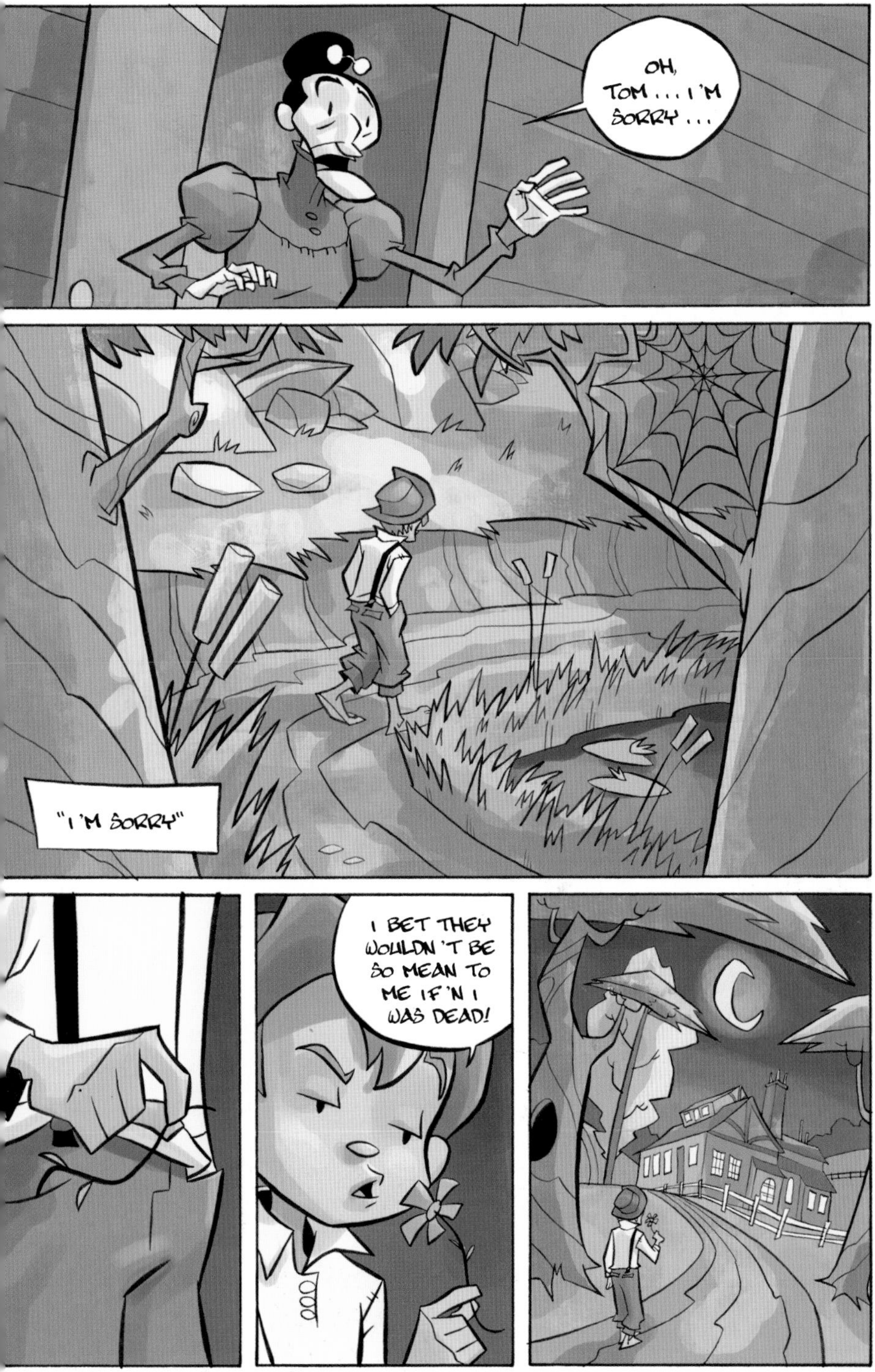
OH, TOM . . . I'M SORRY . . .
"I'M SORRY"
I BET THEY WOULDN'T BE SO MEAN TO ME IF'N I WAS DEAD!

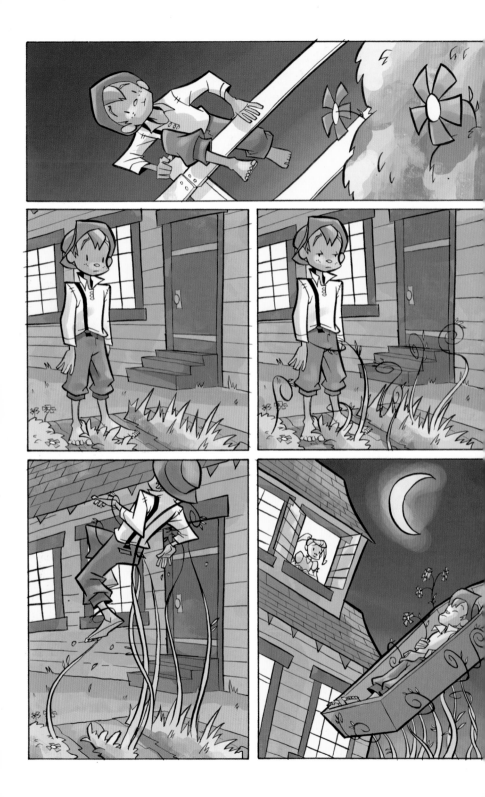

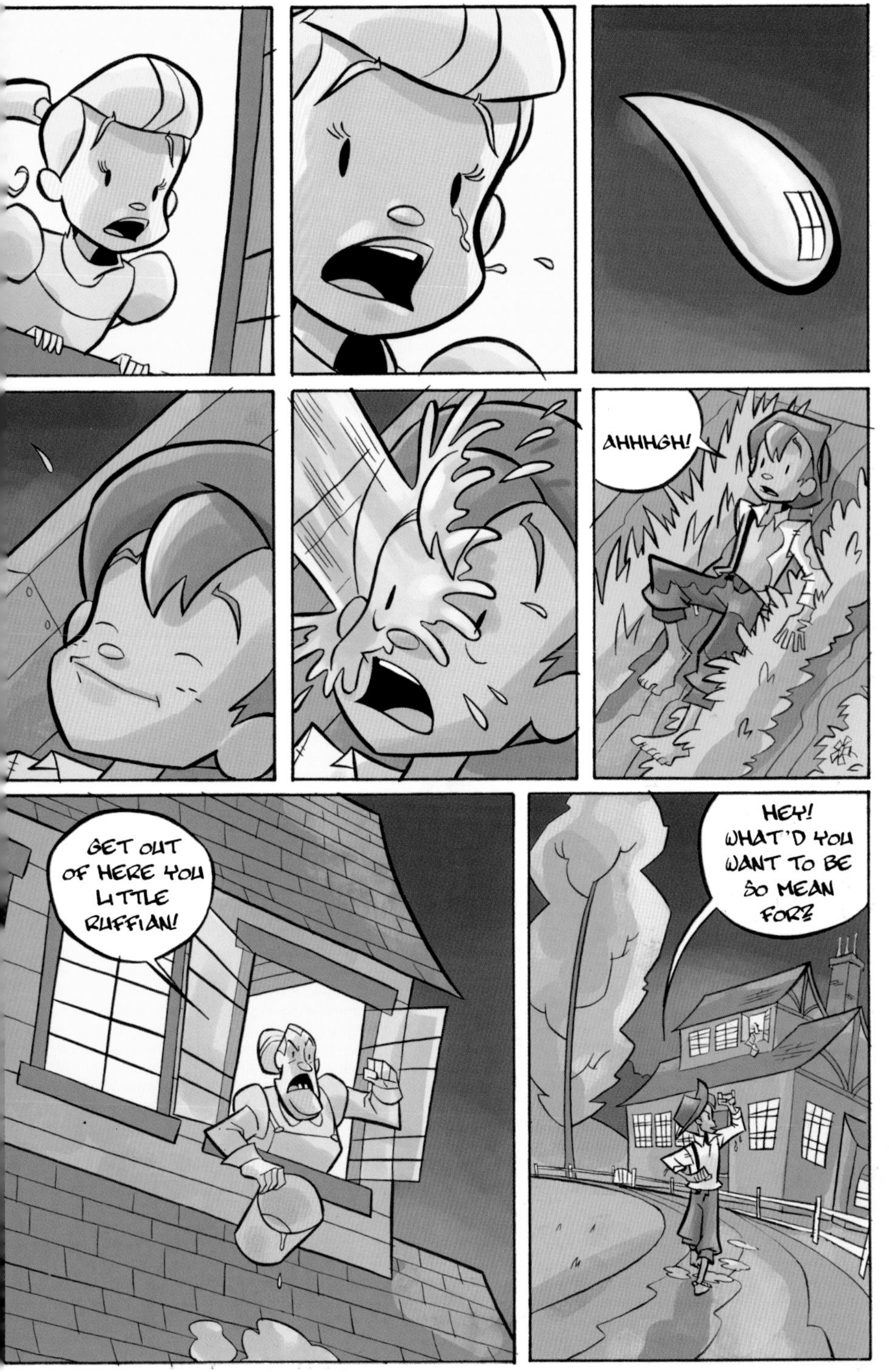
AHHHGH!
GET OUT OF HERE YOU LITTLE RUFFIAN!
HEY! WHAT'D YOU WANT TO BE SO MEAN FOR?

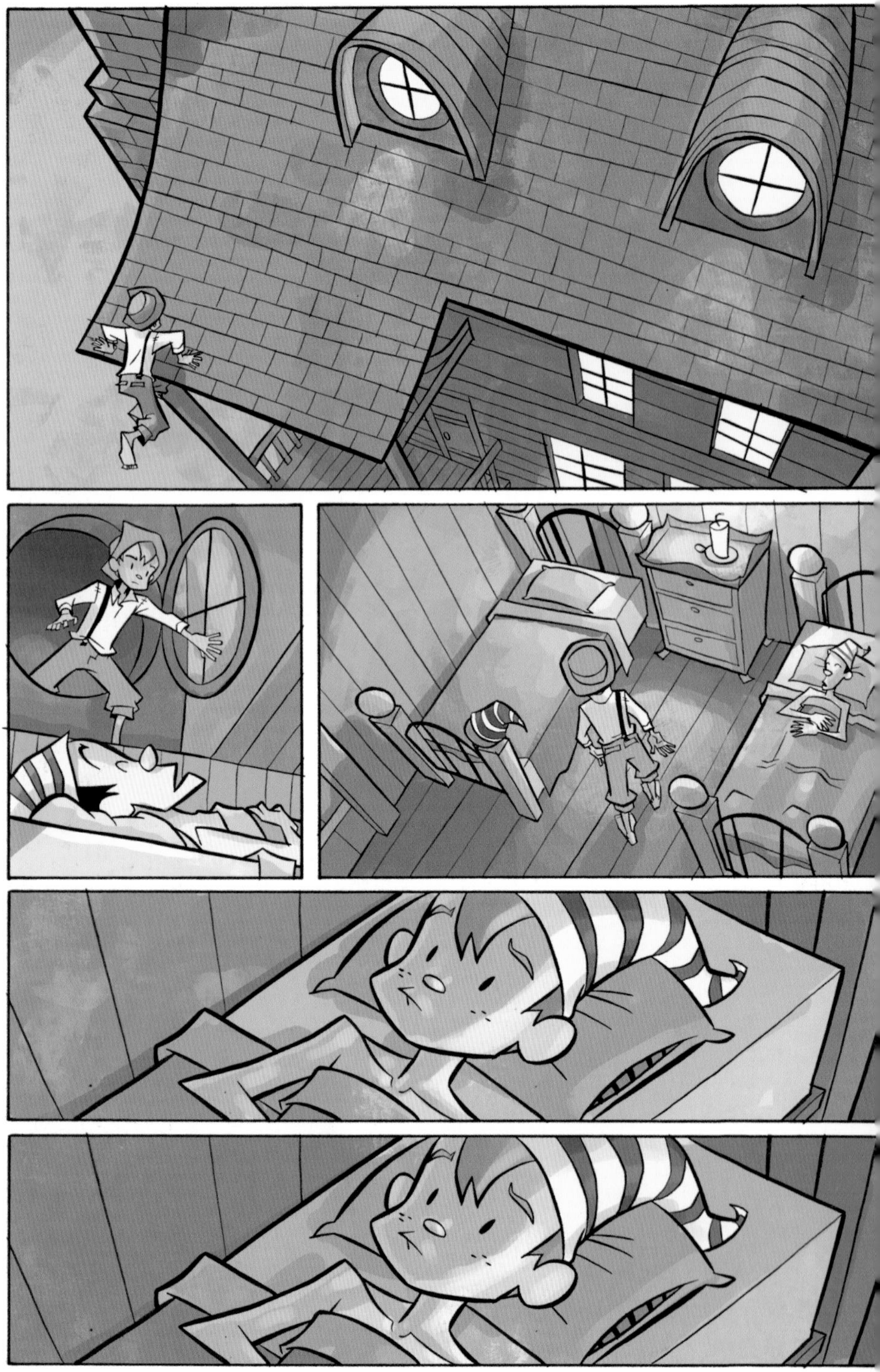

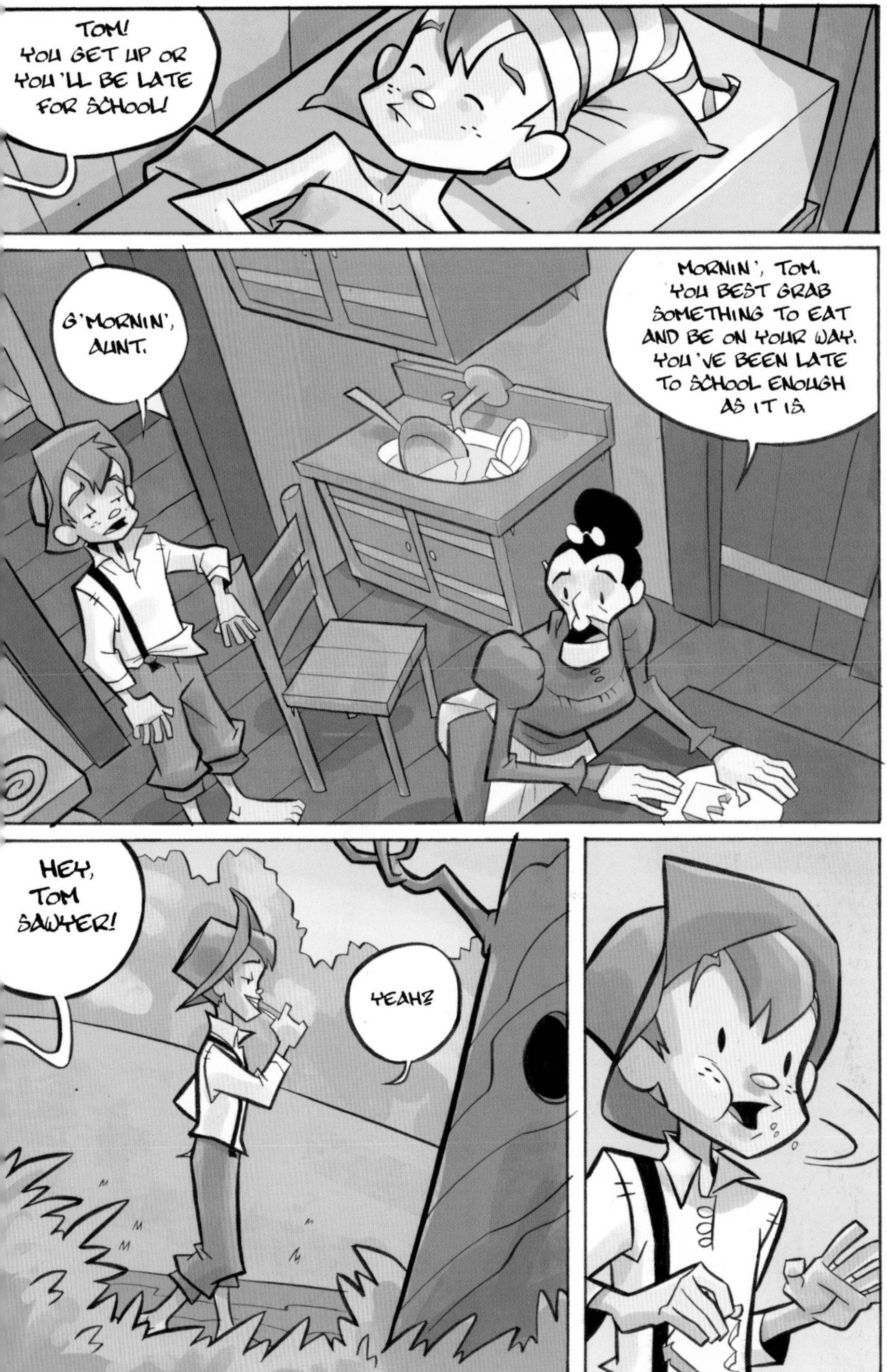
TOM!
YOU GET UP OR YOU'LL BE LATE FOR SCHOOL!
G'MORNIN', AUNT.
MORNIN', TOM. YOU BEST GRAB SOMETHING TO EAT AND BE ON YOUR WAY. YOU'VE BEEN LATE TO SCHOOL ENOUGH AS IT IS.
HEY, TOM SAWYER!
YEAH?

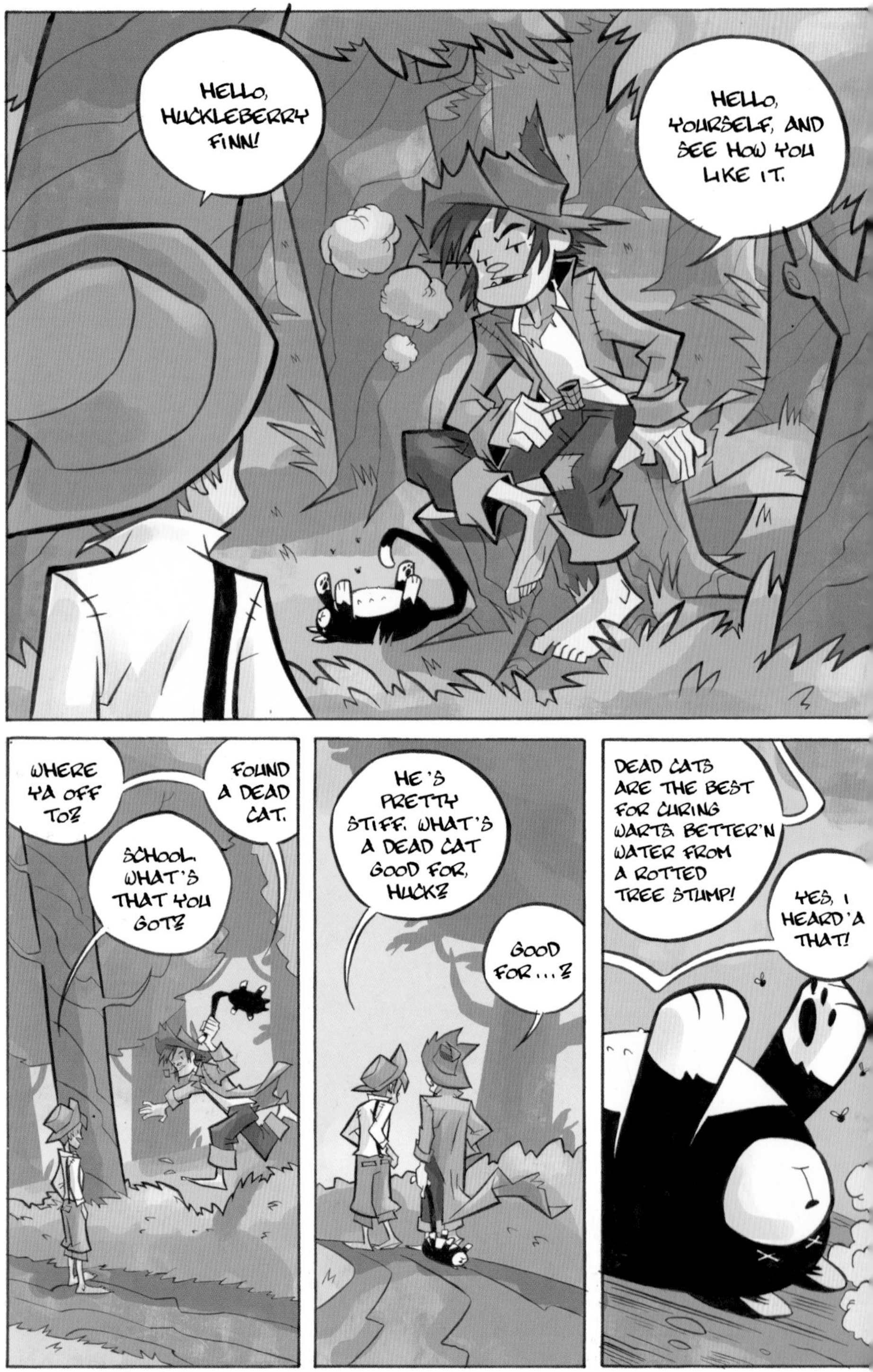
HELLO, HUCKLEBERRY FINN!
HELLO, YOURSELF, AND SEE HOW YOU LIKE IT.
WHERE YA OFF TO?
FOUND A DEAD CAT.
SCHOOL. WHAT'S THAT YOU GOT?
HE'S PRETTY STIFF. WHAT'S A DEAD CAT GOOD FOR, HUCK?
GOOD FOR...?
DEAD CATS ARE THE BEST FOR CURING WARTS. BETTER'N WATER FROM A ROTTED TREE STUMP!
YES, I HEARD'A THAT!

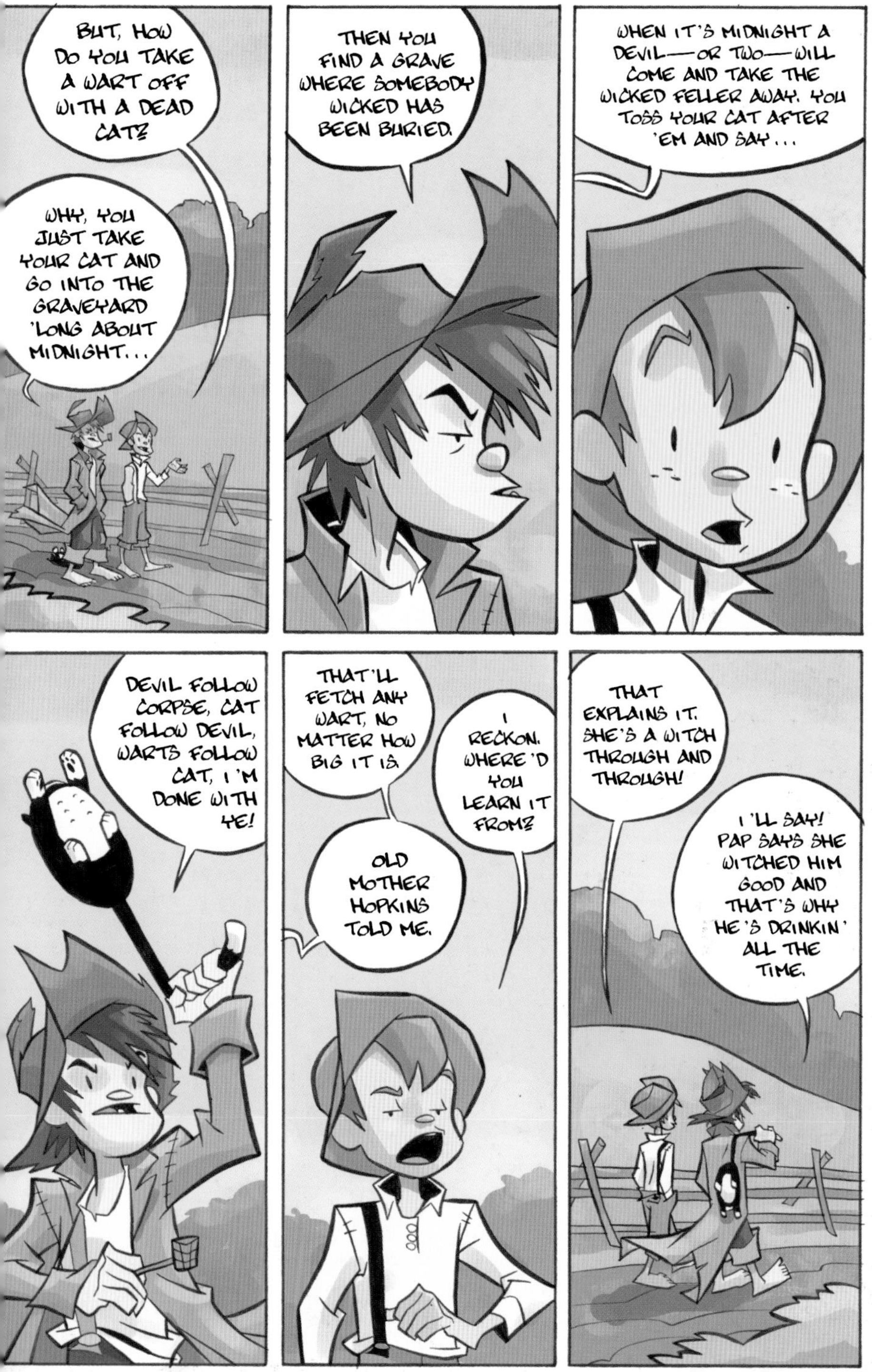
BUT, HOW DO YOU TAKE A WART OFF WITH A DEAD CAT?
WHY, YOU JUST TAKE YOUR CAT AND GO INTO THE GRAVEYARD 'LONG ABOUT MIDNIGHT...
THEN YOU FIND A GRAVE WHERE SOMEBODY WICKED HAS BEEN BURIED.
WHEN IT'S MIDNIGHT A DEVIL—OR TWO—WILL COME AND TAKE THE WICKED FELLER AWAY. YOU TOSS YOUR CAT AFTER 'EM AND SAY...
DEVIL FOLLOW CORPSE, CAT FOLLOW DEVIL, WARTS FOLLOW CAT, I'M DONE WITH YE!
THAT'LL FETCH ANY WART, NO MATTER HOW BIG IT IS.
I RECKON. WHERE'D YOU LEARN IT FROM?
OLD MOTHER HOPKINS TOLD ME.
THAT EXPLAINS IT. SHE'S A WITCH THROUGH AND THROUGH!
I'LL SAY! PAP SAYS SHE WITCHED HIM GOOD AND THAT'S WHY HE'S DRINKIN' ALL THE TIME.

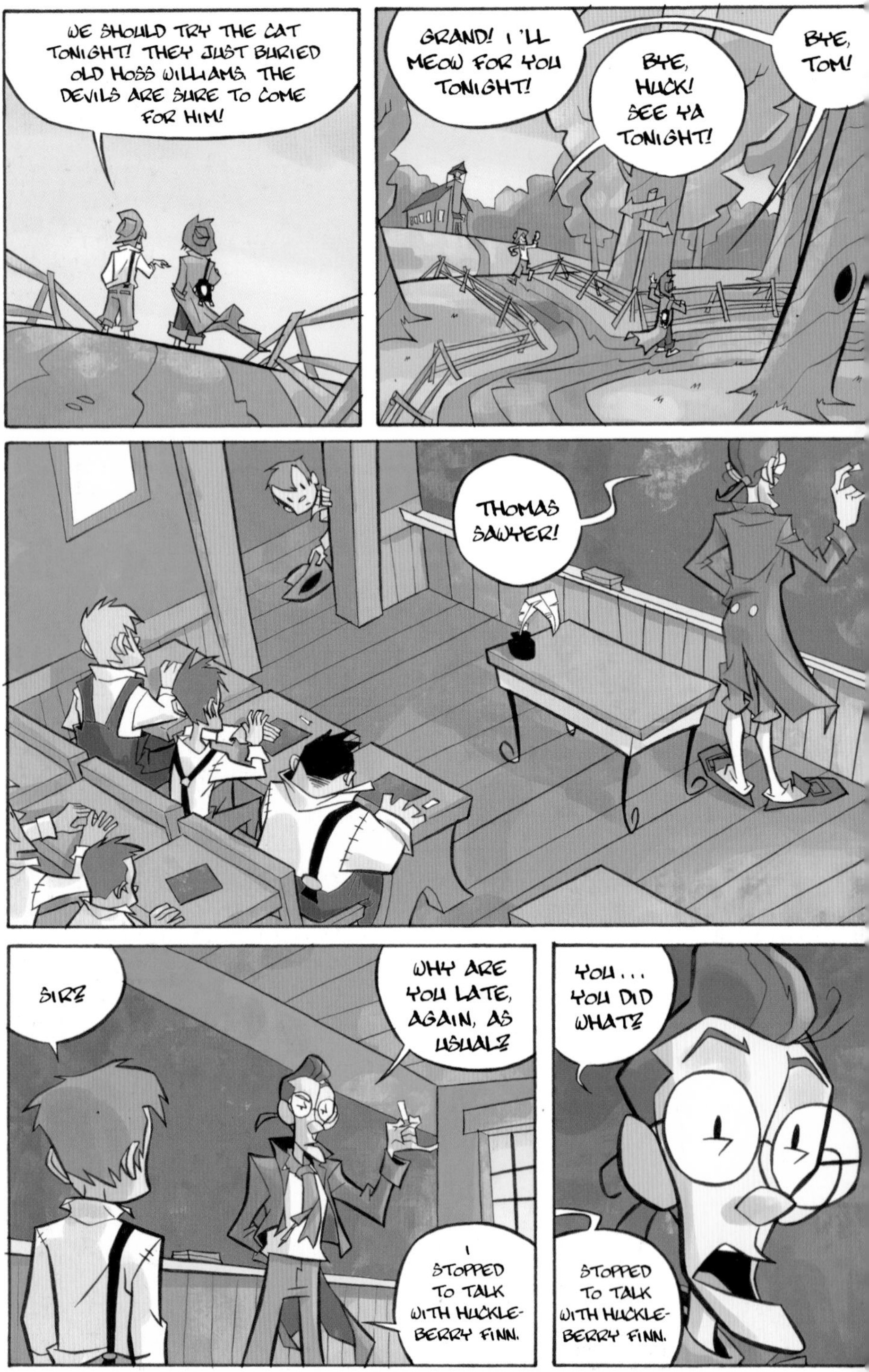

WE SHOULD TRY THE CAT TONIGHT! THEY JUST BURIED OLD HOSS WILLIAMS. THE DEVILS ARE SURE TO COME FOR HIM!
GRAND! I'LL MEOW FOR YOU TONIGHT!
BYE, HUCK! SEE YA TONIGHT!
BYE, TOM!
THOMAS SAWYER!
SIR?
WHY ARE YOU LATE, AGAIN, AS USUAL?
I STOPPED TO TALK WITH HUCKLE-BERRY FINN.
YOU... YOU DID WHAT?
STOPPED TO TALK WITH HUCKLE-BERRY FINN.

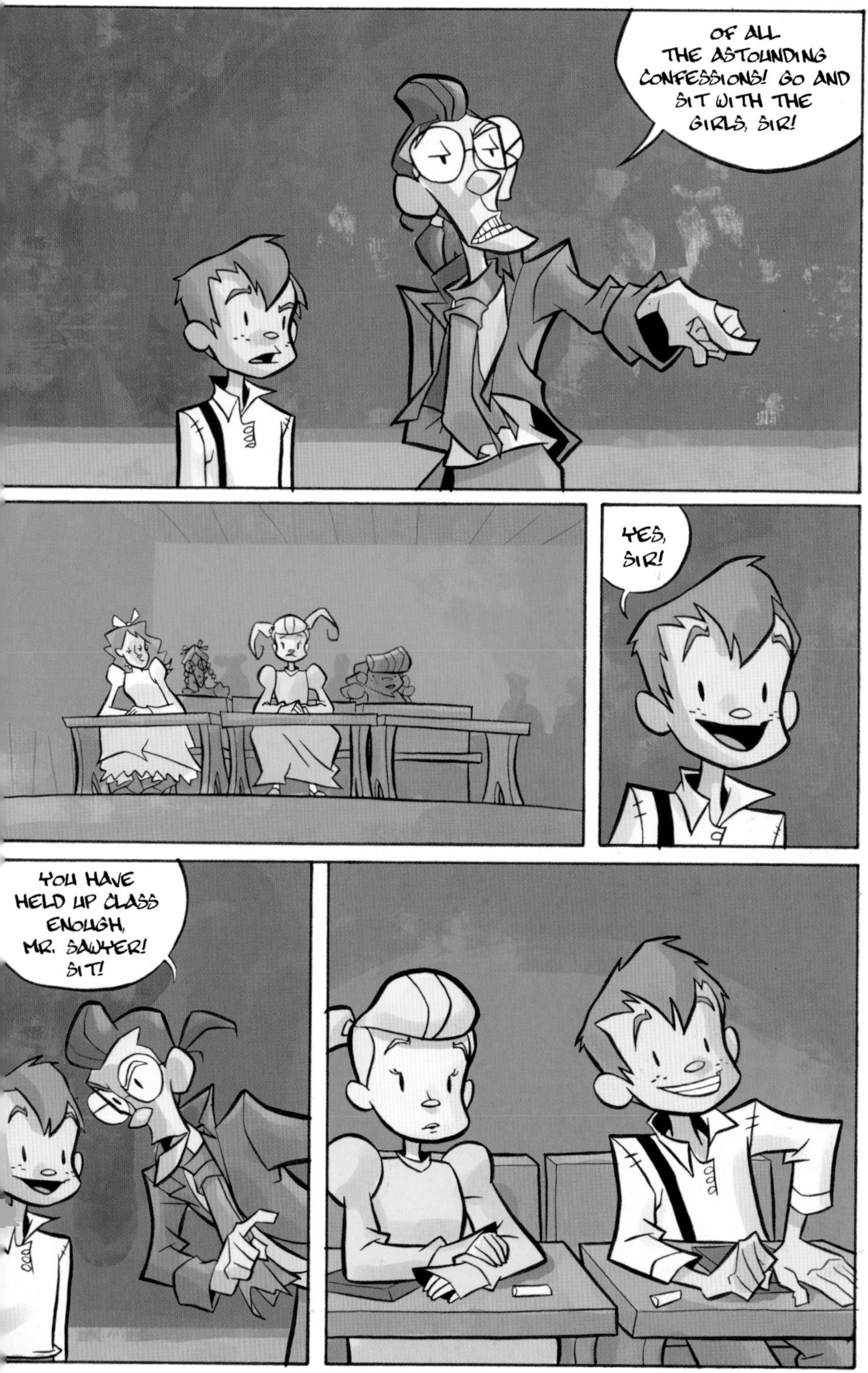
OF ALL THE ASTOUNDING CONFESSIONS! GO AND SIT WITH THE GIRLS, SIR!
YES, SIR!
YOU HAVE HELD UP CLASS ENOUGH, MR. SAWYER! SIT!

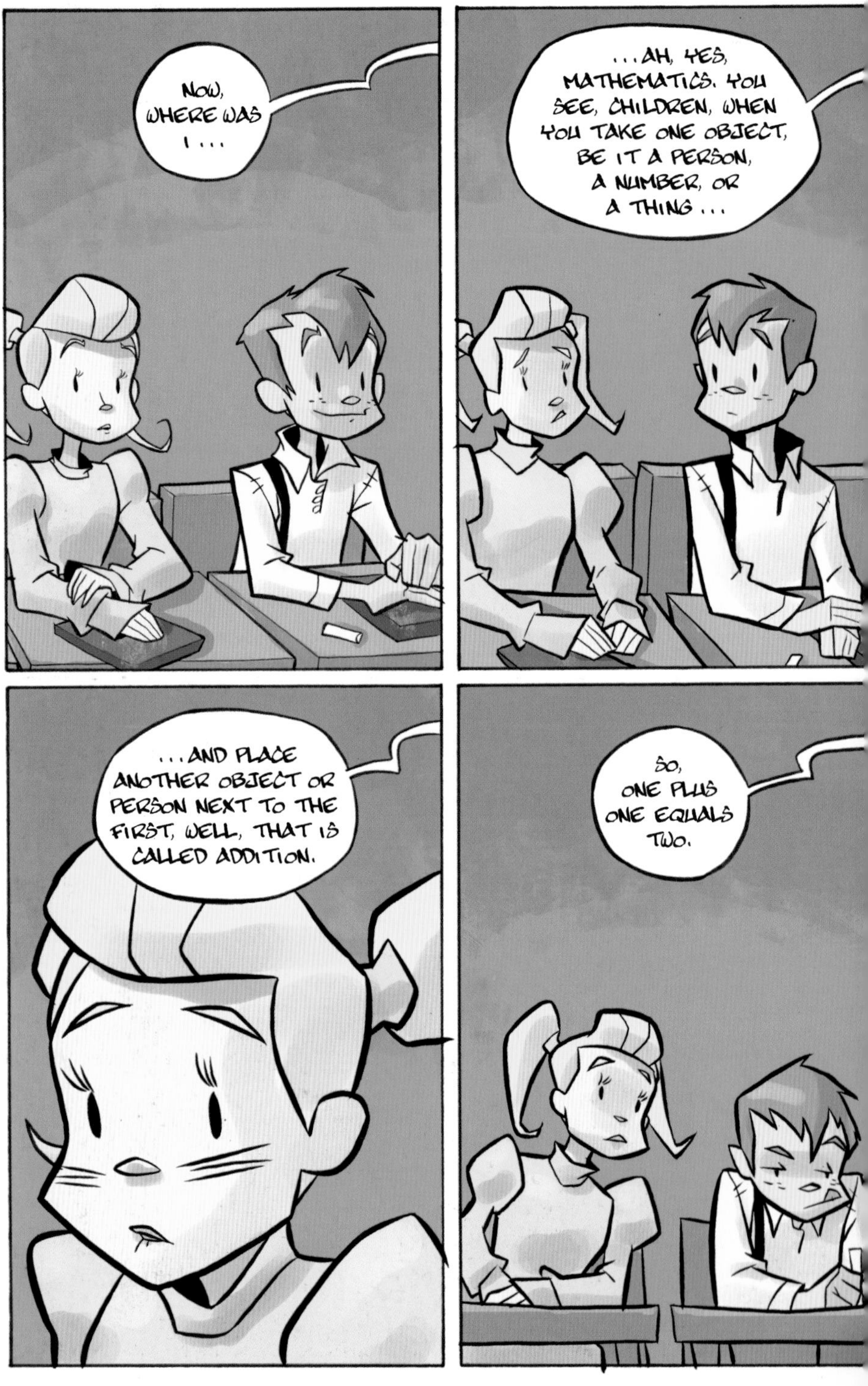
NOW, WHERE WAS I . . .
. . . AH, YES, MATHEMATICS. YOU SEE, CHILDREN, WHEN YOU TAKE ONE OBJECT, BE IT A PERSON, A NUMBER, OR A THING . . .
. . . AND PLACE ANOTHER OBJECT OR PERSON NEXT TO THE FIRST, WELL, THAT IS CALLED ADDITION.
SO, ONE PLUS ONE EQUALS TWO.

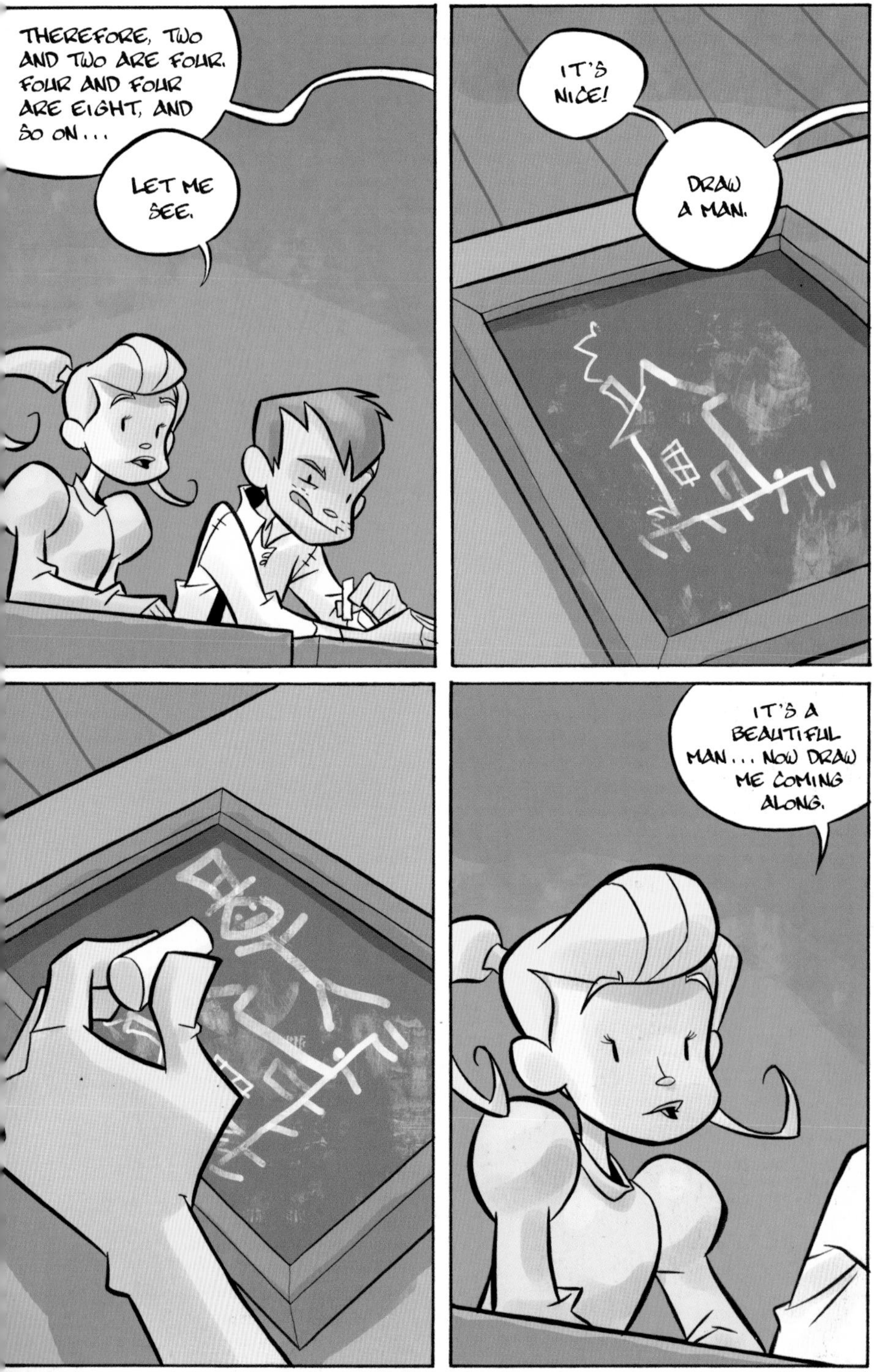
THEREFORE, TWO AND TWO ARE FOUR. FOUR AND FOUR ARE EIGHT, AND SO ON . . .
LET ME SEE.
IT'S NICE!
DRAW A MAN.
IT'S A BEAUTIFUL MAN . . . NOW DRAW ME COMING ALONG.

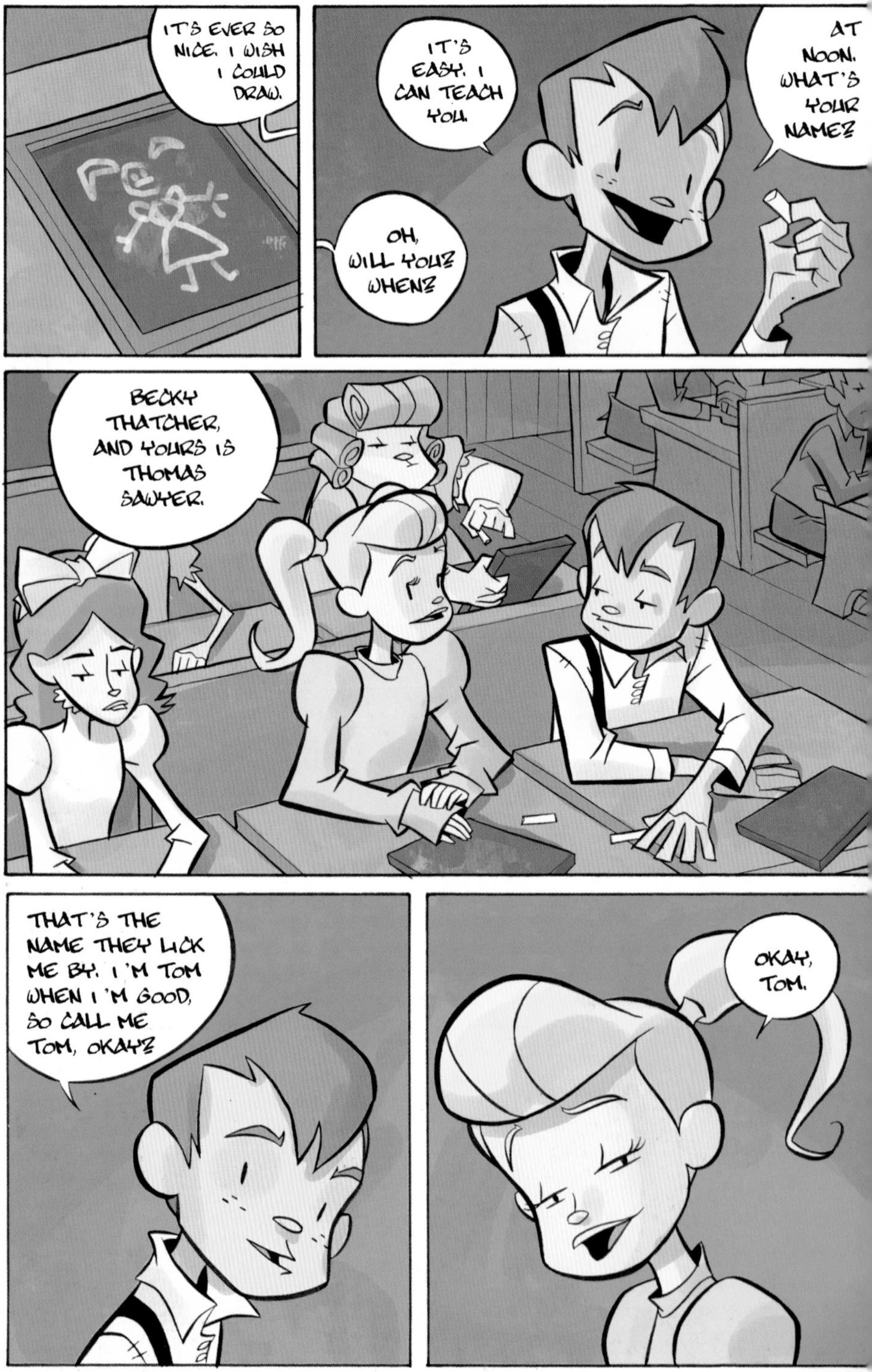
IT'S EVER SO NICE. I WISH I COULD DRAW.
IT'S EASY. I CAN TEACH YOU.
OH, WILL YOU? WHEN?
AT NOON. WHAT'S YOUR NAME?
BECKY THATCHER, AND YOURS IS THOMAS SAWYER.
THAT'S THE NAME THEY LICK ME BY. I'M TOM WHEN I'M GOOD, SO CALL ME TOM, OKAY?
OKAY, TOM.

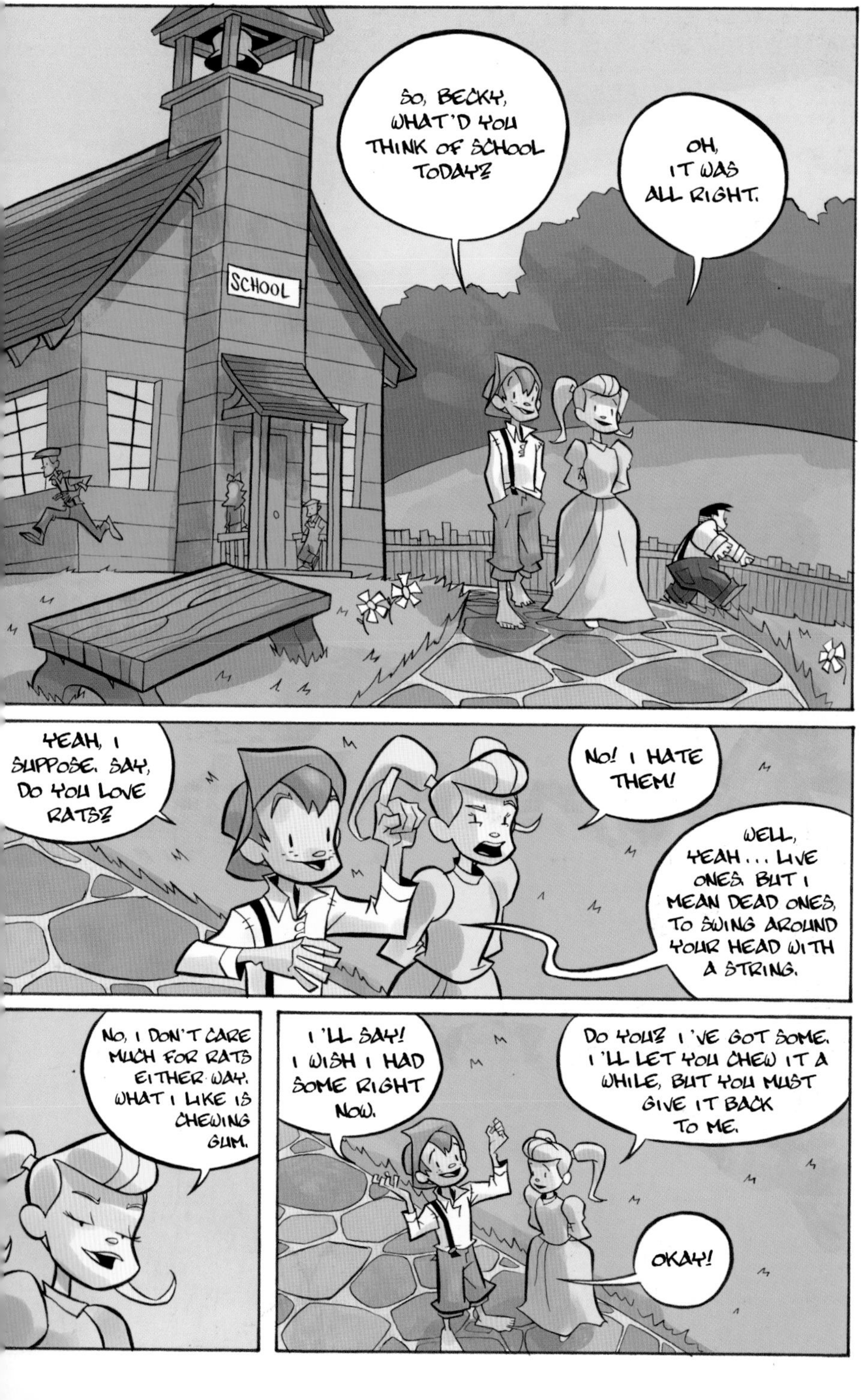
SO, BECKY, WHAT'D YOU THINK OF SCHOOL TODAY?
OH, IT WAS ALL RIGHT.
SCHOOL
YEAH, I SUPPOSE. SAY, DO YOU LOVE RATS?
NO! I HATE THEM!
WELL, YEAH... LIVE ONES. BUT I MEAN DEAD ONES, TO SWING AROUND YOUR HEAD WITH A STRING.
NO, I DON'T CARE MUCH FOR RATS EITHER WAY. WHAT I LIKE IS CHEWING GUM.
I'LL SAY! I WISH I HAD SOME RIGHT NOW.
DO YOU? I'VE GOT SOME. I'LL LET YOU CHEW IT A WHILE, BUT YOU MUST GIVE IT BACK TO ME.
OKAY!

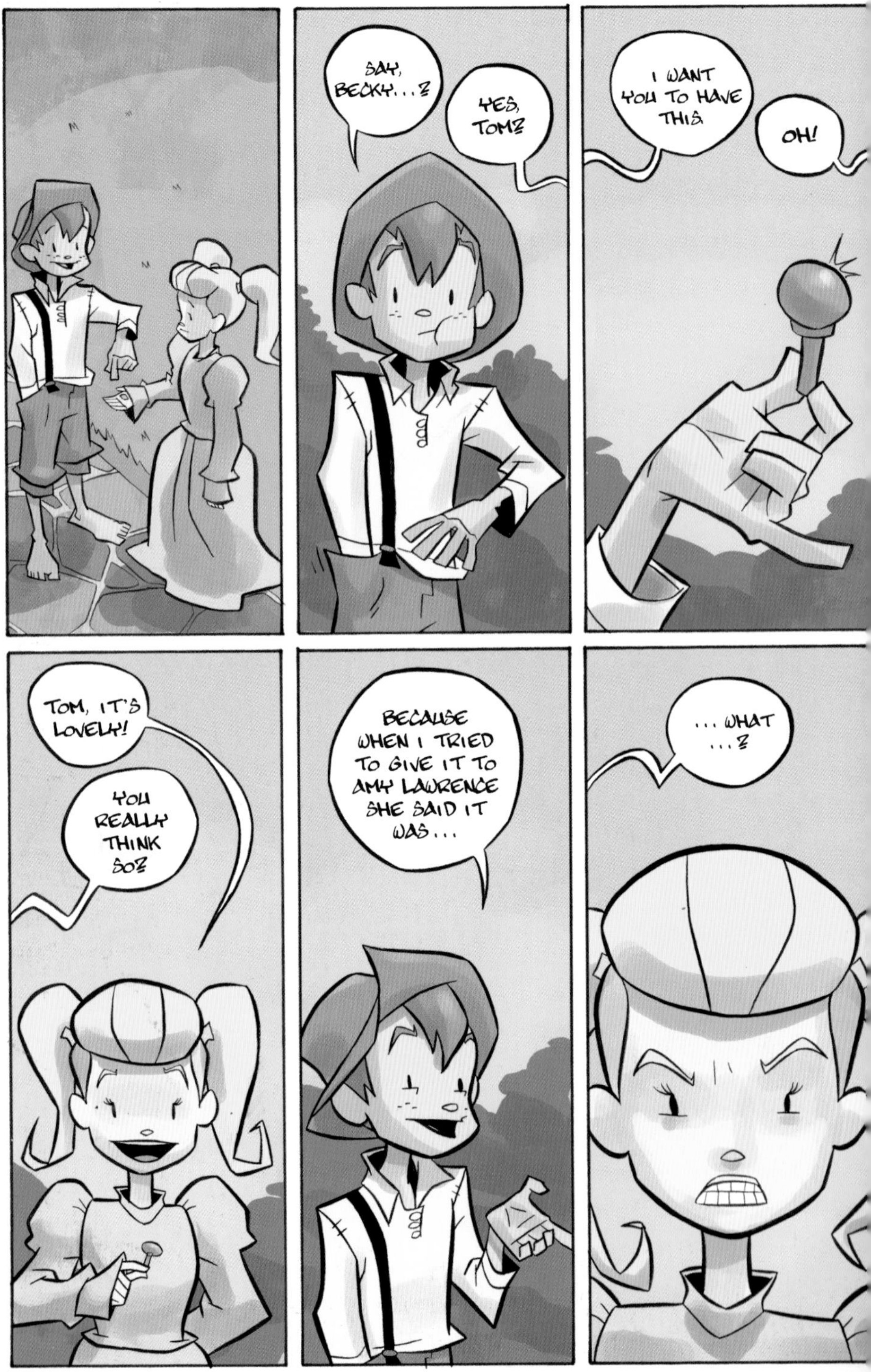
SAY, BECKY...?
YES, TOM?
I WANT YOU TO HAVE THIS.
OH!
TOM, IT'S LOVELY!
YOU REALLY THINK SO?
BECAUSE WHEN I TRIED TO GIVE IT TO AMY LAWRENCE SHE SAID IT WAS...
...WHAT...?

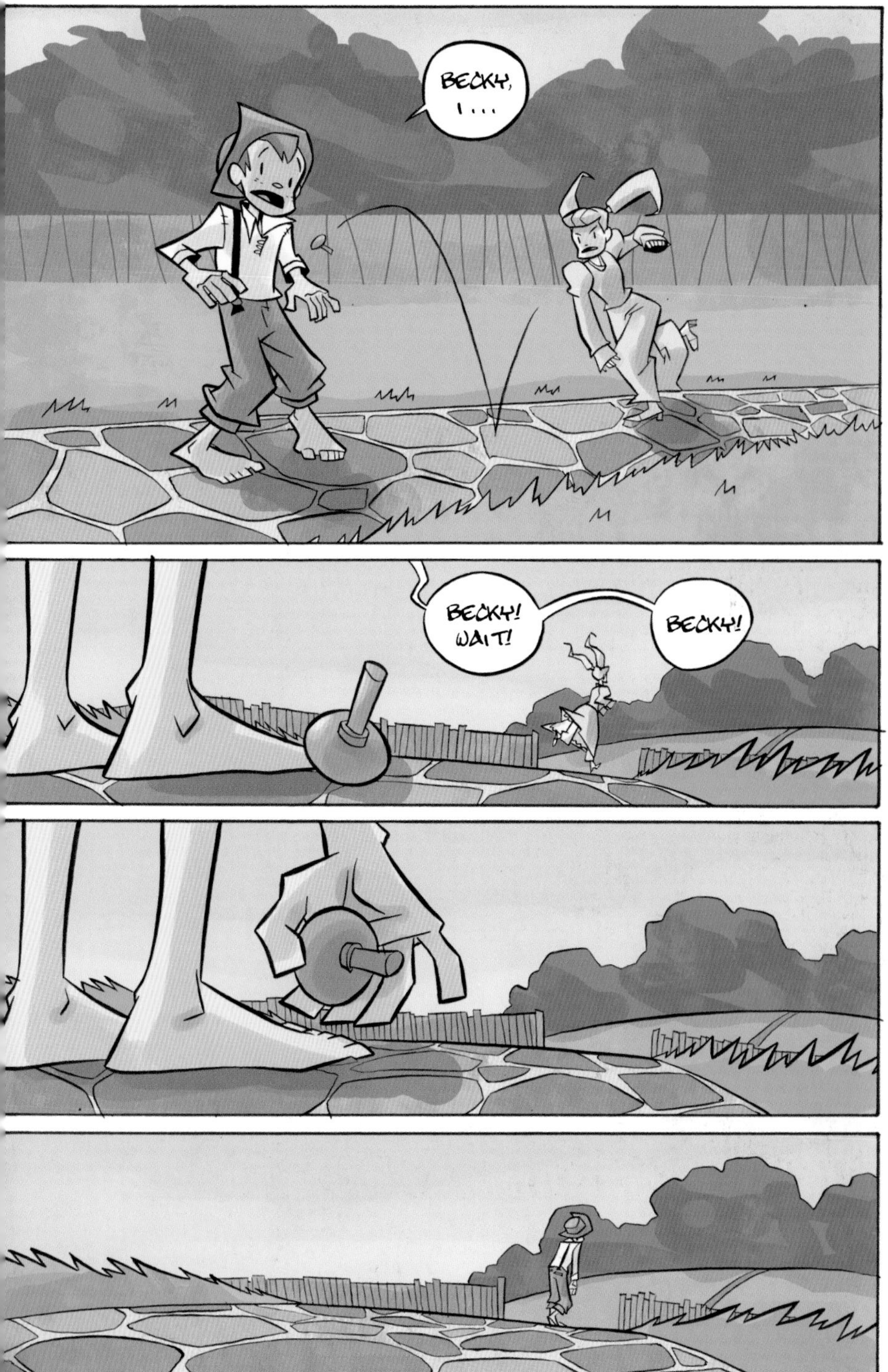
BECKY, I...
BECKY! WAIT!
BECKY!

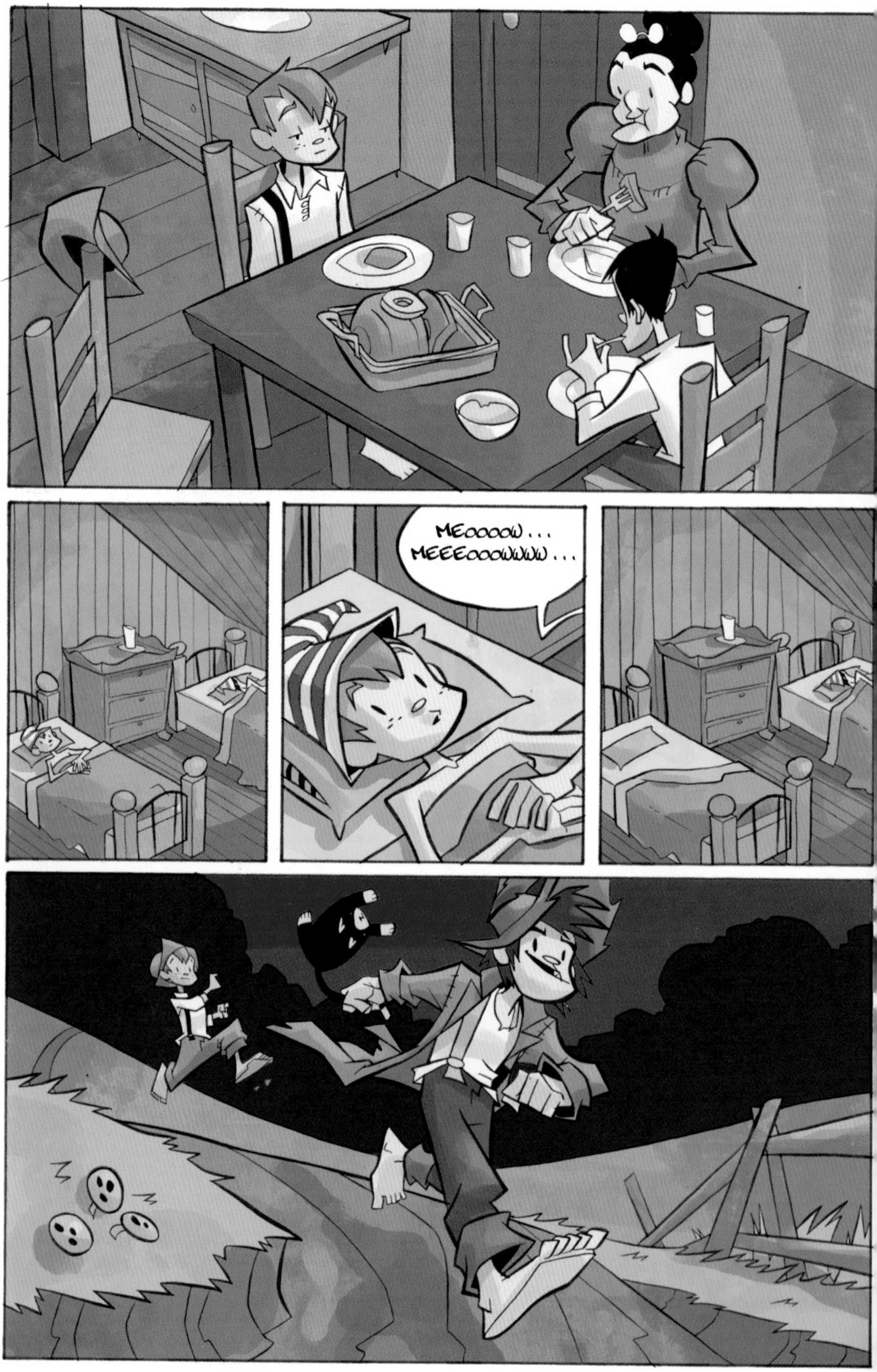
MEooooW...
MEEEoooWWWW...

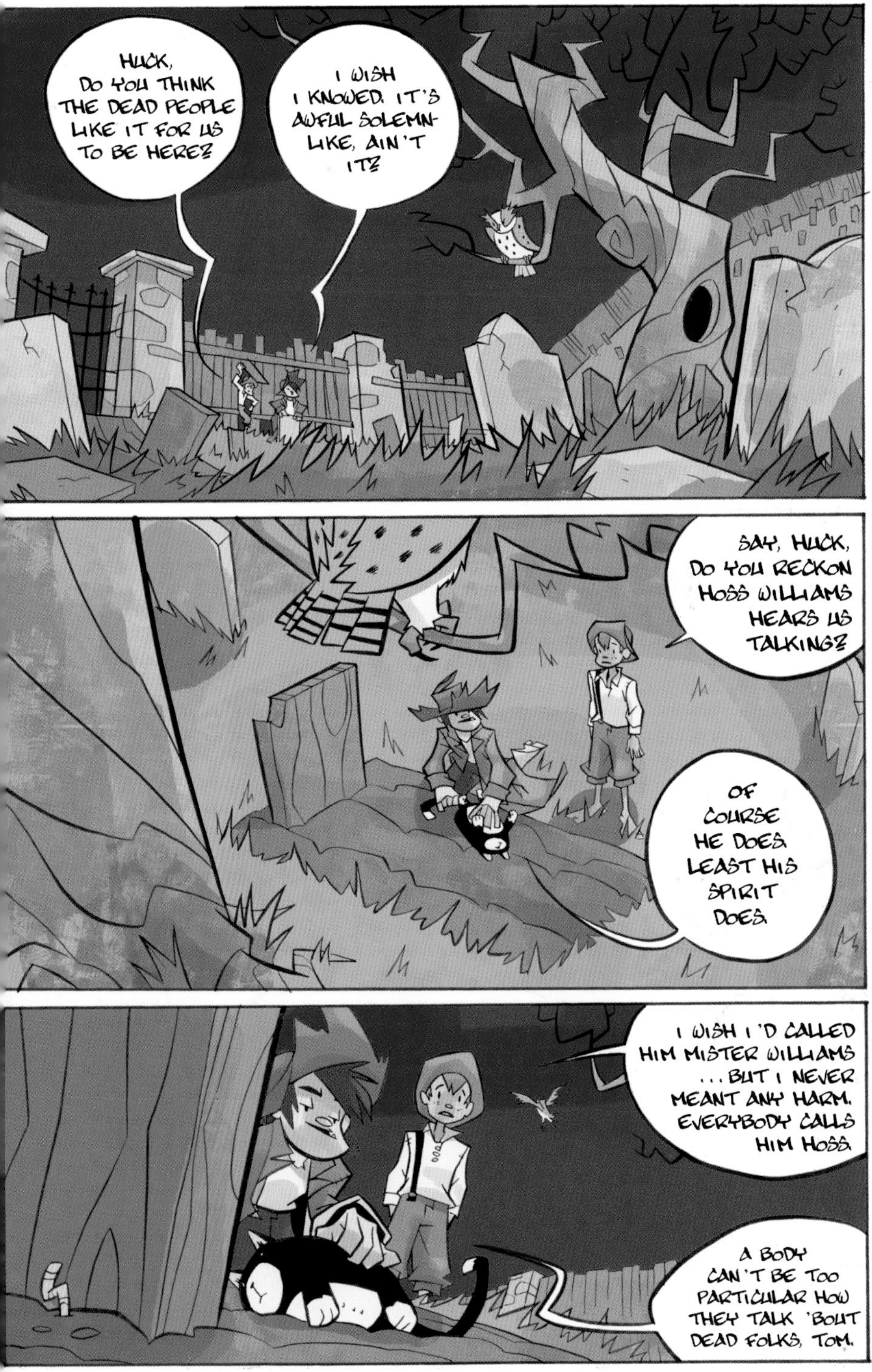
HUCK, DO YOU THINK THE DEAD PEOPLE LIKE IT FOR US TO BE HERE?
I WISH I KNOWED. IT'S AWFUL SOLEMN-LIKE, AIN'T IT?
SAY, HUCK, DO YOU RECKON HOSS WILLIAMS HEARS US TALKING?
OF COURSE HE DOES. LEAST HIS SPIRIT DOES.
I WISH I'D CALLED HIM MISTER WILLIAMS ...BUT I NEVER MEANT ANY HARM. EVERYBODY CALLS HIM HOSS.
A BODY CAN'T BE TOO PARTICULAR HOW THEY TALK 'BOUT DEAD FOLKS, TOM.

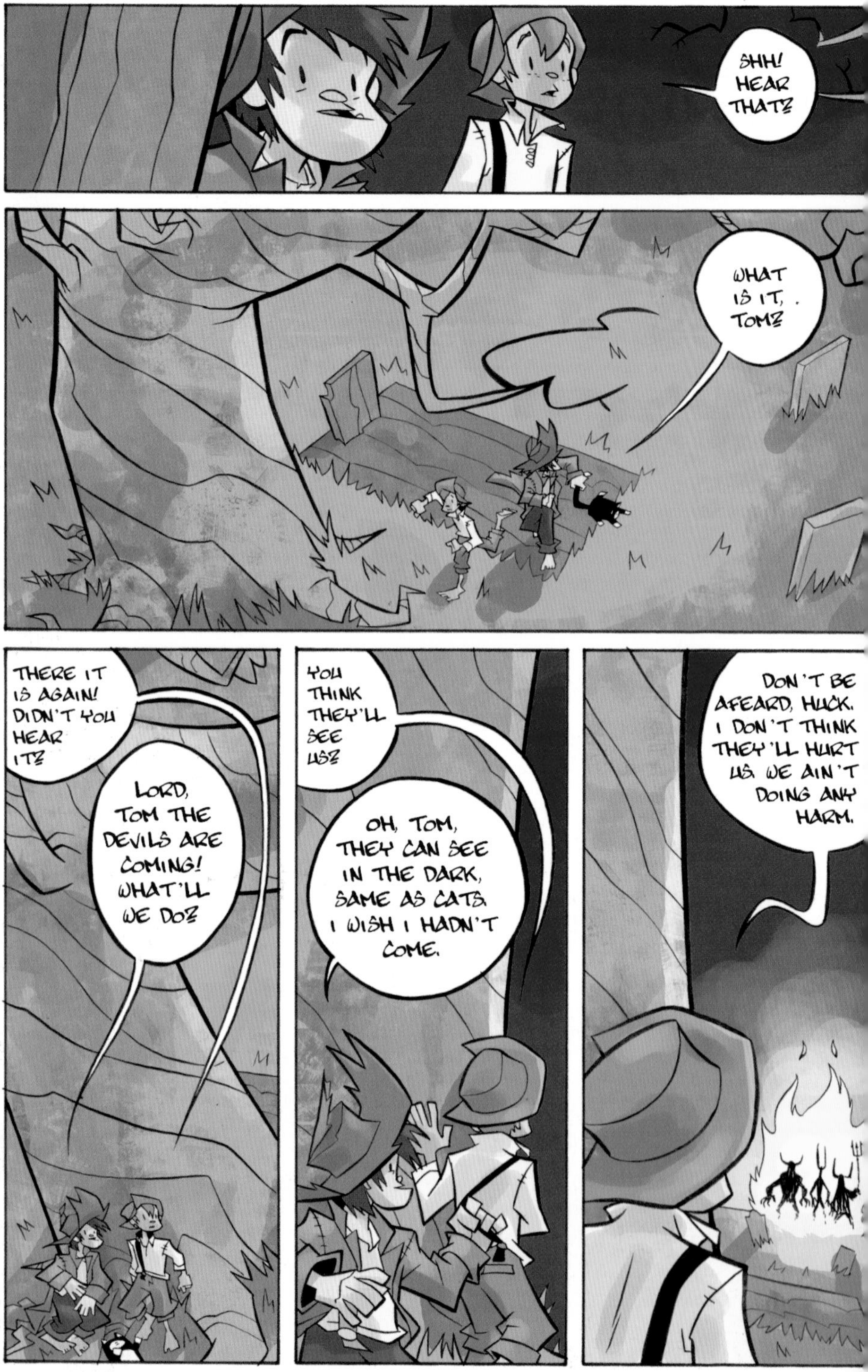
SHH! HEAR THAT?
WHAT IS IT, TOM?
THERE IT IS AGAIN! DIDN'T YOU HEAR IT?
LORD, TOM THE DEVILS ARE COMING! WHAT'LL WE DO?
YOU THINK THEY'LL SEE US?
OH, TOM, THEY CAN SEE IN THE DARK, SAME AS CATS. I WISH I HADN'T COME.
DON'T BE AFEARD, HUCK. I DON'T THINK THEY'LL HURT US. WE AIN'T DOING ANY HARM.

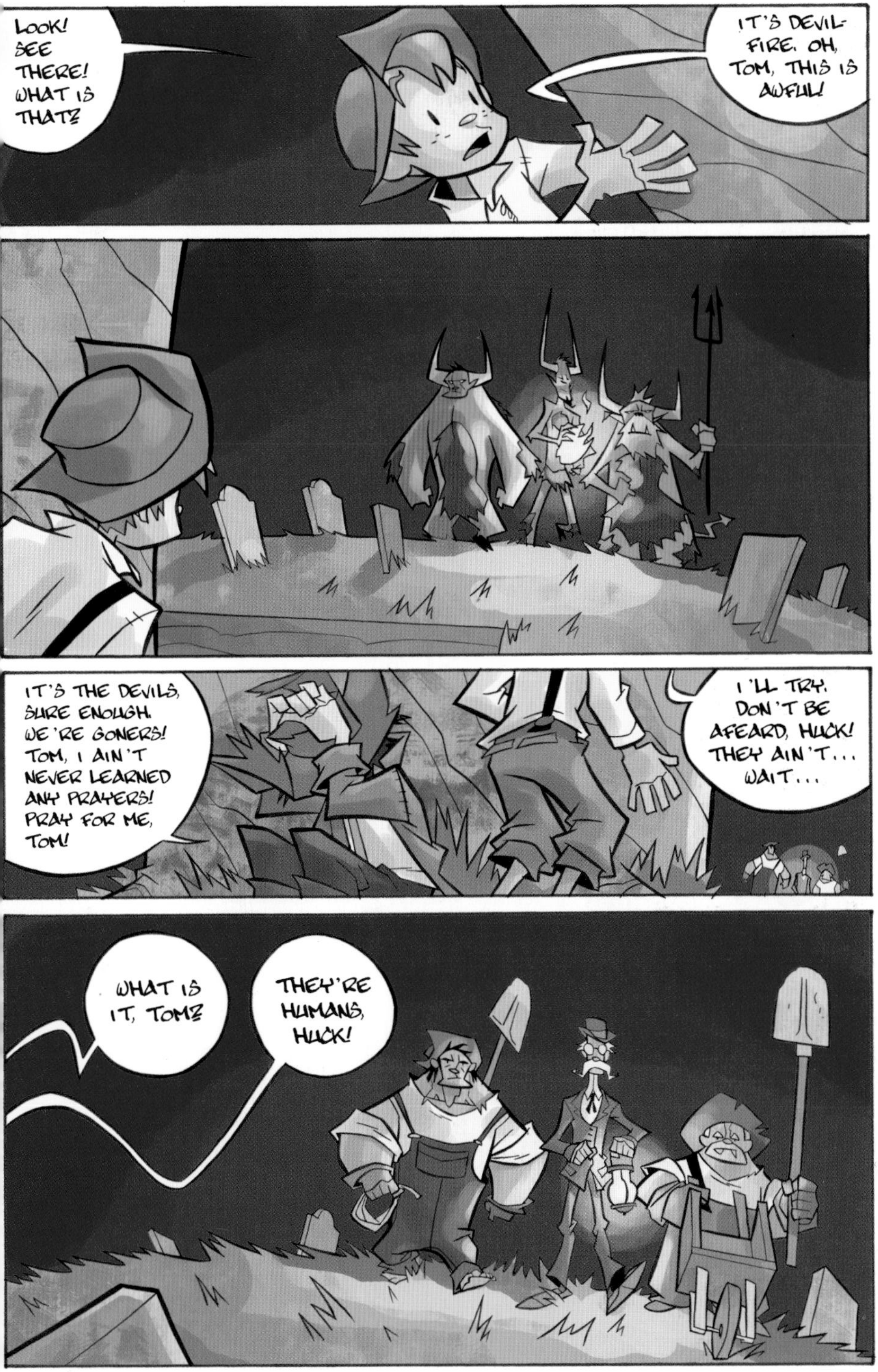
LOOK! SEE THERE! WHAT IS THAT?
IT'S DEVIL-FIRE. OH, TOM, THIS IS AWFUL!
IT'S THE DEVILS, SURE ENOUGH. WE'RE GONERS! TOM, I AIN'T NEVER LEARNED ANY PRAYERS! PRAY FOR ME, TOM!
I'LL TRY. DON'T BE AFEARD, HUCK! THEY AIN'T... WAIT...
WHAT IS IT, TOM?
THEY'RE HUMANS, HUCK!

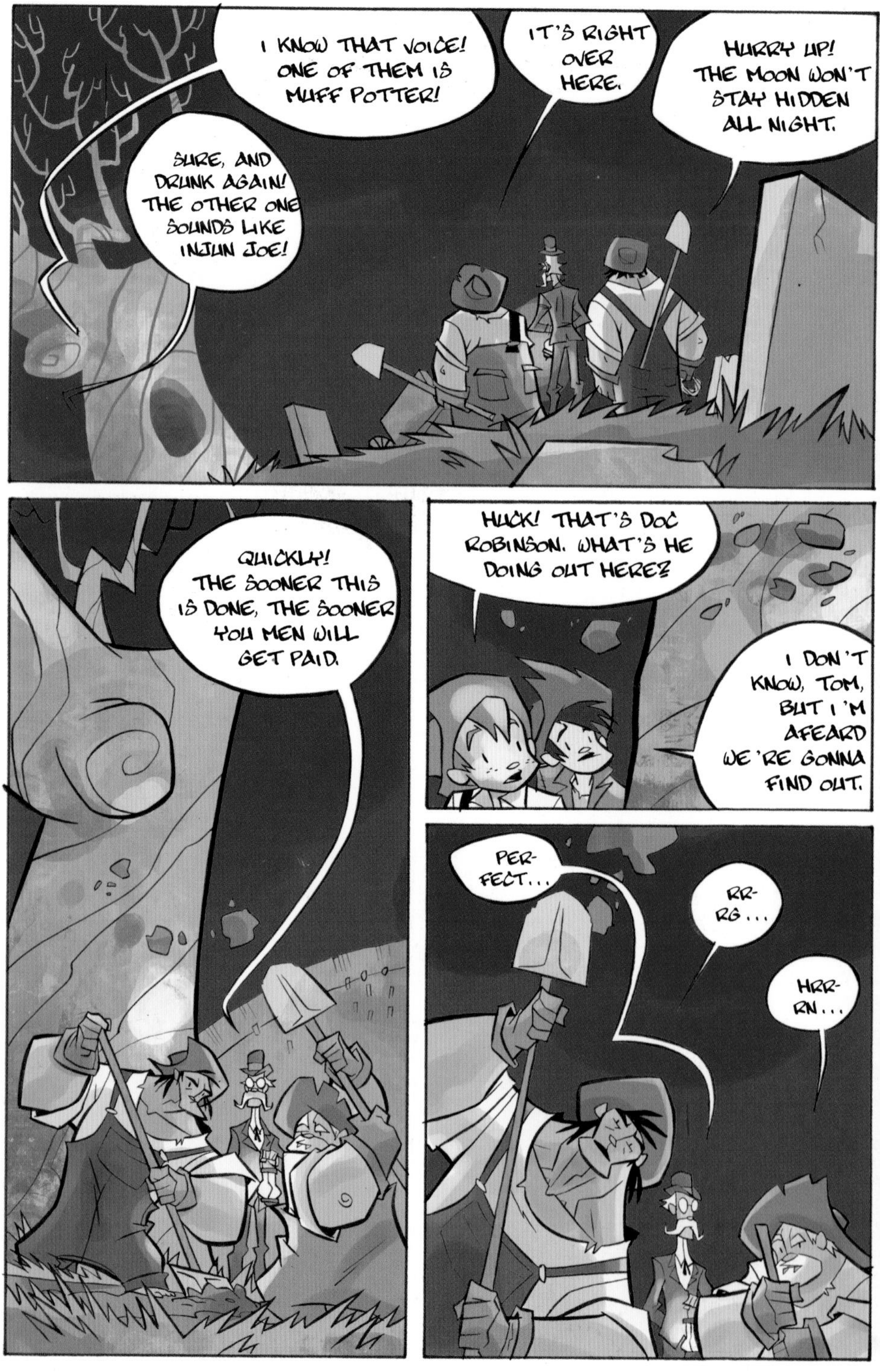
I KNOW THAT VOICE! ONE OF THEM IS MUFF POTTER!
SURE, AND DRUNK AGAIN! THE OTHER ONE SOUNDS LIKE INJUN JOE!
IT'S RIGHT OVER HERE.
HURRY UP! THE MOON WON'T STAY HIDDEN ALL NIGHT.
QUICKLY! THE SOONER THIS IS DONE, THE SOONER YOU MEN WILL GET PAID.
HUCK! THAT'S DOC ROBINSON. WHAT'S HE DOING OUT HERE?
I DON'T KNOW, TOM, BUT I'M AFEARD WE'RE GONNA FIND OUT.
PER-FECT...
RR-RG...
HRR-RN...

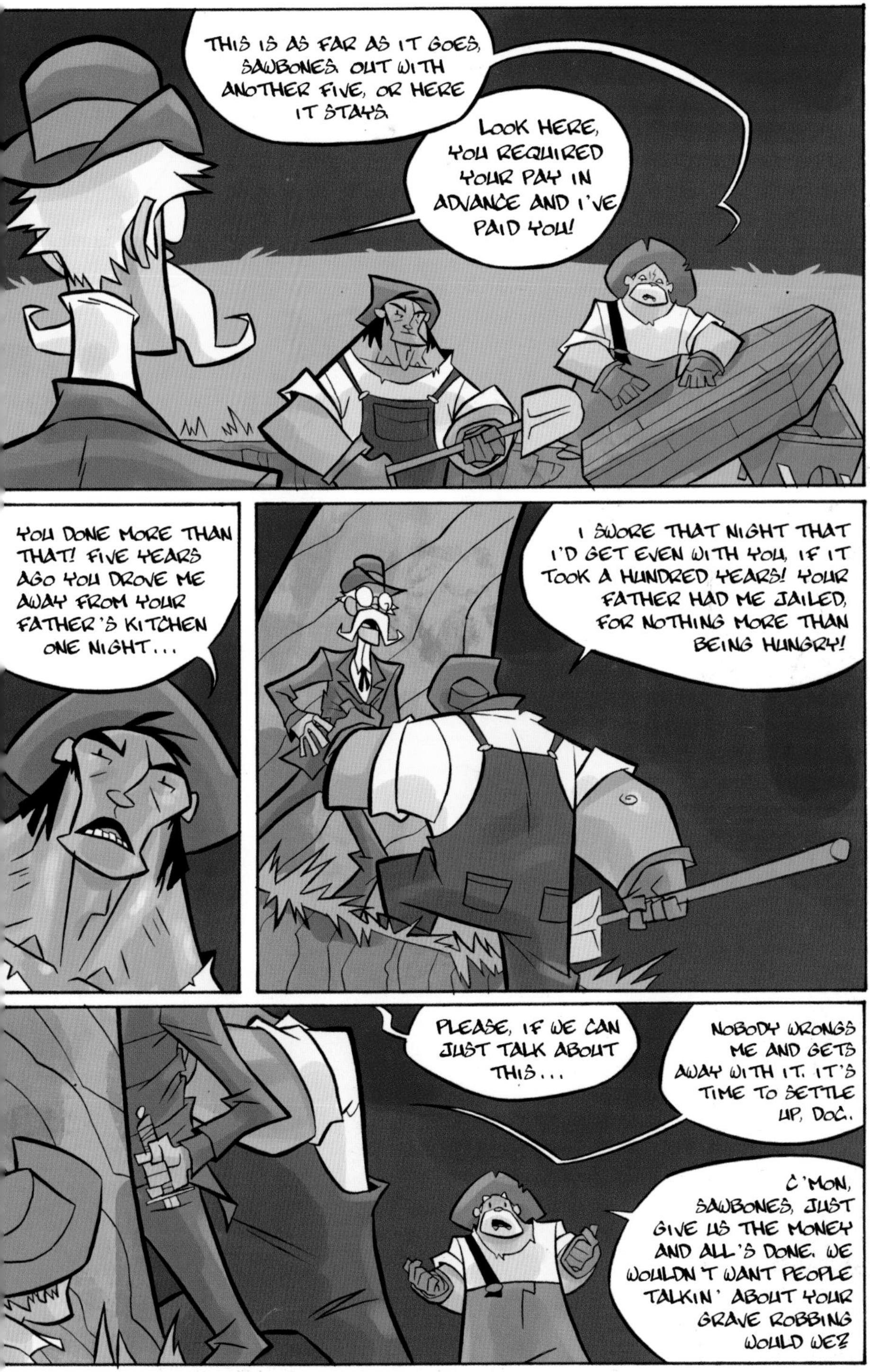
THIS IS AS FAR AS IT GOES, SAWBONES. OUT WITH ANOTHER FIVE, OR HERE IT STAYS.
LOOK HERE, YOU REQUIRED YOUR PAY IN ADVANCE AND I'VE PAID YOU!
YOU DONE MORE THAN THAT! FIVE YEARS AGO YOU DROVE ME AWAY FROM YOUR FATHER'S KITCHEN ONE NIGHT...
I SWORE THAT NIGHT THAT I'D GET EVEN WITH YOU, IF IT TOOK A HUNDRED YEARS! YOUR FATHER HAD ME JAILED, FOR NOTHING MORE THAN BEING HUNGRY!
PLEASE, IF WE CAN JUST TALK ABOUT THIS...
NOBODY WRONGS ME AND GETS AWAY WITH IT. IT'S TIME TO SETTLE UP, DOC.
C'MON, SAWBONES, JUST GIVE US THE MONEY AND ALL'S DONE. WE WOULDN'T WANT PEOPLE TALKIN' ABOUT YOUR GRAVE ROBBING WOULD WE?

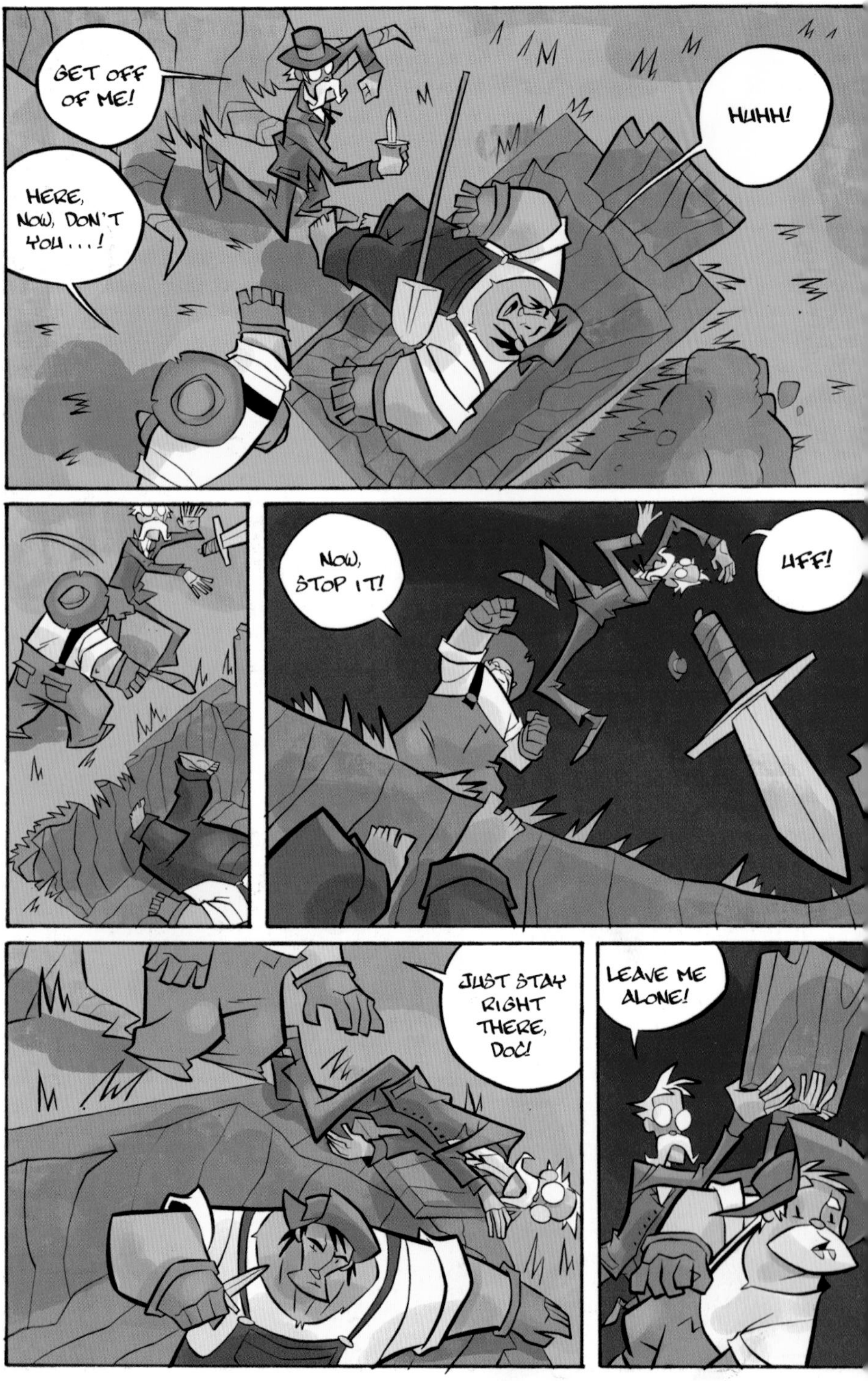
GET OFF OF ME!
HERE, NOW, DON'T YOU...!
HUHH!
NOW, STOP IT!
UFF!
JUST STAY RIGHT THERE, DOC!
LEAVE ME ALONE!

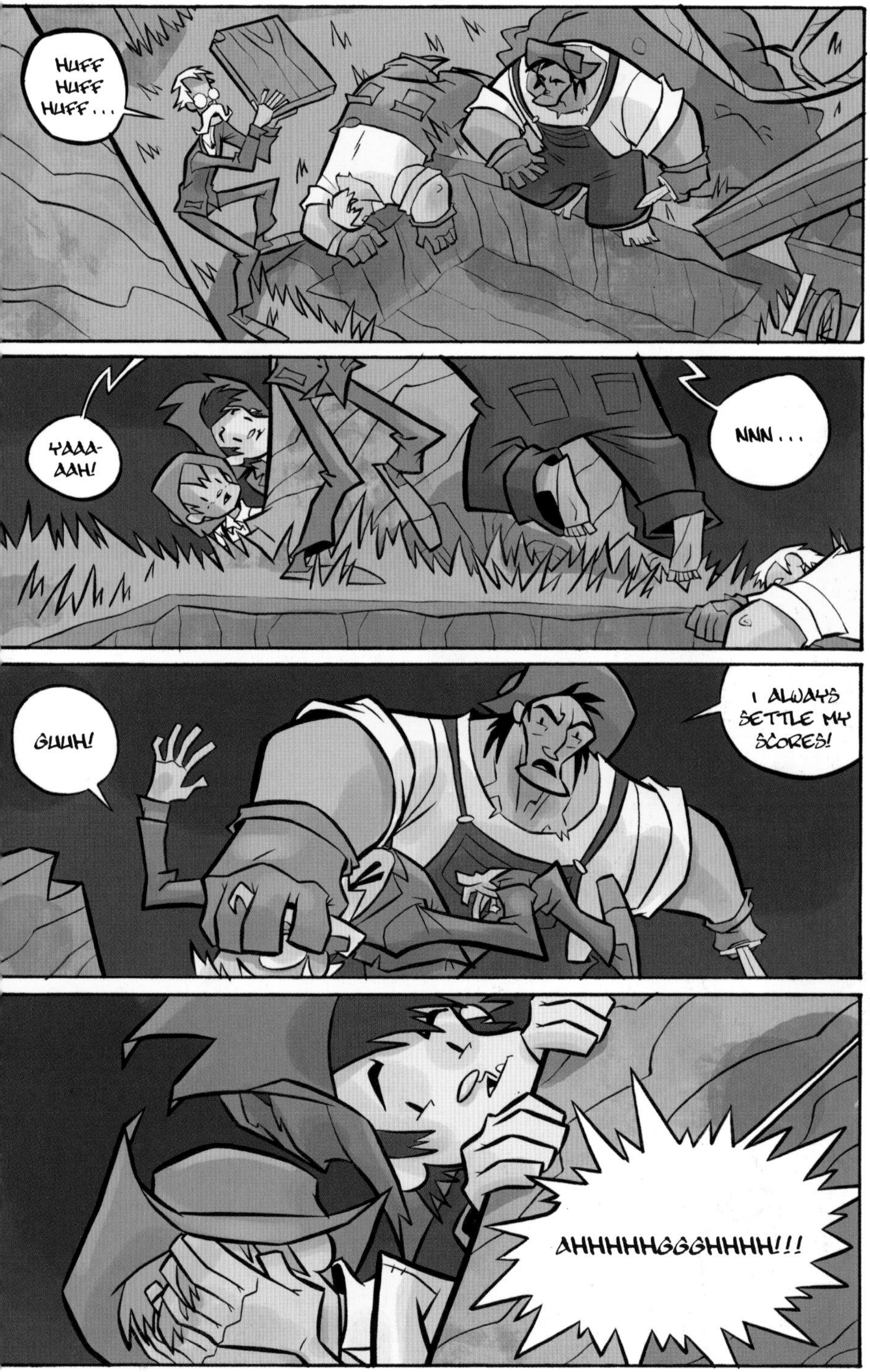
HUFF
HUFF
HUFF . . .
YAAAA-
AAH!
NNN . . .
GUUH!
I ALWAYS
SETTLE MY
SCORES!
AHHHHHGGGHHHH!!!

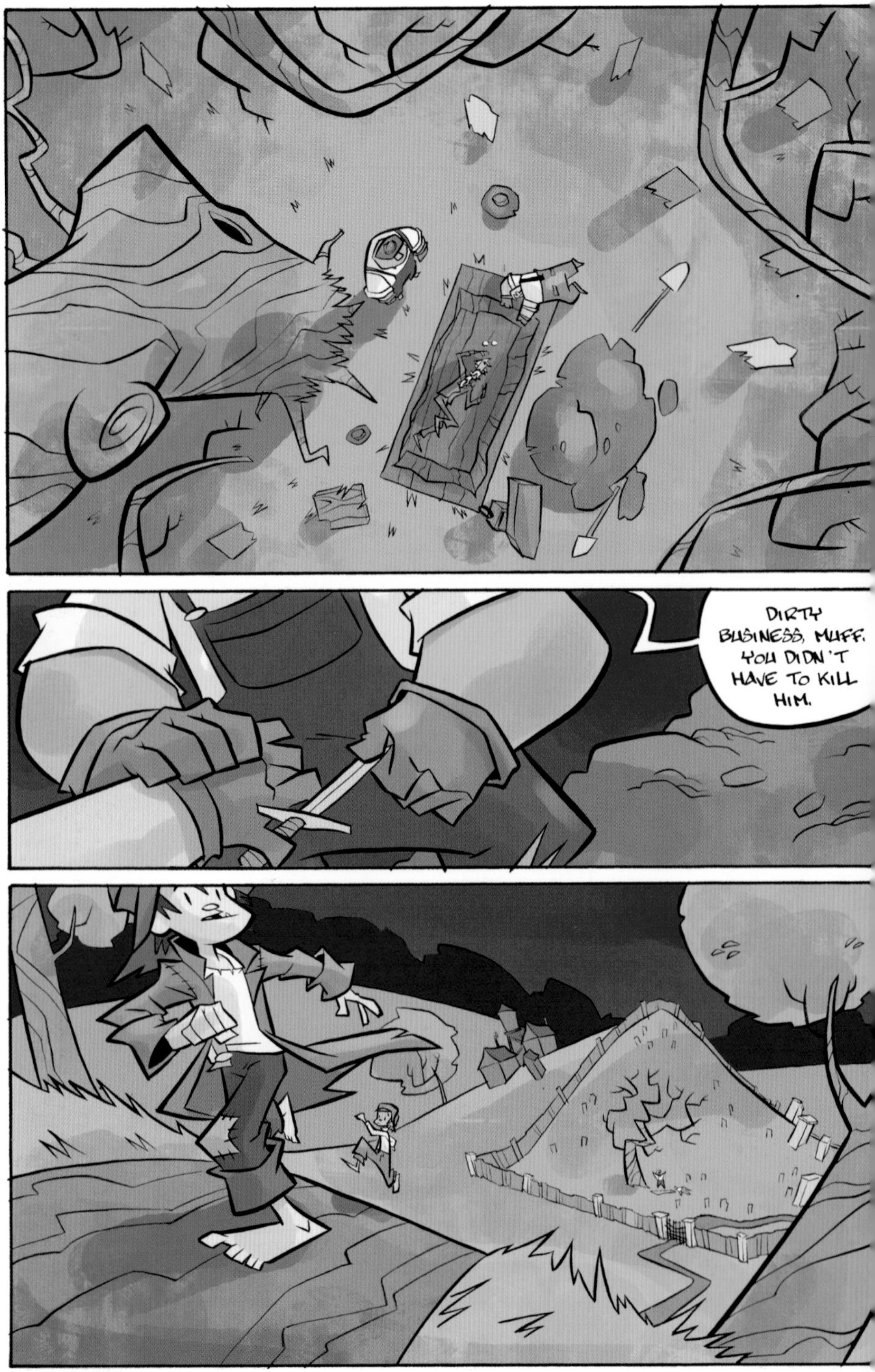
DIRTY BUSINESS, MUFF. YOU DIDN'T HAVE TO KILL HIM.

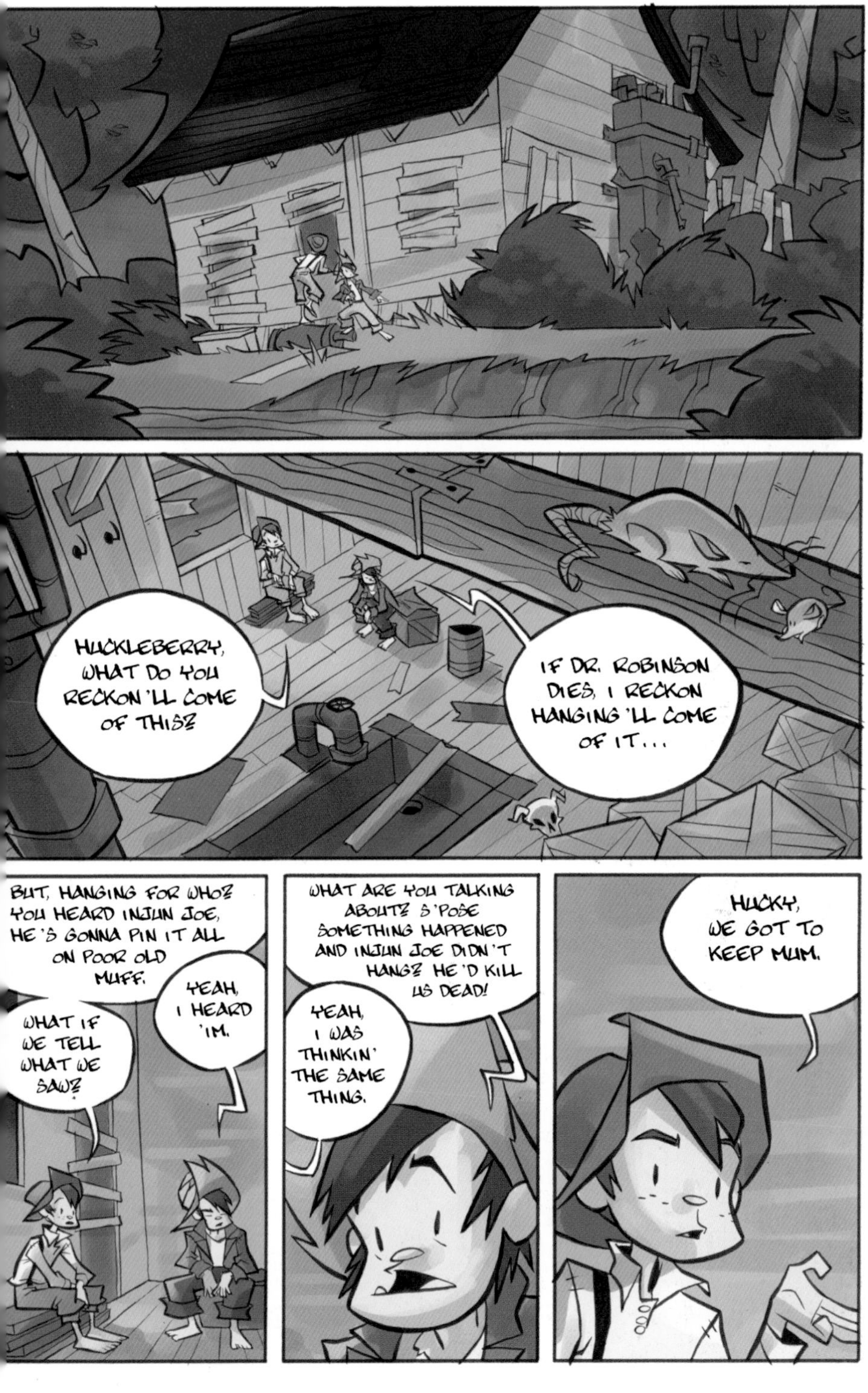
HUCKLEBERRY, WHAT DO YOU RECKON'LL COME OF THIS?
IF DR. ROBINSON DIES, I RECKON HANGING'LL COME OF IT...
BUT, HANGING FOR WHO? YOU HEARD INJUN JOE, HE'S GONNA PIN IT ALL ON POOR OLD MUFF.
YEAH, I HEARD 'IM.
WHAT IF WE TELL WHAT WE SAW?
WHAT ARE YOU TALKING ABOUT? S'POSE SOMETHING HAPPENED AND INJUN JOE DIDN'T HANG? HE'D KILL US DEAD!
YEAH, I WAS THINKIN' THE SAME THING.
HUCKY, WE GOT TO KEEP MUM.

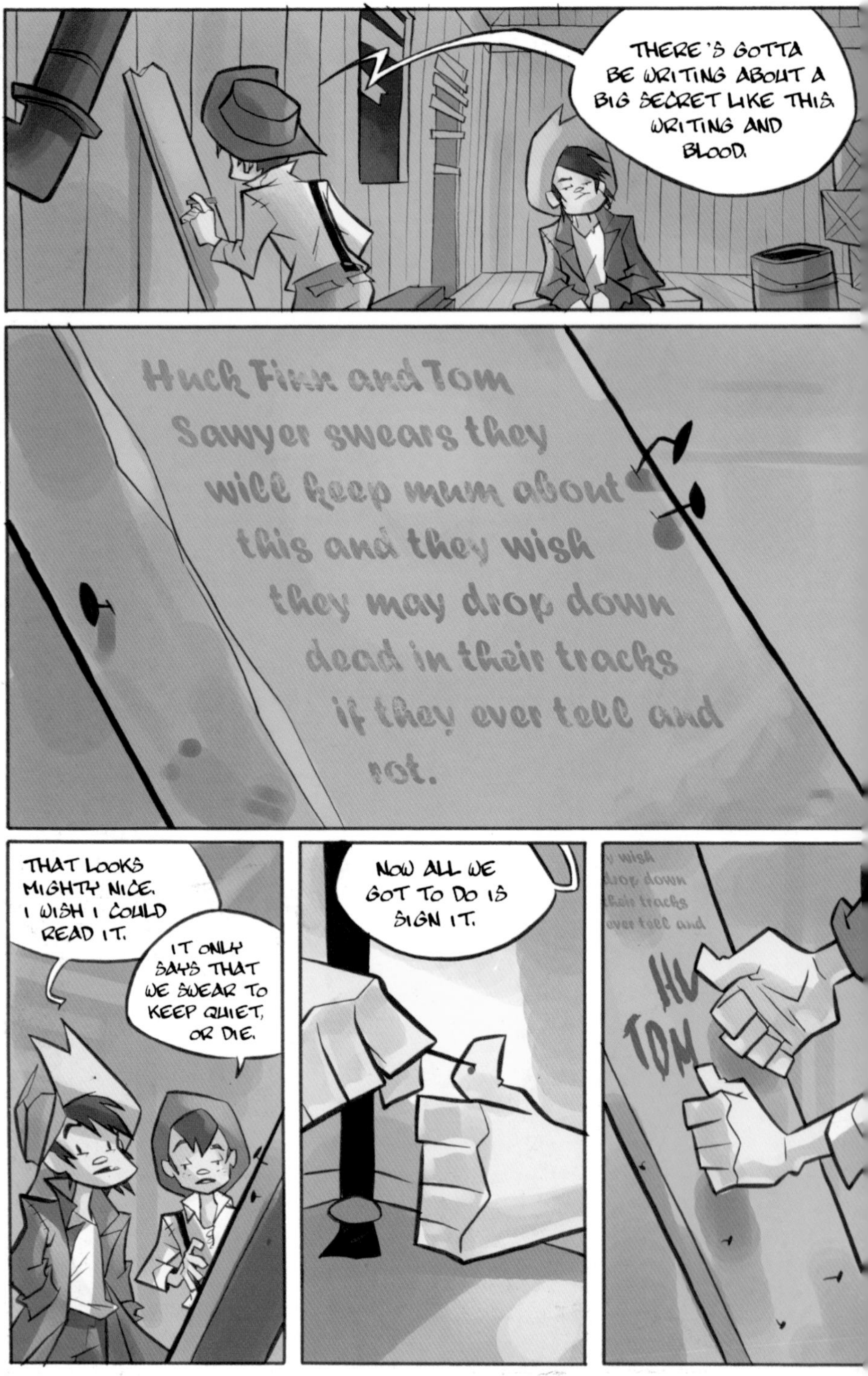
THERE'S GOTTA BE WRITING ABOUT A BIG SECRET LIKE THIS. WRITING AND BLOOD.
Huck Finn and Tom Sawyer swears they will keep mum about this and they wish they may drop down dead in their tracks if they ever tell and rot.
THAT LOOKS MIGHTY NICE. I WISH I COULD READ IT.
IT ONLY SAYS THAT WE SWEAR TO KEEP QUIET, OR DIE.
NOW ALL WE GOT TO DO IS SIGN IT.
HU
TOM

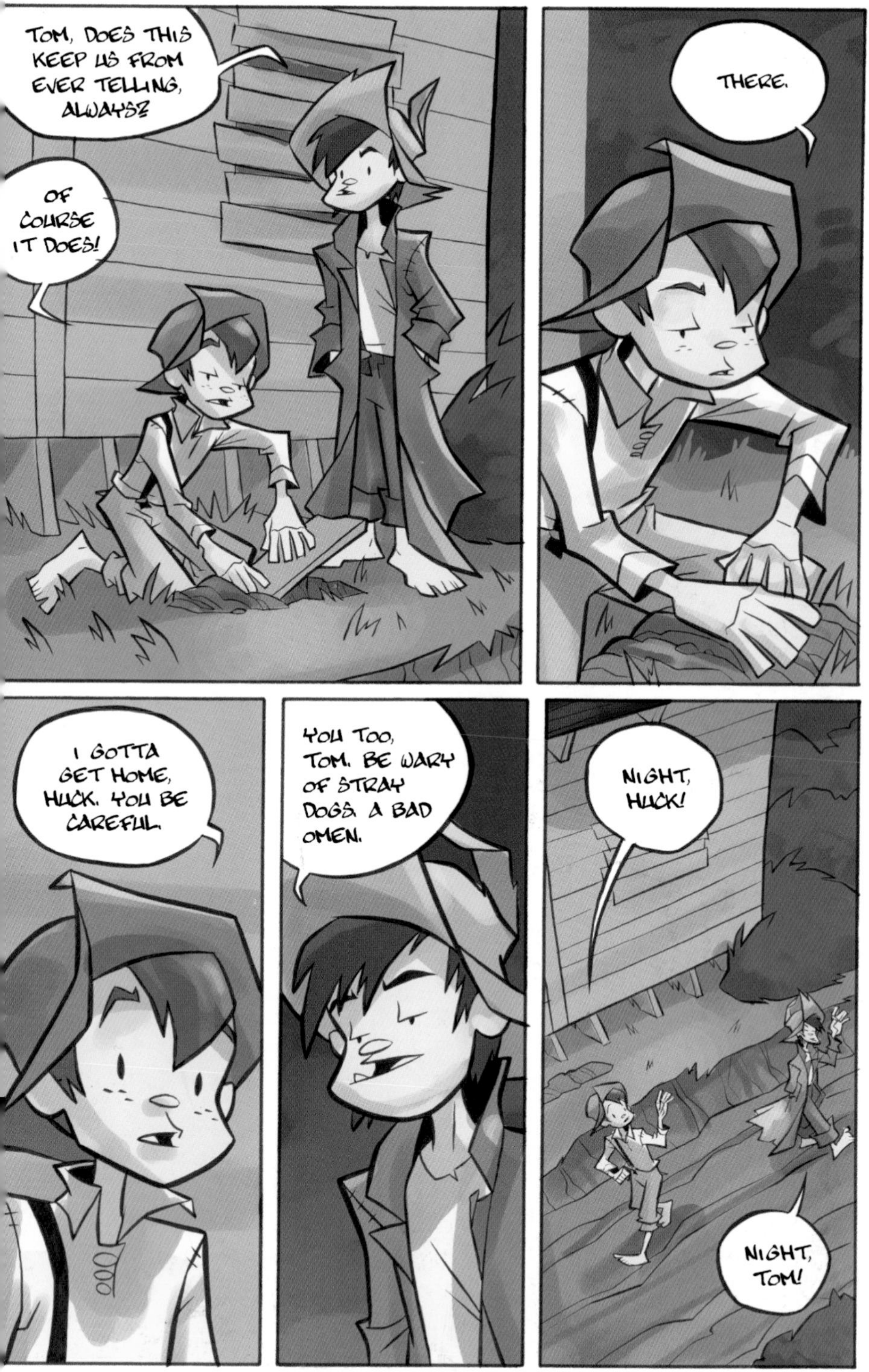
TOM, DOES THIS KEEP US FROM EVER TELLING, ALWAYS?
OF COURSE IT DOES!
THERE.
I GOTTA GET HOME, HUCK. YOU BE CAREFUL.
YOU TOO, TOM. BE WARY OF STRAY DOGS. A BAD OMEN.
NIGHT, HUCK!
NIGHT, TOM!

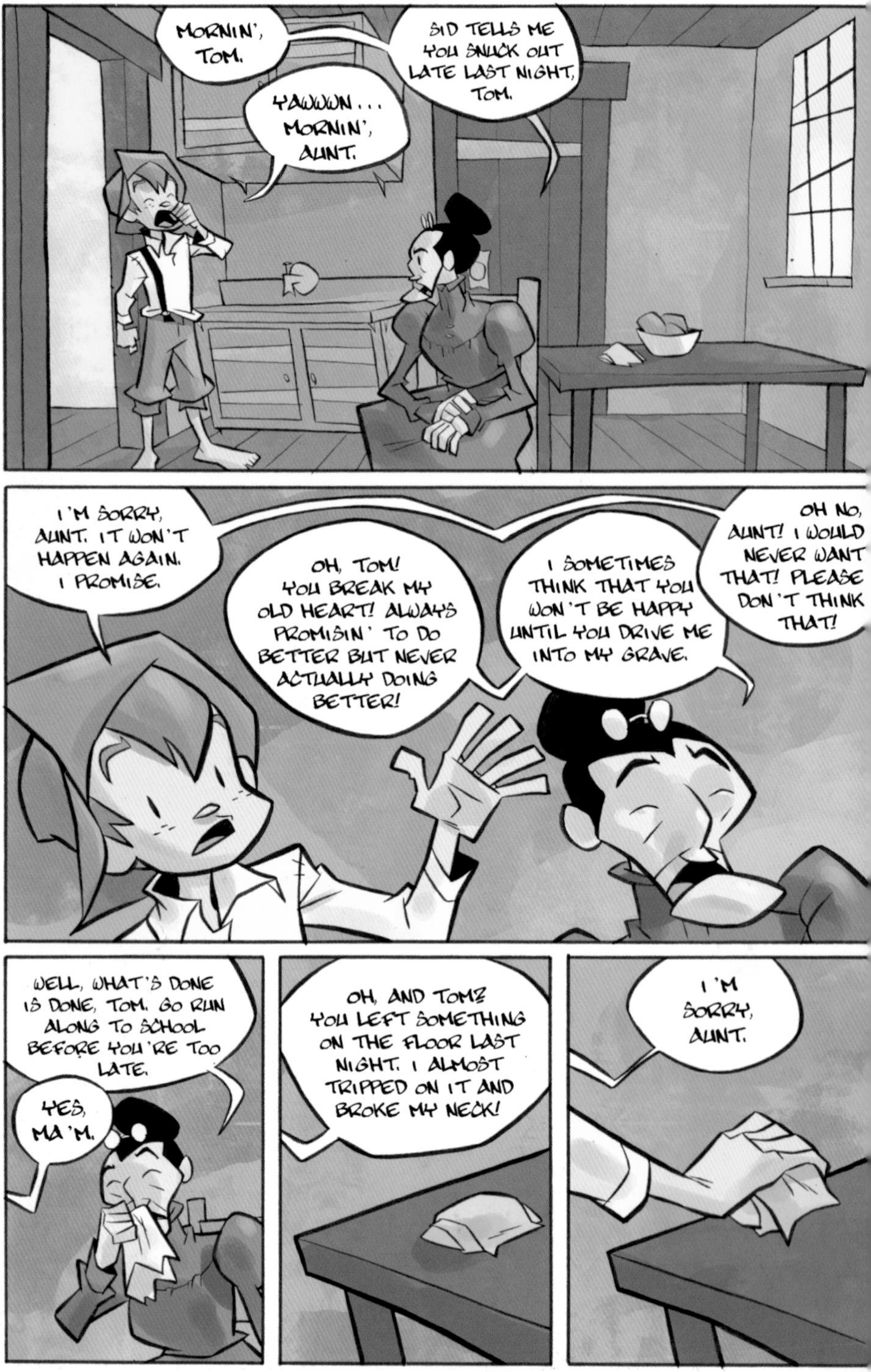
MORNIN', TOM.
YAWWN... MORNIN', AUNT.
SID TELLS ME YOU SNUCK OUT LATE LAST NIGHT, TOM.
I'M SORRY, AUNT. IT WON'T HAPPEN AGAIN. I PROMISE.
OH, TOM! YOU BREAK MY OLD HEART! ALWAYS PROMISIN' TO DO BETTER BUT NEVER ACTUALLY DOING BETTER!
I SOMETIMES THINK THAT YOU WON'T BE HAPPY UNTIL YOU DRIVE ME INTO MY GRAVE.
OH NO, AUNT! I WOULD NEVER WANT THAT! PLEASE DON'T THINK THAT!
WELL, WHAT'S DONE IS DONE, TOM. GO RUN ALONG TO SCHOOL BEFORE YOU'RE TOO LATE.
YES, MA'M.
OH, AND TOM? YOU LEFT SOMETHING ON THE FLOOR LAST NIGHT. I ALMOST TRIPPED ON IT AND BROKE MY NECK!
I'M SORRY, AUNT.

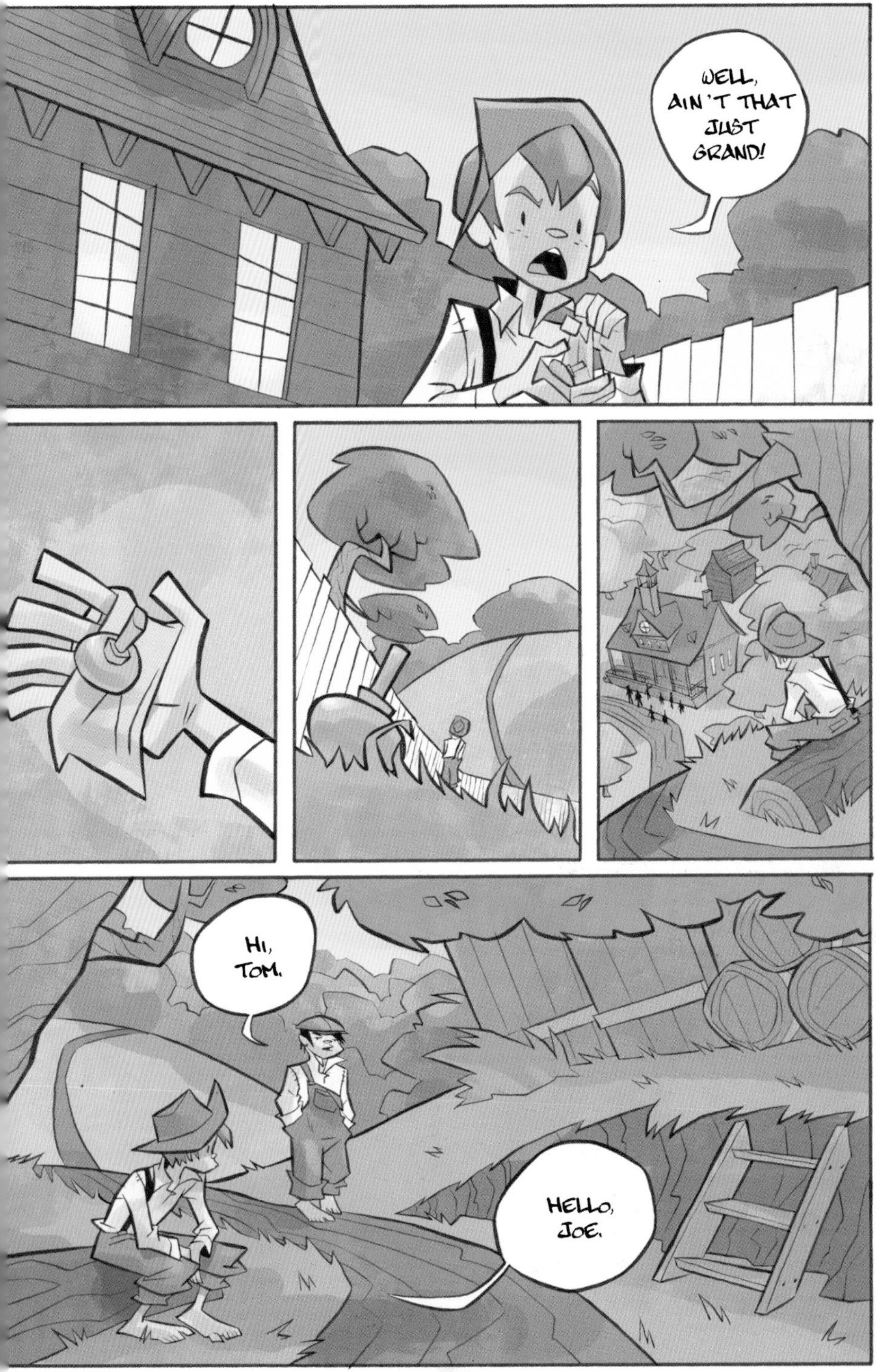
WELL, AIN'T THAT JUST GRAND!
HI, TOM.
HELLO, JOE.

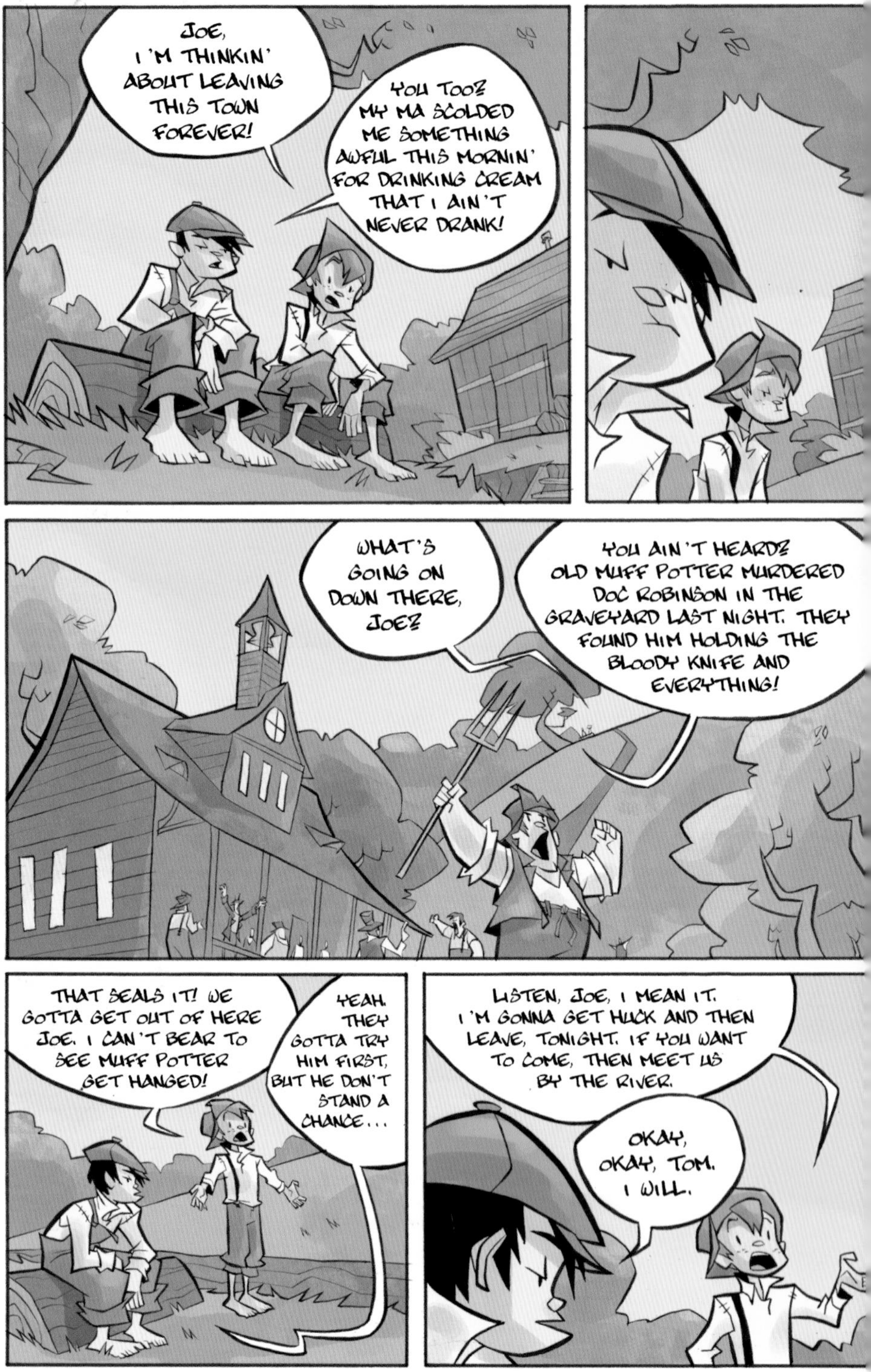
JOE, I'M THINKIN' ABOUT LEAVING THIS TOWN FOREVER!
YOU TOO? MY MA SCOLDED ME SOMETHING AWFUL THIS MORNIN' FOR DRINKING CREAM THAT I AIN'T NEVER DRANK!
WHAT'S GOING ON DOWN THERE, JOE?
YOU AIN'T HEARD? OLD MUFF POTTER MURDERED DOC ROBINSON IN THE GRAVEYARD LAST NIGHT. THEY FOUND HIM HOLDING THE BLOODY KNIFE AND EVERYTHING!
THAT SEALS IT! WE GOTTA GET OUT OF HERE JOE. I CAN'T BEAR TO SEE MUFF POTTER GET HANGED!
YEAH. THEY GOTTA TRY HIM FIRST, BUT HE DON'T STAND A CHANCE...
LISTEN, JOE, I MEAN IT. I'M GONNA GET HUCK AND THEN LEAVE, TONIGHT. IF YOU WANT TO COME, THEN MEET US BY THE RIVER.
OKAY, OKAY, TOM. I WILL.

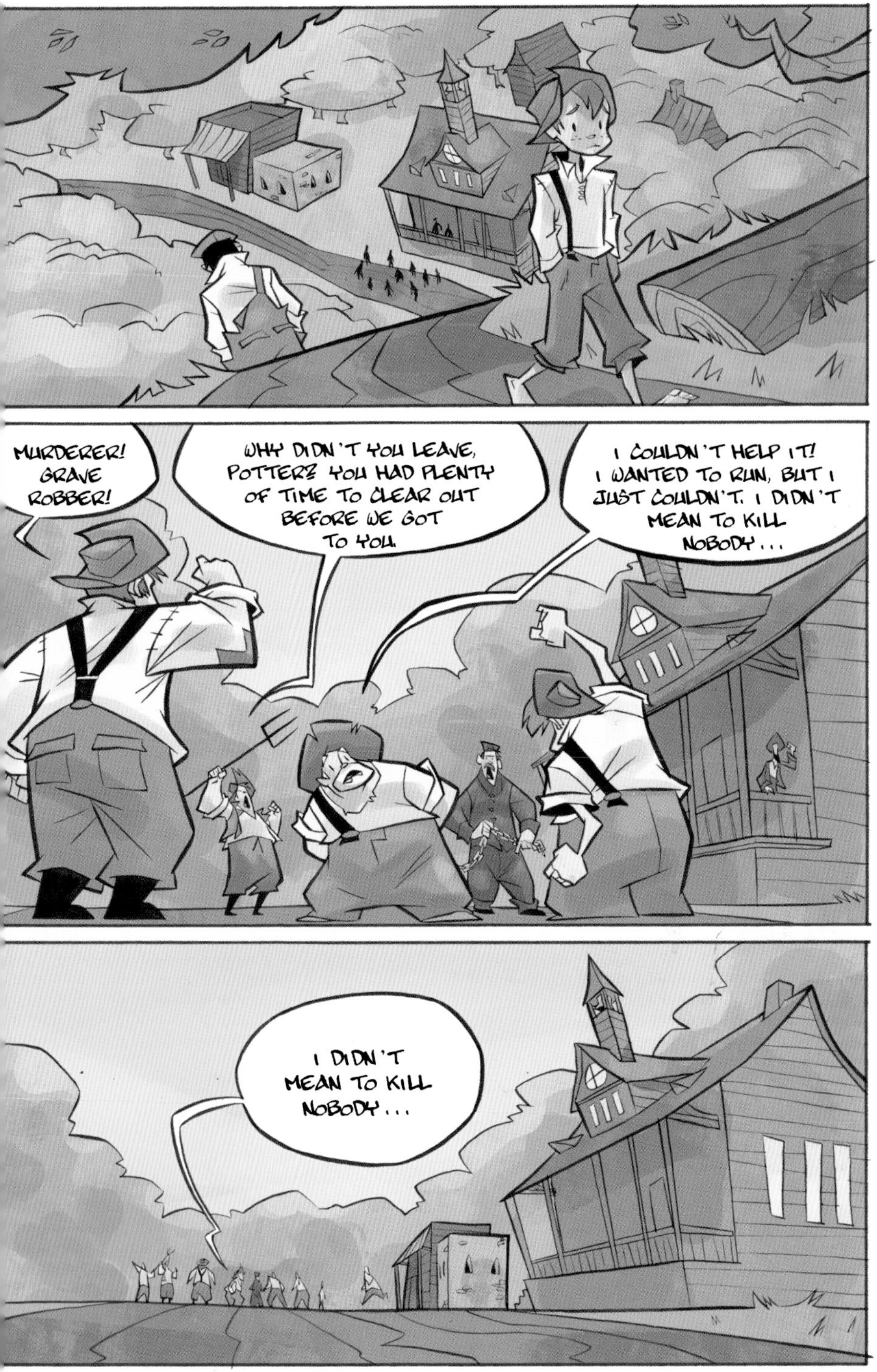
MURDERER! GRAVE ROBBER!
WHY DIDN'T YOU LEAVE, POTTER? YOU HAD PLENTY OF TIME TO CLEAR OUT BEFORE WE GOT TO YOU.
I COULDN'T HELP IT! I WANTED TO RUN, BUT I JUST COULDN'T. I DIDN'T MEAN TO KILL NOBODY...
I DIDN'T MEAN TO KILL NOBODY...

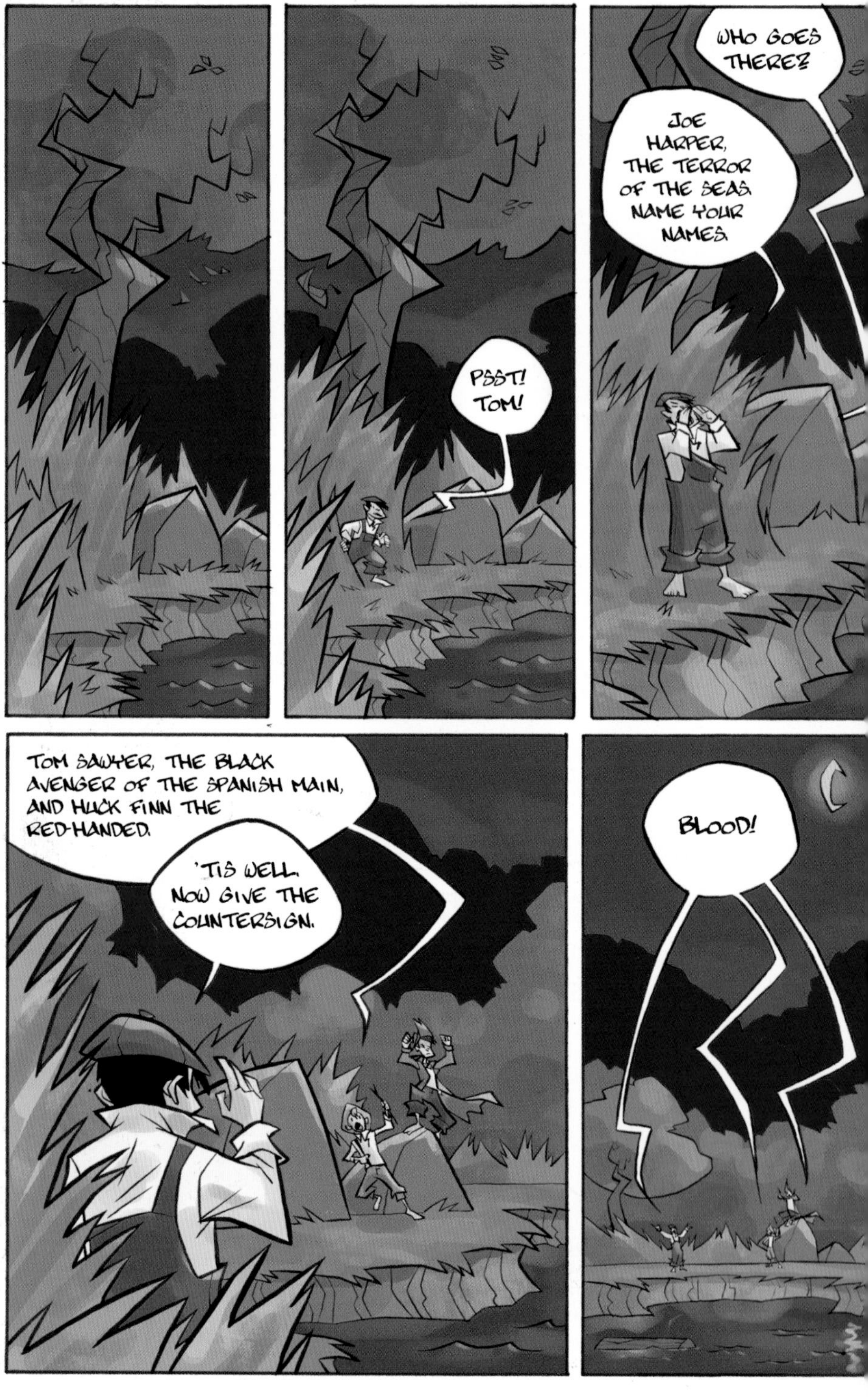
PSST! TOM!
WHO GOES THERE?
JOE HARPER, THE TERROR OF THE SEAS. NAME YOUR NAMES.
TOM SAWYER, THE BLACK AVENGER OF THE SPANISH MAIN, AND HUCK FINN THE RED-HANDED.
'TIS WELL. NOW GIVE THE COUNTERSIGN.
BLOOD!

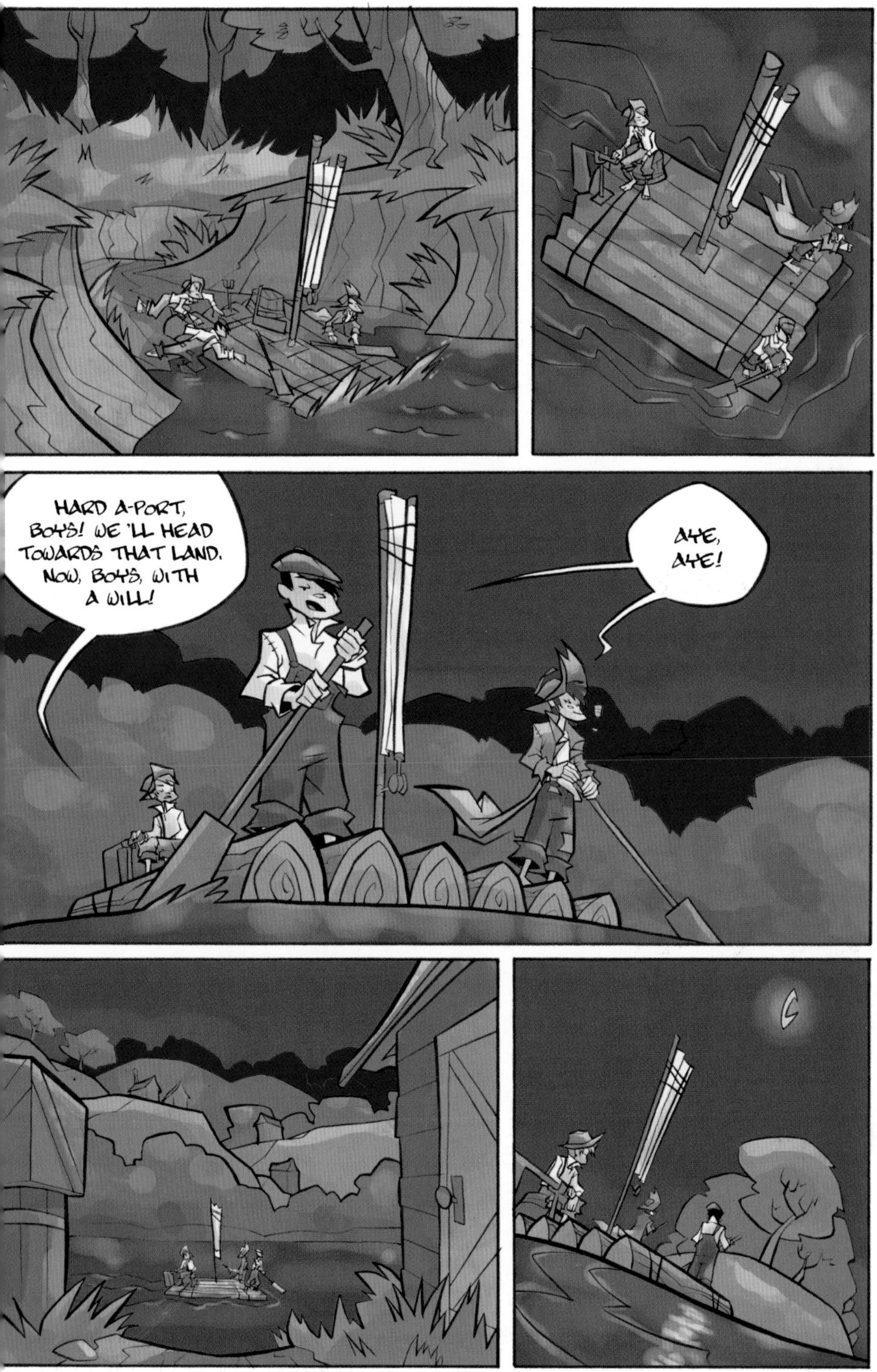
HARD A-PORT, BOYS! WE'LL HEAD TOWARDS THAT LAND. NOW, BOYS, WITH A WILL!
AYE, AYE!

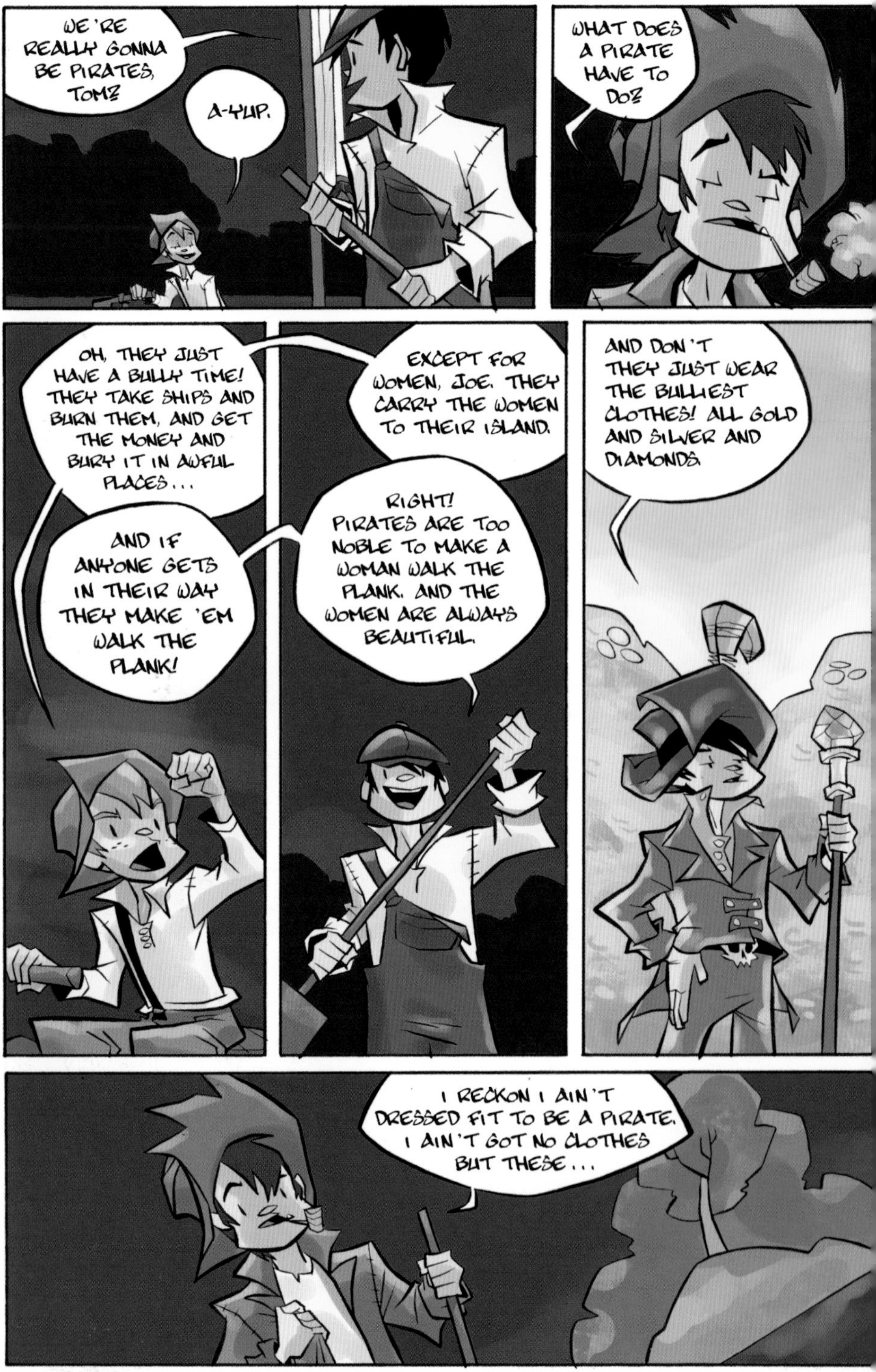
WE'RE REALLY GONNA BE PIRATES, TOM?
A-YUP.
WHAT DOES A PIRATE HAVE TO DO?
OH, THEY JUST HAVE A BULLY TIME! THEY TAKE SHIPS AND BURN THEM, AND GET THE MONEY AND BURY IT IN AWFUL PLACES...
EXCEPT FOR WOMEN, JOE. THEY CARRY THE WOMEN TO THEIR ISLAND.
AND IF ANYONE GETS IN THEIR WAY THEY MAKE 'EM WALK THE PLANK!
RIGHT! PIRATES ARE TOO NOBLE TO MAKE A WOMAN WALK THE PLANK. AND THE WOMEN ARE ALWAYS BEAUTIFUL.
AND DON'T THEY JUST WEAR THE BULLIEST CLOTHES! ALL GOLD AND SILVER AND DIAMONDS.
I RECKON I AIN'T DRESSED FIT TO BE A PIRATE. I AIN'T GOT NO CLOTHES BUT THESE...

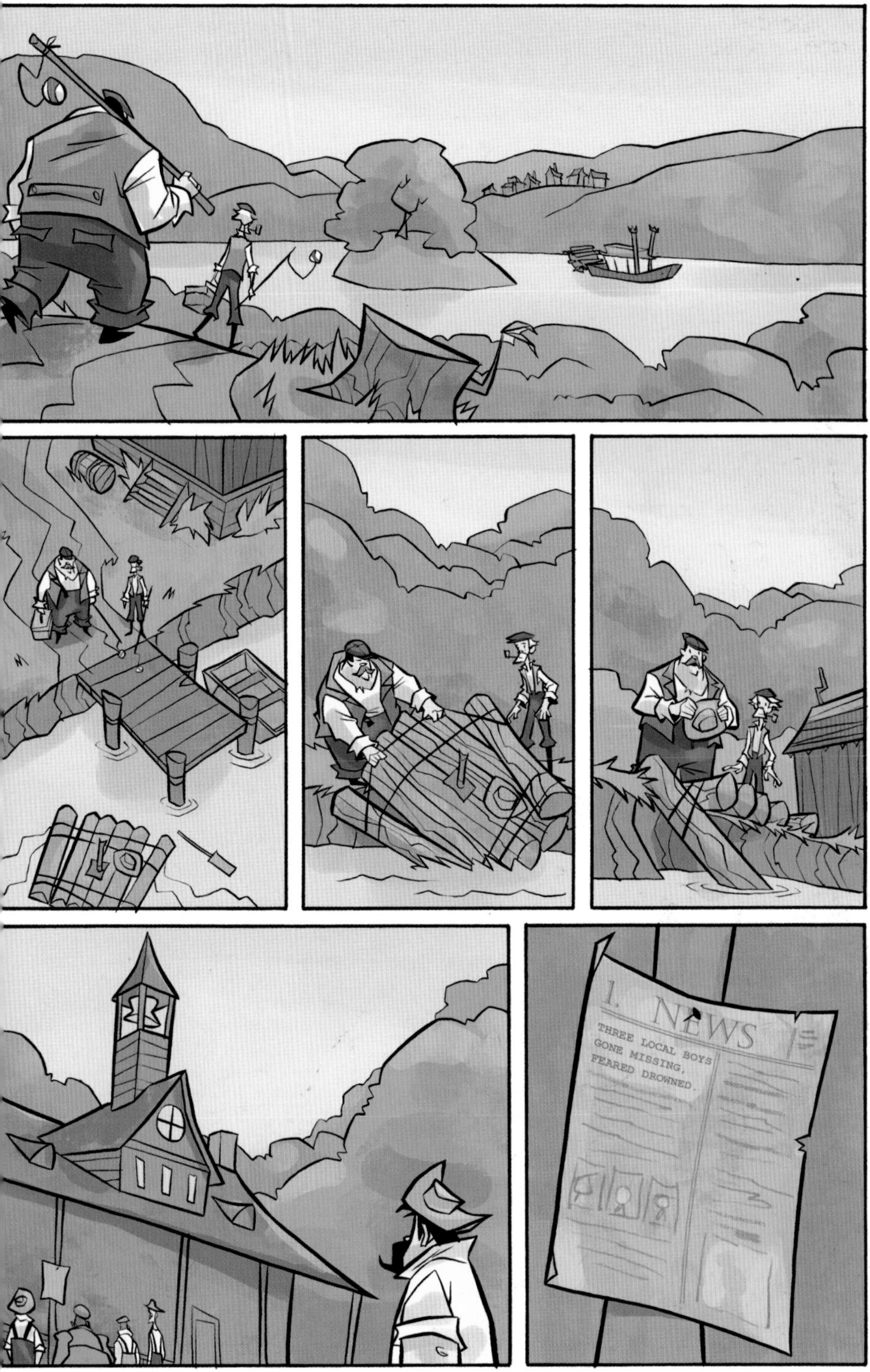

1.
NEWS
THREE LOCAL BOYS GONE MISSING, FEARED DROWNED.

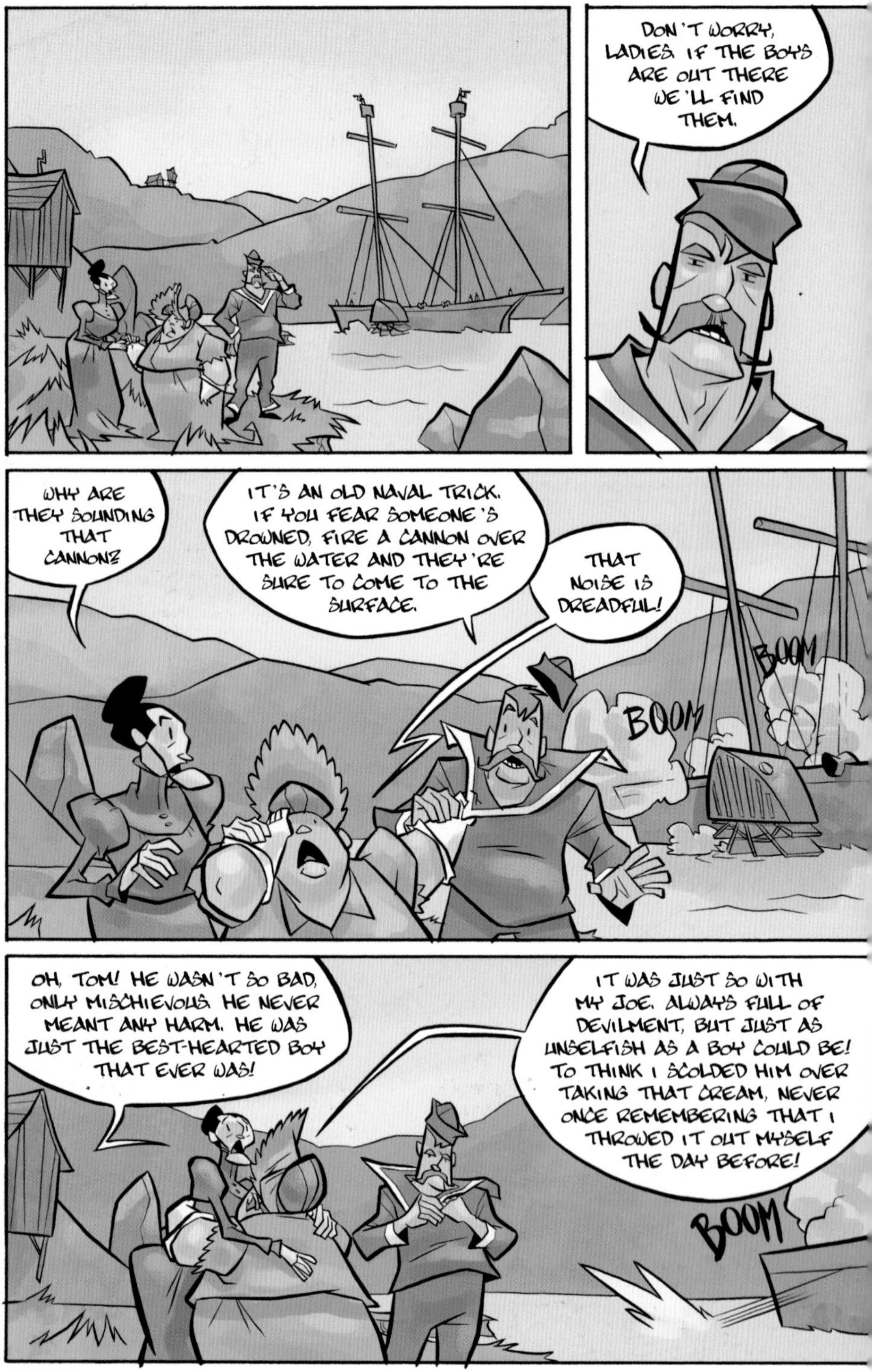
DON'T WORRY, LADIES. IF THE BOYS ARE OUT THERE WE'LL FIND THEM.
WHY ARE THEY SOUNDING THAT CANNON?
IT'S AN OLD NAVAL TRICK. IF YOU FEAR SOMEONE'S DROWNED, FIRE A CANNON OVER THE WATER AND THEY'RE SURE TO COME TO THE SURFACE.
THAT NOISE IS DREADFUL!
BOOM
BOOM
OH, TOM! HE WASN'T SO BAD, ONLY MISCHIEVOUS. HE NEVER MEANT ANY HARM. HE WAS JUST THE BEST-HEARTED BOY THAT EVER WAS!
IT WAS JUST SO WITH MY JOE. ALWAYS FULL OF DEVILMENT, BUT JUST AS UNSELFISH AS A BOY COULD BE! TO THINK I SCOLDED HIM OVER TAKING THAT CREAM, NEVER ONCE REMEMBERING THAT I THROWED IT OUT MYSELF THE DAY BEFORE!
BOOM

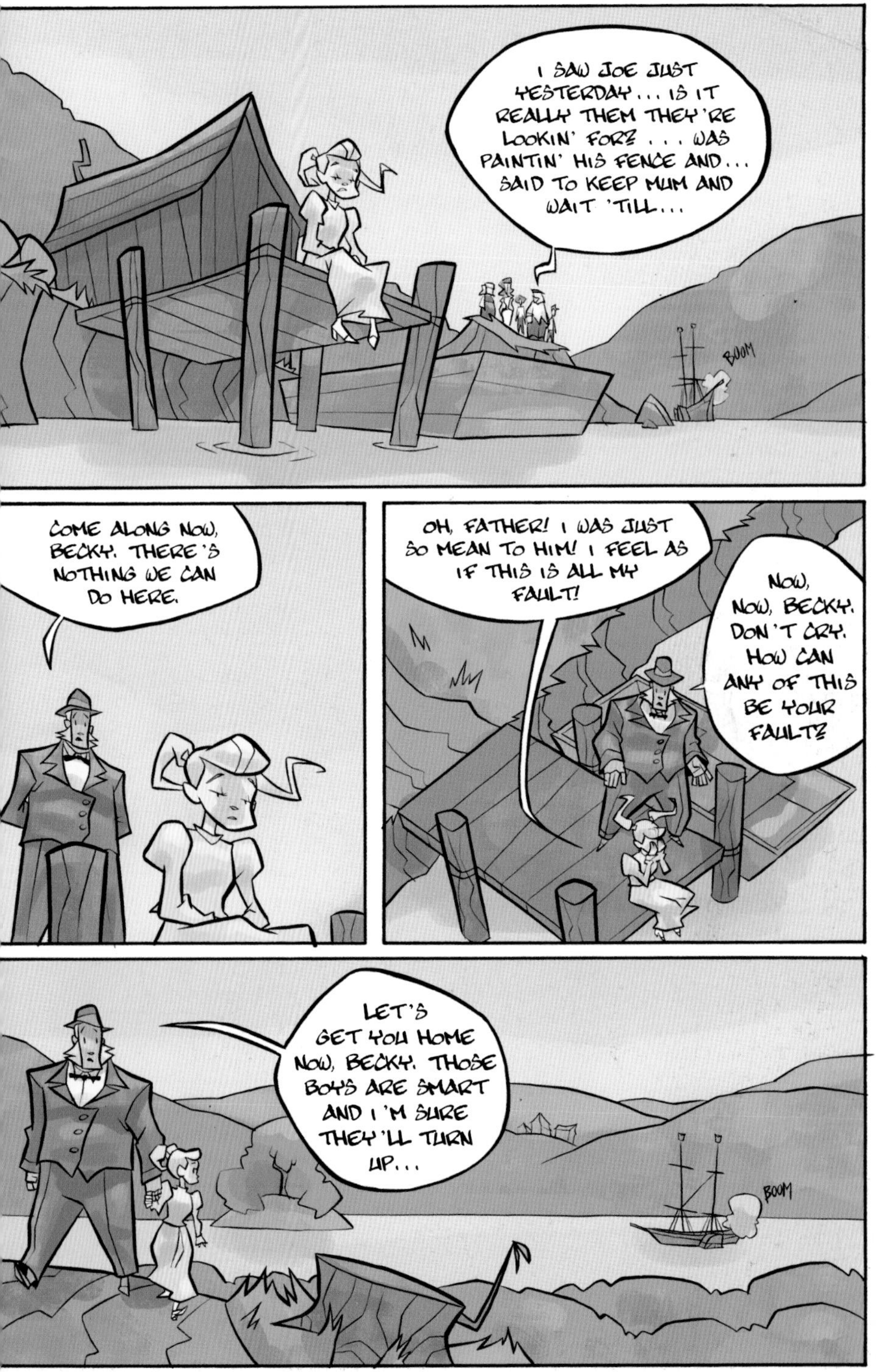
I SAW JOE JUST YESTERDAY... IS IT REALLY THEM THEY'RE LOOKIN' FOR? ... WAS PAINTIN' HIS FENCE AND... SAID TO KEEP MUM AND WAIT 'TILL...
BOOM
COME ALONG NOW, BECKY. THERE'S NOTHING WE CAN DO HERE.
OH, FATHER! I WAS JUST SO MEAN TO HIM! I FEEL AS IF THIS IS ALL MY FAULT!
NOW, NOW, BECKY. DON'T CRY. HOW CAN ANY OF THIS BE YOUR FAULT?
LET'S GET YOU HOME NOW, BECKY. THOSE BOYS ARE SMART AND I'M SURE THEY'LL TURN UP...
BOOM

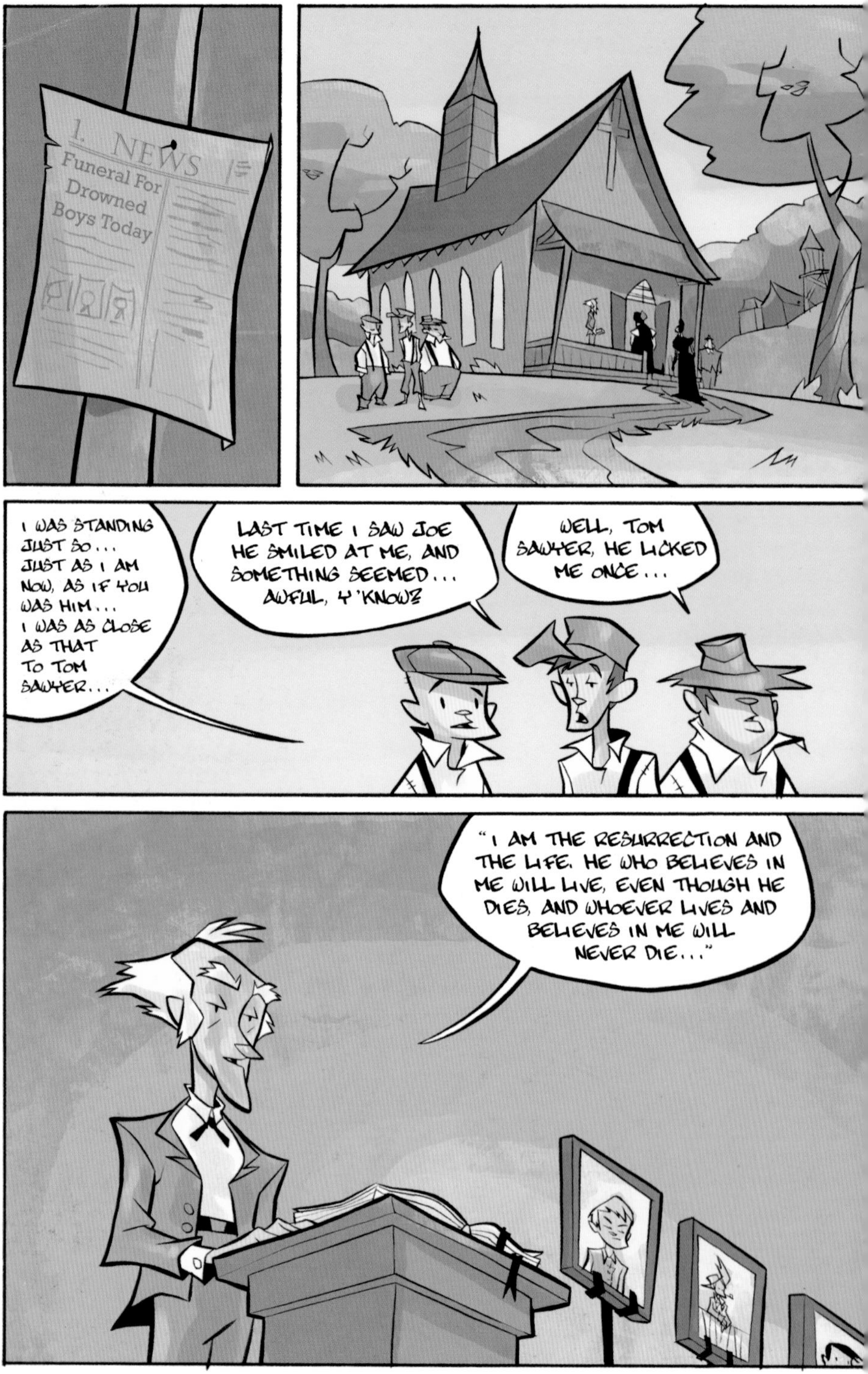
1. NEWS
Funeral For Drowned Boys Today
I WAS STANDING JUST SO... JUST AS I AM NOW, AS IF YOU WAS HIM... I WAS AS CLOSE AS THAT TO TOM SAWYER...
LAST TIME I SAW JOE HE SMILED AT ME, AND SOMETHING SEEMED... AWFUL, Y'KNOW?
WELL, TOM SAWYER, HE LICKED ME ONCE...
"I AM THE RESURRECTION AND THE LIFE. HE WHO BELIEVES IN ME WILL LIVE, EVEN THOUGH HE DIES, AND WHOEVER LIVES AND BELIEVES IN ME WILL NEVER DIE..."

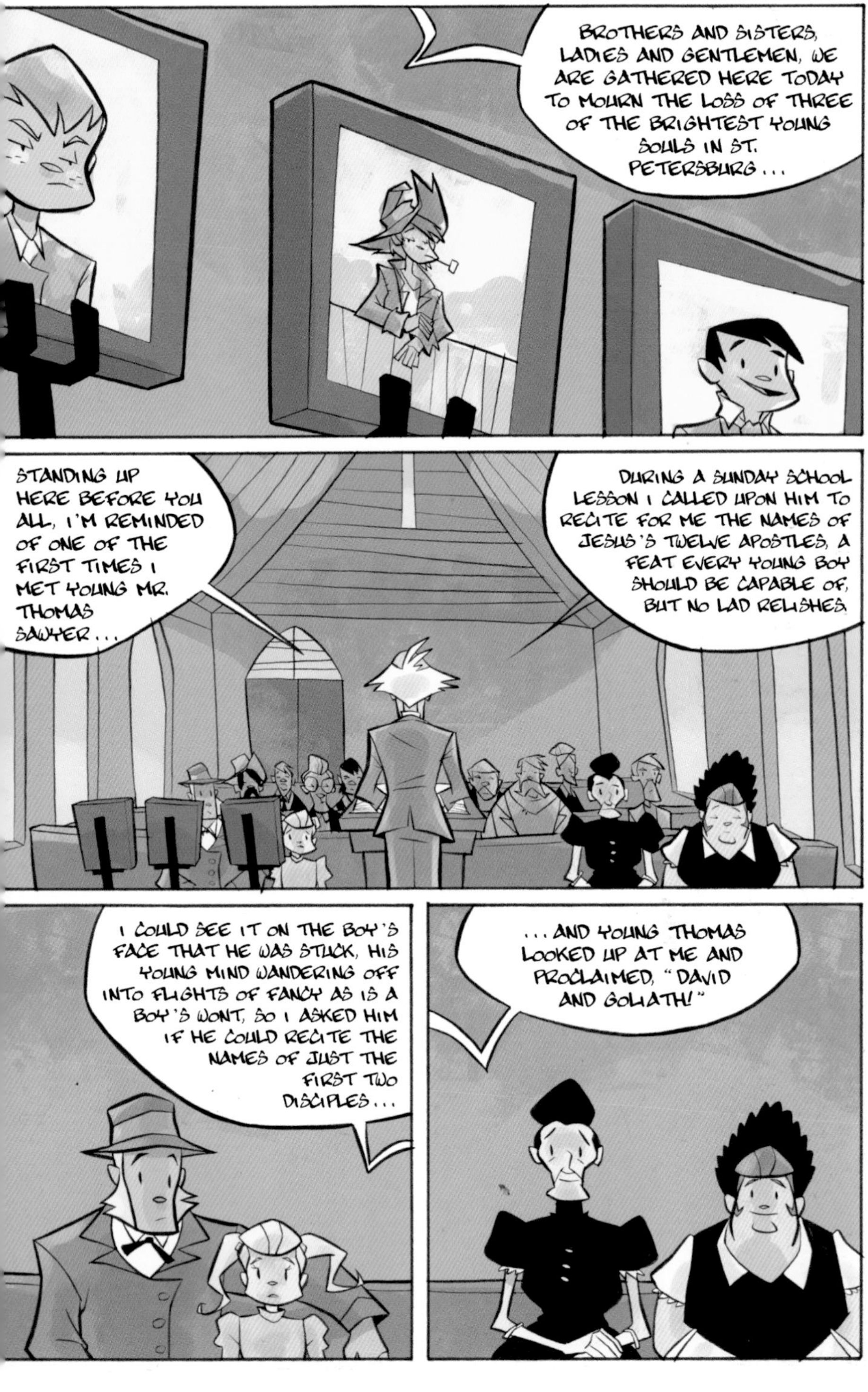
BROTHERS AND SISTERS, LADIES AND GENTLEMEN, WE ARE GATHERED HERE TODAY TO MOURN THE LOSS OF THREE OF THE BRIGHTEST YOUNG SOULS IN ST. PETERSBURG . . .
STANDING UP HERE BEFORE YOU ALL, I'M REMINDED OF ONE OF THE FIRST TIMES I MET YOUNG MR. THOMAS SAWYER . . .
DURING A SUNDAY SCHOOL LESSON I CALLED UPON HIM TO RECITE FOR ME THE NAMES OF JESUS'S TWELVE APOSTLES, A FEAT EVERY YOUNG BOY SHOULD BE CAPABLE OF, BUT NO LAD RELISHES.
I COULD SEE IT ON THE BOY'S FACE THAT HE WAS STUCK, HIS YOUNG MIND WANDERING OFF INTO FLIGHTS OF FANCY AS IS A BOY'S WONT, SO I ASKED HIM IF HE COULD RECITE THE NAMES OF JUST THE FIRST TWO DISCIPLES . . .
. . . AND YOUNG THOMAS LOOKED UP AT ME AND PROCLAIMED, "DAVID AND GOLIATH!"

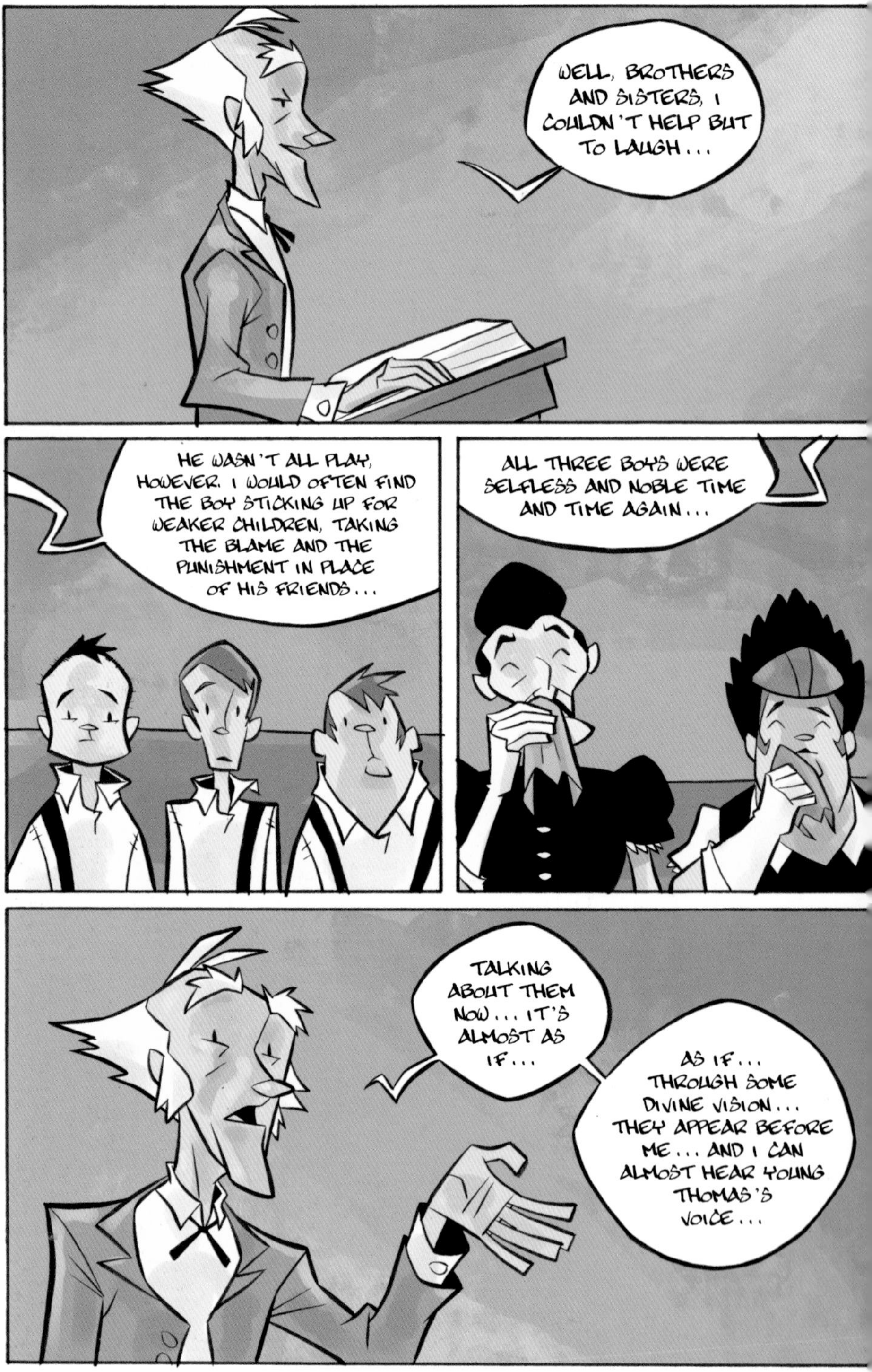
WELL, BROTHERS AND SISTERS, I COULDN'T HELP BUT TO LAUGH...
HE WASN'T ALL PLAY, HOWEVER. I WOULD OFTEN FIND THE BOY STICKING UP FOR WEAKER CHILDREN, TAKING THE BLAME AND THE PUNISHMENT IN PLACE OF HIS FRIENDS...
ALL THREE BOYS WERE SELFLESS AND NOBLE TIME AND TIME AGAIN...
TALKING ABOUT THEM NOW... IT'S ALMOST AS IF...
AS IF... THROUGH SOME DIVINE VISION... THEY APPEAR BEFORE ME... AND I CAN ALMOST HEAR YOUNG THOMAS'S VOICE...

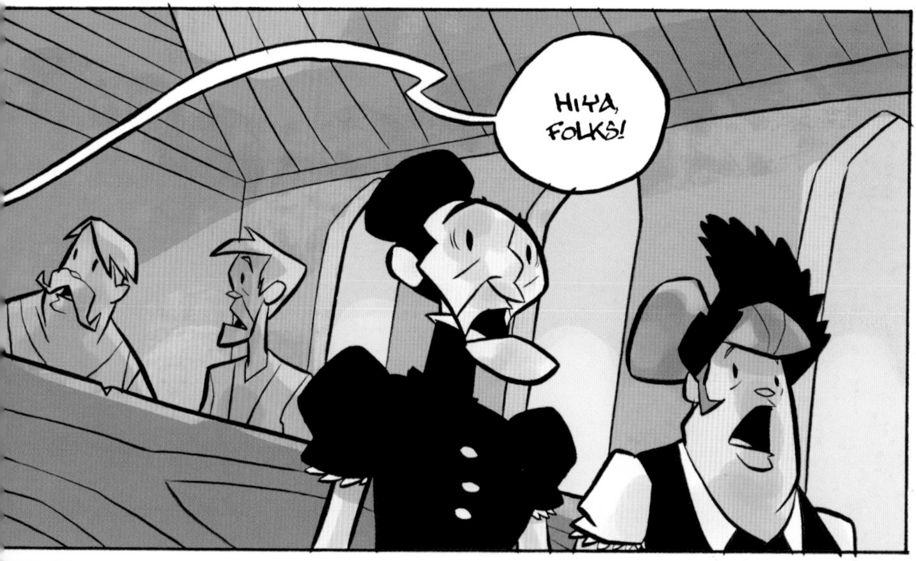
HIYA, FOLKS!

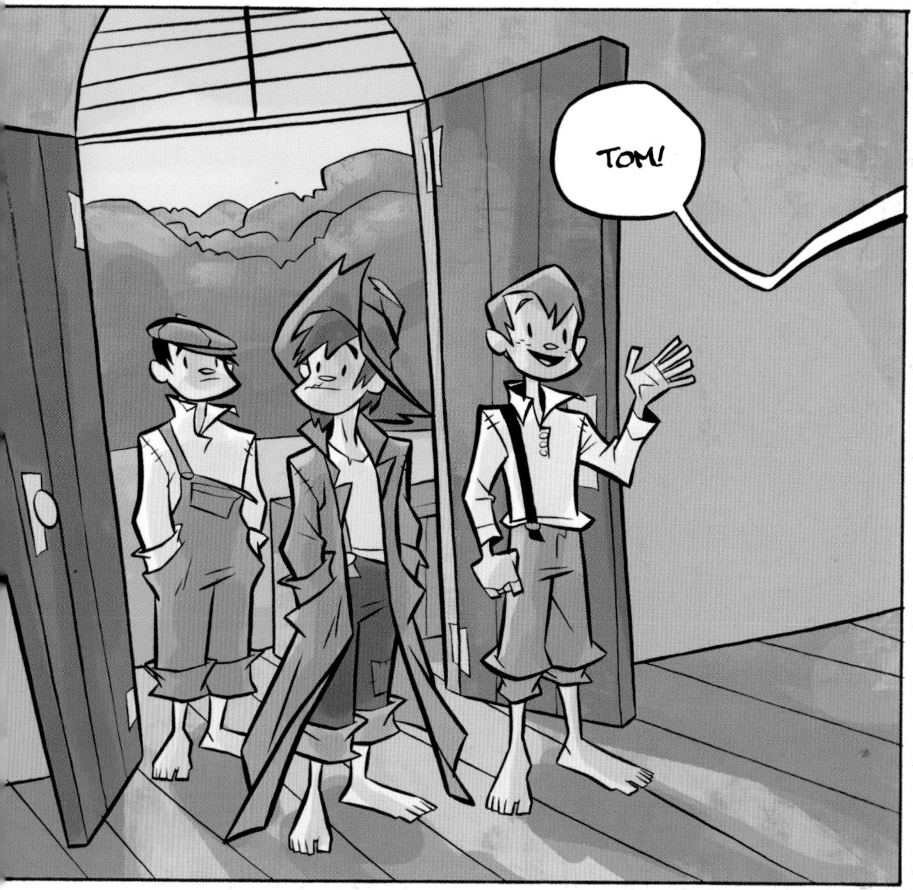
TOM!

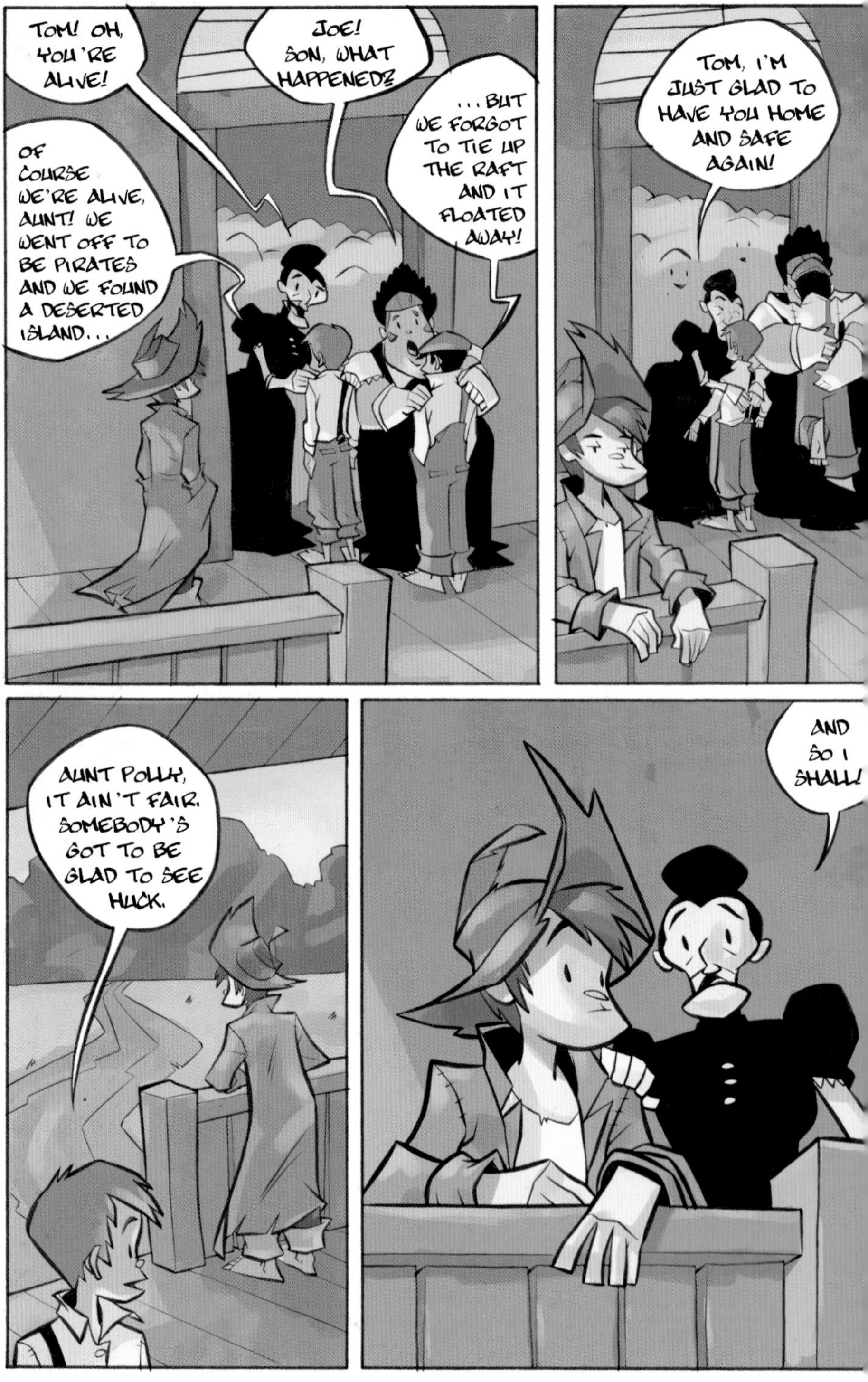
TOM! OH, YOU'RE ALIVE!
JOE! SON, WHAT HAPPENED?
OF COURSE WE'RE ALIVE, AUNT! WE WENT OFF TO BE PIRATES AND WE FOUND A DESERTED ISLAND...
...BUT WE FORGOT TO TIE UP THE RAFT AND IT FLOATED AWAY!
TOM, I'M JUST GLAD TO HAVE YOU HOME AND SAFE AGAIN!
AUNT POLLY, IT AIN'T FAIR. SOMEBODY'S GOT TO BE GLAD TO SEE HUCK.
AND SO I SHALL!

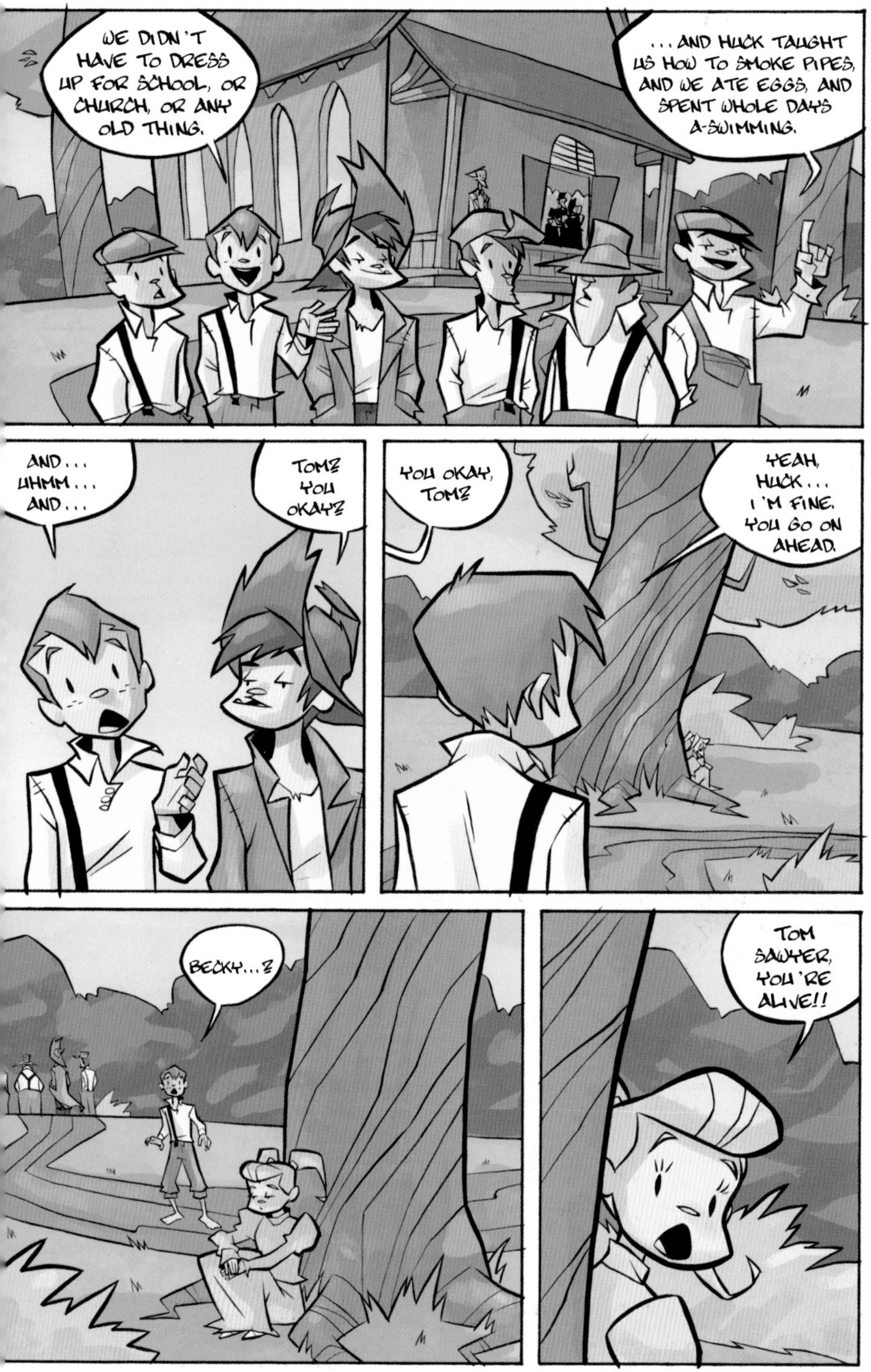
WE DIDN'T HAVE TO DRESS UP FOR SCHOOL, OR CHURCH, OR ANY OLD THING.
...AND HUCK TAUGHT US HOW TO SMOKE PIPES, AND WE ATE EGGS, AND SPENT WHOLE DAYS A-SWIMMING.
AND... UHMM... AND...
TOM? YOU OKAY?
YOU OKAY, TOM?
YEAH, HUCK... I'M FINE. YOU GO ON AHEAD.
BECKY...?
TOM SAWYER, YOU'RE ALIVE!!

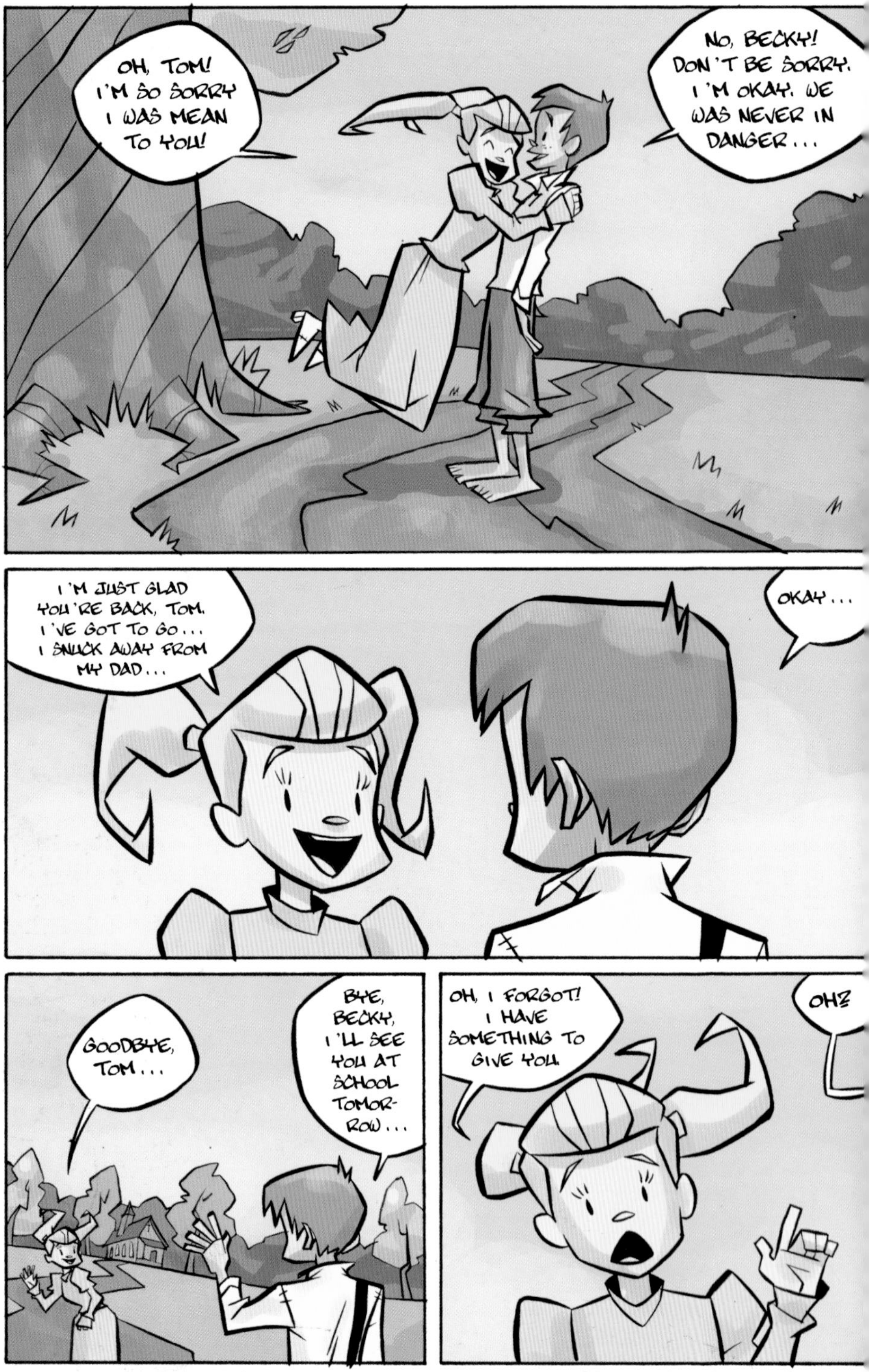
OH, TOM! I'M SO SORRY I WAS MEAN TO YOU!
NO, BECKY! DON'T BE SORRY. I'M OKAY. WE WAS NEVER IN DANGER...
I'M JUST GLAD YOU'RE BACK, TOM. I'VE GOT TO GO... I SNUCK AWAY FROM MY DAD...
OKAY...
GOODBYE, TOM...
BYE, BECKY, I'LL SEE YOU AT SCHOOL TOMOR-ROW...
OH, I FORGOT! I HAVE SOMETHING TO GIVE YOU.
OH?

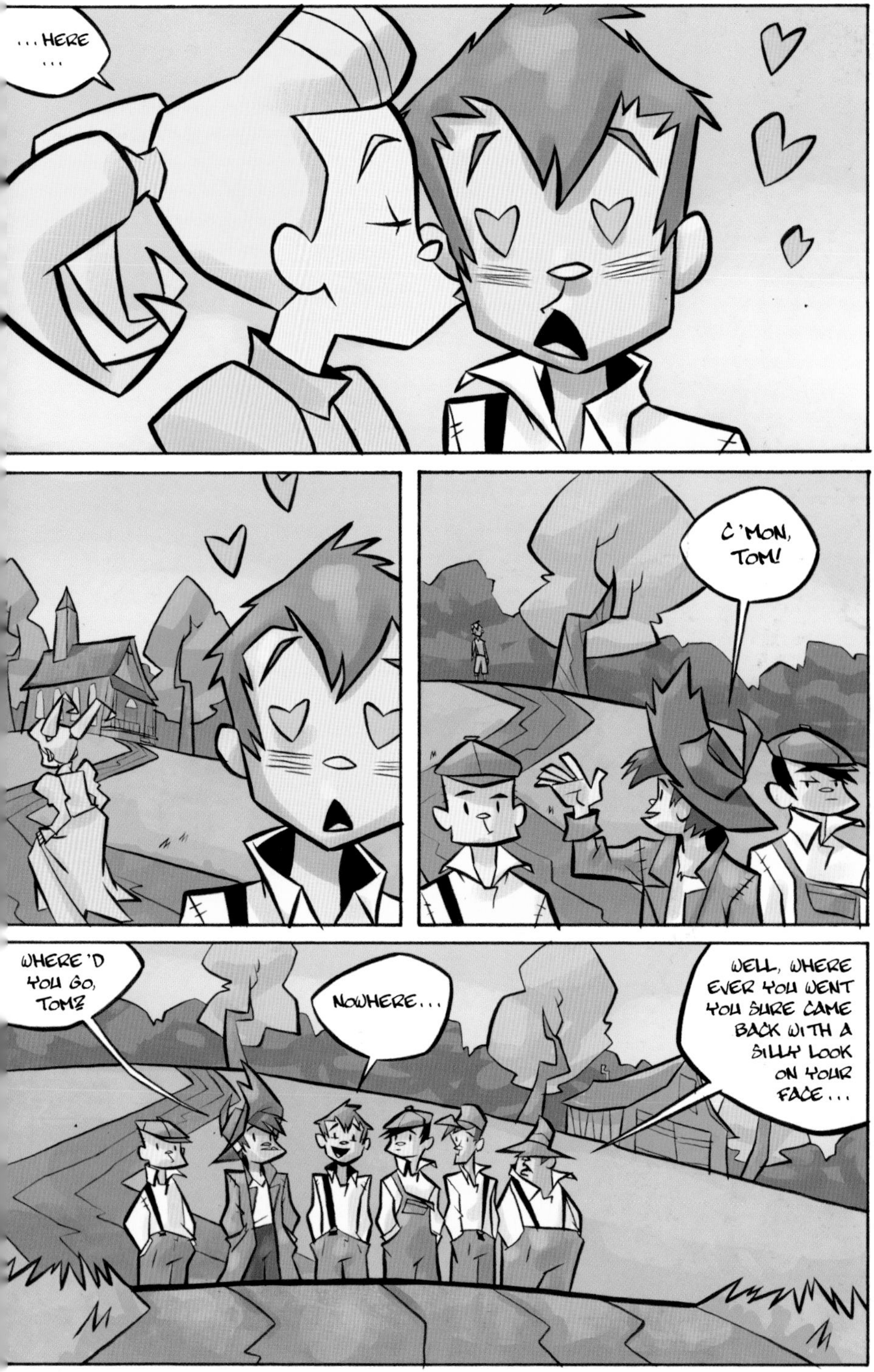
...HERE
...
C'MON, TOM!
WHERE'D YOU GO, TOM?
NOWHERE...
WELL, WHERE EVER YOU WENT YOU SURE CAME BACK WITH A SILLY LOOK ON YOUR FACE...

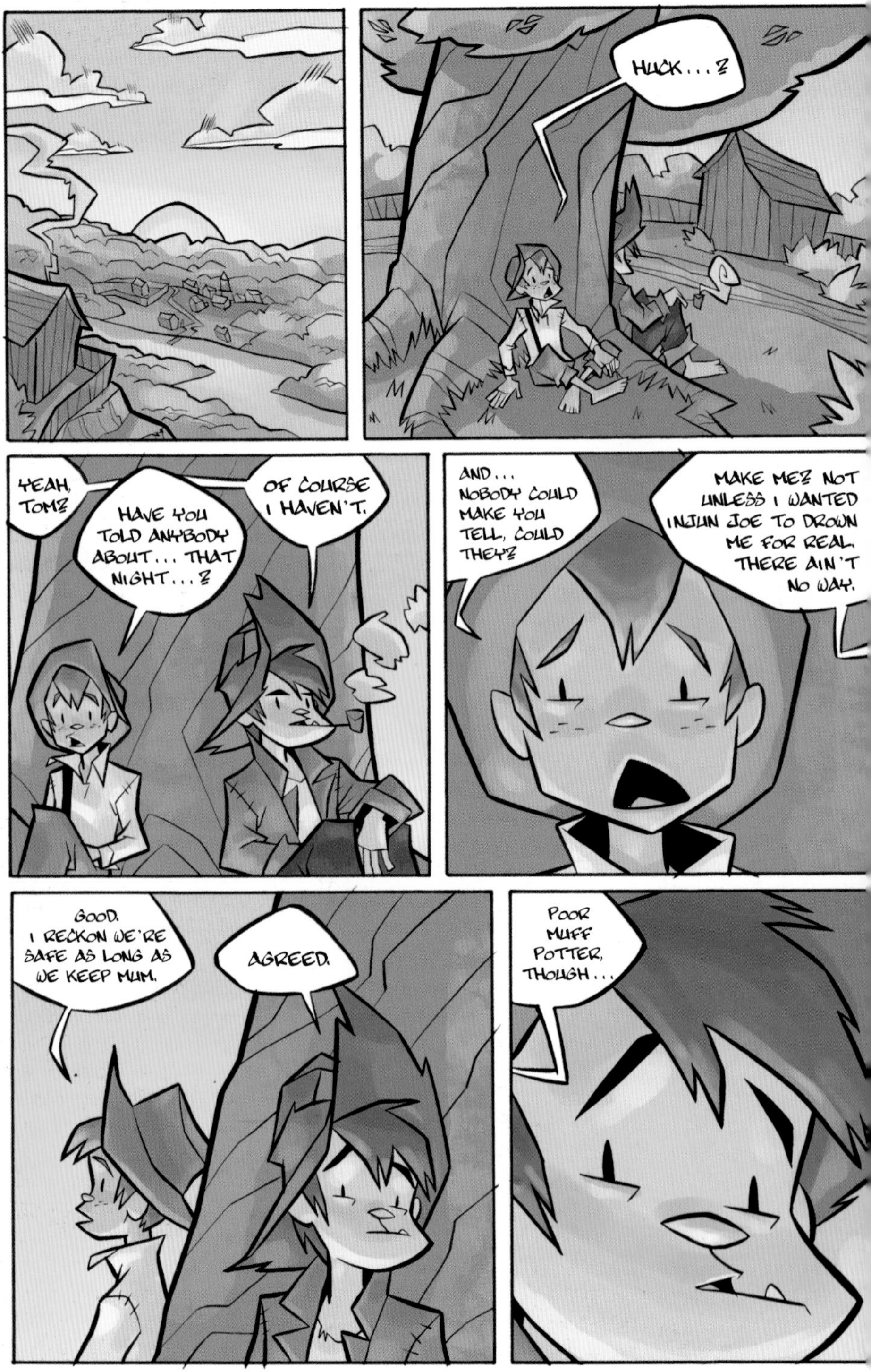
HUCK...?
YEAH, TOM?
HAVE YOU TOLD ANYBODY ABOUT... THAT NIGHT...?
OF COURSE I HAVEN'T.
AND... NOBODY COULD MAKE YOU TELL, COULD THEY?
MAKE ME? NOT UNLESS I WANTED INJUN JOE TO DROWN ME FOR REAL. THERE AIN'T NO WAY.
GOOD. I RECKON WE'RE SAFE AS LONG AS WE KEEP MUM.
AGREED.
POOR MUFF POTTER, THOUGH...

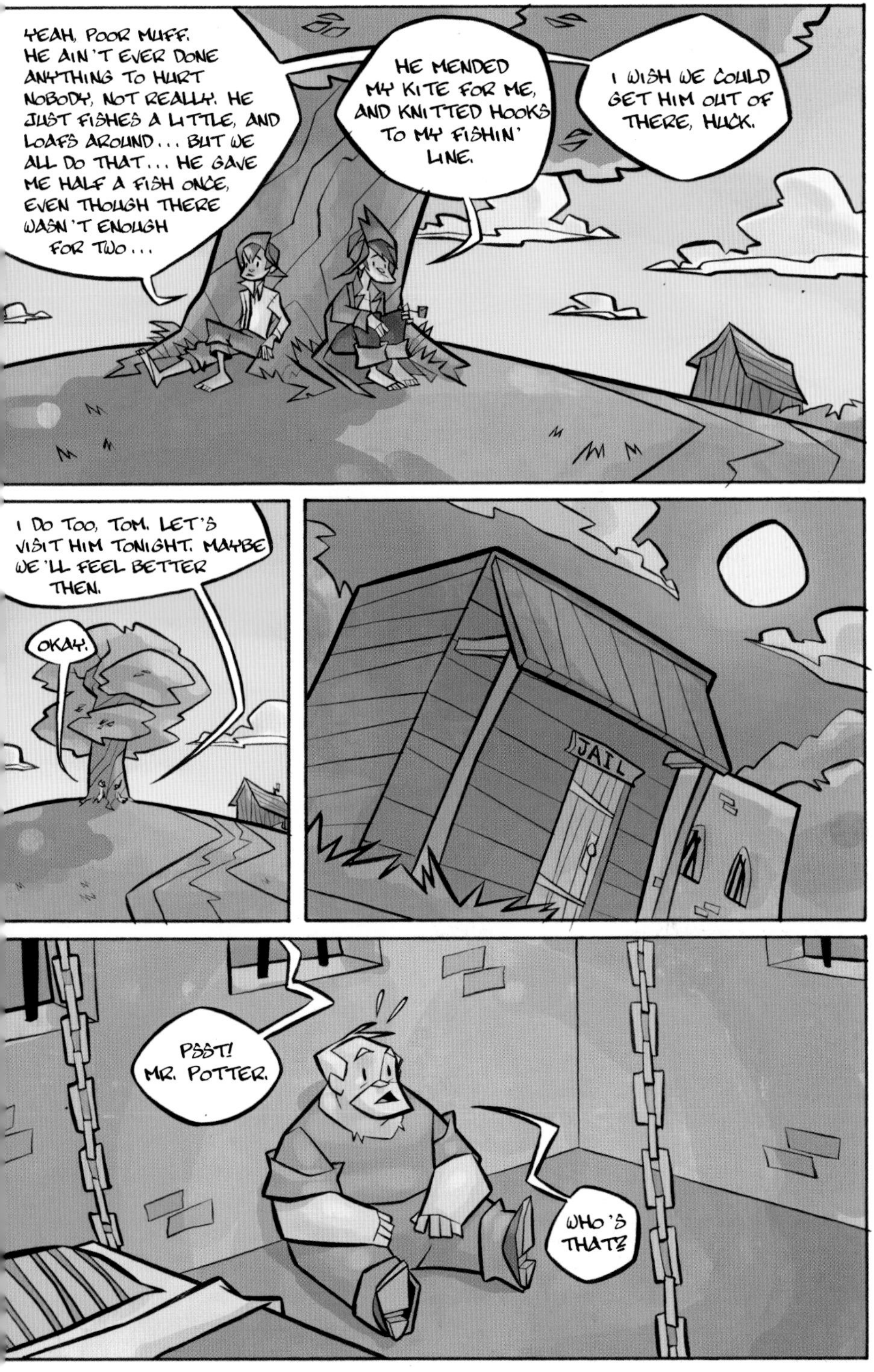
YEAH, POOR MUFF. HE AIN'T EVER DONE ANYTHING TO HURT NOBODY, NOT REALLY. HE JUST FISHES A LITTLE, AND LOAFS AROUND... BUT WE ALL DO THAT... HE GAVE ME HALF A FISH ONCE, EVEN THOUGH THERE WASN'T ENOUGH FOR TWO...
HE MENDED MY KITE FOR ME, AND KNITTED HOOKS TO MY FISHIN' LINE.
I WISH WE COULD GET HIM OUT OF THERE, HUCK.
I DO TOO, TOM. LET'S VISIT HIM TONIGHT. MAYBE WE'LL FEEL BETTER THEN.
OKAY.
JAIL
PSST! MR. POTTER.
WHO'S THAT?

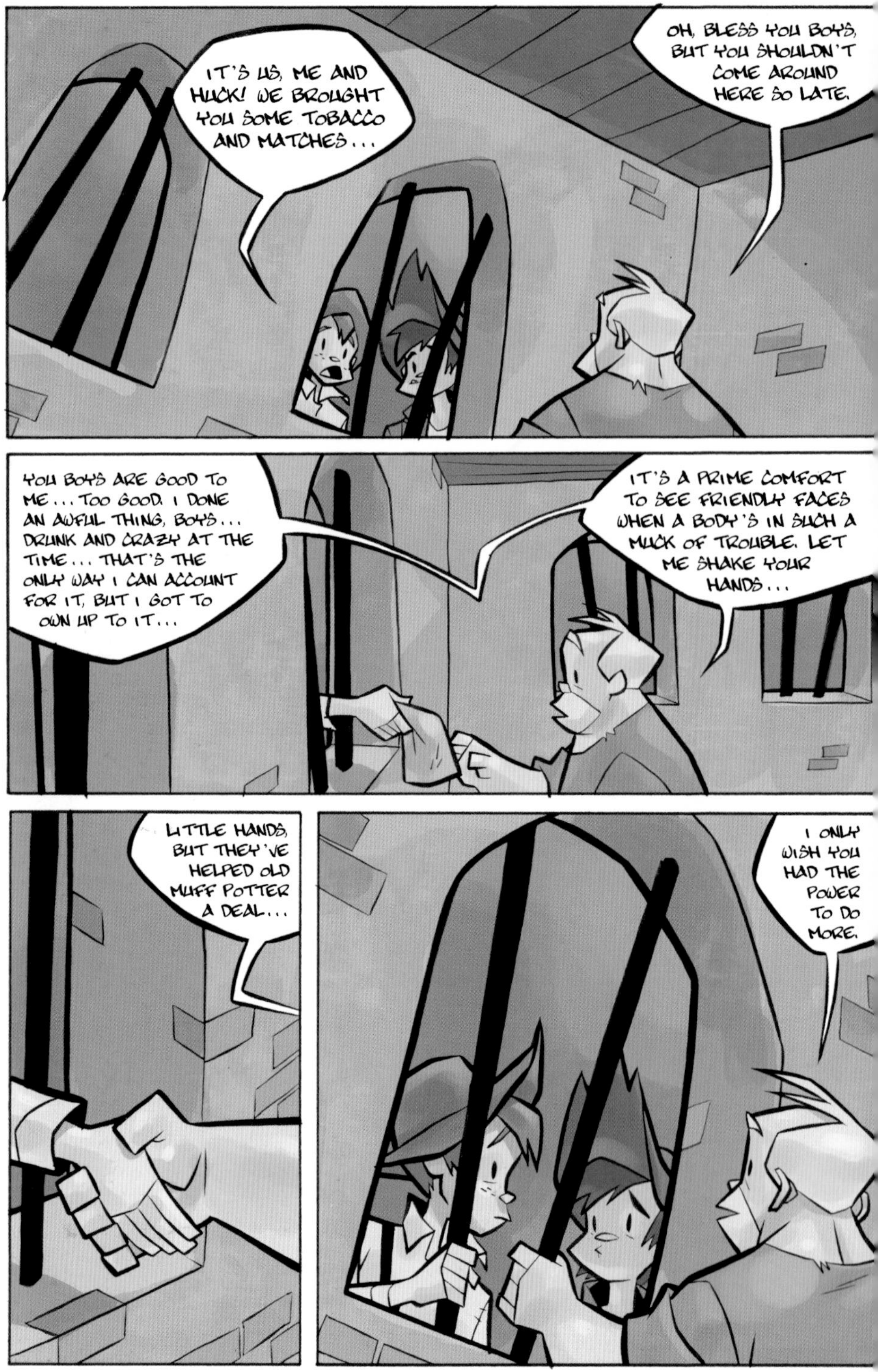
IT'S US, ME AND HUCK! WE BROUGHT YOU SOME TOBACCO AND MATCHES...
OH, BLESS YOU BOYS, BUT YOU SHOULDN'T COME AROUND HERE SO LATE.
YOU BOYS ARE GOOD TO ME... TOO GOOD. I DONE AN AWFUL THING, BOYS... DRUNK AND CRAZY AT THE TIME... THAT'S THE ONLY WAY I CAN ACCOUNT FOR IT, BUT I GOT TO OWN UP TO IT...
IT'S A PRIME COMFORT TO SEE FRIENDLY FACES WHEN A BODY'S IN SUCH A MUCK OF TROUBLE. LET ME SHAKE YOUR HANDS...
LITTLE HANDS, BUT THEY'VE HELPED OLD MUFF POTTER A DEAL...
I ONLY WISH YOU HAD THE POWER TO DO MORE.

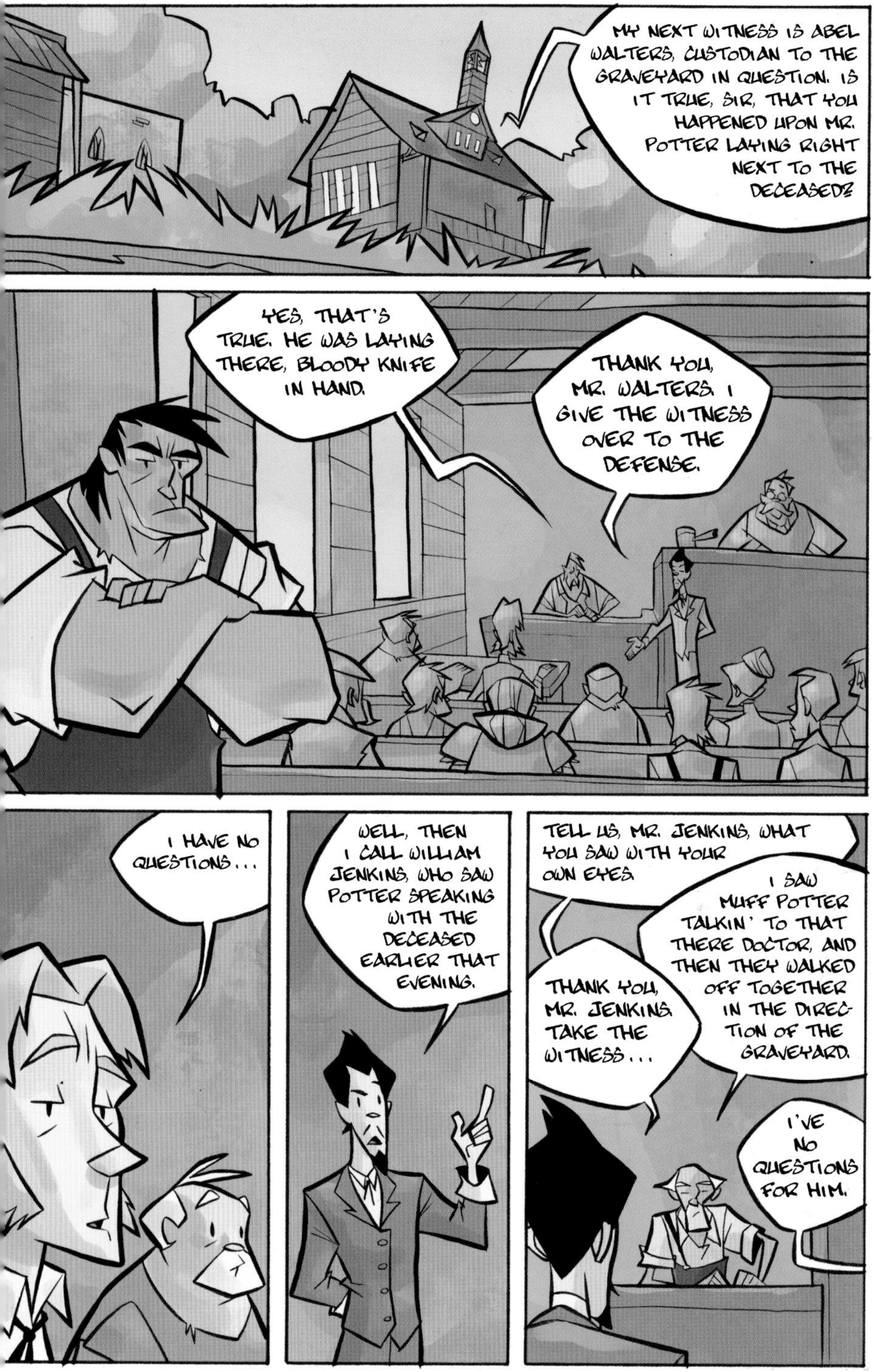
MY NEXT WITNESS IS ABEL WALTERS, CUSTODIAN TO THE GRAVEYARD IN QUESTION. IS IT TRUE, SIR, THAT YOU HAPPENED UPON MR. POTTER LAYING RIGHT NEXT TO THE DECEASED?
YES, THAT'S TRUE. HE WAS LAYING THERE, BLOODY KNIFE IN HAND.
THANK YOU, MR. WALTERS. I GIVE THE WITNESS OVER TO THE DEFENSE.
I HAVE NO QUESTIONS...
WELL, THEN I CALL WILLIAM JENKINS, WHO SAW POTTER SPEAKING WITH THE DECEASED EARLIER THAT EVENING.
TELL US, MR. JENKINS, WHAT YOU SAW WITH YOUR OWN EYES.
I SAW MUFF POTTER TALKIN' TO THAT THERE DOCTOR, AND THEN THEY WALKED OFF TOGETHER IN THE DIRECTION OF THE GRAVEYARD.
THANK YOU, MR. JENKINS. TAKE THE WITNESS...
I'VE NO QUESTIONS FOR HIM.

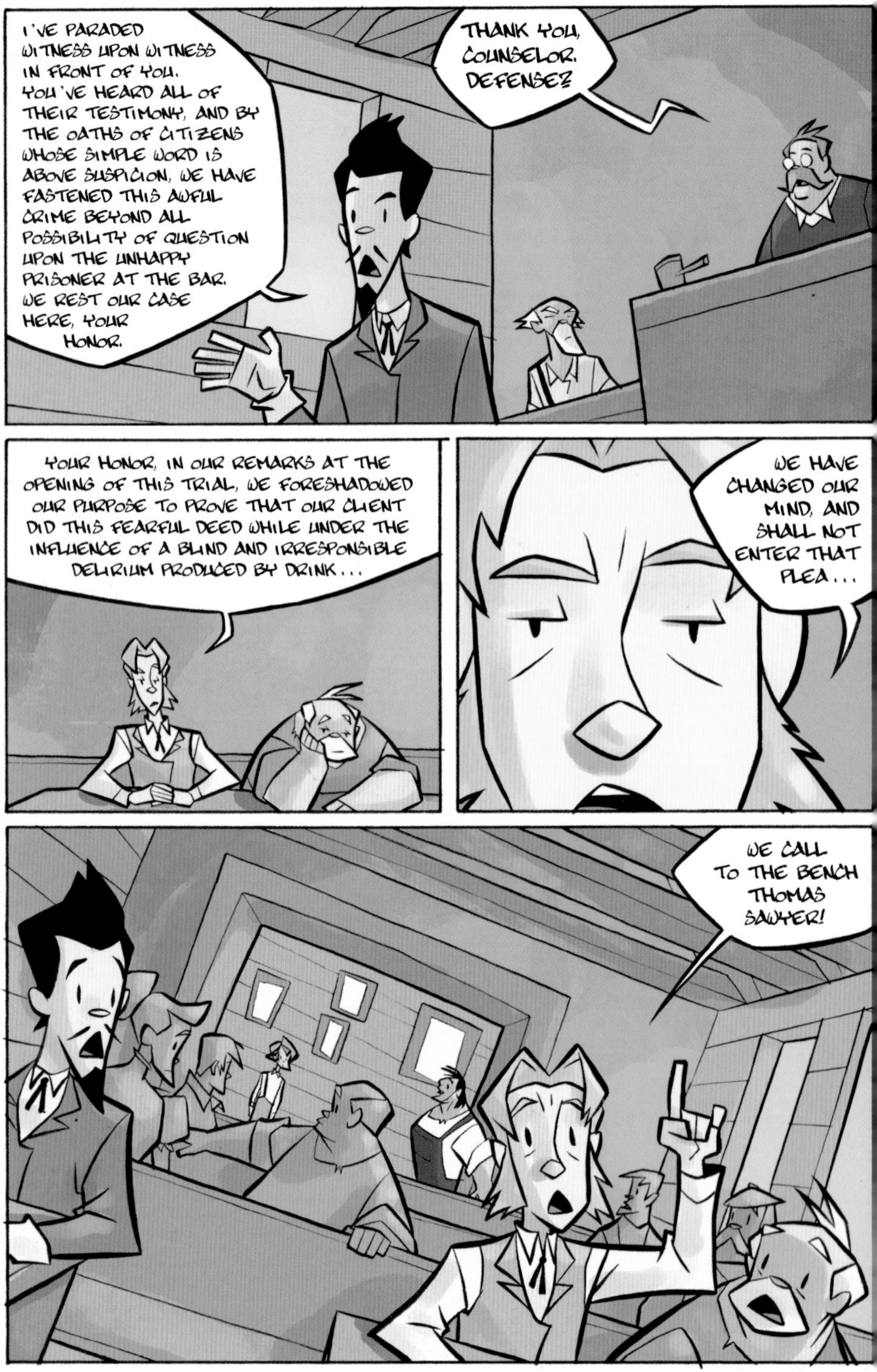
I'VE PARADED WITNESS UPON WITNESS IN FRONT OF YOU. YOU'VE HEARD ALL OF THEIR TESTIMONY, AND BY THE OATHS OF CITIZENS WHOSE SIMPLE WORD IS ABOVE SUSPICION, WE HAVE FASTENED THIS AWFUL CRIME BEYOND ALL POSSIBILITY OF QUESTION UPON THE UNHAPPY PRISONER AT THE BAR. WE REST OUR CASE HERE, YOUR HONOR.
THANK YOU, COUNSELOR. DEFENSE?
YOUR HONOR, IN OUR REMARKS AT THE OPENING OF THIS TRIAL, WE FORESHADOWED OUR PURPOSE TO PROVE THAT OUR CLIENT DID THIS FEARFUL DEED WHILE UNDER THE INFLUENCE OF A BLIND AND IRRESPONSIBLE DELIRIUM PRODUCED BY DRINK...
WE HAVE CHANGED OUR MIND, AND SHALL NOT ENTER THAT PLEA...
WE CALL TO THE BENCH THOMAS SAWYER!

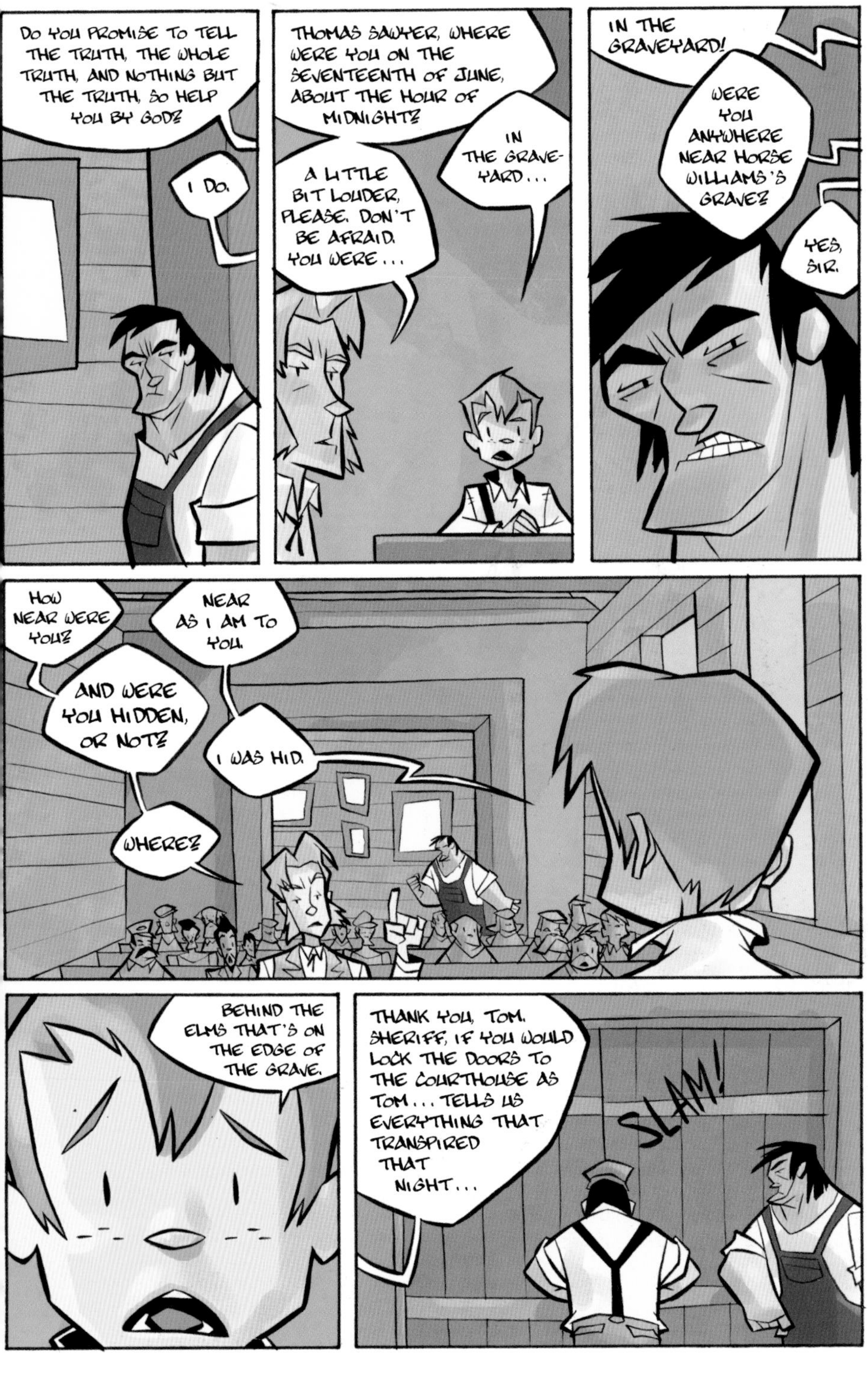
Do you promise to tell the truth, the whole truth, and nothing but the truth, so help you by God?
I do.
Thomas Sawyer, where were you on the seventeenth of June, about the hour of midnight?
In the grave-yard...
A little bit louder, please. Don't be afraid. You were...
In the graveyard!
Were you anywhere near Horse Williams's grave?
Yes, sir.
How near were you?
Near as I am to you.
And were you hidden, or not?
I was hid.
Where?
Behind the elms that's on the edge of the grave.
Thank you, Tom. Sheriff, if you would lock the doors to the courthouse as Tom... tells us everything that transpired that night...
SLAM!

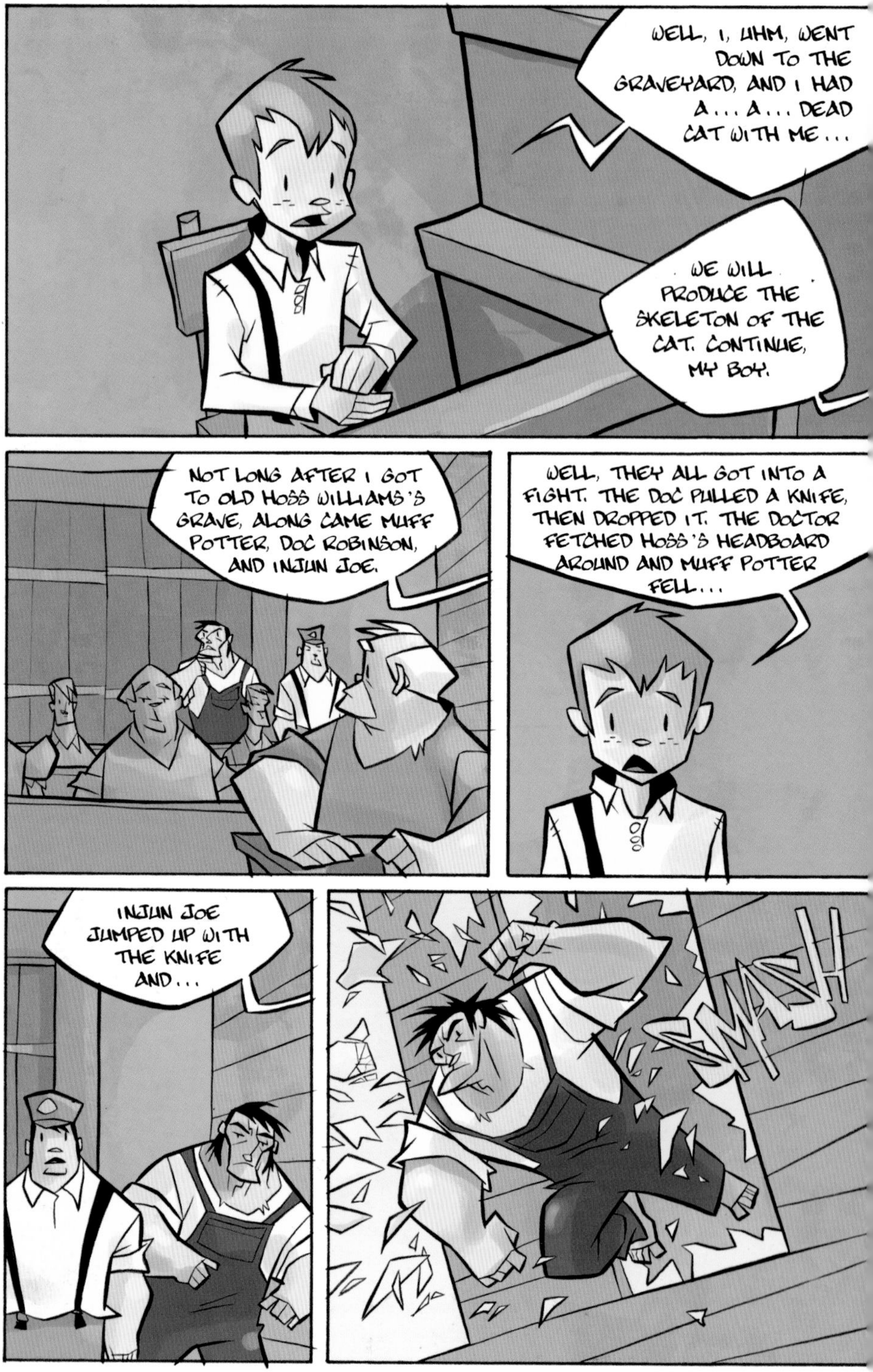
WELL, I, UHM, WENT DOWN TO THE GRAVEYARD, AND I HAD A . . . A . . . DEAD CAT WITH ME . . .
WE WILL PRODUCE THE SKELETON OF THE CAT. CONTINUE, MY BOY.
NOT LONG AFTER I GOT TO OLD HOSS WILLIAMS'S GRAVE, ALONG CAME MUFF POTTER, DOC ROBINSON, AND INJUN JOE.
WELL, THEY ALL GOT INTO A FIGHT. THE DOC PULLED A KNIFE, THEN DROPPED IT. THE DOCTOR FETCHED HOSS'S HEADBOARD AROUND AND MUFF POTTER FELL . . .
INJUN JOE JUMPED UP WITH THE KNIFE AND . . .
SMASH

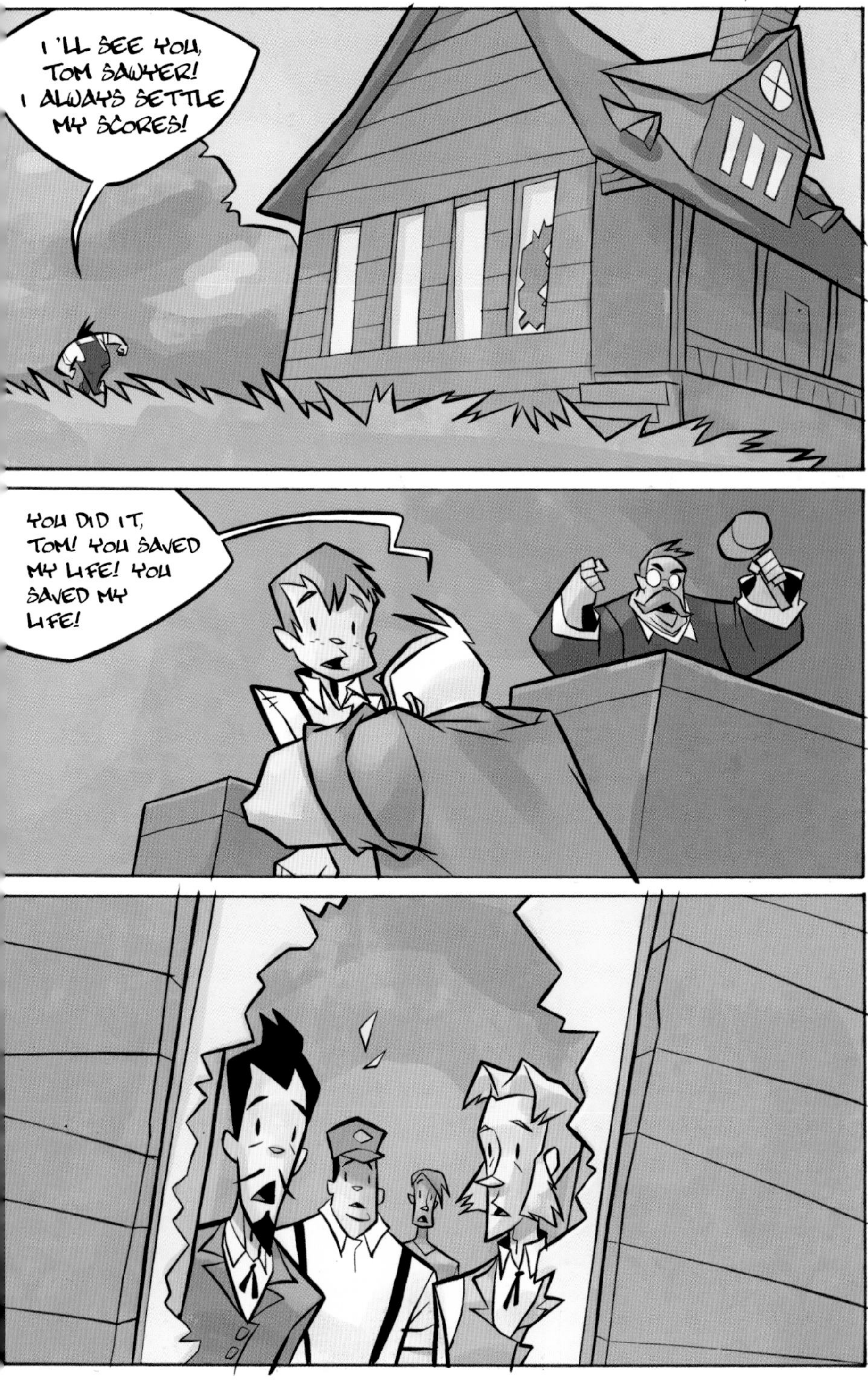
I'LL SEE YOU, TOM SAWYER! I ALWAYS SETTLE MY SCORES!
YOU DID IT, TOM! YOU SAVED MY LIFE! YOU SAVED MY LIFE!

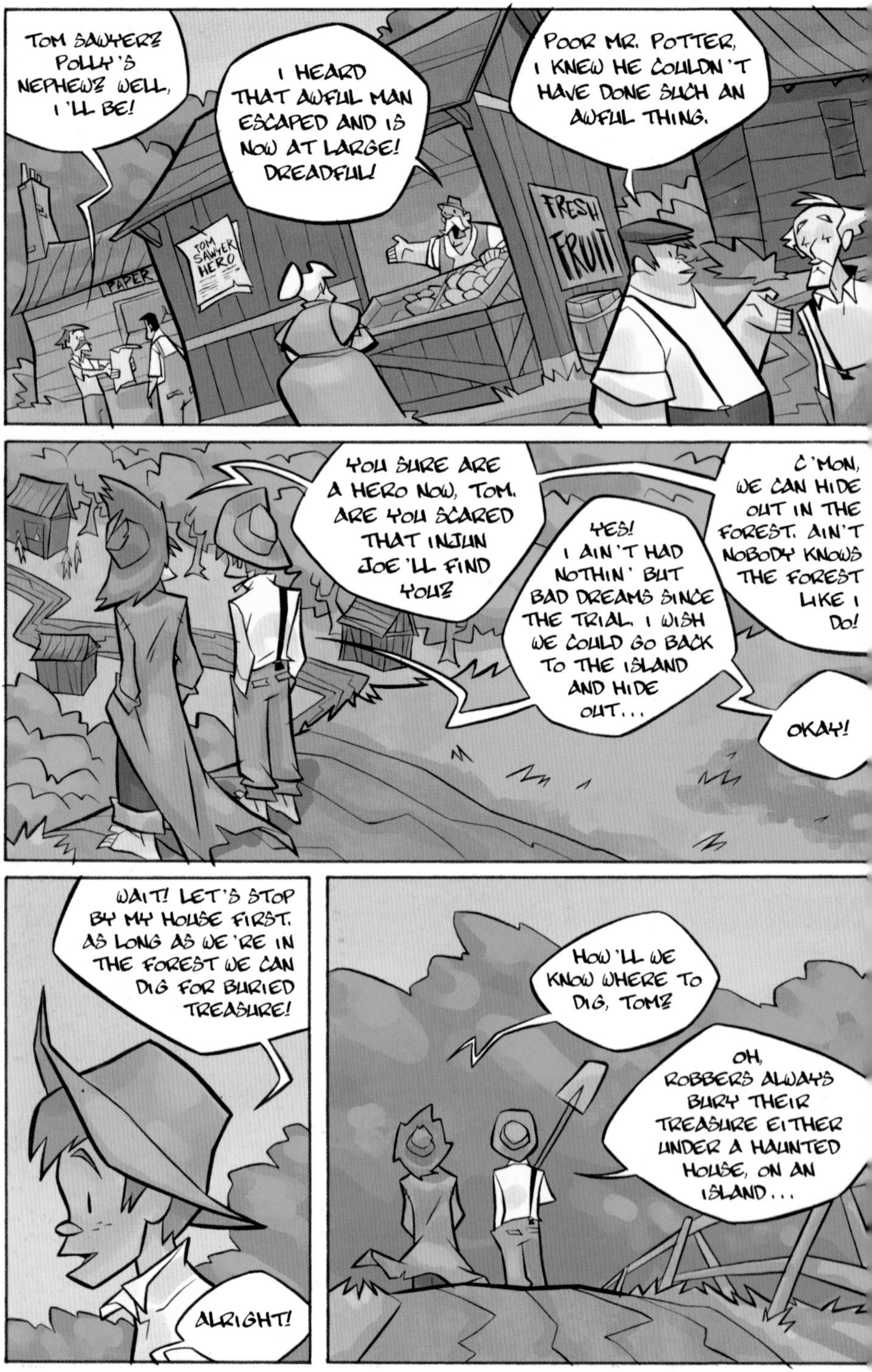
TOM SAWYER? POLLY'S NEPHEW? WELL, I'LL BE!
I HEARD THAT AWFUL MAN ESCAPED AND IS NOW AT LARGE! DREADFUL!
POOR MR. POTTER, I KNEW HE COULDN'T HAVE DONE SUCH AN AWFUL THING.
PAPER
TOM SAWYER HERO
FRESH FRUIT
YOU SURE ARE A HERO NOW, TOM. ARE YOU SCARED THAT INJUN JOE'LL FIND YOU?
YES! I AIN'T HAD NOTHIN' BUT BAD DREAMS SINCE THE TRIAL. I WISH WE COULD GO BACK TO THE ISLAND AND HIDE OUT...
C'MON, WE CAN HIDE OUT IN THE FOREST. AIN'T NOBODY KNOWS THE FOREST LIKE I DO!
OKAY!
WAIT! LET'S STOP BY MY HOUSE FIRST. AS LONG AS WE'RE IN THE FOREST WE CAN DIG FOR BURIED TREASURE!
ALRIGHT!
HOW'LL WE KNOW WHERE TO DIG, TOM?
OH, ROBBERS ALWAYS BURY THEIR TREASURE EITHER UNDER A HAUNTED HOUSE, ON AN ISLAND...

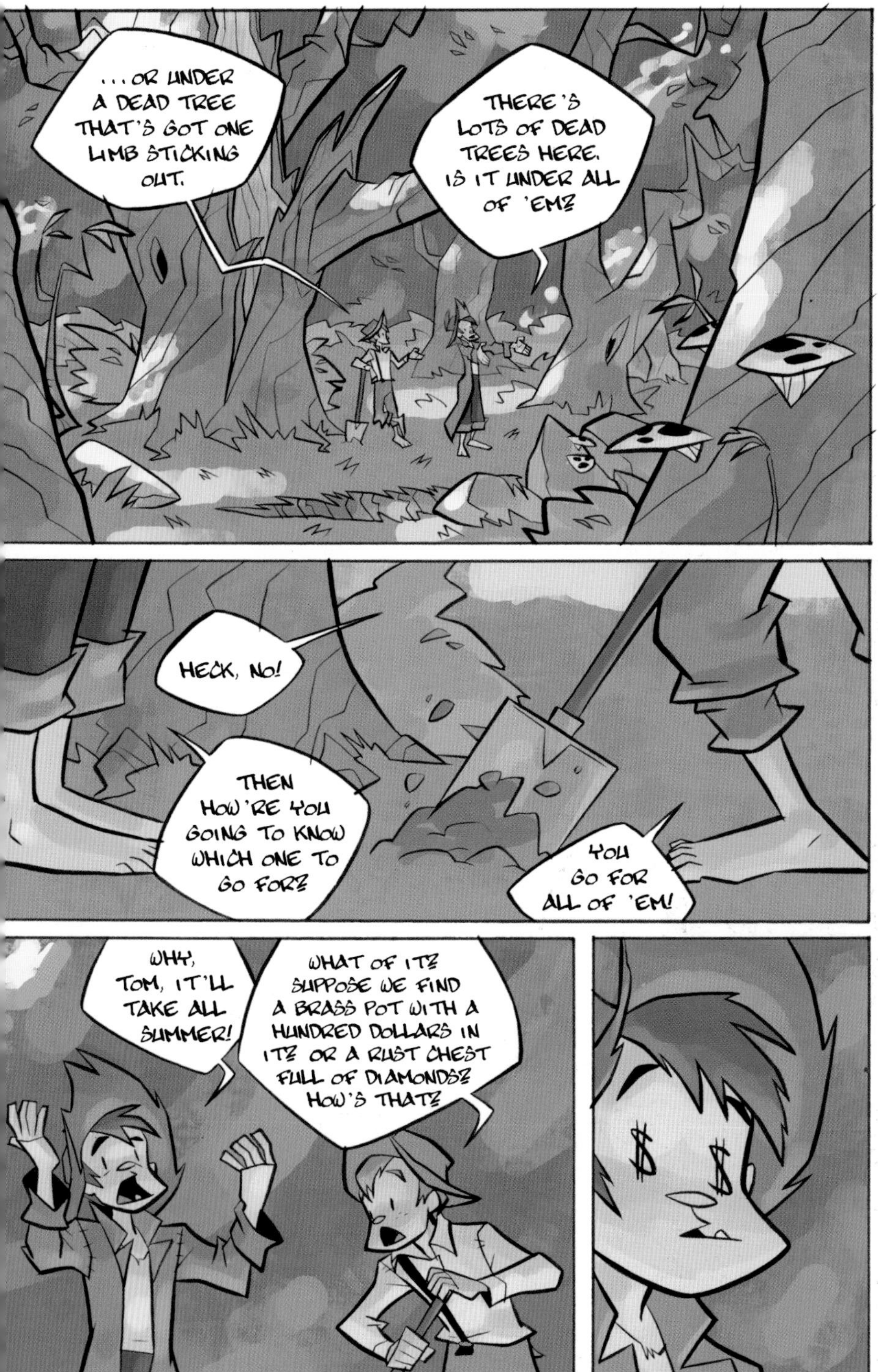
...OR UNDER A DEAD TREE THAT'S GOT ONE LIMB STICKING OUT.
THERE'S LOTS OF DEAD TREES HERE. IS IT UNDER ALL OF 'EM?
HECK, NO!
THEN HOW'RE YOU GOING TO KNOW WHICH ONE TO GO FOR?
YOU GO FOR ALL OF 'EM!
WHY, TOM, IT'LL TAKE ALL SUMMER!
WHAT OF IT? SUPPOSE WE FIND A BRASS POT WITH A HUNDRED DOLLARS IN IT? OR A RUST CHEST FULL OF DIAMONDS? HOW'S THAT?

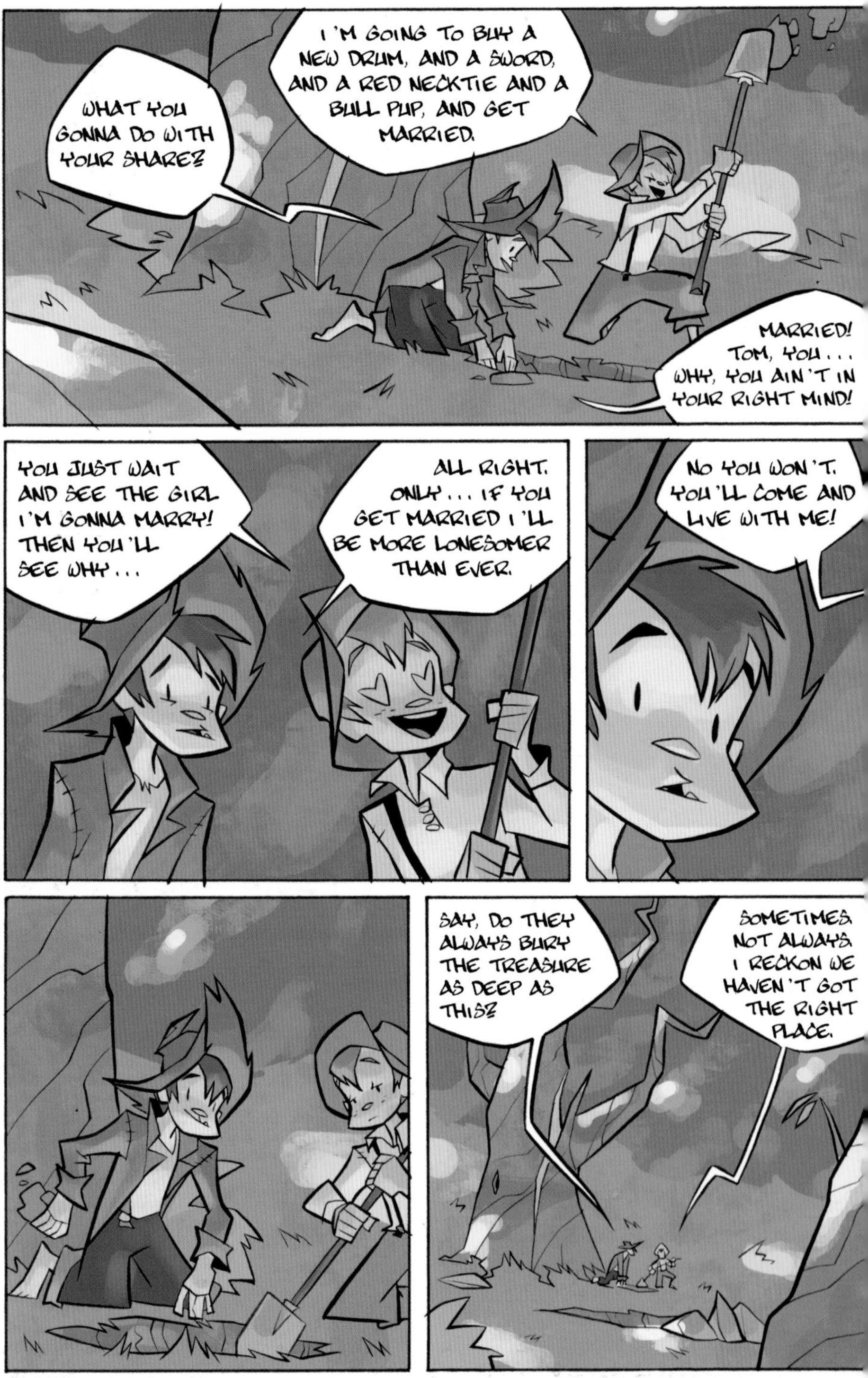
WHAT YOU GONNA DO WITH YOUR SHARE?
I'M GOING TO BUY A NEW DRUM, AND A SWORD, AND A RED NECKTIE AND A BULL PUP, AND GET MARRIED.
MARRIED! TOM, YOU . . . WHY, YOU AIN'T IN YOUR RIGHT MIND!
YOU JUST WAIT AND SEE THE GIRL I'M GONNA MARRY! THEN YOU'LL SEE WHY . . .
ALL RIGHT. ONLY . . . IF YOU GET MARRIED I'LL BE MORE LONESOMER THAN EVER.
NO YOU WON'T. YOU'LL COME AND LIVE WITH ME!
SAY, DO THEY ALWAYS BURY THE TREASURE AS DEEP AS THIS?
SOMETIMES. NOT ALWAYS. I RECKON WE HAVEN'T GOT THE RIGHT PLACE.

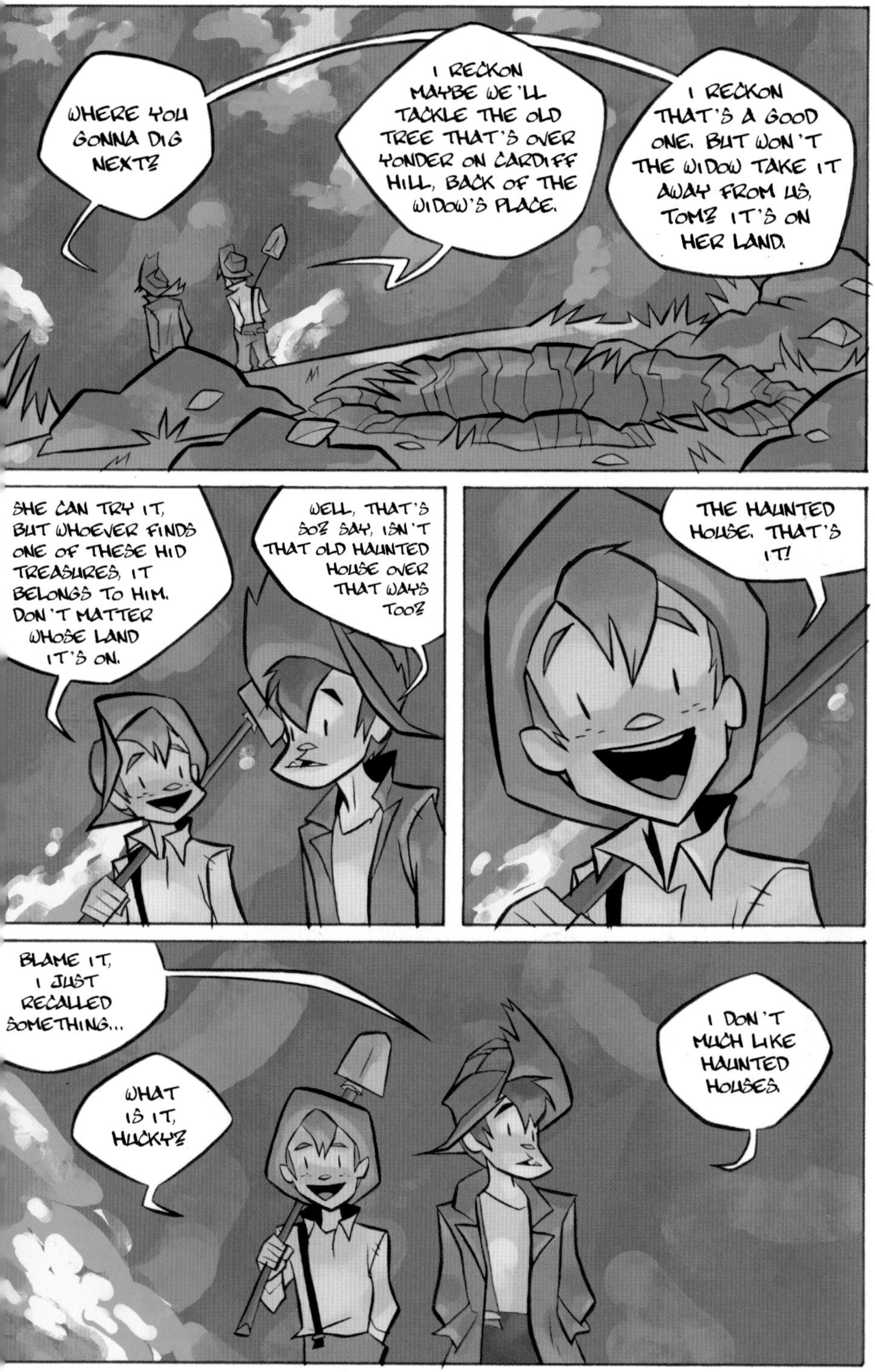
WHERE YOU GONNA DIG NEXT?
I RECKON MAYBE WE'LL TACKLE THE OLD TREE THAT'S OVER YONDER ON CARDIFF HILL, BACK OF THE WIDOW'S PLACE.
I RECKON THAT'S A GOOD ONE. BUT WON'T THE WIDOW TAKE IT AWAY FROM US, TOM? IT'S ON HER LAND.
SHE CAN TRY IT, BUT WHOEVER FINDS ONE OF THESE HID TREASURES, IT BELONGS TO HIM. DON'T MATTER WHOSE LAND IT'S ON.
WELL, THAT'S SO? SAY, ISN'T THAT OLD HAUNTED HOUSE OVER THAT WAYS TOO?
THE HAUNTED HOUSE. THAT'S IT!
BLAME IT, I JUST RECALLED SOMETHING...
WHAT IS IT, HUCKY?
I DON'T MUCH LIKE HAUNTED HOUSES.

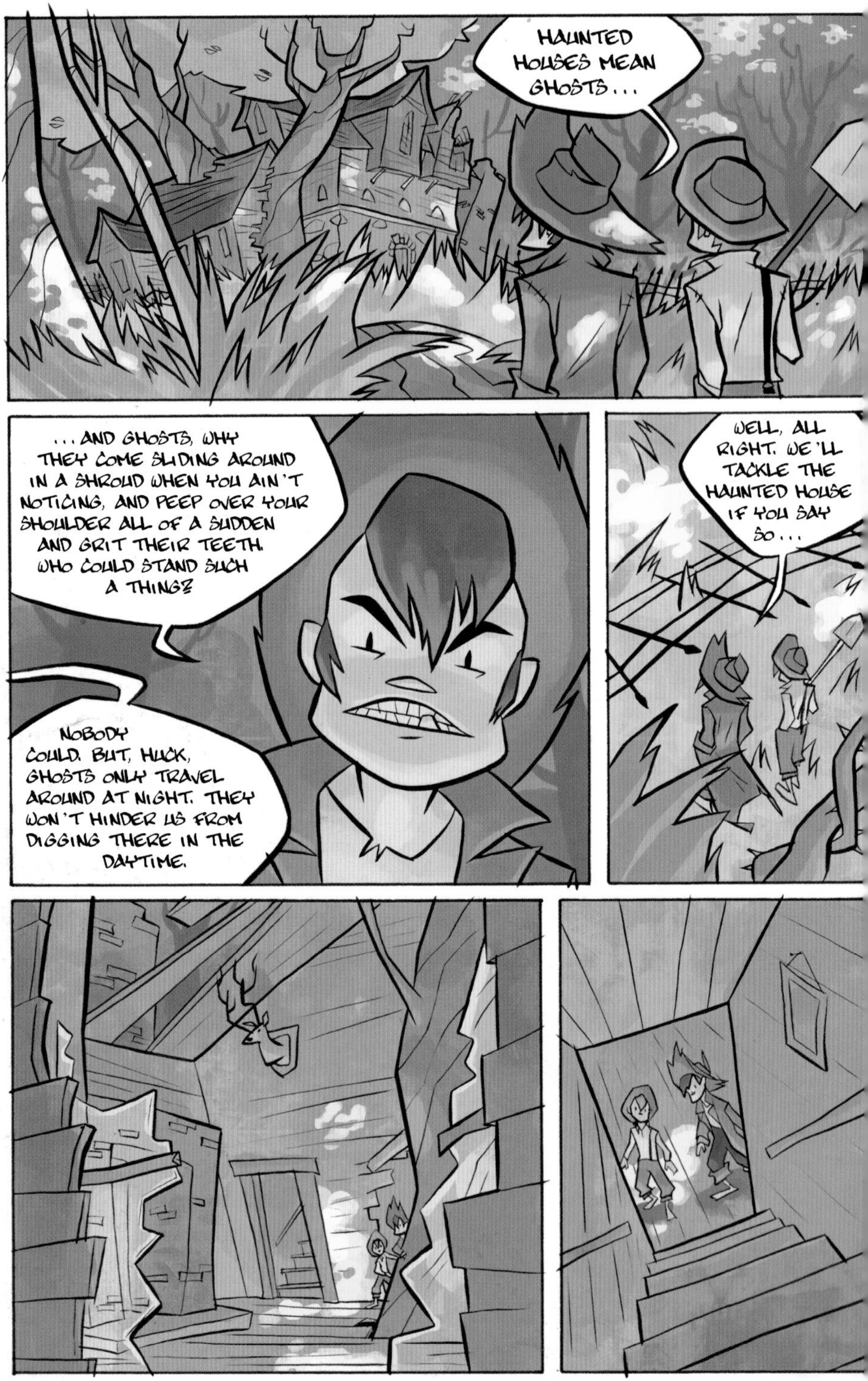
HAUNTED HOUSES MEAN GHOSTS . . .
. . . AND GHOSTS, WHY THEY COME SLIDING AROUND IN A SHROUD WHEN YOU AIN'T NOTICING, AND PEEP OVER YOUR SHOULDER ALL OF A SUDDEN AND GRIT THEIR TEETH. WHO COULD STAND SUCH A THING?
NOBODY COULD. BUT, HUCK, GHOSTS ONLY TRAVEL AROUND AT NIGHT. THEY WON'T HINDER US FROM DIGGING THERE IN THE DAYTIME.
WELL, ALL RIGHT. WE'LL TACKLE THE HAUNTED HOUSE IF YOU SAY SO . . .

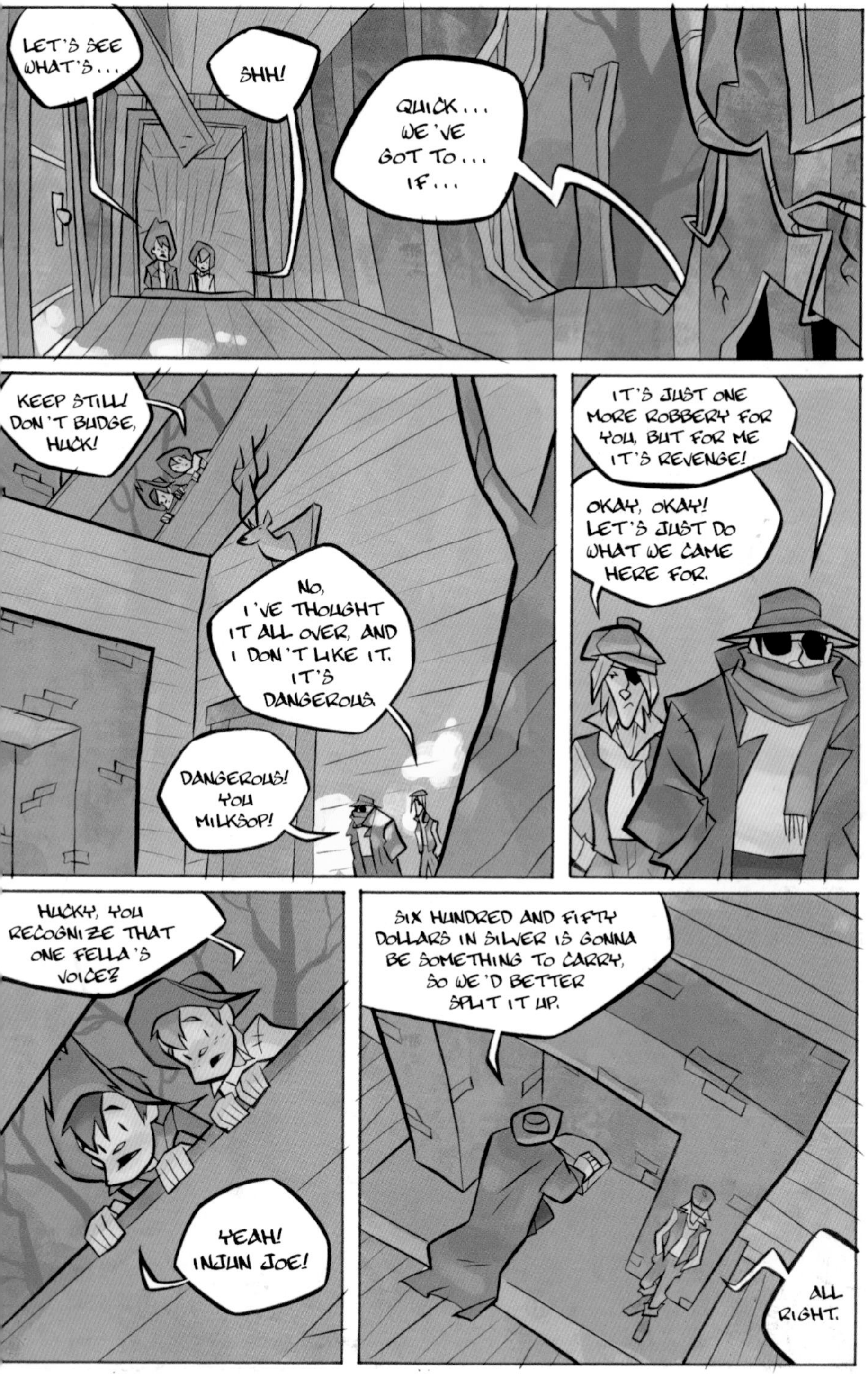
LET'S SEE WHAT'S...
SHH!
QUICK... WE'VE GOT TO... IF...
KEEP STILL! DON'T BUDGE, HUCK!
NO, I'VE THOUGHT IT ALL OVER, AND I DON'T LIKE IT. IT'S DANGEROUS.
DANGEROUS! YOU MILKSOP!
IT'S JUST ONE MORE ROBBERY FOR YOU, BUT FOR ME IT'S REVENGE!
OKAY, OKAY! LET'S JUST DO WHAT WE CAME HERE FOR.
HUCKY, YOU RECOGNIZE THAT ONE FELLA'S VOICE?
YEAH! INJUN JOE!
SIX HUNDRED AND FIFTY DOLLARS IN SILVER IS GONNA BE SOMETHING TO CARRY, SO WE'D BETTER SPLIT IT UP.
ALL RIGHT.

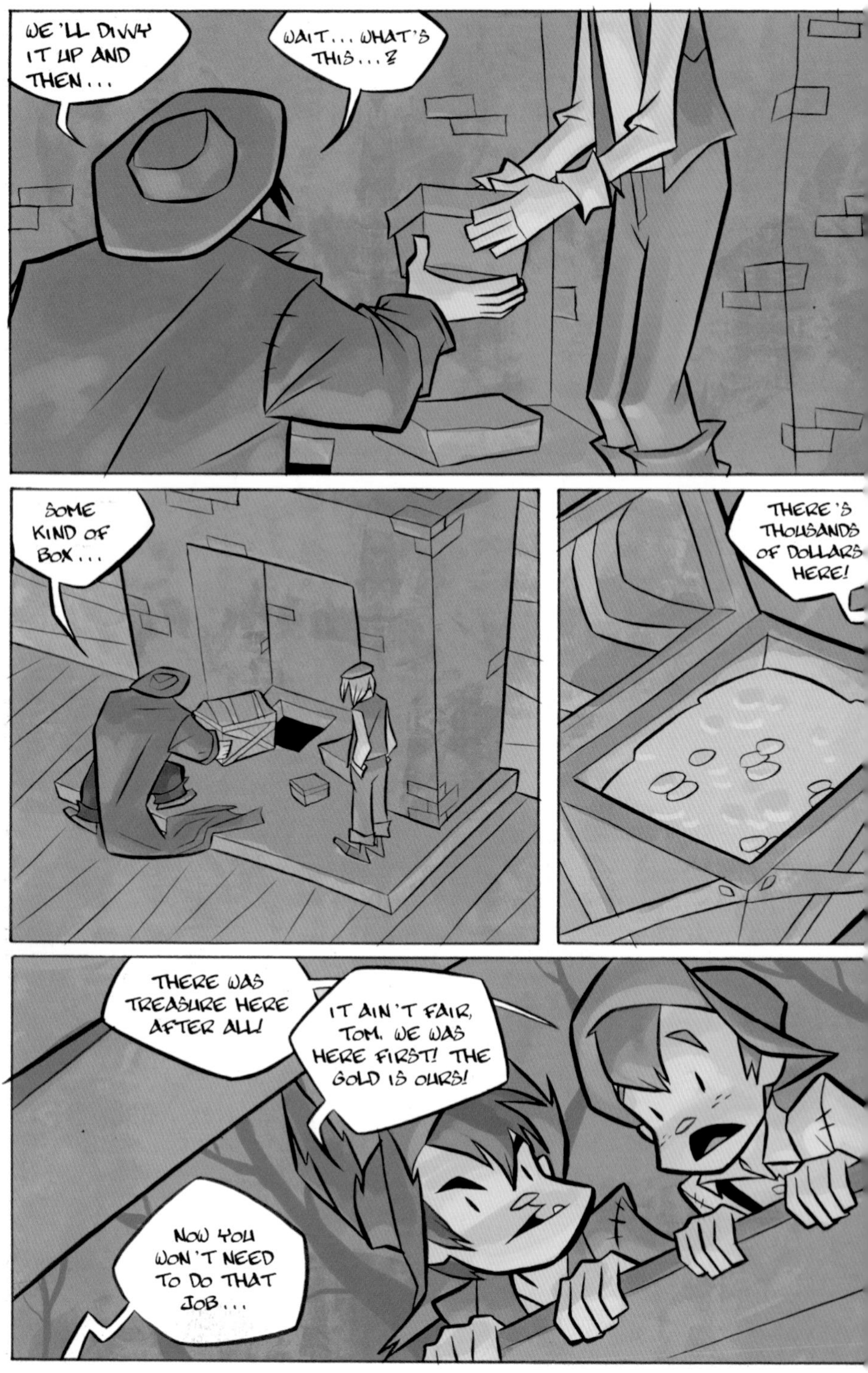
WE'LL DIVVY IT UP AND THEN...
WAIT... WHAT'S THIS...?
SOME KIND OF BOX...
THERE'S THOUSANDS OF DOLLARS HERE!
THERE WAS TREASURE HERE AFTER ALL!
IT AIN'T FAIR, TOM. WE WAS HERE FIRST! THE GOLD IS OURS!
NOW YOU WON'T NEED TO DO THAT JOB...

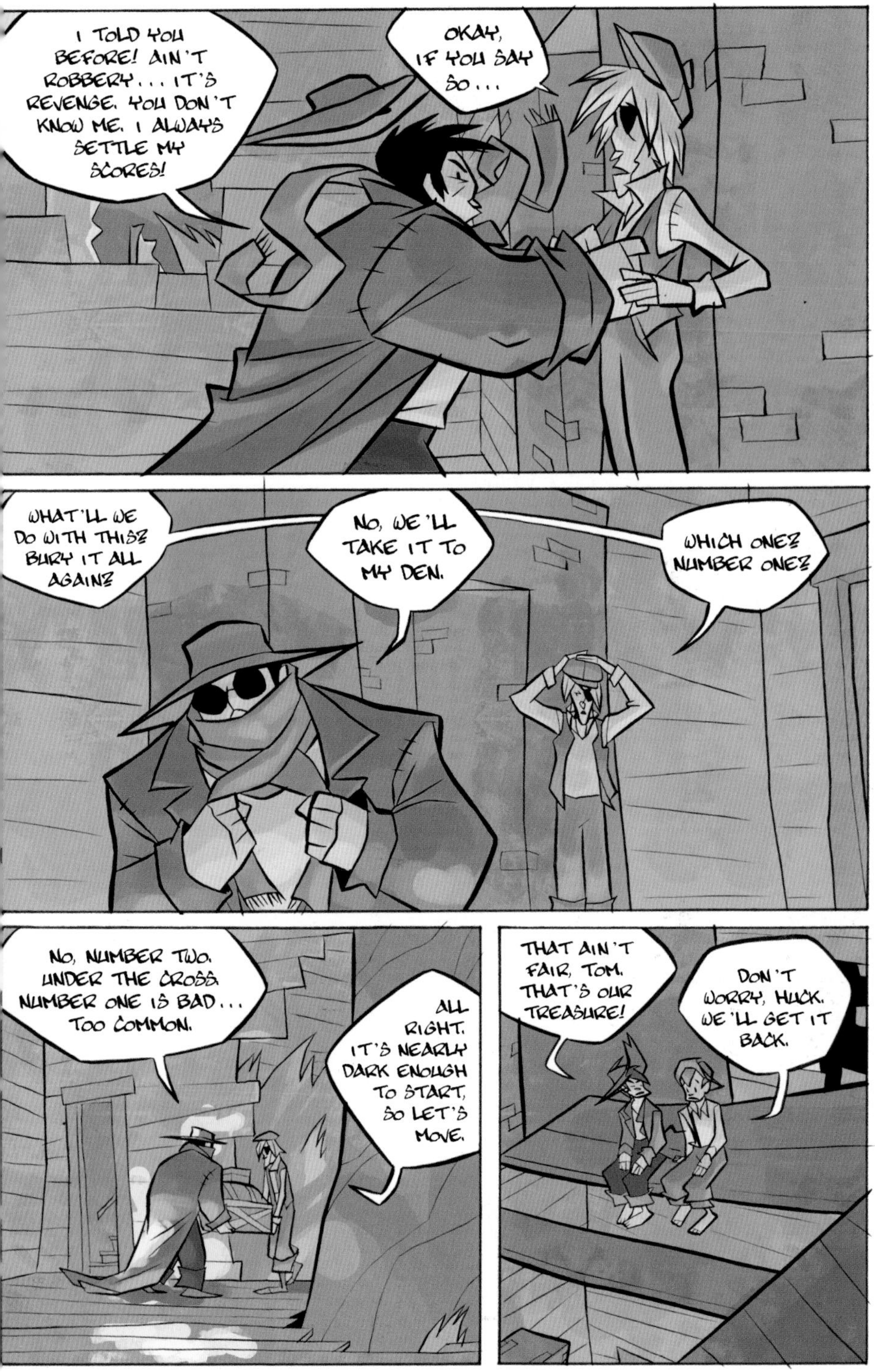
I TOLD YOU BEFORE! AIN'T ROBBERY... IT'S REVENGE. YOU DON'T KNOW ME. I ALWAYS SETTLE MY SCORES!
OKAY, IF YOU SAY SO...
WHAT'LL WE DO WITH THIS? BURY IT ALL AGAIN?
NO, WE'LL TAKE IT TO MY DEN.
WHICH ONE? NUMBER ONE?
NO, NUMBER TWO. UNDER THE CROSS. NUMBER ONE IS BAD... TOO COMMON.
ALL RIGHT. IT'S NEARLY DARK ENOUGH TO START, SO LET'S MOVE.
THAT AIN'T FAIR, TOM. THAT'S OUR TREASURE!
DON'T WORRY, HUCK. WE'LL GET IT BACK.

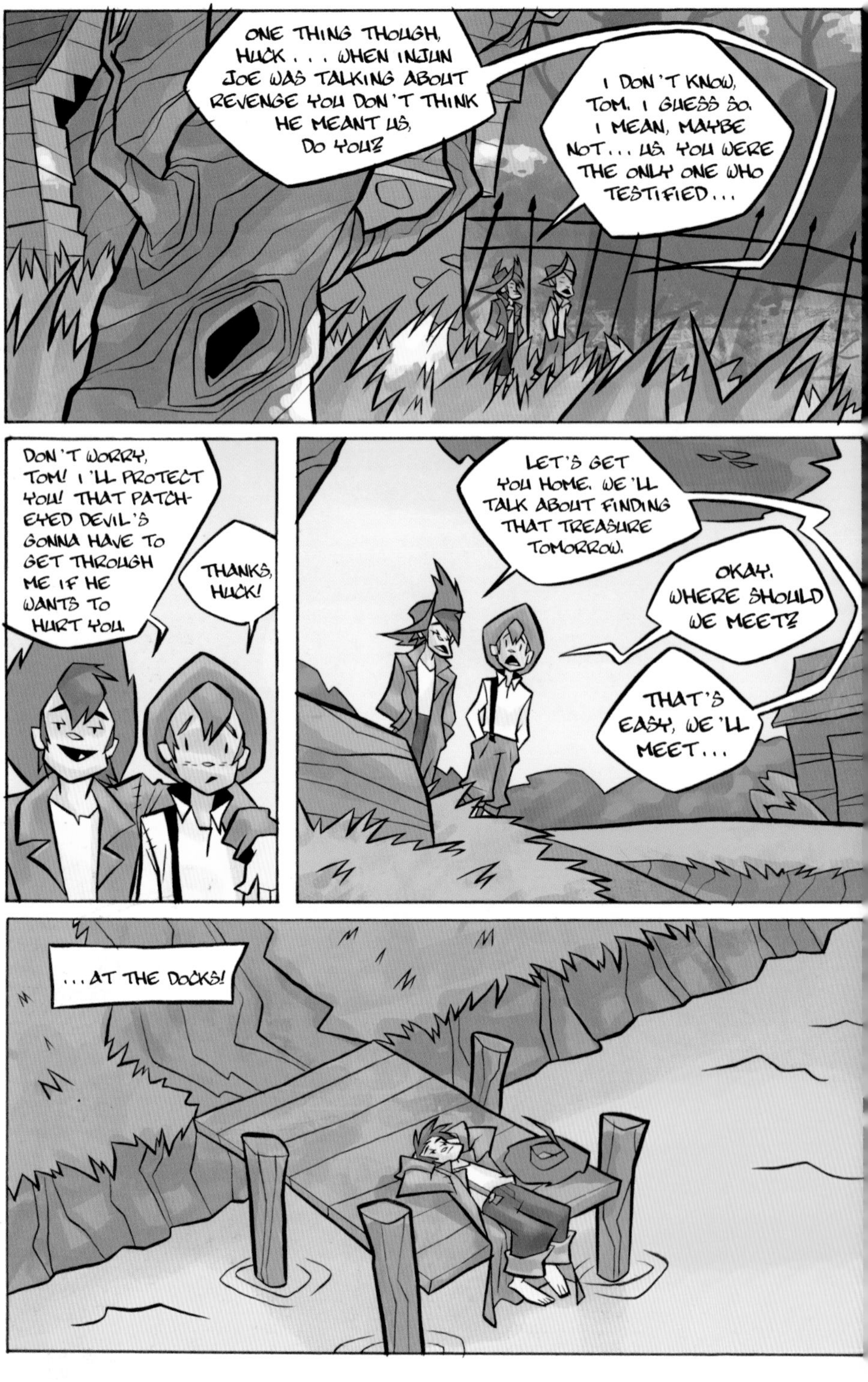
ONE THING THOUGH, HUCK . . . WHEN INJUN JOE WAS TALKING ABOUT REVENGE YOU DON'T THINK HE MEANT US, DO YOU?
I DON'T KNOW, TOM. I GUESS SO. I MEAN, MAYBE NOT... US. YOU WERE THE ONLY ONE WHO TESTIFIED...
DON'T WORRY, TOM! I'LL PROTECT YOU! THAT PATCH-EYED DEVIL'S GONNA HAVE TO GET THROUGH ME IF HE WANTS TO HURT YOU.
THANKS, HUCK!
LET'S GET YOU HOME. WE'LL TALK ABOUT FINDING THAT TREASURE TOMORROW.
OKAY. WHERE SHOULD WE MEET?
THAT'S EASY, WE'LL MEET...
...AT THE DOCKS!

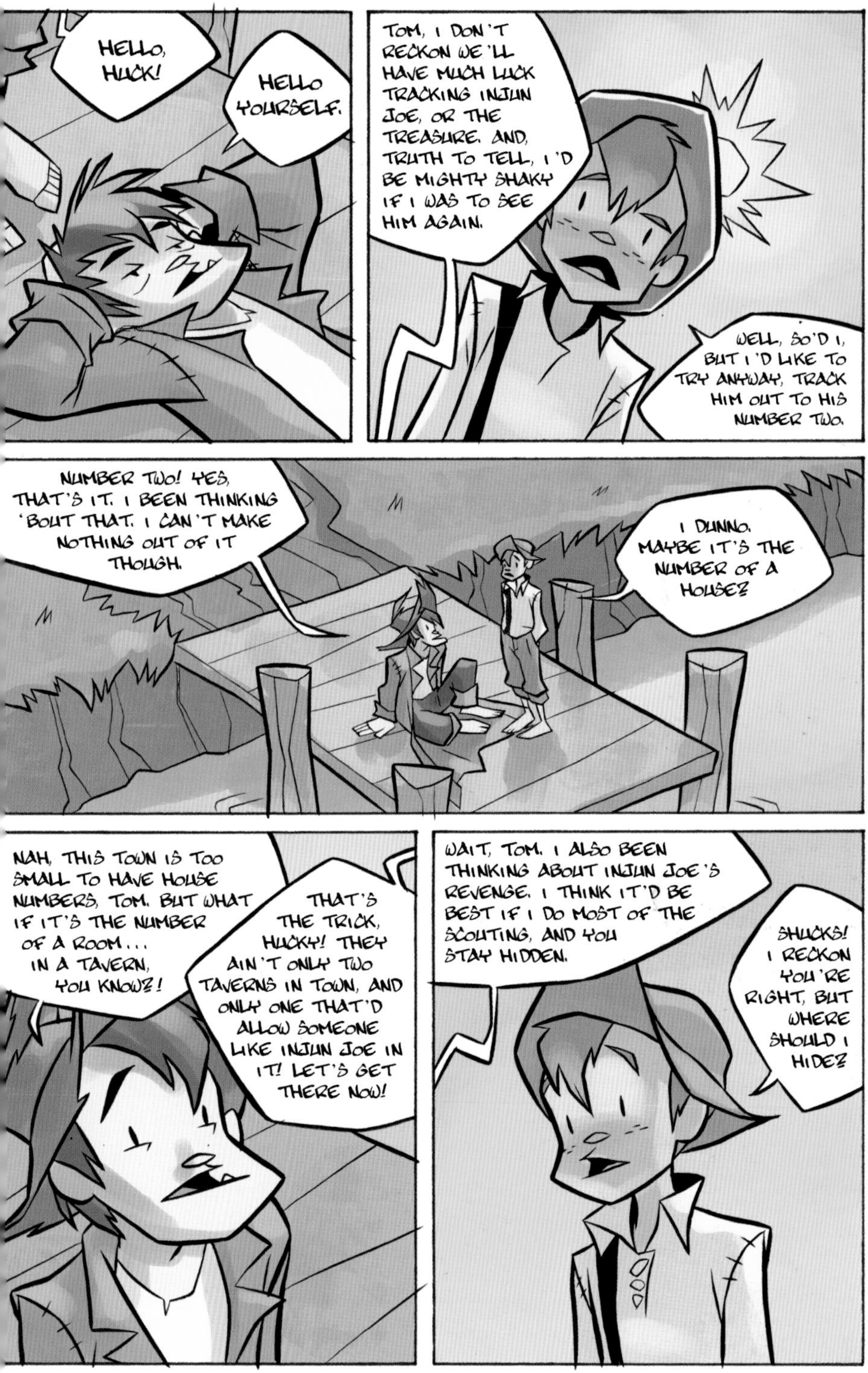
HELLO, HUCK!
HELLO YOURSELF.
TOM, I DON'T RECKON WE'LL HAVE MUCH LUCK TRACKING INJUN JOE, OR THE TREASURE. AND, TRUTH TO TELL, I'D BE MIGHTY SHAKY IF I WAS TO SEE HIM AGAIN.
WELL, SO'D I, BUT I'D LIKE TO TRY ANYWAY, TRACK HIM OUT TO HIS NUMBER TWO.
NUMBER TWO! YES, THAT'S IT. I BEEN THINKING 'BOUT THAT. I CAN'T MAKE NOTHING OUT OF IT THOUGH.
I DUNNO. MAYBE IT'S THE NUMBER OF A HOUSE?
NAH, THIS TOWN IS TOO SMALL TO HAVE HOUSE NUMBERS, TOM. BUT WHAT IF IT'S THE NUMBER OF A ROOM... IN A TAVERN, YOU KNOW?!
THAT'S THE TRICK, HUCKY! THEY AIN'T ONLY TWO TAVERNS IN TOWN, AND ONLY ONE THAT'D ALLOW SOMEONE LIKE INJUN JOE IN IT! LET'S GET THERE NOW!
WAIT, TOM. I ALSO BEEN THINKING ABOUT INJUN JOE'S REVENGE. I THINK IT'D BE BEST IF I DO MOST OF THE SCOUTING, AND YOU STAY HIDDEN.
SHUCKS! I RECKON YOU'RE RIGHT, BUT WHERE SHOULD I HIDE?

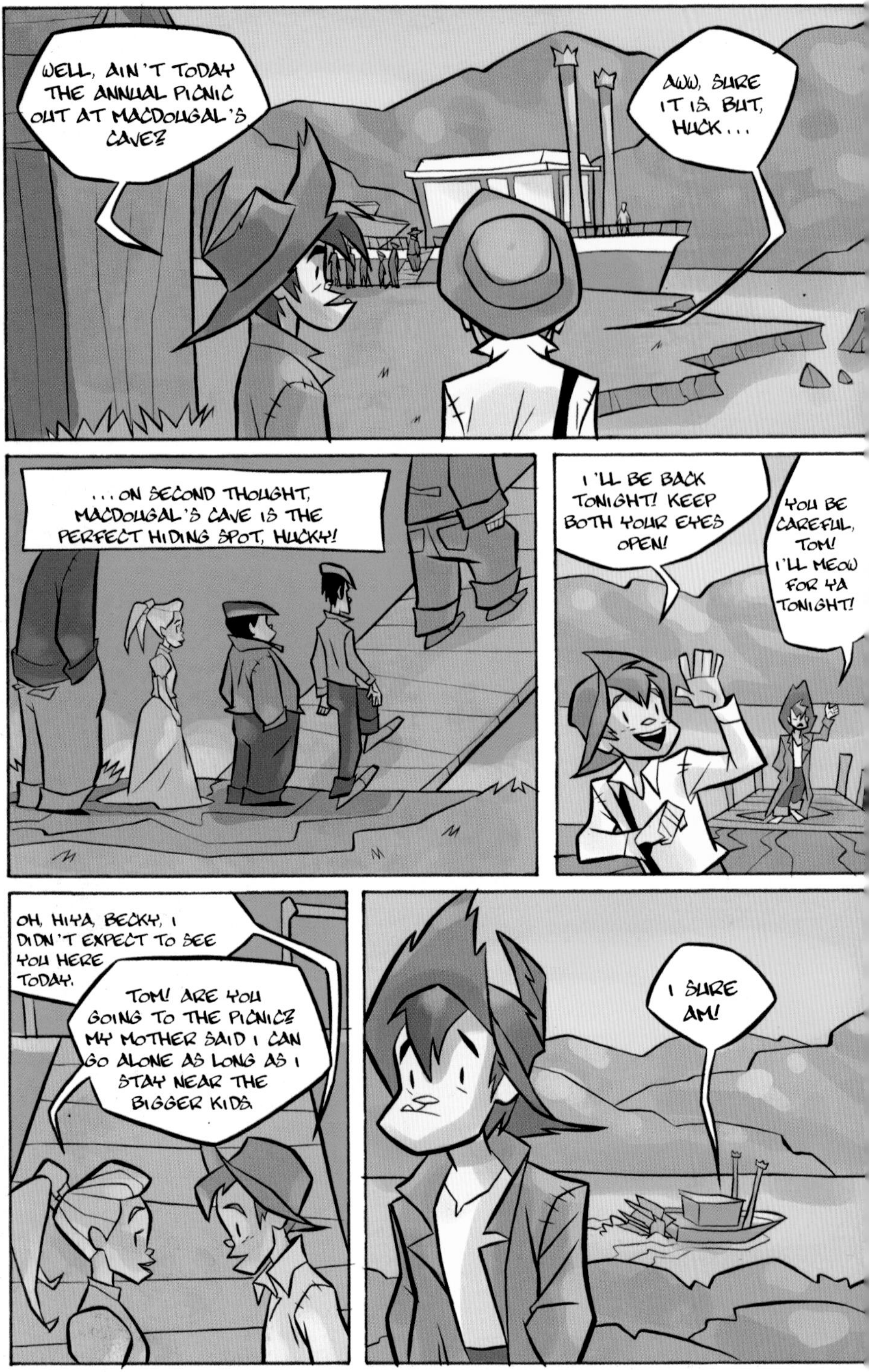
WELL, AIN'T TODAY THE ANNUAL PICNIC OUT AT MACDOUGAL'S CAVE?
AWW, SURE IT IS. BUT, HUCK...
...ON SECOND THOUGHT, MACDOUGAL'S CAVE IS THE PERFECT HIDING SPOT, HUCKY!
I'LL BE BACK TONIGHT! KEEP BOTH YOUR EYES OPEN!
YOU BE CAREFUL, TOM! I'LL MEOW FOR YA TONIGHT!
OH, HIYA, BECKY, I DIDN'T EXPECT TO SEE YOU HERE TODAY.
TOM! ARE YOU GOING TO THE PICNIC? MY MOTHER SAID I CAN GO ALONE AS LONG AS I STAY NEAR THE BIGGER KIDS.
I SURE AM!

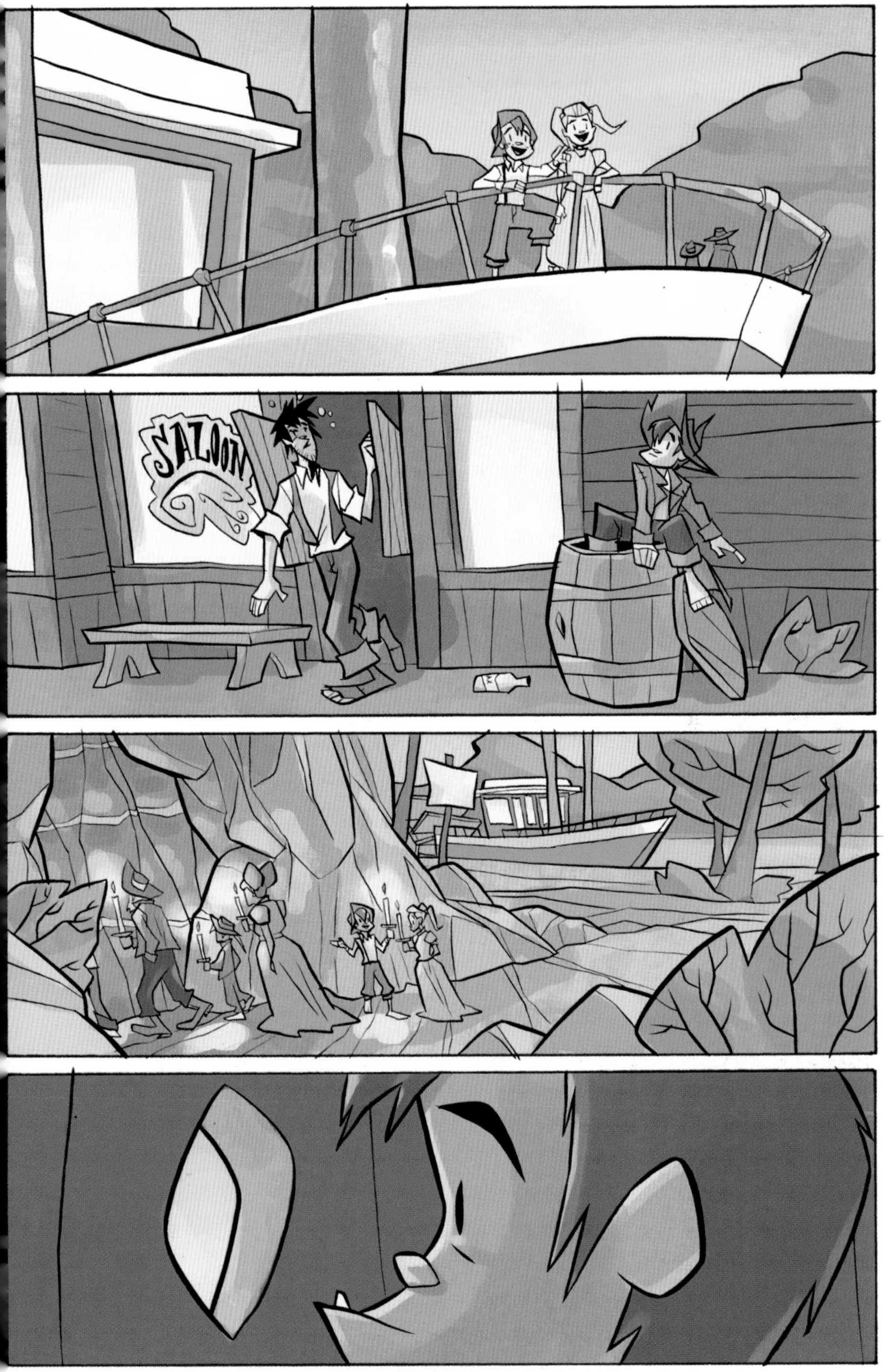
SALOON

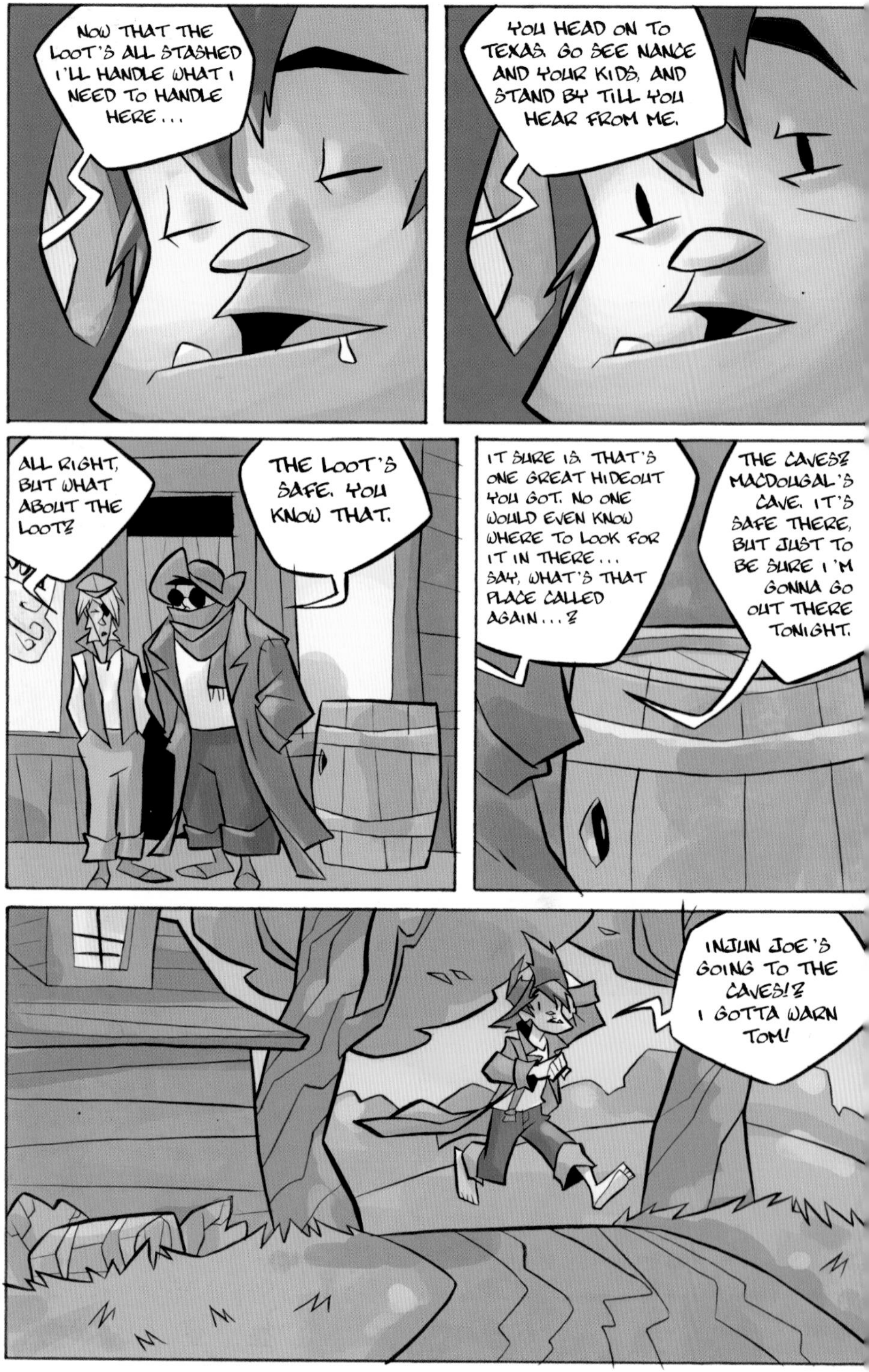
NOW THAT THE LOOT'S ALL STASHED I'LL HANDLE WHAT I NEED TO HANDLE HERE...
YOU HEAD ON TO TEXAS. GO SEE NANCE AND YOUR KIDS, AND STAND BY TILL YOU HEAR FROM ME.
ALL RIGHT, BUT WHAT ABOUT THE LOOT?
THE LOOT'S SAFE. YOU KNOW THAT.
IT SURE IS. THAT'S ONE GREAT HIDEOUT YOU GOT. NO ONE WOULD EVEN KNOW WHERE TO LOOK FOR IT IN THERE... SAY, WHAT'S THAT PLACE CALLED AGAIN...?
THE CAVES? MACDOUGAL'S CAVE. IT'S SAFE THERE, BUT JUST TO BE SURE I'M GONNA GO OUT THERE TONIGHT.
INJUN JOE'S GOING TO THE CAVES!? I GOTTA WARN TOM!

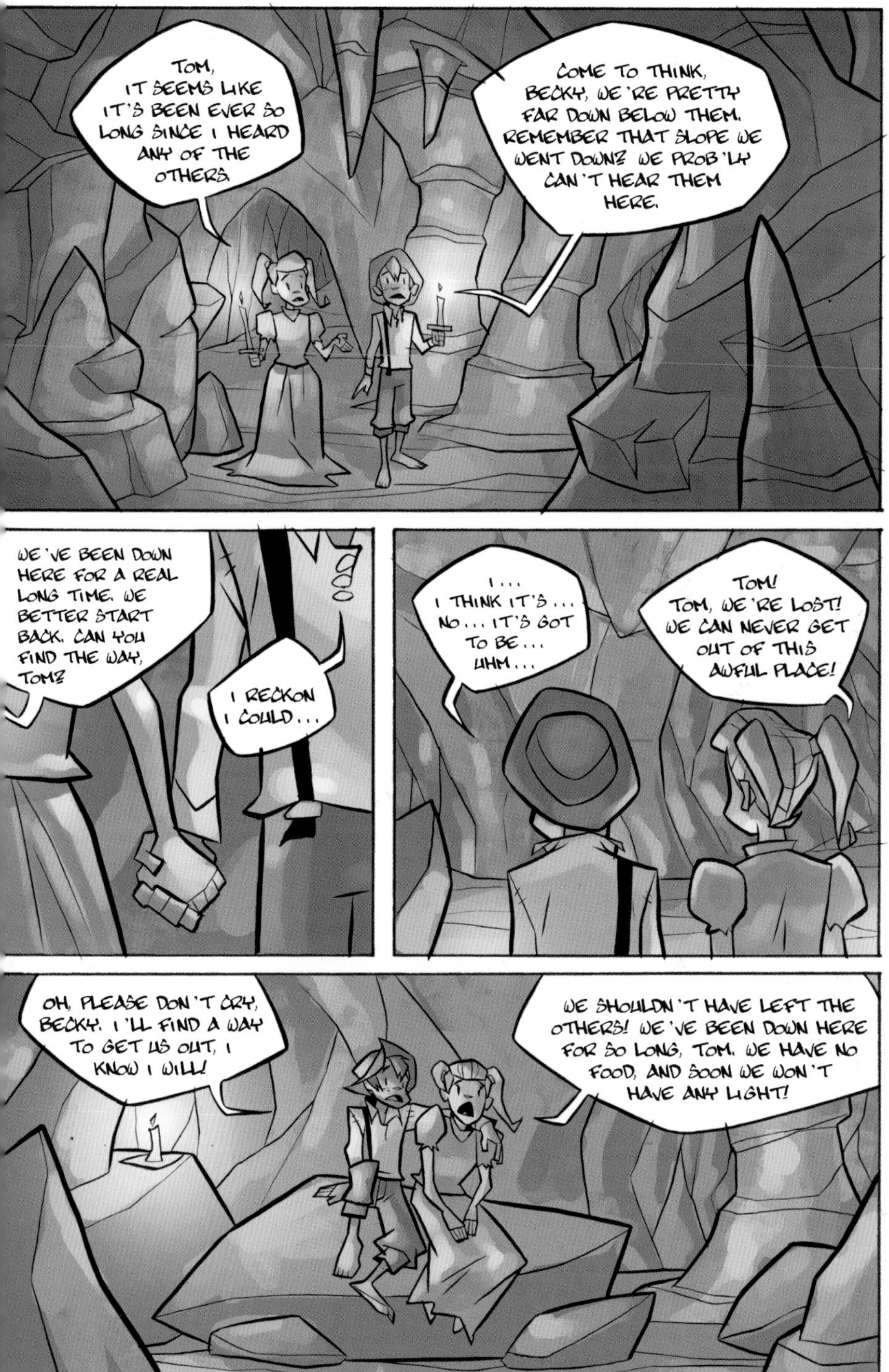
TOM, IT SEEMS LIKE IT'S BEEN EVER SO LONG SINCE I HEARD ANY OF THE OTHERS.
COME TO THINK, BECKY, WE'RE PRETTY FAR DOWN BELOW THEM. REMEMBER THAT SLOPE WE WENT DOWN? WE PROB'LY CAN'T HEAR THEM HERE.
WE'VE BEEN DOWN HERE FOR A REAL LONG TIME. WE BETTER START BACK. CAN YOU FIND THE WAY, TOM?
I RECKON I COULD...
I... I THINK IT'S... NO... IT'S GOT TO BE... UHM...
TOM! TOM, WE'RE LOST! WE CAN NEVER GET OUT OF THIS AWFUL PLACE!
OH, PLEASE DON'T CRY, BECKY. I'LL FIND A WAY TO GET US OUT, I KNOW I WILL!
WE SHOULDN'T HAVE LEFT THE OTHERS! WE'VE BEEN DOWN HERE FOR SO LONG, TOM. WE HAVE NO FOOD, AND SOON WE WON'T HAVE ANY LIGHT!

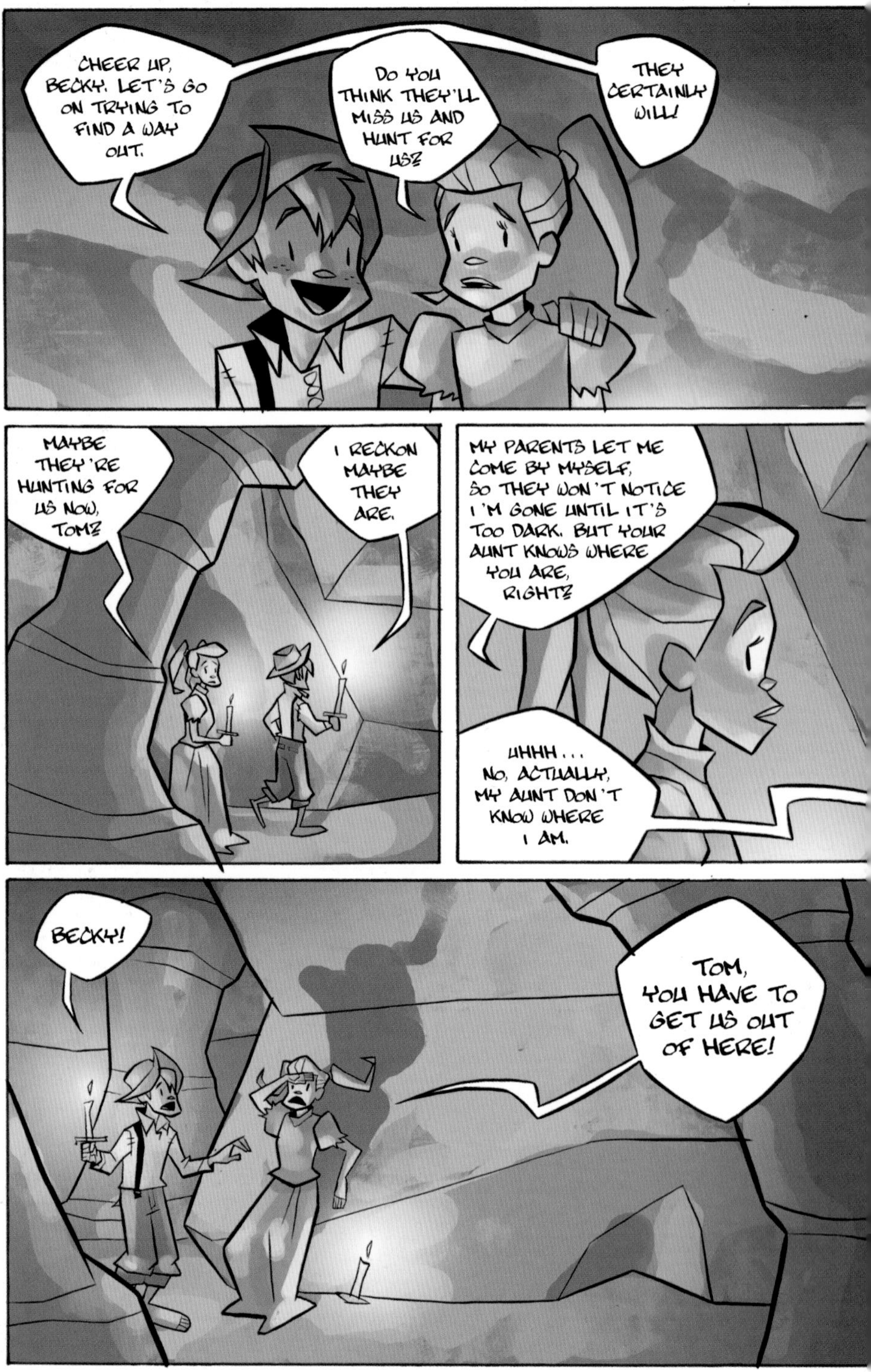
CHEER UP, BECKY. LET'S GO ON TRYING TO FIND A WAY OUT.
DO YOU THINK THEY'LL MISS US AND HUNT FOR US?
THEY CERTAINLY WILL!
MAYBE THEY'RE HUNTING FOR US NOW, TOM?
I RECKON MAYBE THEY ARE.
MY PARENTS LET ME COME BY MYSELF, SO THEY WON'T NOTICE I'M GONE UNTIL IT'S TOO DARK. BUT YOUR AUNT KNOWS WHERE YOU ARE, RIGHT?
UHHH... NO, ACTUALLY, MY AUNT DON'T KNOW WHERE I AM.
BECKY!
TOM, YOU HAVE TO GET US OUT OF HERE!

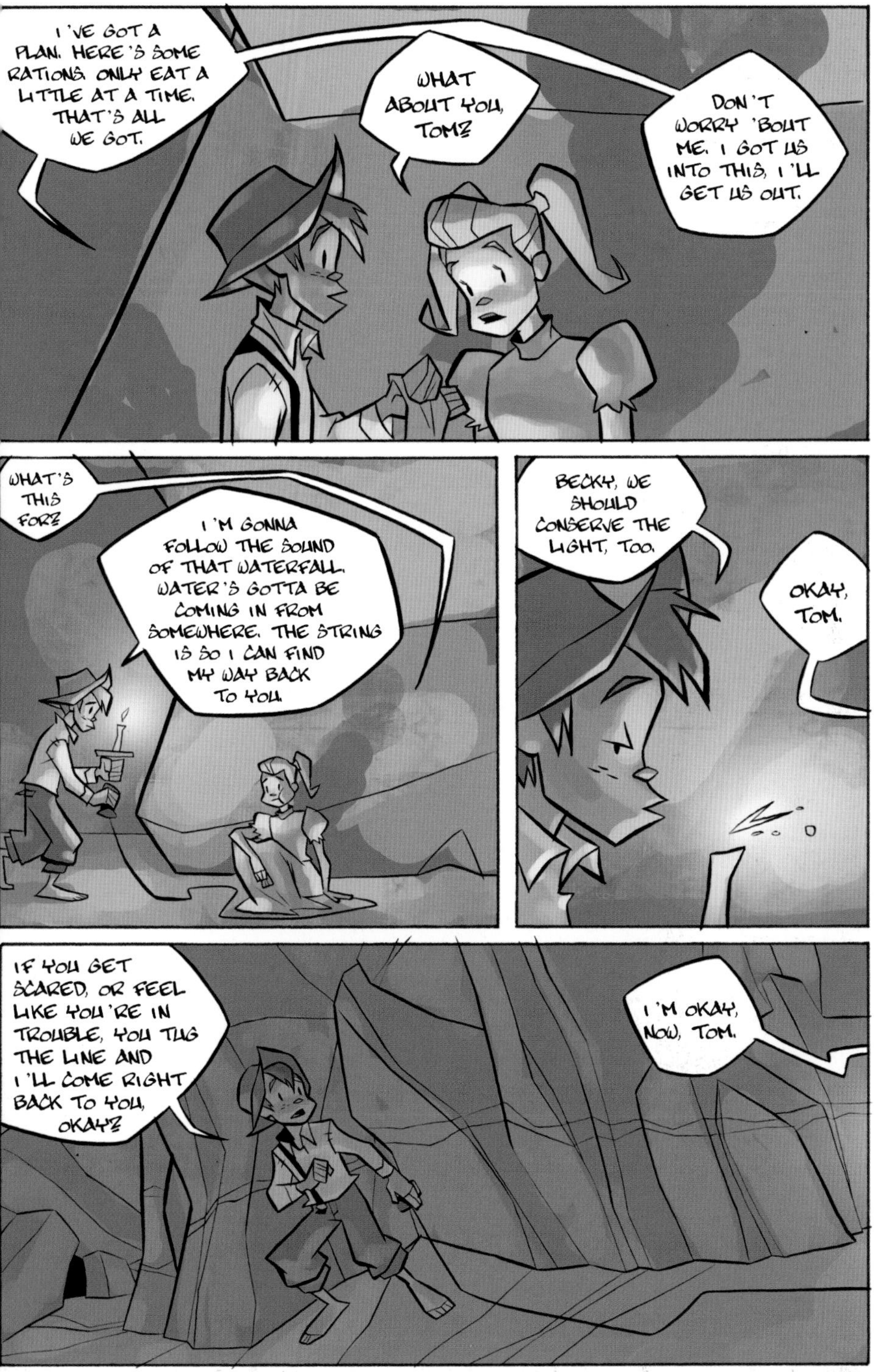

I'VE GOT A PLAN. HERE'S SOME RATIONS. ONLY EAT A LITTLE AT A TIME. THAT'S ALL WE GOT.
WHAT ABOUT YOU, TOM?
DON'T WORRY 'BOUT ME. I GOT US INTO THIS, I'LL GET US OUT.
WHAT'S THIS FOR?
I'M GONNA FOLLOW THE SOUND OF THAT WATERFALL. WATER'S GOTTA BE COMING IN FROM SOMEWHERE. THE STRING IS SO I CAN FIND MY WAY BACK TO YOU.
BECKY, WE SHOULD CONSERVE THE LIGHT, TOO.
OKAY, TOM.
IF YOU GET SCARED, OR FEEL LIKE YOU'RE IN TROUBLE, YOU TUG THE LINE AND I'LL COME RIGHT BACK TO YOU, OKAY?
I'M OKAY, NOW, TOM.

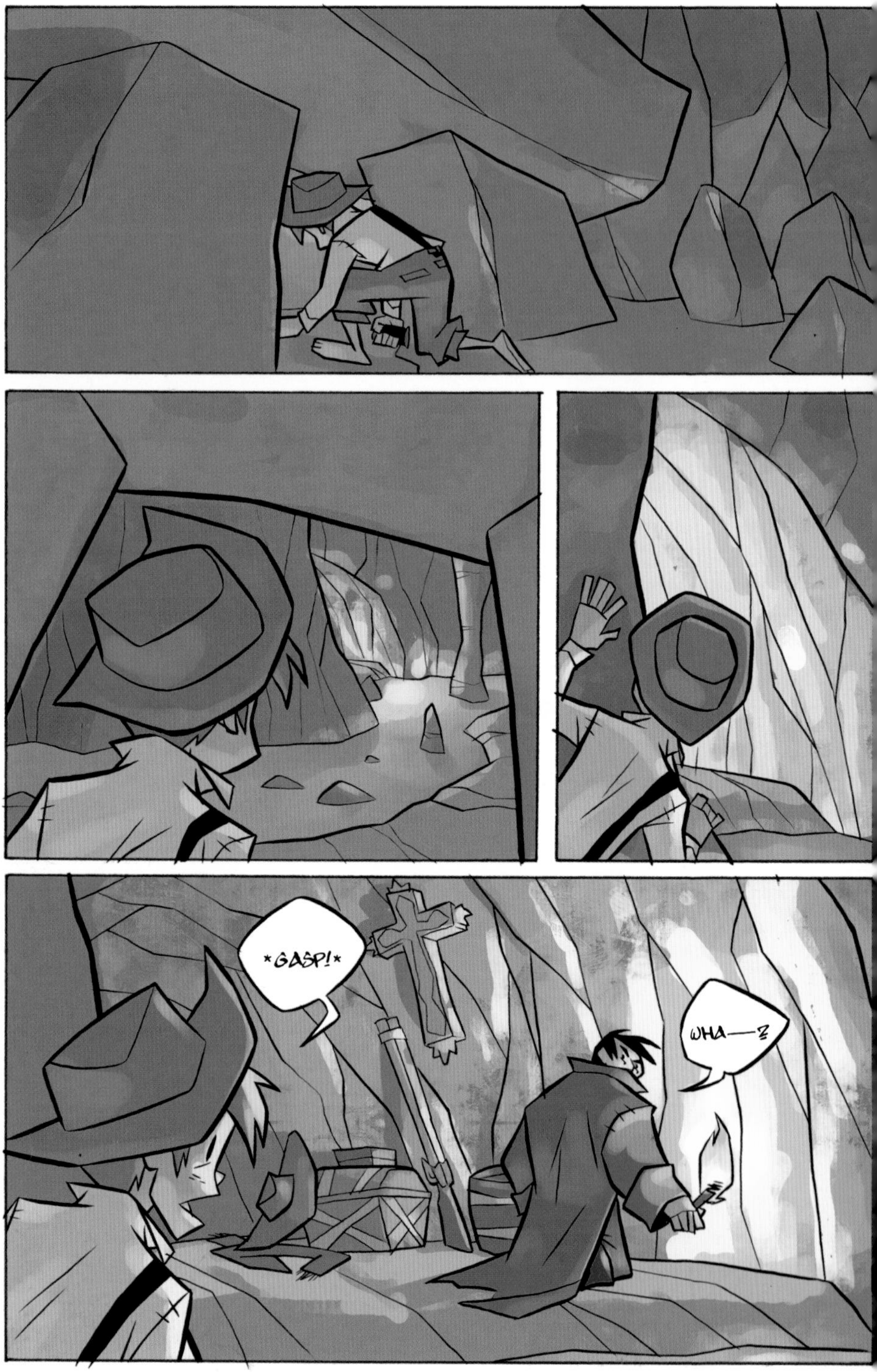
GASP!
WHA—?

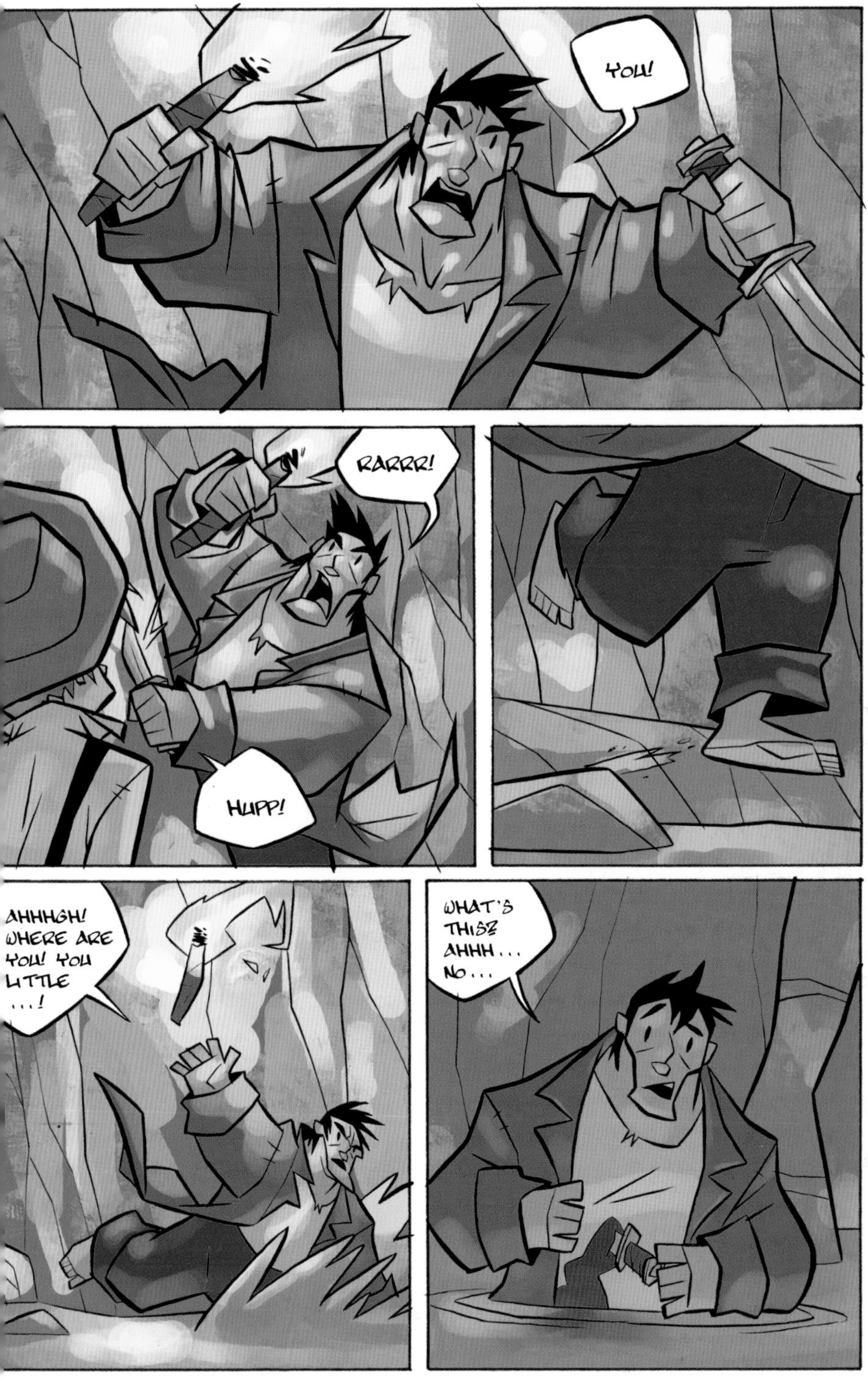
YOU!
RARRR!
HUPP!
AHHHGH! WHERE ARE YOU! YOU LITTLE ...!
WHAT'S THIS? AHHH... NO...

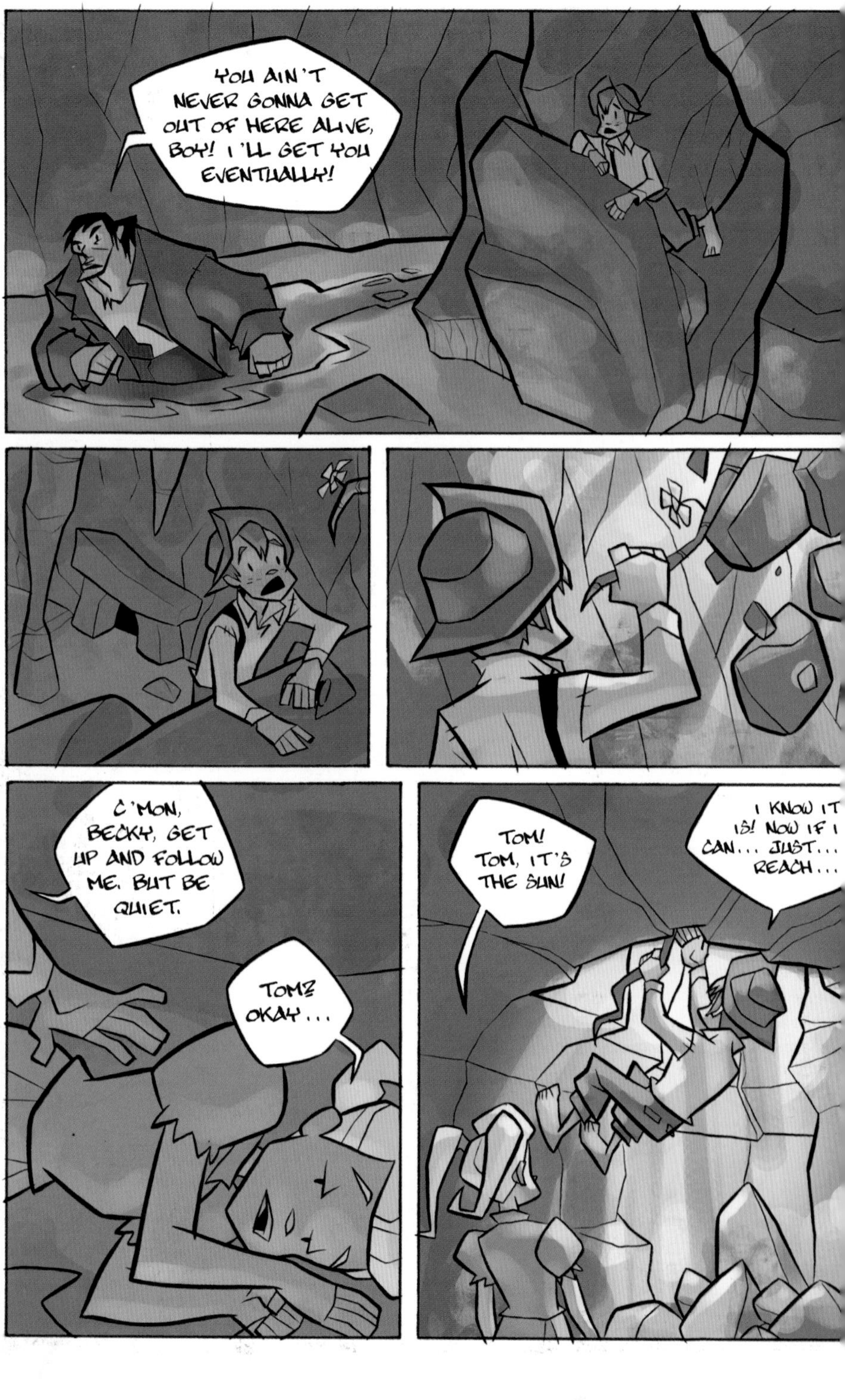
YOU AIN'T NEVER GONNA GET OUT OF HERE ALIVE, BOY! I'LL GET YOU EVENTUALLY!
C'MON, BECKY, GET UP AND FOLLOW ME. BUT BE QUIET.
TOM? OKAY...
TOM! TOM, IT'S THE SUN!
I KNOW IT IS! NOW IF I CAN... JUST... REACH...

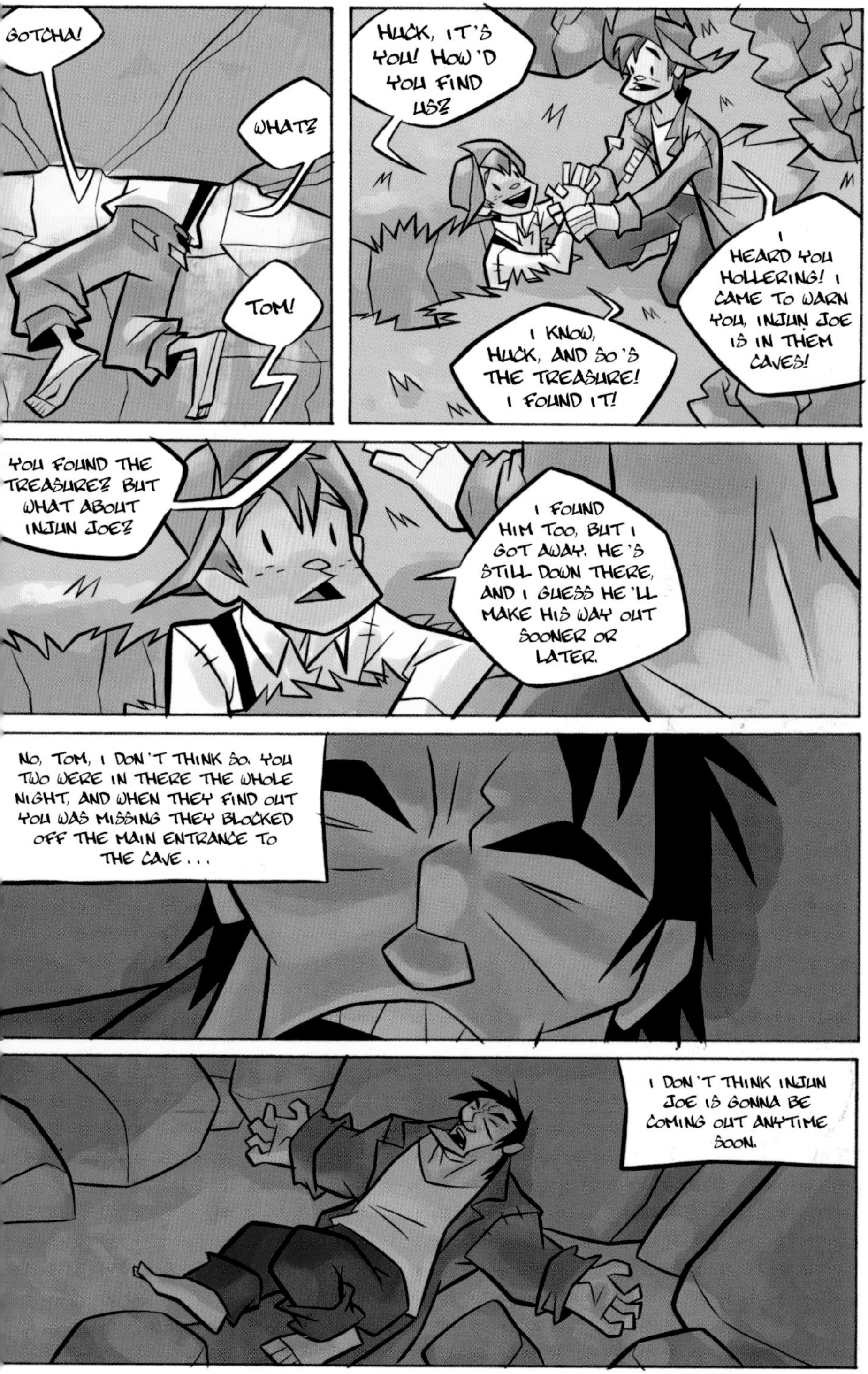
GOTCHA!
WHAT?
TOM!
HUCK, IT'S YOU! HOW'D YOU FIND US?
I HEARD YOU HOLLERING! I CAME TO WARN YOU, INJUN JOE IS IN THEM CAVES!
I KNOW, HUCK, AND SO'S THE TREASURE! I FOUND IT!
YOU FOUND THE TREASURE? BUT WHAT ABOUT INJUN JOE?
I FOUND HIM TOO, BUT I GOT AWAY. HE'S STILL DOWN THERE, AND I GUESS HE'LL MAKE HIS WAY OUT SOONER OR LATER.
NO, TOM, I DON'T THINK SO. YOU TWO WERE IN THERE THE WHOLE NIGHT, AND WHEN THEY FIND OUT YOU WAS MISSING THEY BLOCKED OFF THE MAIN ENTRANCE TO THE CAVE . . .
I DON'T THINK INJUN JOE IS GONNA BE COMING OUT ANYTIME SOON.

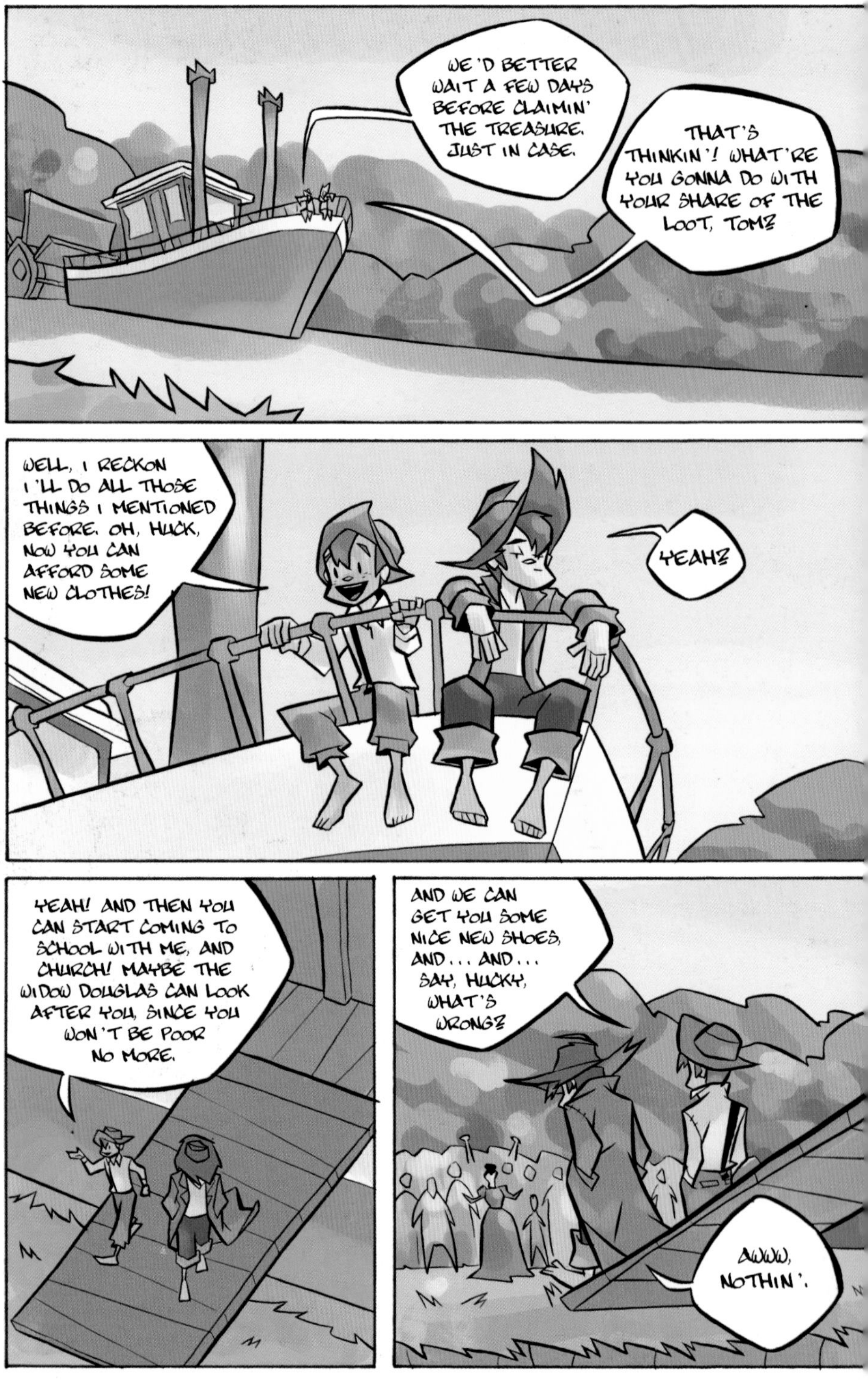
WE'D BETTER WAIT A FEW DAYS BEFORE CLAIMIN' THE TREASURE. JUST IN CASE.
THAT'S THINKIN'! WHAT'RE YOU GONNA DO WITH YOUR SHARE OF THE LOOT, TOM?
WELL, I RECKON I'LL DO ALL THOSE THINGS I MENTIONED BEFORE. OH, HUCK, NOW YOU CAN AFFORD SOME NEW CLOTHES!
YEAH?
YEAH! AND THEN YOU CAN START COMING TO SCHOOL WITH ME, AND CHURCH! MAYBE THE WIDOW DOUGLAS CAN LOOK AFTER YOU, SINCE YOU WON'T BE POOR NO MORE.
AND WE CAN GET YOU SOME NICE NEW SHOES, AND... AND... SAY, HUCKY, WHAT'S WRONG?
AWWW, NOTHIN'.

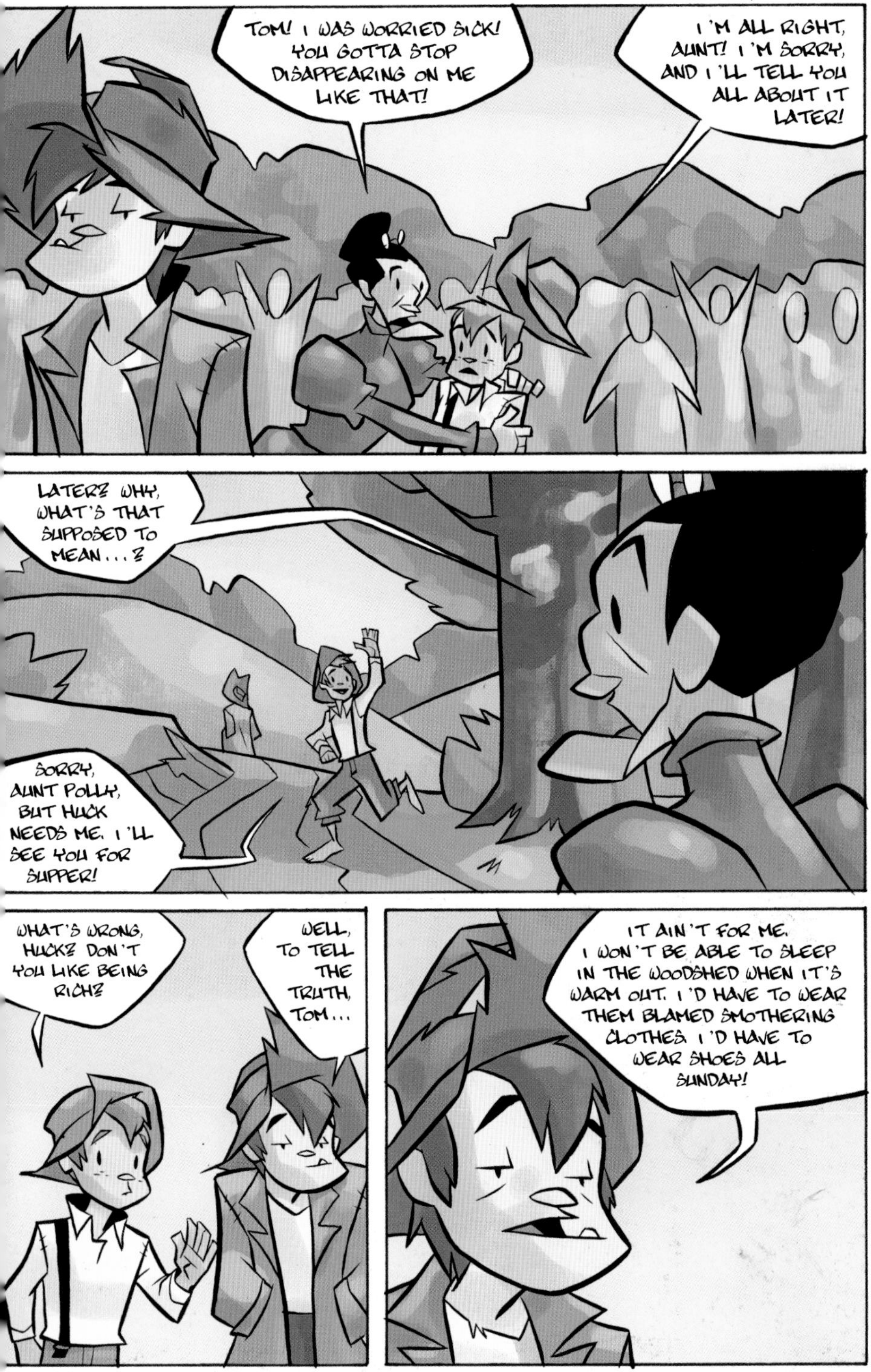
TOM! I WAS WORRIED SICK! YOU GOTTA STOP DISAPPEARING ON ME LIKE THAT!
I'M ALL RIGHT, AUNT! I'M SORRY, AND I'LL TELL YOU ALL ABOUT IT LATER!
LATER? WHY, WHAT'S THAT SUPPOSED TO MEAN...?
SORRY, AUNT POLLY, BUT HUCK NEEDS ME. I'LL SEE YOU FOR SUPPER!
WHAT'S WRONG, HUCK? DON'T YOU LIKE BEING RICH?
WELL, TO TELL THE TRUTH, TOM...
IT AIN'T FOR ME. I WON'T BE ABLE TO SLEEP IN THE WOODSHED WHEN IT'S WARM OUT. I'D HAVE TO WEAR THEM BLAMED SMOTHERING CLOTHES. I'D HAVE TO WEAR SHOES ALL SUNDAY!

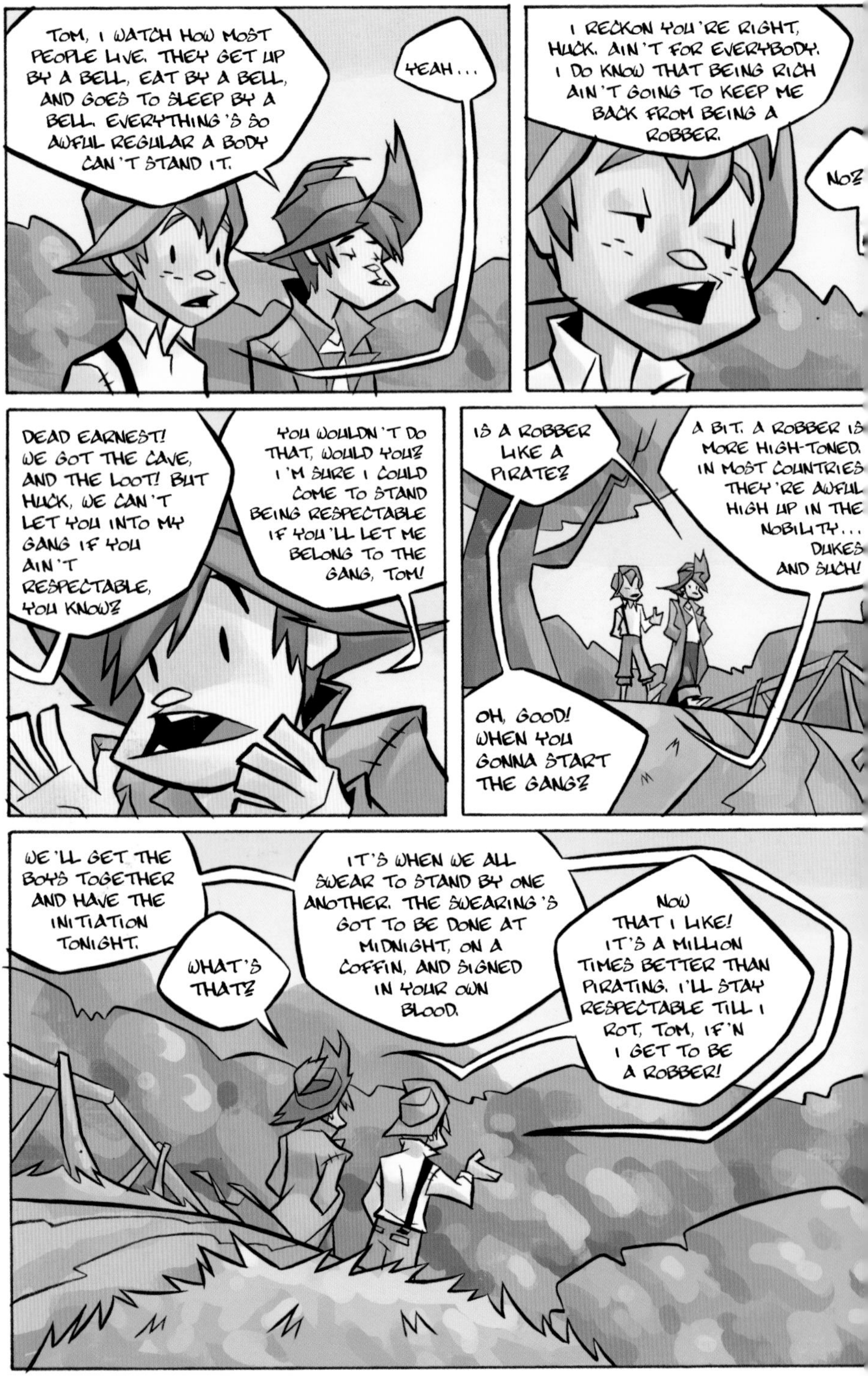
TOM, I WATCH HOW MOST PEOPLE LIVE. THEY GET UP BY A BELL, EAT BY A BELL, AND GOES TO SLEEP BY A BELL. EVERYTHING'S SO AWFUL REGULAR A BODY CAN'T STAND IT.
YEAH...
I RECKON YOU'RE RIGHT, HUCK. AIN'T FOR EVERYBODY. I DO KNOW THAT BEING RICH AIN'T GOING TO KEEP ME BACK FROM BEING A ROBBER.
NO?
DEAD EARNEST! WE GOT THE CAVE, AND THE LOOT! BUT HUCK, WE CAN'T LET YOU INTO MY GANG IF YOU AIN'T RESPECTABLE, YOU KNOW?
YOU WOULDN'T DO THAT, WOULD YOU? I'M SURE I COULD COME TO STAND BEING RESPECTABLE IF YOU'LL LET ME BELONG TO THE GANG, TOM!
IS A ROBBER LIKE A PIRATE?
A BIT. A ROBBER IS MORE HIGH-TONED. IN MOST COUNTRIES THEY'RE AWFUL HIGH UP IN THE NOBILITY... DUKES AND SUCH!
OH, GOOD! WHEN YOU GONNA START THE GANG?
WE'LL GET THE BOYS TOGETHER AND HAVE THE INITIATION TONIGHT.
WHAT'S THAT?
IT'S WHEN WE ALL SWEAR TO STAND BY ONE ANOTHER. THE SWEARING'S GOT TO BE DONE AT MIDNIGHT, ON A COFFIN, AND SIGNED IN YOUR OWN BLOOD.
NOW THAT I LIKE! IT'S A MILLION TIMES BETTER THAN PIRATING. I'LL STAY RESPECTABLE TILL I ROT, TOM, IF'N I GET TO BE A ROBBER!

ABOUT
MARK TWAIN

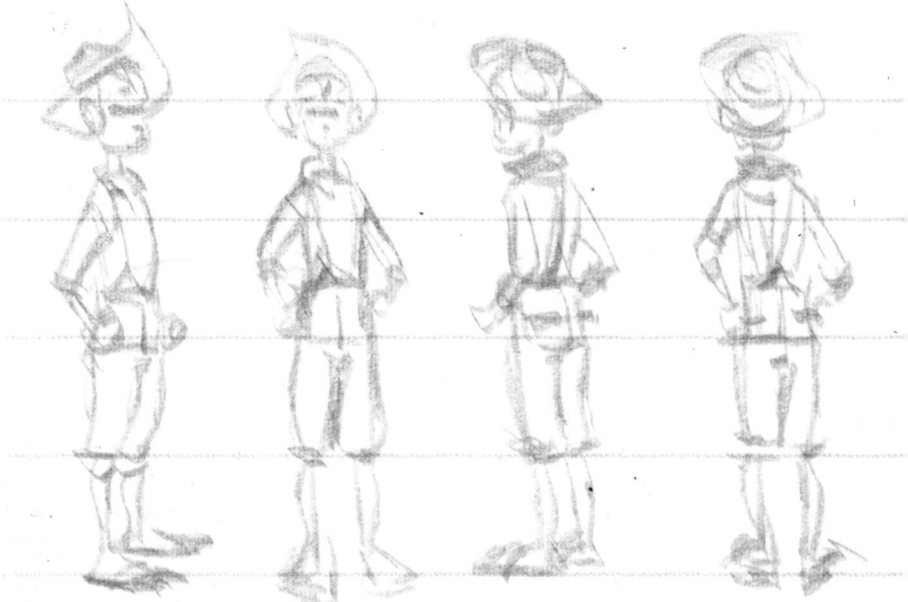

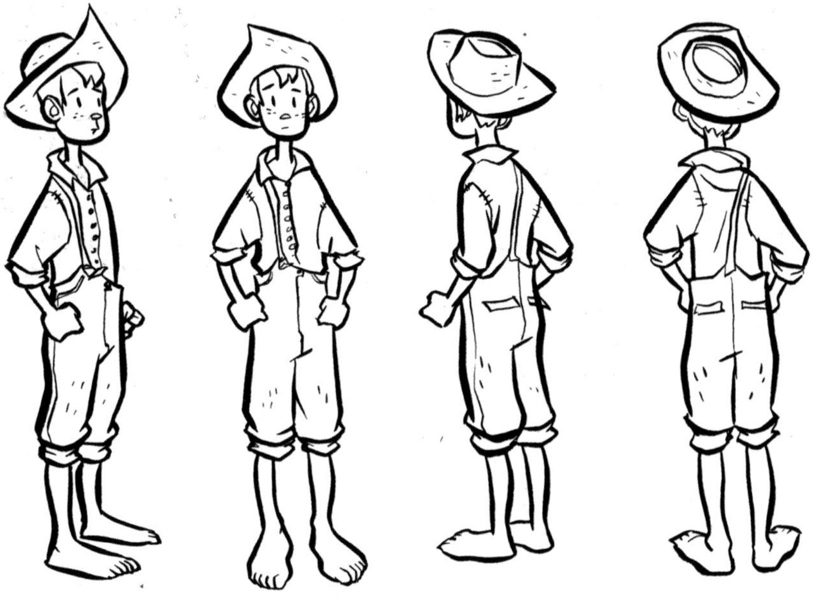

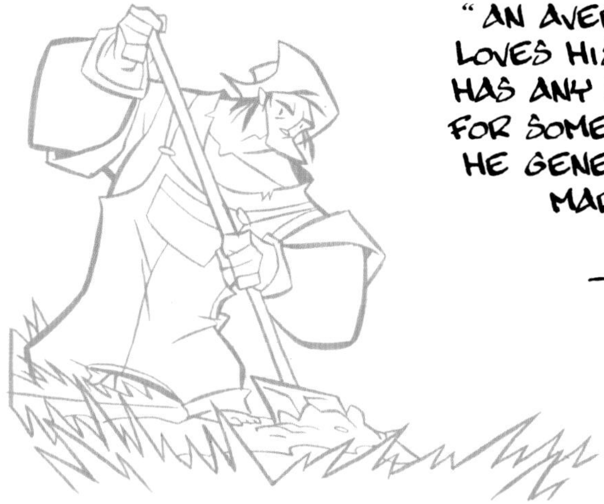

"AN AVERAGE AMERICAN LOVES HIS FAMILY. IF HE HAS ANY LOVE LEFT OVER FOR SOME OTHER PERSON, HE GENERALLY SELECTS MARK TWAIN."

—THOMAS EDISON

MARK TWAIN IS THE WELL-KNOWN PSEUDONYM OF AMERICAN WRITER, HUMORIST, NOVELIST AND LECTURER SAMUEL LANGHORNE CLEMENS, BORN THE SIXTH OF SEVEN CHILDREN ON NOVEMBER 30, 1835 IN FLORIDA, MISSOURI. CLEMENS' FAMILY THEN MOVED TO THE PORT TOWN OF HANNIBAL WHEN HE WAS FOUR.

DURING HIS EARLY TEENS, HE WORKED AS AN APPRENTICE PRINTER, HAVING LEFT SCHOOL AFTER COMPLETING FIFTH GRADE. AT SIXTEEN, HE BEGAN WRITING HUMOROUS ARTICLES AND NEWSPAPER SKETCHES. BY THE AGE OF EIGHTEEN, CLEMENS HAD LEFT HANNIBAL TO WORK AS A PRINTER IN NEW YORK, PHILADELPHIA, ST. LOUIS AND CINCINNATI.

AT THE AGE OF 22, CLEMENS RETURNED TO MISSOURI AND WORKED THERE AS A RIVER-BOAT PILOT—THE LIKELY ORIGIN OF HIS FAMOUS PEN NAME "MARK TWAIN. "TWO FATHOMS (12 FT), THE NAUTICAL TERM FOR "SAFE WATER," WAS MEASURED WITH A SOUNDING LINE, AND MARKED BY CALLING OUT "MARK TWAIN." TWAIN HIMSELF NEVER CONFIRMED THE SOURCE OF HIS PEN NAME. CLEMENS CONTINUED TO WORK AS A RIVER BOAT PILOT UNTIL 1861, WHEN THE AMERICAN CIVIL WAR BEGAN.

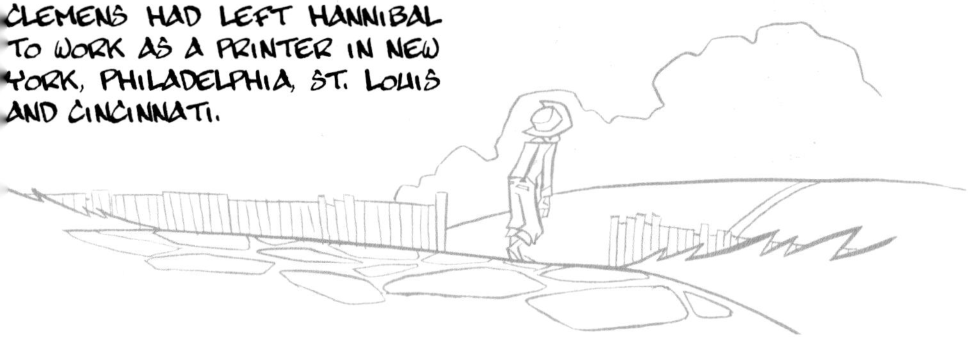

AFTER FAILING AS A SILVER PROSPECTOR, CLEMENS OBTAINED WORK AT A NEWSPAPER IN VIRGINIA CITY CALLED THE "DAILY TERRITORIAL ENTERPRISE," AND ADOPTED THE NAME MARK TWAIN.

BY 1864, TWAIN HEADED TO SAN FRANCISCO TO WRITE FOR THE LOCAL PAPERS. A YEAR LATER HE WAS SENT TO REPORT ON THE SANDWICH ISLANDS IN HAWAII. HIS TRAVEL WRITINGS WERE SO POPULAR THAT, ON HIS RETURN, HE BEGAN A SERIES OF FAMOUS LECTURE TOURS, CEMENTING HIS POPULARITY AS A PUBLIC SPEAKER AND STAGE PRESENCE.

AT THE START OF THE CIVIL WAR, CLEMENS AND HIS FRIENDS FORMED A CONFEDERATE MILITIA CALLED THE MARION RANGERS, WHICH DISBANDED AFTER TWO WEEKS DUE TO LACK OF MILITARY ACTION.

WHILE HIS FRIENDS WENT OFF TO JOIN THE CONFEDERATE ARMY, CLEMENS AND HIS BROTHER, ORION (THE NEWLY APPOINTED SECRETARY TO THE TERRITORIAL GOVERNOR OF NEVADA), HEADED WEST—AN EXPERIENCE THAT CLEMENS CONSIDERED SIGNIFICANT TO HIS FORMATION AS A WRITER AND THAT BECAME THE BASIS FOR A TRAVEL BOOK "ROUGHING IT." SAMUEL AND ORION TRAVELED BY STAGECOACH, AND EXPERIENCED A VARIETY OF MISADVENTURES, INCLUDING THEIR FIRST ENCOUNTER WITH NATIVE AMERICAN TRIBES.

TWAIN HAD BECOME THE MOST POPULAR AMERICAN CELEBRITY OF HIS AGE. HIS FAMOUS FRIENDS INCLUDED INVENTOR, PHYSICIST AND MECHANICAL ENGINEER NIKOLA TESLA, DEAF AND BLIND AUTHOR/ACTIVIST HELEN KELLER, AND AUTHOR ROBERT LOUIS STEVENSON. BY 1873 TWAIN HAD SETTLED DOWN WITH HIS WIFE, OLIVIA, IN A 19-ROOM FARMHOUSE IN HARTFORD, CONNECTICUT, AND IT WAS FROM 1874 TO 1891 THAT TWAIN COMPLETED HIS MOST FAMOUS WORKS. IN 1876 TWAIN PUBLISHED ONE OF HIS MOST ENDEARING NOVELS, "TOM SAWYER."

IN "TOM SAWYER," TWAIN CAPTURED HIS OWN CHILDHOOD MEMORIES OF GROWING UP IN HANNIBAL, MISSOURI, AND BASED MANY OF THE CHARACTERS ON PEOPLE HE KNEW AS A CHILD. TOM, FOR INSTANCE, IS A COMPOSITE OF TWAIN'S CHILDHOOD FRIENDS JOHN BRIGGS AND WILL BOWEN, AND OF HIMSELF. JANE CLEMENS, TWAIN'S MOTHER, WAS HIS MODEL FOR AUNT POLLY, AND HIS BROTHER HENRY WAS THE BASIS FOR SID, THOUGH TWAIN ADMITS THAT HENRY WAS "A MUCH FINER AND BETTER BOY THAN SID EVER WAS."

"NEVER PUT OFF UNTIL TOMORROW THAT WHICH COULD BE DONE THE DAY AFTER TOMORROW."

—MARK TWAIN

"IN WRITING 'TOM SAWYER' I HAD NO IDEA OF LAYING DOWN RULES FOR THE BRINGING UP OF SMALL FAMILIES, BUT MERELY TO THROW OUT HINTS AS TO HOW THEY MIGHT BRING THEMSELVES UP, AND THE BOYS SEEMED TO HAVE CAUGHT THE IDEA NICELY."

—MARK TWAIN

HUCK WAS MODELED AFTER AN "IGNORANT, UNWASHED, AND INSUFFICIENTLY FED" BOY NAMED TOM BLANKENSHIP. BECKY THATCHER HAS HER ROOTS IN LAURA HAWKINS, A GIRL WHO LIVED ACROSS THE STREET FROM TWAIN AND WHO HE HAD A CRUSH ON. THERE WAS ALSO A REAL INJUN JOE, BUT IT IS LIKELY THAT HE WAS JUST A LOAFER AND A DRUNK, NOT THE ARCH-VILLAIN THAT TWAIN PORTRAYED.

CHILDHOOD INFLUENCES ASIDE, TOM SAWYER AND HUCK FINN ARE ALSO BASED ON TWO FAMOUS LITERARY CHARACTERS, DON QUIXOTE AND SANCHO PANZA FROM CERVANTES' "DON QUIXOTE."

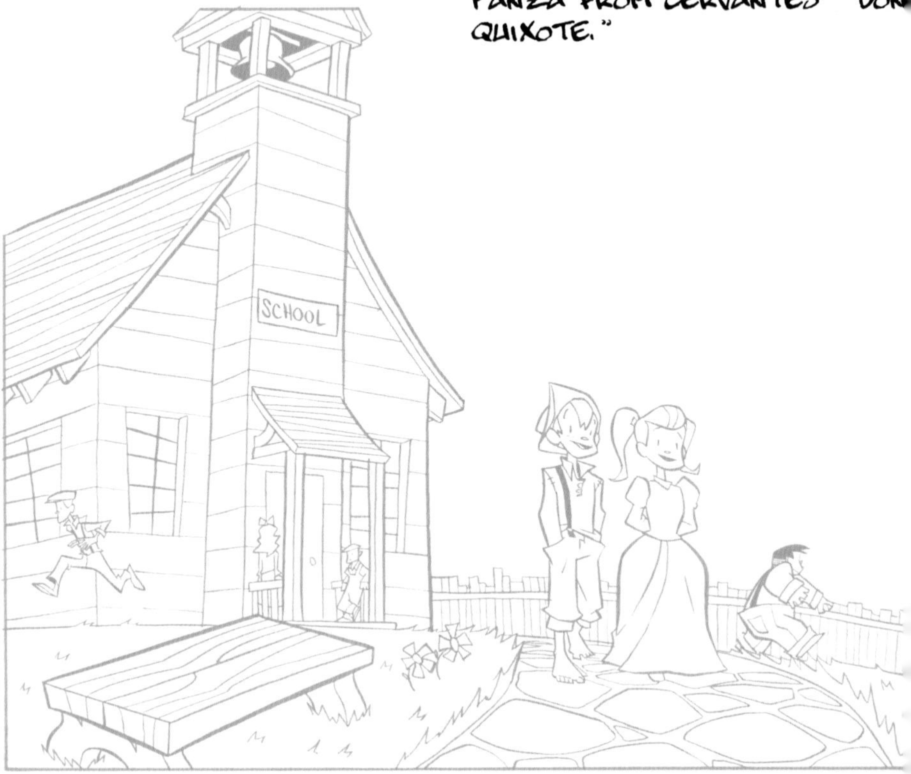
SCHOOL

TWAIN'S ORIGINAL INTENTIONS WERE TO HAVE TOM MATURE AND TRAVEL TO MANY LANDS THROUGHOUT THE PROGRESS OF THE FIRST NOVEL. WHILE TOM APPEARED IN "THE ADVENTURES OF HUCKLEBERRY FINN" (1884), IT WASN'T UNTIL MUCH LATER THAT HIS PLANS FOR HIS YOUNG ADVENTURER WERE REALIZED WHEN HE PUBLISHED "TOM SAWYER ABROAD" (1894) AND "TOM SAWYER, DETECTIVE" (1896). "TOM SAWYER ABROAD" SEES TOM, HUCK AND JIM TRAPPED IN A RUNAWAY BALLOON WITH A MAD SCIENTIST, AND "TOM SAWYER, DETECTIVE" PLANTS THE BOYS BACK IN HANNIBAL, WHERE TOM ATTEMPTS TO SOLVE A MYSTERIOUS MURDER.

ONE OF THE KEY'S TO TWAIN'S POPULARITY WAS HIS ABILITY TO CAPTURE THE LIFESTYLE AND LANGUAGE OF THE COMMON, EVERYDAY PERSON. HE HAD A TRUE EAR FOR COLLOQUIAL SPEECH, AND THE ABILITY TO BRING THAT SPEECH, AND THE LIVES OF ITS SPEAKERS, TO THE WRITTEN PAGE.

IN TWAIN'S TIME, EDUCATION WAS A LUXURY THAT MANY PEOPLE COULDN'T AFFORD. THE BUILDING OF SCHOOL HOUSES AND THE EMPLOYMENT OF TEACHERS WERE COMMUNITY EFFORTS, AND WHILE THE RUDIMENTARY EDUCATIONAL SYSTEM DEPENDED UPON THE COMMUNITY, THE COMMUNITY ALSO DEPENDED UPON THE EDUCATIONAL SYSTEM TO TEACH ITS CHILDREN THE PRACTICAL KNOWLEDGE THEY NEEDED.

CHILDREN WERE TAUGHT BY PURE MEMORIZATION. THE FORMAL CURRICULUM CENTERED AROUND SPELLING, READING, WRITING AND ARITHMETIC, BUT MORE USEFUL SKILLS WERE TAUGHT AS WELL.

"I HAVE NEVER LET MY SCHOOLING GET IN THE WAY OF MY EDUCATION."

—MARK TWAIN

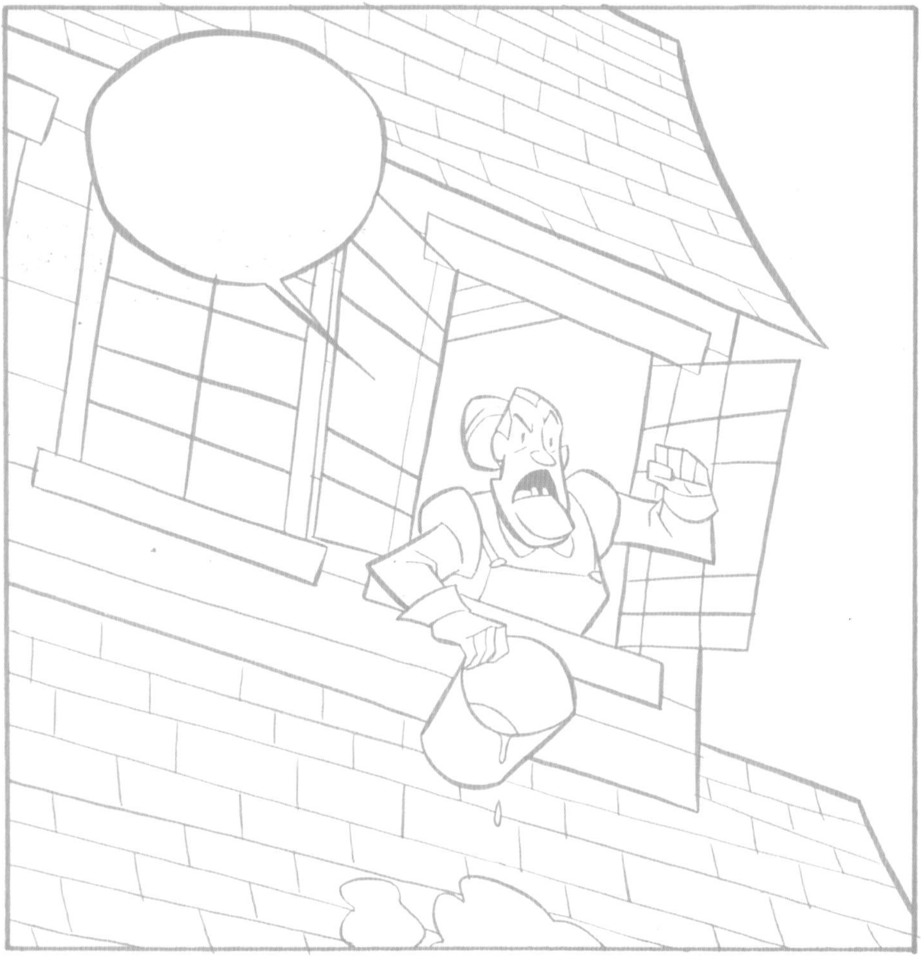

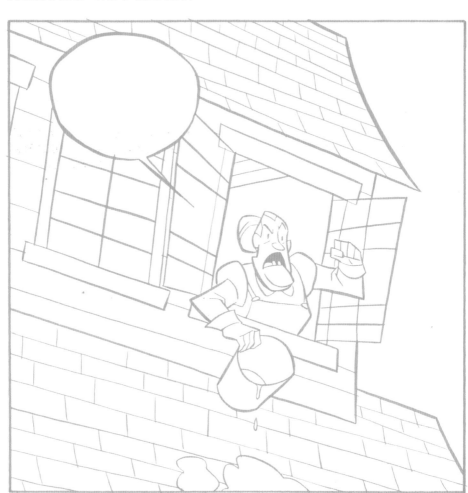

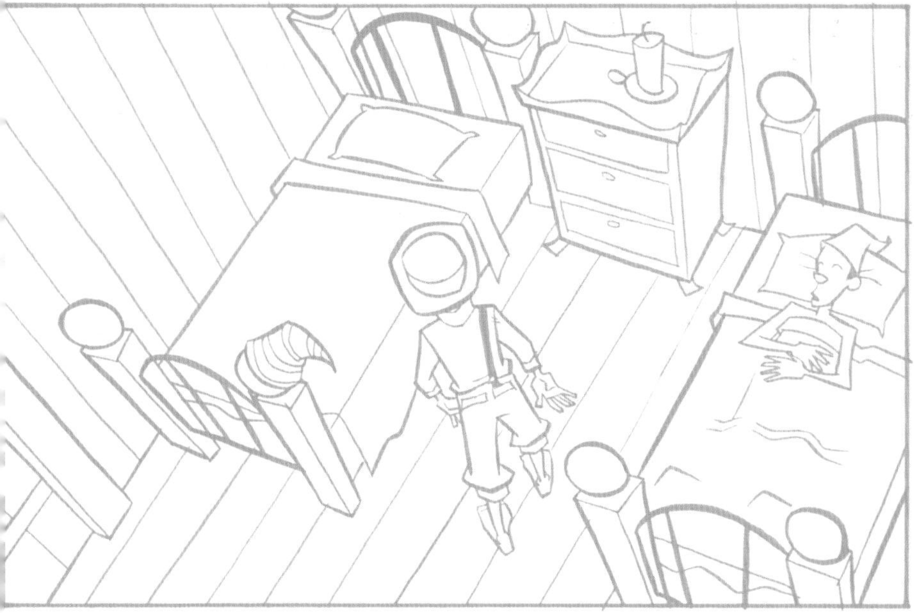

STUDENTS COULD BE EXPECTED TO LEARN HOW TO FARM, SEW, MEND CLOTHES AND DO GENERAL HOUSEWORK, IN ADDITION TO THEIR PENMANSHIP LESSONS. TEXTBOOKS WERE SO RARE THAT MANY SCHOOLS TAUGHT FROM THE BIBLE, WHICH WAS A BOOK MANY FAMILIES OWNED, AND STUDENTS WOULD PRACTICE THEIR LESSONS ON A WRITING SLATE (LIKE A CHALK-BOARD), WHICH WAS CHEAPER AND MORE DURABLE THAN PAPER.

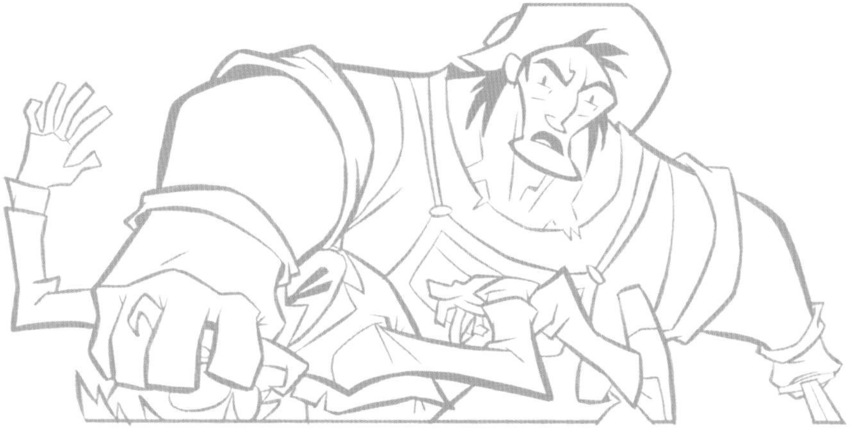

THROUGHOUT HIS LIFETIME TWAIN TRAVELED ALL OVER THE WORLD, OBSERVING AND LEARNING. TRAVEL IN HIS DAY WAS RELEGATED TO HORSE DRAWN COACHES, SHIPS AND BOATS, OR TRAINS. AIR TRAVEL WAS VERY RARE, AND THE AUTOMOBILE INDUSTRY WAS IN ITS INFANCY. RIVERS LIKE THE MISSISSIPI, WHICH TWAIN WORKED ON AS A RIVERBOAT PILOT, WERE IMMENSELY IMPORTANT TO THE NATION'S TRADE AND ECONOMY. IN A LETTER TO HIS CHILDHOOD FRIEND WILL BOWEN, TWAIN WROTE, "THE ONLY REAL, INDEPENDENT & GENUINE GENTLEMEN IN THE WORLD GO QUIETLY UP AND DOWN THE MISSISSIPPI RIVER, ASKING NO HOMAGE OF ANY ONE, SEEKING NO POPULARITY, NO NOTORIETY & NOT CARING A DAMN WHETHER SCHOOL KEEPS OR NOT." ON APRIL 21, 1910, SAM CLEMENS DIED AT THE AGE OF 74 AT HIS HOUSE IN REDDING, CONNECTICUT.

"RUMOURS OF MY DEATH HAVE BEEN GREATLY EXAGGERATED."

—MARK TWAIN

MARK TWAIN WROTE HUNDREDS OF BOOKS, ESSAYS, AND ARTICLES THROUGHOUT HIS LIFE. HERE ARE SOME OF HIS MORE FAMOUS WORKS. IN ADDITION TO "TOM SAWYER" AND OTHER ADVENTURE STORIES, TWAIN WAS ALSO INTERESTED IN POLITICAL REFORM AND CONTINUED TO TRAVEL AND WRITE ABOUT TRAVEL UNTIL HIS DEATH.

(1867) ADVICE FOR LITTLE GIRLS (FICTION)

(1867) THE CELEBRATED JUMPING FROG OF CALAVERAS COUNTY (STORIES)

(1869) THE INNOCENTS ABROAD (NONFICTION TRAVEL)

(1872) ROUGHING IT (NON-FICTION)

(1873) THE GILDED AGE: A TALE OF TODAY (FICTION)

(1875) SKETCHES NEW AND OLD (FICTIONAL STORIES)

(1876) OLD TIMES ON THE MISSISSIPPI (NONFICTION)

(1876) THE ADVENTURES OF TOM SAWYER (FICTION)

(1877) A TRUE STORY AND THE RECENT CARNIVAL OF CRIME (STORIES)

(1880) A TRAMP ABROAD (NONFICTION TRAVEL)

(1882) THE PRINCE AND THE PAUPER (FICTION)

(1883) LIFE ON THE MISSISSIPPI (NONFICTION)

(1884) ADVENTURES OF HUCKLEBERRY FINN (FICTION)

(1889) A CONNECTICUT YANKEE IN KING ARTHUR'S COURT (FICTION)

(1894) TOM SAWYER ABROAD (FICTION)

(1894) PUDD'N'HEAD WILSON (FICTION)

(1896) TOM SAWYER, DETECTIVE (FICTION)

(1897) FOLLOWING THE EQUATOR (NONFICTION TRAVEL)

(1901) EDMUND BURKE ON CROKER AND TAMMANY (POLITICAL SATIRE)

(1902) A DOUBLE BARRELLED DETECTIVE STORY (FICTION)

(1905) KING LEOPOLD'S SOLILOQUY (POLITICAL SATIRE)

(1906) THE $30,000 BEQUEST AND OTHER STORIES (FICTION)

(1935) MARK TWAIN'S NOTEBOOK (PUBLISHED POSTHUMOUSLY)

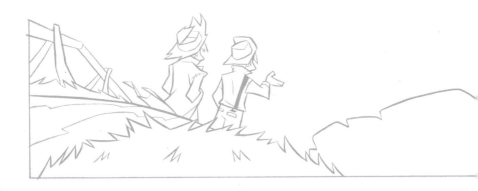